the Day We Met

ROXIE COOPER

EBURY
PRESS

First published by Ebury Press in 2019

1 3 5 7 9 10 8 6 4 2

Ebury Press, an imprint of Ebury Publishing
20 Vauxhall Bridge Road,
London SW1V 2SA

Ebury Press is part of the Penguin Random House group of companies
whose addresses can be found at global.penguinrandomhouse.com

Penguin
Random House
UK

www.penguin.co.uk

A CIP catalogue record for this book is available from the British Library

ISBN 9781529102468

Typeset in 11.75/15.5 pt Adobe Caslon Pro
by Integra Software Services Pvt. Ltd, Pondicherry

Printed and bound in Great Britain by Clays Ltd, Elcograf S.p.A.

Penguin Random House is committed to a sustainable future for
our business, our readers and our planet. This book is made
from Forest Stewardship Council® certified paper.

For Amanda, Sasha and Vicky – who took me apart and put me back together again.

PART ONE

You Do Something To Me

CHAPTER 1

Friday 13 October 2006

Stephanie

I'm not a superstitious person.

One of those people who goes out of their way to avoid walking under ladders, saluting at magpies and all that rubbish – it's a waste of time. I don't think the universe really cares enough to give us a bad day just because we happened to walk under a ladder. Or making the thirteenth day of the month fall on a Friday. But people get worked up about it all, don't they?

If something bad is going to happen, it'll happen regardless of what day it is; whether it's a Friday, a particular month, or which alignment the planets are in.

The clock in the car changes to 5.03 p.m. I'm late.

We've been driving for just under an hour and surely must be almost there now. I hope so, because I can't bear the weight of the silence in this car much longer. Well, it's not complete silence because the radio is on. The volume is set to 'loud enough so that the atmosphere is a little less awkward'. Aerosmith are singing about how they 'Don't Wanna Miss A Thing'.

My head bounces off the headrest as we zoom down the swirly country lanes. He always drives too fast in this car – a baby blue BMW Z3. It's his 'James Bond' car and he likes to show it off at every opportunity.

'Look, I didn't mean it how it came out,' Matt says suddenly, without taking his eyes off the road ahead. The car engine revs up a notch as the words leave his mouth.

Tucking my hands in between my crossed legs, I turn to face him. I'm grateful I'm wearing sunglasses. I always feel less exposed having a disagreement or row when the other person can't see my eyes. It feels like you're giving too much away otherwise.

'How did you mean it, then?' I ask Matt's side profile, in a tone which definitely doesn't suggest I'll be pleased with whatever answer he gives me. 'Because it feels like you're treating me like a kid. *All* of you are treating me like a child and I'm sick of it.'

'I'm so sorry it came out that way, I honestly didn't mean it to,' he says very calmly, which makes me feel like even more of a petulant child. 'We're just looking out for you, that's all.'

'But I can't stand feeling mollycoddled, Matt!' I blurt out. 'It's driving me mad. You just have to trust I'll do the right thing.'

He listens to my words, taking them in as his eyes focus on the road. After a few seconds he nods his head and turns to look at me very briefly.

'No, you're right. Look, I'm just being overprotective because I love you and worry about you. I didn't think it would upset you so much.'

Reaching out, I place my hand on Matt's, which is gripping on to the steering wheel.

'I know,' I say softly, leaning towards him. 'I'm sorry. I'm just a bit ... nervous.'

He takes my hand off the wheel and pops it back on my knee, giving it a little squeeze.

My fiancé. His sparkly blue eyes were the first thing I noticed about him. Big, caring eyes which creased at the corners when he smiled. He's naturally blond, like me. People always comment on it, saying we look Swedish or something and how we will produce beautiful children 'when the time comes'. He styles his hair into a David Beckham-esque messy do which is all the rage at the moment.

'Well, that's the last time I tell *you* to lay off the booze!' Matt says, throwing a cheeky glance my way. You need to learn to live with humour in these situations, I guess.

'Look, no need to worry,' I tell him. 'I'm not going to drink anything. I haven't touched anything since April.'

Has it really been that long? It's weird to think that, until six months ago, Matt and I had been living the crazy, fast-paced life in London. Now we live in a quiet Cambridgeshire village, around the corner from my dad and sister. And I do mean *quiet*. That's quite an adjustment to make when you're twenty-six years old.

I'm not quite sure how the Stephanie I know ended up here – agreeing to spend the weekend on an Art and Photography Weekend Workshop in an upmarket country house about an hour away from where I live. The old Steph would be outraged.

It is beautiful here in the autumn, though. Although I've been living in London since I was eighteen, the countryside is where I grew up and it feels like home. It reminds me of my mum. I love everything about it: the colours, the crisp breeze, even the sound of it – yes, it has a sound. I want to get married in autumn, but Matt insists it has to be a summer wedding because of a whole load of reasons that aren't really important to me – better photos, guests prefer summer weddings, they're more of an 'occasion'. So, next year, on Saturday 14 July 2007, I'll become Mrs Stephanie Bywater.

As we leave the country roads and enter a quaint village, the rapid deceleration of the car makes me feel sick. Or maybe it's nerves. Driving past beautiful houses with oak trees in the garden, we see a sign indicating Heathwood Hall is coming up on the right.

'You gonna be OK here all weekend, baby?' Matt asks, nodding at the sign.

'I hope so,' I say enthusiastically, even though I feel scared. I haven't been left alone for more than a few hours for six months.

'Look, don't be hard on yourself,' Matt tells me. 'This weekend is about relaxing and finding yourself again.'

The sunglasses prevent Matt from seeing my eyes filling with tears.

Don't cry. Not now.

'And besides,' he goes on, 'this course sounds great for you! Art, photography and ... erm, all that. All the stuff you used to love doing.'

'Yeah, can't wait for the "all that" part!' I laugh. 'So, what are you going to do while I'm gone?'

'Playing rugby tomorrow. Gym Sunday. Gotta get this body in shape. Never too early to start looking good for the wedding, Steph,' he says, laughing, taking his left hand off the wheel and making his bicep pop. The smooth, curved lines of his toned arm are visible through his thin, long-sleeved top, which I playfully run my fingers down.

'Lucky me!' I whisper. 'Ooh! We're here!'

The car indicator starts to click as we turn into Heathwood Hall. Late afternoon October light casts a low sun over the road ahead, which is lined with an avenue of old oak trees exploding with red, orange and yellow leaves. Creeping up the drive, I remove my glasses to peek at the building which slowly reveals itself. The brochure describes it as a 'nineteenth-century

Jacobean-style mansion house'. The front of the building faces out towards the rolling landscape and hills, and a pretty terrace is the feature point, hosting a beautiful fountain.

Matt parks just outside reception which is at the side of the building and hauls all my stuff out of the boot.

'Listen,' he says, wrapping his arms around my waist, 'have fun, and let's get that Stephanie I fell in love with back. Love you.'

'Love you, too,' I say, moving closer to him. Taking my face in his hands, he smiles at me for a moment before landing a little kiss on my forehead.

'See you Sunday, call me if you need anything,' he reels off, walking back to his car, 'and don't get into any trouble!'

'Me? Never!' I shout back.

Turns out Dad has booked me into The Starlight Room here, which is also the most expensive. It's a suite, so wildly indulgent and a bit unnecessary when you're solo, but I appreciate the sentiment. After sitting on the four-poster bed with my coat on for fifteen minutes, staring at the fireplace, I figure I should probably get a move on.

Jumping in the shower in an attempt to relax, I'm hoping that I'll feel brave enough to attend the obligatory welcome drinks in the bar followed by dinner. I honestly don't know if I can manage it. I don't know how many times I can repeat the same snippet of small talk with people. Everyone will ask why I'm here, because everyone is here for a reason.

I feel it coming on as soon as I step out the shower. Panic attacks have become a frequent thing in the past few months and I've been given various methods to cope with them, but they keep coming back. It's the creeping nature of them I can't stand. The slow-moving panic slides into your throat, like smoke in the dirty bars of days gone by, and once you've clocked it, there's no way back. Any attempt to start breathing normally is wasted, because you just get more worked up.

Gripping on to the sink in the bathroom to the point where my knuckles turn white, I stare hard at my blurred reflection in the misty mirror, concentrating on breathing. My soaking wet hair is scraped back, leaving my make-up free face looking pale and exposed. My skin, already hot from the shower, becomes even more so. A sticky film covers my body as anxiety gushes out of it. Every bit of oxygen in my lungs feels like it's being squeezed out at the rate of a balloon which has been blown up and then quickly let go. What a pathetic sight. I can't even come away for two nights on my own without falling apart.

When I eventually get myself under control and dry my hair, I make the decision to call Matt and tell him to pick me up.

I can't do this.

Big, hot tears stream from my eyes as I run around the room, trying to locate my phone. I eventually find it, but there's no signal. I just want to go home. Taking deep breaths, I grab my coat, put my boots on and leave the room on a quest to find somewhere that gets service.

Rushing down the sweeping staircase back to reception, I'm going so fast I almost trip up several times on the wooden steps. Reaching the bottom, I run straight to the reception area.

And that's when I see him.

CHAPTER 2

Jamie

The fire crackles and fizzes with furious intent. It's one of those huge fireplaces you get in places like these, grand and imposing. Standing in front of it, I feel the force of its heat, which is a sharp contrast to the icy draft creeping in from somewhere.

As I stand gazing at the sign above the fireplace, the stillness of the moment is interrupted by the sound of footsteps approaching. And that's when I see her.

She bursts into reception and we exchange a brief, momentary glance.

Turning my eyes back to the sign above the fireplace, I sense her presence as she walks around me. I watch her out of the corner of my eye, see her fidgeting about in her pockets, looking at her phone and blowing her nose at the reception desk. She sighs, loudly. I'm unsure as to whether she's in need of help or just an irate guest who should be left alone.

'Erm, there's nobody on the desk. I'm waiting too,' I tell her, trying to be helpful.

'Oh, right. OK, I'll wait,' she says quietly, turning around to face me. She tucks her long blonde hair behind her ears and wraps her coat around her more tightly. Her face is stained with tears, her big green eyes are filled with sadness. She stands with her arms folded, frowning slightly, staring at the floor.

'Do you agree with that?' I ask.

'Excuse me?' she replies, looking a little confused.

'You agree with that?' I ask again, nodding at the wooden plaque above the hearth. She looks up to see what I'm referring to. It's a large dark piece of wood which has been ornately carved with intricate decoration. Inscribed into the wood, in gold, it reads:

You meet your fate on the road you take to avoid it

The tiniest of smiles appears on her face.

'No,' she says. 'Do you?'

'Sure do. You're not a fate-believer?'

'Not really. Well, I suppose I used to be, back when I was a kid. But not any more.'

'That sounds like a sad story.'

'Yeah, natural cynic here, I'm afraid,' she says and shrugs.

'You don't think things happen for a reason? More a believer in coincidence, are you?' I ask.

She studies the sign for a few moments, unaware she's doing a 'thinking' face. The sparks and pops coming from the fire are the only sounds breaking the silence.

'I'm not really much of a believer in anything, to be honest,' she finally says. 'It's a beautiful piece, though.'

I smile, turning to look at her. 'You think so? What do you like about it?'

'It's so intricate. The lines are so smooth in that bottom bit,' she says, pointing up at the sign, 'but that bit, there … the roses or flowers; how do you even carve that into wood? It's incredible.'

'It certainly is,' I agree. 'I actually love how it's asymmetrical. Probably quite an unconventional move for when it was created, I'd imagine. Adds to its quirkiness.'

'Yes!' she smiles, enthusiastically. 'Look at that bit in the middle. It looks like a Celtic design or a knot or something.'

'Ah!' I say, looking up at the intertwining lines of wood which twist around the sign, like vines, meeting at the top and forming a beautiful maze-like design. 'That's a true lover's knot. It represents love, affection and friendship in art.'

She nods in appreciation of what I've just said, but I can tell she's just being polite.

'Nah, you're still not buying it, are you? Still a non-believer?' I wince at her.

'Yep!' she laughs, looking towards reception.

13

'Are you in a hurry to check out?' I ask her.

'Yes. Well, no. Kind of. I can't get any phone signal and I need to call someone and tell them to pick me up.'

'Oh, you won't get any phone signal in here. It's a nightmare,' I tell her. 'There is literally one hotspot in the entire place you can get a signal if you know where it is. I can show you if you want?'

'That would be brilliant! Thank you,' she says, gratefully.

I usher her outside and down the steps.

'Thanks so much for this,' she says. 'I'm not putting you out, am I? Are you checking out or just arriving?'

'Just arrived after a long drive from Manchester.'

'I was trying to place your accent. I was going to say Leeds but I am awful with dialects.'

'*Leeds*?' I yelp, completely outraged. 'Wish I'd never offered to help you now!'

She laughs as we reach the terrace. It's all lit up, the glow from the rooms inside pouring out at intervals across the façade. The huge fountain I'm taking her to stands in front of it. Beautifully ornate, stone leaves and roses adorn the tiers, weaving around the structure like snakes. A frozen young woman dances on the top holding a flute-type thing. Her dress swirls, her arms are wild.

'Wow! That's gorgeous,' she says, looking at the fountain. 'I bet it's stunning when it's switched on.'

'Well, this is your hotspot. Try it.'

She reaches into her coat pocket and brings her phone out. The white background illuminates her face when she sparks it into action.

'You were right! One tiny bar of signal!' she says, calling someone and holding the phone to her ear.

I suddenly feel like I'm intruding, so slowly back away and head towards reception.

'Typical!' she shouts, as I spin around, facing her again. 'I go to all this trouble to make a phone call and … straight to voicemail. I'll try again in a few minutes.'

'Want some company?' I ask. 'I really feel like I ought to see this mission through.'

'If you want …' she says, sitting on the edge of the fountain, facing out into the darkness where the hills are. I take a seat next to her.

'So, are you coming or going?'

'Good question!' She laughs, gently. 'I have no idea,' she says, running her hands through her hair, before clasping them together on her knees. 'I only arrived a few hours ago but I might leave tonight.'

'OK … Are you here on your own?'

'Yes. Well, no. I'm supposed to be here with a group. Doing an art thing. But I don't think I'm up to it,' she says quietly, checking her phone.

'Why not?'

She goes quiet, peering down at the stone floor and tapping the tip of her boots together before answering.

'I've had a tough time recently. I had a bit of a breakdown six months ago and I'm trying to get over it.'

'Ah, OK. I'm so sorry.'

She casts a polite smile my way. The kind of smile which says, 'I know there's nothing you can say to that'.

'So, what do you actually want that you don't have?'

'What do you mean?' she asks, frowning.

'Well, generally, if things are bad in your life it's because you need or want something you currently don't have. What's *your* thing?'

She gazes out into the darkness in front of us, searching for an answer. The light from the hall shines intimately on to her face.

'I honestly have no idea,' she says, eventually, shaking her head. 'I mean, I have everything I want – a supportive family, a great job, I'm getting married next year …'

'I think there's a difference between what we *need* and what we *want* and it's up to you to figure out what the difference is.'

'Maybe I'm just being a brat and need to be more grateful for what I have,' she says, rather forcefully.

'Nah,' I shoot back. 'I reckon there's probably a lot going on between the lines you haven't figured out yet. But you will. Sure of it.'

'Maybe,' she says and then laughs, putting her hands in her coat pockets in an attempt to keep warm.

'What's so funny?' I smile.

'You just remind me of someone who would say something like that, that's all.'

Playfully narrowing my eyes at her, which makes her laugh even more, I change the subject.

'So, how come you're doing this art course anyway?'

'Art – well, mainly photography – used to be a huge hobby of mine years ago, so my family booked me on to it. Thought it would help me find myself.'

'Well, for what it's worth, I think you should do the course. It sounds like something you could get a lot out of. Art has an amazing knack of soothing the soul.'

'You think so?' she asks, tilting her head with surprise in her voice. 'I wouldn't have had you down as an art bod. Arty types are quite flamboyant and you look too …'

'Too what?'

She looks me up and down. I'm worried I look scruffy – I haven't shaved in a few days, and because I'm dark-haired, this means I already have something between stubble and beard.

'Normal …' she says, eventually.

I laugh. 'Well, I wouldn't have had you down as being as "broken" as you say you are. I guess appearances can be deceptive, can't they?'

'I suppose so.' She smiles. 'So, what are you here for?'

'Just here with some friends for the weekend,' I tell her. 'Listen, why don't you sleep on it and decide tomorrow?'

Just then, her phone starts to ring. She picks it out of her pocket and looks at the screen, before quickly glancing at me.

'You better take that. It was lovely to meet you – oh, I'm Jamie,' I say quickly, shuffling off back towards the hall.

'Stephanie,' she replies with a smile as she answers the phone.

Easels, pencils, charcoals and acrylic paints are scattered around. Some heaters have been placed in the room, presumably so that the life model doesn't freeze to death when she comes out. The warm air roars as it circulates around us.

'Hi, everyone! My name is Jamie Dobson and I'll be running this fine-art workshop ...'

Each of the participants watches me as they sit behind their workstations, eager to get started. They nod along, impressed with my credentials as I tell them I'm twenty-eight years old and gained a First Class degree from Central Saint Martins, won prestigious internships with well-known artists and have exhibited regionally. And then I notice her at the back of the room, smiling at me.

'So, you decided to stay after all?' I ask, going over as soon as my intro finishes.

She laughs, shaking her head in disbelief. 'What can I say? You talked me into it.'

We spend the next few hours drawing various life pieces: an arrangement of items in the middle of the room, some fruit and then a life model.

'Please don't look, it's rubbish. I'm terrible at life drawing,' Stephanie says, trying to cover her easel as I make my way around the class.

'No, you're not. I love what you've done with light on that bit. Well done!'

'The bit where I've just coloured it in black around the chair, you mean? That's not the point of the assignment, is it, though?!'

'The point is to interpret what you see. Not draw a perfect nose, or pair of hands,' I tell her. 'And besides, shadows are actually a very important part of pencil and charcoal drawing.'

I reach out and place my finger about a centimetre away from the left part of her jaw, as if telling her to tilt it up slightly.

'When you draw a face, you don't draw a line,' I explain, drawing my finger parallel to the edge of her face. Her green eyes watch mine the whole time. 'A lot of drawing is just as much about depicting what you *don't* see as what you do see.'

She laughs, gently. 'I don't really understand that.'

'Sometimes, you can only see what's there when you draw around it … when you see what's in the shadows. You see?'

'Yes,' she whispers.

'Jamie, could you take a look at this hand for me? I've messed it up!' a man shouts from the other side of the room.

Our eyes flicker towards each other once more, before I head off to see my other students, leaving her to find shadows to draw.

After a day of workshops, all I want to do is go outside and get some fresh air. I love teaching, but it's full on. Walking out into the grounds at the front of the Hall, I see someone sitting on the bench under the huge oak tree. I smile when I realise it's Stephanie again.

'Strike a pose!' she shouts, pointing a camera in my direction.

I stop and stand, hands in my pockets, all my weight on one leg, looking off into the distance. My best catalogue model impersonation.

''Ow's this, love?' I yell back, in my thickest Mancunian accent, channelling my inner moody Liam Gallagher.

'Marvellous, darling! Next stop, Milan!' she shouts back as I walk over to where she's sitting.

'Do you mind if I join you?' I ask, gesturing towards the empty space on the bench next to her.

'No, not at all,' she replies, taking out her iPod earbuds and shoving them into her coat pocket.

'I'm glad you decided to stay.'

'Yeah, me too. It wasn't anywhere near as bad as I thought it would be. And I feel proud of myself.'

'You should be. I mean, I don't know why, but you should be.'

'But I can't believe you didn't tell me you were a teacher on this bloody course!'

I turn to her, laughing.

'Nah,' I say, shrugging. 'It was irrelevant. Far better I was the cool stranger you opened up to. You might not have decided to stay if you'd known you'd see me again.'

'Erm, who said I thought you were cool?'

'I'm an artist, so of *course* I'm cool! No, you're actually right. I'm just an art geek who never made it as a proper artist. I'm happy watching from the sidelines, though.'

'What? Oh shut up!' she squeals, playfully nudging me with her elbow. 'I've heard all about your credentials, you told us yourself.'

'Maybe,' I say, laughing. 'Listen, do you fancy a drink? I could go grab a bottle and bring it out. Fetch some blankets. It's a stunning night for stargazing.'

She looks up to admire the sky which is getting darker by the minute, going quiet for a few seconds.

'Stephanie?'

'Yeah? Erm, sorry,' she says. 'A drink. Yeah, just one glass though. Don't want to be hungover tomorrow!'

'OK, then!' I say, jumping up and walking back towards the Hall, before turning back to shout, 'What colour? Red or white?'

21

'White!' she calls. 'I hate red!'

'Me too!' I shout back.

I manage to borrow some of those huge, thick tartan blankets you get in these places, so we wrap them around ourselves and Stephanie tucks her hair in at the back, but it remains loose around her face. I made her promise not to tell anyone I used such a blanket on the basis that I was supposed to be a 'hard northerner' and I was only doing it to make her feel better.

We don't stop talking and laughing. Our lives are so different – I went to a rough comp, she attended fee-paying independent schools – but we have so many similarities with our love for art, literature and music. We both even despise Queen – the band, not the monarch. 'I love "Bohemian Rhapsody", Jamie,' she says, 'but I don't get the other stuff. It's just screaming and drama.'

As predicted, it's a really clear night and the stars shine brightly.

'So am I allowed to ask what actually happened a few months ago? Because you seem to have it all quite together now.'

She shrugs. 'It's a bit of a long story, really. I just lost myself for a while.'

'Vague. Nice,' I joke, doing an 'OK' sign with my fingers as I wink.

'Yeah, I do vague well, don't you think?'

'So very well,' I agree. 'How did the rest of your family react?'

'Now, that is a difficult one to answer.'

'Why?'

'My family don't like talking about things. We have elephants in our rooms and we don't discuss them.'

'Has it always been like that?'

'No,' she replies, taking a large gulp of wine. 'Anyway, tell me about your family. Folks? Brothers? Sisters?'

'Only child. Mum still lives in Manchester. Dad walked out on us when I was little. I haven't seen him since I was ten.'

'Oh, I'm sorry ...'

'It is what it is.'

'His loss, I'm sure,' she says, upbeat, to try and lighten the tone of the conversation, which has descended into rather deep waters on all fronts. 'Anyway, now you have to tell me more about you.'

'There's not much to say. Pretty much just working at the school and creating my own stuff when I can. I use the garage as a workshop.'

'Oh, how marvellous that you can keep doing your own stuff,' she says, enthusiastically. 'So, what's the dream?'

'My dream?'

'Yes.'

I think about it for a few seconds, gazing up at the sky as I consider my answer.

'To work as an artist professionally and make a living from it. My best mate, Cal, is a designer. Hardly earns anything at the moment but he will make it at some point. He at least gets manages to get his stuff out there. Me, him and my wife were best friends at uni.'

'Oh, it must be so important to be married to someone who gets the art thing,' Stephanie says. 'What's her name?'

'Helen. And oh, yeah! She absolutely loves that I'm creative.'

'I can imagine. How long have you been together?'

I smile at her. 'Since we were eighteen.'

'Oh, really? That's amazing!'

'We met at Saint Martins. She's an incredible designer and works in advertising in Manchester.'

'Oh, OK, so she went down the more commercial route?'

'Yes, she's much more level-headed than I am. I'm the classic bohemian romantic artist, I'm afraid.'

'So, when did you get married?'

'Three years ago. No kids yet – everyone always asks,' I say, rolling my eyes.

'No rush, I'm sure. I'm not planning on going down that route for a while,' she agrees, taking a sip of wine.

'Anyway …' I nudge her arm. 'What's *your* dream? I see from the enormous rock on your finger you're engaged. Big fancy wedding planned?'

'A big wedding next July, yes,' she says, bringing her hand closer to her face as the diamond sparkles in the light coming from the Hall.

'Is that the kind of wedding you've always wanted?'

'It'll be really beautiful. It's in this gorgeous castle about an hour away which has got a moat and everything. Matt found it and thought it would be perfect,' she gushes.

'How did you meet Matt?'

'It was about four years ago when I lived in London. At a party. I mean, in all honesty, it was when I was going through a bad time but didn't realise that until later on,' she explains, wrapping her blanket around her more tightly. 'But he stuck with me through it all. He works for our family company, as a sales manager. I work there too, as marketing manager."

'And you're happy?'

'Yes, of course!' she answers, looking at me like I'm demented for even asking such a thing. 'I mean, I've got the ring, we've set the date, we've invited one hundred of our closest family and friends—'

'Only one hundred?'

'And, besides,' she says, laughing, 'Matt is such a great guy. When he looks at me he sees security, safety, a wife, the future mother of his children ...'

'I'm sure he sees what I do – a smart, funny, intelligent, beautiful young woman.'

'No,' she quickly shoots back, glancing at me. 'Matt *looks* at me. He doesn't *see* me. There's a difference.'

Her eyes suddenly leave my face; she doesn't know where to look.

'Yes,' I say quietly, 'there is.'

We are both still, silent. Her eyes are drawn back to mine. It's that moment when you can just feel a connection with someone, when your heart starts to beat a little quicker. There is suddenly a ravine of uncertainty between us in the inches between our faces. It feels like a lifetime, but like most intense moments, it actually only lasts a few seconds. We've been chattering away for so long, and now it's silent. The only thing I can hear is our breathing, the pace of which has dramatically increased. As our faces inch closer, I feel the faintest brush of her mouth on my lips. And then we simultaneously jump away from each other.

The silence continues, only this time it's filled with awkwardness and embarrassment.

'Jesus! Erm, I'm so sorry,' I say, placing my glass on the grass and removing my blanket.

'No, I'm sorry!' she replies. 'God, what the hell happened?'

'I've no idea. We've probably just had too much to drink,' I say, lying. Neither of us are particularly drunk, but I need to say something because I have no clue about what just happened. 'I should go.'

Standing up, I take a few deep breaths and edge away from her.

'Yes, of course. You go, I'll stay here for a bit.'

'Sure you'll be OK?' I ask, running my hands through my hair.

'Yeah, I'm sure,' she says, raising her knees up to her chest on the bench.

'OK, well. I'll probably see you tomorrow before you leave.'

'Night, Jamie.'

I got no more than a few hours' sleep.

What. The. Fuck?

That near kiss.

What the hell was I thinking? What were both of us thinking? I've never, ever done anything like that before. Thank God we stopped it before anything happened. I shouldn't have let it get to that stage to start with. But I was having such a great time with her. She was just someone I wanted to get to know. There's something about her …

I don't see her the next day. She isn't in any of my workshops.

When the course is over and checkout time arrives, the reception area is packed with people. Everyone gathers next to the fireplace and I can't help but peer up at the sign on the wall which sparked our first conversation. A smile sweeps across my face as I wait to hand my keys in.

27

Roxie Cooper

'Jamie?'

I turn around to see Stephanie, looking much happier than she was last time she was here. Her cheekbones are accentuated when she smiles, her nose is slightly upturned and wiggles slightly when she talks.

She's beautiful.

'Stephanie! Are you off now?'

'Yes, Matt is outside. Just wanted to say goodbye.'

'Ah! OK!' I smile, hiding a weird disappointment I can't quite work out. 'Well, it's been lovely knowing you, albeit briefly.'

'You too,' she smiles back, her eyes locked on to mine.

'And best of luck with everything. Keep up the drawing, you've got potential,' I tell her.

'I will. Perhaps I'll come back next year,' she says, picking her bag up and walking towards the main door.

I stand motionless for a few seconds, wondering whether to say anything. Who am I to be dishing out life advice? And especially to someone I've known for less than forty-eight hours? Oh fuck it. I'll never see her again.

'Steph!'

She turns around, with the door half-open as I quickly run over.

'I just wanted to say …'

'Yeah?' she whispers.

28

'People will see you if you let them in, you know.'

Smiling very gently, she kisses me on my cheek. 'Thank you, Jamie.'

I watch her walk down the steps and into the car park. I watch a blond-haired man get out of his sporty blue convertible and hug her before putting her bag in the boot. And then I watch her take one last glance back at the door I'm looking through before getting into the car.

CHAPTER 3

Saturday 18 August 2007

Stephanie

I check out my reflection from all angles in the full-length mirror on the hotel room wall. I want to look nice, obviously. But it's also important the dress has enough 'give' in it because I'm going to stuff my face with food and do not want to be breathing in all night.

Running my hands over the pretty broderie anglaise skater dress, I do a half twirl to assess its swishiness. Glancing over my shoulder in the mirror reflection, I compare it to the other two dresses I brought which are hanging off the edge of the bed. A woman of indecision, that's me. Having just arrived back from Thailand on honeymoon, my skin is the most tanned it's been in years, so I've gone for three dresses I hardly ever wear on account of them clashing with my usually ivory-white exterior. An emerald-green, silky, fitted high-neckline affair which brings out my eyes; a dressy yellow floral thing that I bought in a sale and have never worn; and this one, which I opt for.

The view is spectacular from the fifth floor. Even though Leeds is a modern city, it retains a character about it. The boutique hotel we are staying in has been renovated from an old mill and has ancient beams on the ceilings, wooden pillars in the middle of the room and uneven walls.

'Come on, birthday girl!' he says, popping his head around the bathroom door as the smell of deodorant wafts into the bedroom. It's overpowering in this heat we've been having. 'Get a move on! We want to go for a wander before dinner.'

'All right, keep your hair on!' I roll my eyes at Matt. 'It's all that shopping's worn me out.'

'Yeah, worn my wallet out too.'

I playfully stick my tongue out at him, before carrying on getting ready.

Sitting in front of the dressing table, I add the last touches of make-up. My green eyes are my 'thing', apparently. They're described as cat-like, which I usually emphasise with liquid eyeliner. Not sure about the rest of me, though. I wouldn't say I'm anything special to look at. My nose has a little upturned bit at the end I could do without and both Ebony and I have our mum's figure – not skinny, but we have a decent shape. We have hips and boobs that will probably become an issue as we get older if we don't look after ourselves. But, for the moment, we are thankful for them.

I add a bit of red lipstick and, reaching into my toiletry bag for the finishing touch, pull out my perfume.

There was always something so comforting about the one Mum had. She'd use just the right amount: a quick spritz on each side of her neck and then on her wrist, before gently rubbing the other one on it. Then, dramatically spraying a cloud into the air above her.

That was my favourite part.

I'd dance about in the falling plume of a mixture of floral- and fruit-smelling particles as they landed in my waist-length golden hair in an explosion of jasmine, apricot, vanilla and amber, giggling with my sister as we helped her pick out a dress for the important dinner she was going to with my dad. She went to a lot of them.

'Oooh! No, my sweeties! That's no good for dancing in!' she'd say, scowling at a dress we'd be dragging out of the wardrobe that, by anyone else's standards, would be more than adequate, but not for my mum.

'How about this one …?' she'd say.

'Yes!' Ebony and I would shriek, watching her slip into the most beautiful, sparkliest, floor-length gown you've ever clapped eyes on in your life, rather like a magician's assistant's.

My amazing mummy.

She always looked beautiful and full of life. The red lipstick – her trademark feature – contrasted against her natural blonde hair. Just like mine does.

It was Matt's idea to come to Leeds for my birthday weekend. I'd never been before, but he said we should explore more of the north. The furthest I've ever been is Durham and that's only because Ebony studied Law there and while I spent many a drunken weekend visiting the pubs of Newcastle, we never once visited Durham Cathedral, which I feel terrible about now. Students, eh?

I thought of Jamie on the journey here. I remembered how outraged he was when I placed his accent as Leeds and laughed to myself. I wonder what he's up to these days. I've found myself thinking about him often, actually.

It's a beautiful, hazy summer evening, bustling with people. Matt and I hold hands, like newlyweds do, pottering around The Calls, a lovely old part of central Leeds. Sunglasses on, we've dressed well, we look good.

The restaurant we are eating at for my birthday dinner is in a huge, old post office building. Large chandeliers hang from the ceiling. Curved booths covered with velour line the walls, with smaller tables filling out the middle. I adore the buzz of restaurants and watching everyone. Matt calls me nosy but I just like watching them interact. You can tell so much by what people don't say to each other.

Matt fiddles about on his phone as I order some wine.

'We agreed no phones – can you put it away?' I ask. He's always messing about with something on there.

'I'm just checking in on Facebook,' he says, as if I'm so ridiculous for even asking. His fingers type quickly for another few seconds and he pops his phone back in his pocket. 'Right, baby, all yours.'

The food is delicious here. Matt got the recommendation from a client and he wasn't wrong. It's one of those meals which is long and drawn out – my favourite kind.

'Do you fancy some cocktails after?' I ask Matt. 'Doesn't feel right finishing the evening without one after being on holiday.'

'Erm, Steph,' he says in a serious tone, 'I think if you're after one of Kiko's pina colada specials, you'll struggle here.'

I burst out laughing. 'Oh, they were special, weren't they? I just can't get over how much stuff he put in them.'

'It was 20 per cent drink and 80 per cent bloody jungle in there.' he responds and laughs. 'And don't forget the sparklers. *And* the fact he served them to us in a porcelain duck!'

'Oh, the whole thing was so much fun, wasn't it?'

'Gorgeous.' He smiles. 'But we've got more to come. The next stage – we need to get house-hunting.'

'We can certainly see what's out there. It's exciting.'

'So, when do you think we should think about kids?' he asks, oh-so-matter-of-factly, popping some Tuscan calamari into his mouth.

'We're only just married, Matt. Don't you think we should enjoy this time together? What's the rush? Besides, I've been doing really well and a baby is a very big change,' I tell him, rotating my wedding ring with my left thumb and trying to bat away the sick feeling which swirls up in my stomach.

'There's no rush, but it's expected, isn't it? The next natural step,' he states. 'How is therapy going? You don't really talk about it much.'

'Well, that's kind of the point. It's private,' I say, abruptly. 'But, yes, it's going well.'

Matt nods. 'Good. Well, that's the main thing. What's she like?'

'Jane?' I reply, almost shocked he's asking about her. We never, ever talk about Jane.

'Yeah. Does she sit in a white coat, asking you to sit on a couch?'

'What? And makes me tell her all about my mother?' I say.

He doesn't respond and I don't blame him. I look away, feeling immediate regret for that unnecessary comment.

'Sorry, baby. I just don't want to talk about any of that,' I apologise. 'Not this weekend.'

'Don't worry. I shouldn't have brought it up,' he says, reaching for my hand. 'It's fine. And I'm sure you'll get better eventually. Let's change the subject.'

When the main course arrives, we're playing my favourite game: 'What's Their Story?' The rules are simple: select groups/couples and, going on how they're acting and talking with each other, come up with what their story is.

So far, Matt has decided that the group of four men to our right is actually an assassination team sent to sort out the raucous group of women at the opposite end of the restaurant going by the filthy looks they keep shooting in their direction. He does hilarious voiceovers when each of them talks, which makes my wine go down the wrong way. He really does make me howl sometimes.

'What about them?' he asks, gesturing to a couple sitting on a table to our left.

They look about our age. She's wearing a pretty hot-pink dress with a sweetheart neckline. Her dark hair is wavy, obviously affected by the humidity, but it looks effortlessly styled and her make-up is understated. He sits opposite her, wearing a white polo shirt. His hair is virtually black, as is the stubble on his face, and he's wearing some of those nerdy but cool black-rimmed glasses. They're chatting away to each other in a way which suggests they hold an intimacy nobody else in this room understands. It's like nobody else is here. Their eyes dance about with each other and she occasionally glances down at her lap, before quickly meeting his gaze again. It's hypnotic.

'He's planning on getting some with her tonight,' Matt proclaims.

The guy reaches out for his date's hand. She meets it halfway across the table. They don't hold hands, their fingers just caress and play with each other. Slowly. Sensually. The entire time, their eyes flirt with each other. I'd love to know what they're saying. The candle on the table adds a closeness to the scene and I feel awkward, watching what's clearly such an intimate moment for them.

'No way,' I say, turning to Matt. 'It's more than that.'

'I'm telling you,' he says, rolling his eyes, 'he'll be in her knickers tonight.'

'I've absolutely no doubt of that. But they're in a relationship. They have a connection. Bloody look at them!'

Matt gawps at the couple with no thought whatsoever for subtlety, before turning back to me and reiterating he was correct to start with.

'Still in the honeymoon period,' he declares. 'Between one and three dates. Tops. You don't get all smoochy like that beyond the first few dates.'

Don't you? A little part of me feels so sad when Matt says this. Because I look at them and a part of me wants to feel like that.

But maybe Matt's right. Some people just aren't like that. Matt and I were never like that. We had a honeymoon period, sure. But it was more about laughs, wanting to spend loads of time together, staying up chatting until late – that kind of stuff. Some people just aren't about the swoons – and that's OK.

But how do you know you're the absolute happiest you can be? What does 'happiness' even feel like?

'It's the *best* day of your life', 'I got to marry my *best* friend'; that's what they always say. Everything is simply the *best* on your wedding day. I imagine these people spending the entire day, grinning from ear to ear, simply unable to believe they've married this incredible person. Is that how it's supposed to be? Does it last thereafter? Is *that* happiness? Or does it morph into more of a contentedness? Is that acceptable? Is that 'settling'?

'I guess you're right,' I say and smile.

After five courses I am fit to burst and don't think I need to eat for at least another week. Leaning back in my chair, I'm relieved I went for the skater dress.

'Right, present time!' Matt declares, producing a cream envelope from his jacket pocket.

'What?' I reply, confused. 'This weekend is my birthday present. And besides, my birthday isn't even for another few days yet.'

'It's just a little extra one. And, in any case, you got me the watch last year for my thirtieth which must have cost you a fortune.'

'It's not a competition, Matt. And I knew you'd love it, which is all that matters,' I say, glancing at the gift I bought him which is wrapped around his wrist. I had it engraved: 'Love you, M. From your S. Xx'. He never takes it off.

'Open it!' he urges, grinning like an excited child.

I reach into the envelope and pull out a small pamphlet. I know what it is as soon as I see the venue emblazoned across the top. Catching my breath, I take a minute to compose myself before responding.

'You got so much out of it last year which is why I'm sending you back again in October,' he says, proud of himself.

'Heathwood Hall Art Workshop ...'

A flutter of excitement builds in my tummy which I try to ignore.

'Thank you so much! I love it!' I say, leaning over to give him a kiss.

'Well, you came back last year raving about it and it was nice to see you smiling again,' he very astutely observes. 'Even though you had the minor indiscretion ... but we'll forget that.'

'What?'

'You. Drinking, even though you said you wouldn't.'

'Oh. Yes,' I sigh. Matt could tell I'd had a drink when he picked me up in the Heathwood Hall car park and asked me about before we'd even left the grounds. I explained it was no more than two glasses of wine and I was absolutely fine, but I still felt terrible about it – especially after the performance in the car on the way there. Still, he promised not to tell Dad and Ebony, thank God.

I nip to the loo before we leave. When I leave the cubicle, I see the loved-up, wild-haired girl washing her hands.

Catching her eye in the mirror, we share a smile.

'I love your dress,' I say. 'It really suits you.'

'Thank you,' she replies, quickly glancing down at it.

'It's gorgeous. Special occasion?' I ask, inquisitively.

'Yes, actually,' she admits, reapplying her lipstick. 'Anniversary!'

'Oh! How lovely,' I reply, a little bit more eager than I should be. Ha! I was right. Even if it was six months, it's still an anniversary. 'Congratulations!'

'Thanks! Been married two years this weekend!' she says, grinning from ear to ear. She almost giggles when she says it, she's that thrilled.

My mouth almost drops open. I go from smug to envious in two seconds flat.

'Wow! That's brilliant. Good for you. Have a fabulous weekend!' I gush, before hurrying out the bathroom and telling Matt I fancy some cocktails somewhere.

A few hours later we're lying in a pile of white, crumpled sheets. The windows have been flung open in a desperate attempt to get some air into the room which smells of sex and my perfume.

'How did you know I was the one?' I ask Matt as he rearranges the cotton sheet over us. He always gets too hot in the summer.

'What do you mean?'

'What made me different to everyone else?' I ask. 'What was it about *me*?'

'You were great fun,' he says after thinking about it.

'OK, *were* is past tense, and anyone can be fun.'

'Well, you'll admit yourself you've had a hard time lately. Doesn't mean I love you less, babe.'

'Oh, thanks!'

'Oh, come on! What's brought this on?'

'Nothing,' I lie. 'Just be nice to know.'

'You're hot, fun, always up for a laugh, lovely,' he reels off. 'Can I stop now? I'm so tired!'

Smart, funny, intelligent, beautiful.

'Yes, goodnight ...' I turn over on my side, away from him. He's snoring within seconds.

I can't sleep. It's funny how your brain works when you're lying in bed. Thoughts flit about like electrical sparks on a switchboard, unrelated and yet somehow all linked together, like a chain reaction ...

I walked over to her as she sat at her dressing table, one of those French ones with three mirrors on it and loads of drawers, placing a diamond choker around her neck.

'I want to be just like you when I'm older, Mum!' I whispered into her ear, giggling after I'd said it. I was so in awe of her.

'You will be, baby. I love you so very much,' she told me, kissing my forehead and wiping the resulting red lipstick smudge off as she laughed.

'But, who will I marry? Will they love me like Dad loves you?' I asked.

I watched her face from all angles in the three-way mirror as she considered her answer.

'Darling, Stephanie. You'll know when you find the one you're meant to be with, and you know how?' Mum teased. I hung on to her every word, watching her immaculately made-up face as she spoke to me.

'You'll be in a crowded room, talking to other people and he won't be able to take his eyes off you. He will love you even though you're not perfect, because none of us are. He will love you because you're perfectly imperfect. That's how Daddy loves me.'

I looked at her, a bit confused. 'What does "perfectly imperfect" mean?' I asked, screwing my face up, wondering whether I'd said it right.

Her face softened slightly, her smile faded, 'It just means you're human and you make mistakes sometimes.'

'But how will he find me?'

'He just will. Because everyone has a someone they're meant for and you're just kind of thrown together by the

universe whether you like it or not. It makes sure you find each other – trust me on that,' she said and winked.

But how can you be sure if the person you're with *is* that person? I mean, it's not something you think to ask when you're twelve years old, is it?

And it's too late to ask her now, because she's gone.

CHAPTER 4

Friday 12 October 2007

Stephanie

I arrive at Heathwood Hall, late afternoon. Alone and on time. Has it really been a year since I was here? It's not as picturesque as last time I arrived. Grey and drizzly clouds gather over the hills, threatening miserable weather for the weekend.

The reception area buzzes with participants waiting to check in. I recognise some of them. Then my eyes are drawn to the sign on the wall.

You meet your fate on the road you take to avoid it

I feel a tap on my right shoulder. Spinning around, I see him standing in front of me. He looks just the same as he did last year: same rugged features, icy blue eyes which contrast to his dark hair, and the black shirt he's wearing emphasises his tall, broad frame.

'Jamie, hi!'

He smells so familiar – an infusion of mint, lavender and sandalwood.

'You returned!' he says, smiling, putting his hands in the pockets of his jeans. 'It's great to see you. How have you been?'

'Good, thanks! I've even been working on my drawing.'

'Have you now?' he asks, raising his eyebrows.

'Yes!' I say proudly. 'Lots of drawing shadows and things which aren't there.'

I actually have been practising. Dad bought me a whole load of art supplies for Christmas and I wasted no time in putting them to use.

'And married now, I see,' he says, nodding towards my platinum wedding band, imprisoned on my hand by the engagement ring.

'Yes. Got married in July and it rained – so much for a summer wedding!'

'Ah well, English weather, I suppose,' he sympathises.

'Quite!'

Our eyes have been locked on each other the whole time.

'Anyway, I'd better go to do some prep before my first workshop tomorrow.'

I smile. 'Yes, of course. Good to see you.'

It's only when he leaves that I feel the blush in my cheeks fade and my heart rate return to normal.

*

After dumping my bags, I slope downstairs to the bar and chat to the others, intermittently glancing over at Jamie. It's a very civilised affair, with people talking about their favourite pieces of art and the odd bit of politics. I feel a bit displaced, and despite feeling the urge to grab the nearest bottle of wine, I stick to having one glass.

I somehow end up in a group who have wild opinions on Jackson Pollock, including Jamie. I watch him talk with such passion about art. He uses his entire body to express himself: his hands wave about, his eyes are animated, he leans forward, inviting everyone in to listen. And they do. It's compelling. His eyes captivate everyone in the group, including me.

After the mini art lecture, everyone goes up to the bar to get a drink, leaving me and Jamie in the corner of the room. I can't stop smiling at him.

'What?' he says, grinning back at me.

'You love what you do, don't you?'

'Don't you?' he asks, quizzically.

'I don't love being a marketing manager like that, no!' I say, laughing.

'There'll be something you have the same passion for. You just have to find it and then do it. Everyone has something.'

'Just like that?' I shrug, with an air of bewilderment.

'Yes,' he says, taking a drink out of his beer. 'You look very nice tonight, by the way.'

'Thank you.' I peek down at my leopard-print, polo-neck fitted top which is tucked into my hipster bootcut jeans. 'I wasn't sure if it was too … Shania Twain?'

'Well, I ain't got a flash car, brains or particularly brilliant hair, so I can't imagine you're impressed much.'

We both laugh, reaching for our drinks, getting comfortable on the sofa.

'So, tell me about the wedding,' he says.

'Ooh, yes! So—'

'Jamie – so sorry to interrupt you – could I borrow you for five minutes?' Bob, the course leader asks, popping out of nowhere.

Jamie flashes me a little smile and mouths 'sorry' as he's dragged off. It's getting late, anyway, so I head back to my room to get ready for tomorrow's workshops.

Pulling the curtains back the next morning reveals an overcast autumn day.

The photography workshop is first. We attend a quick seminar with our tutor, Tom, before going outside and taking some shots. This is the workshop I really enjoy. I love capturing things on film – a moment frozen in time. You can capture a tree blowing in the wind and you'll never see it in the same way again. The break of a wave crashes differently every single time. But it's people I love watching the most. Like the couple in the restaurant I saw with Matt.

There's something about witnessing a split second of a moment and having that on film. Expressions of people together. Expressions of joy, anger, sadness, happiness, disappointment, desire ... because you'll never capture that same emotion again, in the same way. The way their eyes crease, or their mouths move. It's different every single time.

Reaching the front of the Hall, I see some of the teachers chatting outside. Tom is gesturing towards the front of the building, talking about something.

'How are you getting on, Steph?' he asks.

'Oh, fine!' I respond, holding one of my iPod earbuds just outside my ear. 'I was just wondering, can we photograph people as part of this?'

'Yes, of course. As long as they don't mind. I think everyone is doing their own thing, though.'

'I'll help you out if you want?' Jamie says.

'I just want to get some natural shots with some scenery in the background.'

'Sure, happy to help. I've got a spare half hour.'

We walk into the grounds, past the tree where we had that moment together last year. I wonder if he's thinking about it as we walk by, and try to think of something to say, just to take my mind off it. I ask how his year has been and he tells me some funny stories about his pupils, his holiday to Greece and that his best friend, Cal, got married in Vegas. 'Did it without even telling me – the bastard!' he says.

'Right, so … how do you want to do this?' he asks. It feels like there's only us for miles. It's so quiet, you pick up on people's voices more.

'Can you just, you know, look out into the hills? Look like you're amazed by them,' I say, laughing, holding the camera up to my face, taking a deep breath. Jamie does a comedic shocked expression.

'No, a bit too much. Can you tone it down a bit, please?'

'Sorry, Mario Testino!' he says, deadpan. He looks out towards the hills, away from me and I take a second before I click, just to admire his jaw, which appears prominent through the lens. His hair, swept back from his face, is untamed, merging perfectly into the scenery we find ourselves in. It's mainly straight, but curls very slightly at the nape of his neck. His broad frame stands firm in the centre of the photo. He is the definition of tall, dark and handsome. He is what women would probably describe as rugged, but in a very clean, sexy way.

Click!

'You know, my mum always said that more words are spoken in a silent, captured image than in a full conversation if you take it at the right moment,' I go on, gesturing for him to move forwards as I walk.

'She's absolutely right. It's exactly the same for portraits, I find. They speak a thousand words. Very powerful stuff. Is your mum into all this, then?'

'What?'

49

'Photography? Art?'

'Oh …' I say, caught off guard, which is ridiculous seeing as I brought it up. 'No. Well, yes, she was. She died.'

'Oh, Stephanie. I'm really sorry.'

'Don't worry, it's fine. It was a long time ago now. I was only thirteen.'

'It's hard when a parent leaves when you're a kid. Doesn't really matter if they died or just fucked off for good. It changes the dynamic.'

'It really does …'

'When my dad left, I blamed my mum for so long. Wasn't her fault, obviously. But it made me so angry. I didn't have brothers or sisters so I dealt with it myself. I put all of my anger into art and that's what got me through. Art was my outlet, I suppose. I'd spend all of my free time in the art block, not wanting to go home. I'd spend hours sketching, painting. Became fascinated with drawing people … portraits.'

'I get that,' I say. 'I turned to music.'

'Ahhh! So that's why you always have your iPod on?' he asks.

'Yes,' I reply, finding it hard to hide the surprise in my voice that he noticed such a thing. 'I suppose it's my comfort blanket, my escape. In fact, when I was a teenager I used to—'

I cut myself off before going any further. No way am I telling him that. I've never even told Matt or Ebony I used to do that.

'What?' He looks confused.

'Oh, nothing,' I say lightly, swishing my hand around, to change the subject. Narrowing his eyes, he peers at me suspiciously, like he knows I'm hiding something. I return the look with a cheeky smile.

'I have to listen to music when I'm painting,' he admits, walking alongside me as I stop him occasionally to take a photo by placing a hand on his arm. 'It's important. Like the art, it becomes part of you.'

'Yes, I can relate to that.' I look at him through the lens of my camera. He stands, looking at the ground with his hands in his pockets, his hair falling just on to his cheekbones. 'So, what's your relationship like with your mum now?'

'Much better. I feel terrible for putting her through those teenage years, but it was a hard time for us both. Only later on, as an adult, could I properly grasp how hard it was for her. How is your relationship with your dad?'

'It's never quite recovered from Mum dying, to be honest. I think a part of him died with her. We get on well, but it's not the same. Nowhere near.'

Jamie nods, as though he understands where I'm coming from. He's unbelievably easy to talk to about this stuff.

'Anyway, how about I take a few photos of you?' he asks.

'No,' I reply, firmly. 'I take pictures, I don't like being in them.'

'OK.' He smiles. 'Actually, was that a spot of rain?' Jamie says, looking up to the sky. 'Let's take a few more quick photos and head back before it starts pouring.'

The evening is the same format as last year. I engage in polite conversation with the other course members, but it's Jamie who seems most interested in what I'm doing. I catch him glancing at me from another table throughout the meal. That smile he manages to hypnotise you with becomes even more captivating against the backdrop of candlelight and a glass or two of sauvignon blanc.

Once the meal ends, people start splintering off but I don't want to go back to my room yet, so I head to the bar for another drink.

'Why are we the only people ever here under the age of thirty?' Jamie asks, joining me.

'Because art is an old person's hobby?' I say and laugh.

'Excuse me, darling! Would you mind awfully ...?' An older woman and her friend totally interrupt by standing between us, clearly a bit pissed and wanting to gush at Jamie about how marvellous the workshop he did for them today was.

'Not at all! He's all yours.' I gesture towards him.

Before he knows it, they're dragging him off having bought him a whisky and he's mouthing 'help me' over his shoulder. Laughing, I raise my glass to him, but I'm actually relieved. It's probably for the best I'm not around him when I've had a drink.

I'm quite happy sitting alone next to the fire. I pull the sleeves of my top down over my hands, like teenagers do. I never grew out of that.

'Right, come on. We've got to go,' Jamie whispers urgently in my right ear.

'See you managed to escape then,' I say, giggling.

'For now. Come on, let's go outside'

'OK, I'll grab a bottle of white.' I smile, punching away all thoughts in my head which are telling me this is a very bad idea.

We pass the fountain with the dancing lady and we're just about to dash to the tree when heavy rain starts slamming out of the sky, bouncing off the floor. It's the kind of rain which drenches you in seconds and you don't know whether to be amused by it or furious.

'Shit! Plan B?' he shouts, screwing his face up and narrowing his eyes so he can see me through the sheet-like rain.

'Back to the bar?' I scream.

'We never get a conversation finished in there!'

Before I even have time to think about what I'm saying, I suggest it.

'My room? It's a suite, so it's got sofas and tables!'

'Yep! Let's go!'

We dash inside and up the sweeping staircase to The Starlight Room. Rainwater drips off the pair of us as I fumble around for the key.

*

Roxie Cooper

The thing being with Jamie is that time passes so quickly. It's ridiculous how much we've got in common and how much he makes me laugh. For hours, we've been sitting on the sofa in my room, listening to the thunder and watching the lightning outside. Only one lamp, on the side table next to the bed, supplies light to the room. It radiates a soft, intimate feel around us, fitting with the old building and weather outside.

I'm curled up in one corner of the sofa, knees up to my chest. Jamie sits inches away, extending his arm along the back of the sofa, so that his fingers occasionally sweep past my hair. The white shirt he's wearing contrasts against his dark features and he's rolled the sleeves up. The top few buttons are undone. He wears it with jeans and looks much more like a model than an artist.

'I'm glad you came back, I've been wondering how you were getting on,' he says.

'I wasn't planning on it. My husband was the one who booked it, actually.'

'Oh, OK,' he replies, looking slightly disappointed. 'Well, anyway, looks like the universe wanted you back here, Little Miss Cynical.'

I laugh at him. 'You and your universe nonsense again.'

'Shhh! It can hear you!' he says, putting his index finger against his mouth in a bid to get me to zip it.

'Anyway, I'd better get moving,' he says, looking at his watch. 'Don't want you losing out on your beauty sleep.'

'Yes, I didn't even realise the time,' I lie. As the last hour or so wore on, I've started to feel a little more awkward, wondering how this was going to end.

We both get up off the sofa, standing opposite each other. All manner of thoughts start rapidly whooshing through my head. Do I hug him? Kiss him on the cheek? Do I dare get that close to him?

'Well, I've had a great night ... again,' I tell him, walking him out. What an understatement.

'Me too,' he says.

The short walk over to the door fills me with sadness and dread. What if this is the last time I ever see him? He might not come back next year. I want to say ... *something* to him; absolutely no idea what. I wonder if he's thinking the same.

He gets there first and reaches out for the handle. Then he stops.

Turning around to face me so that I'm right in front of him, he's closer than a friend would be. But he doesn't look freaked out by it, and nor does he look away. He stares right into my eyes. Neither of us say anything. I have to tilt my head to look at him.

His fingers slide through the front of my hair, behind my ears. He gently places his hands on either side of my neck. My heart races as I move closer to him. Our mouths get nearer and just before they touch, we stop for a few seconds.

Millimetres away from each other. We make a choice. This is the moment to turn back, or change everything.

The kiss starts soft and slow. It builds and swirls deeper into an urgent, passionate one within seconds. Like our mouths were meant to be together. He uses his weight to turn us around, placing me against the door, pressing up to me with his body. I put my arms around his waist, pulling him closer. He gently bites my bottom lip. All I can think is just how amazing he is, and this feels. We both start instinctively moving towards the huge bed.

I lie down and he kisses my neck; sensual, soft, tender kisses. His body presses against me as I wrap my legs around him.

And then he breaks away, abruptly. I take a deep breath, as does he. He lies next to me, his hands covering his mouth. Silence hangs in the air but I don't want to be the one to break it. I don't know what to say.

'Look, Stephanie … my God, I'm so sorry,' he says. 'I'm not that guy. Fuck, I'm so sorry.'

'I know you're not,' I interrupt.

'Never in ten years have I ever …'

'I believe you.'

'But … fuck …' he says, looking at me. 'There's something about *you* I can't get out of my head. I can't imagine walking out of here and not seeing you again, talking to you. I know that sounds crazy. I know …'

I try to reassure him. 'It doesn't at all. I feel the same.'

'And I know I've only met you twice, but I don't know … I need to see you again.'

He needs to see me again.

'Well, there's always the same weekend next year?' I suggest.

'Well, possibly. Hopefully.'

'What do you mean?'

'I'm not sure if it will be running next year; it's in the balance at the moment. Bob isn't in great health and he's unsure if he can run it any more.'

'Oh,' I say, trying hard to hide my disappointment. 'Well, why don't we exchange phone numbers? That way if it's not on we can do something else?'

My God, what will he think of me? I've been married for three months. What the fuck am I playing at? It's like all rational thought has gone out of the window and the only important thing at this moment in time is how I can see this person again.

'I mean, if you want to?' I go on. 'And we don't even have to do anything. God, not that I'd expect to do anything. Fuck. I don't even know what *this* is … but we could maybe stay friends?' I'm torn between cringing and feeling utterly wrenched apart at never seeing Jamie again.

'I should say I can't ever see you again,' he says, looking right at me. 'But I can't. And I can't explain it. And I know it's wrong. I know that sounds utterly mad …'

'I feel it too,' I say, nodding my head. 'It could be our little … thing. This weekend every year. We meet and catch up, as friends …?'

Friends.

That last word lingers in the air, lazily floating above us, like smoke from a cigarette.

'Yes.' And he smiles in such a way that his eyes brighten and dimples by the side of his mouth cave in. 'I'd like that.'

CHAPTER 5

Thursday 21 August 2008

Jamie

'Mr Dobson! Look! I got an A*!' Katie yells, running towards me and waving a piece of white paper in her right hand.

'What? Let's see …' I beam at her as she thrusts the exam results in my face. I already know she attained the top mark – and rightly so – but I'm not taking this moment away from her. She's earned it.

'That's incredible! Congratulations!'

'Sir! Look what I got!' Louise says, yanking on my arm, impatiently.

'Get in! You worked so hard for that C, Lou. So proud of you!' Her face lights up and some of my other pupils run over.

This is why I love my job.

GCSE results day is nerve-wracking. Yes, we have targets to hit and numbers to think about. But for me these concerns come second to these kids' expectations and hopes. I don't have children, but I feel like they're all mine when they're waiting for their results; when I know how much hard work they've put in over the year. When their place at art college depends on them getting the right grades. They did brilliantly this year and I couldn't have been prouder. Watching them jump up and down, squealing with delight, was a pure joy. I always arrive early and load up on coffee, assessing the results before the pupils arrive. It's useful in knowing who to watch out for and excruciating discovering which ones will be disappointed. But it's the best feeling in the world when they run up to you, desperate to tell you their news. It chokes me up.

The school hall always starts off quiet, just whispers and the sound of pupils calmly walking in. It's quickly replaced with shrieks and shouts bouncing around the walls. It's utter chaos, but I love it – I always wait until all my pupils have been and gone. And as a teacher at the school I'm on hand to deal with *any* kid who needs support. We are one big family.

My students' passion was infectious, so after being at school all morning, I came home and did some painting of my own. I love the summer holidays for that. It's the only time I can properly create stuff. Music on, a few beers, a beautiful, sunny day. Perfect.

'To you, Class of 2008!' I say, hissing the top of the beer bottle off and casting it into the recycling bin next to the back door. The cold beer slides down my throat with incredible ease in this heat. It's still stupidly warm, even at 5.45 p.m. But if I've ever earned an early finish, it's today.

I decided to do a BBQ for me and Helen tonight, so I've bought all the meats, made a salad, some fancy pesto pasta thing (got it from *Jamie Oliver*) and even stuffed peppers. I thought we could eat outside on such a gorgeous night and she's been working so hard lately.

I'm relaxing in the garden when she suddenly appears at the back door, saying something I can't hear over Oasis blaring out loud on the Bose speakers.

'Sorry, baby, what did you say? I didn't hear you come in.' I turn the music right down.

'I said you look like you've had a good day!' Helen nods towards the recycling box, which has three beer bottles in it. It was recycling day yesterday.

'I'm celebrating, aren't I?'

'Yes, I'm very proud of you,' she coos, hugging me. 'Another successful year under your belt.'

'Yes, I can't believe it! Highest number of A*s I've ever had.'

Wrapping my arms around Helen's waist, I bury my face into her dark brown hair which is tied up in some kind of knot thing. It smells of her.

'I know,' she says, pulling back and resting her hands on my shoulders. 'Well done! And because you're so clever, I've booked us a table at that new Thai place on Deansgate. Table reserved for seven-thirty so you'd better get a move on.'

'No need,' I tell her proudly. 'I'm doing a BBQ.'

'Oh,' she says, peering over my shoulder. 'Right, so you are. Well, you haven't put the meat on yet. We could save it and do it tomorrow. I really fancy this place – it's had amazing reviews and I only got the reservation because they had a cancellation.'

'I've done a full spread and it's a lovely evening for sitting out,' I reply, casting my eyes over the garden. I've worked really hard on it the last few days. I'm not an expert by any means, but I'm fairly handy with a pair of shears and can work a lawnmower.

'Well, it was my treat, but if you'd rather stay in, up to you,' she says, smiling, removing her arms from around my neck. 'I'm going to get changed, I'll be down in a bit.'

I've always loved doing BBQs. Meals always taste better when they're cooked or eaten outside. Fact of life.

Looking over the banquet I've prepared for us on the wooden garden table, it's a great summer feast. I take a picture of it on my phone and send it to Cal with the caption 'Not just a pretty face'. He immediately replies: 'And not even that, mate!'. Twat.

Helen comes back down in a long summer dress, her sunglasses resting on the top of her head. I hand her a glass of chilled white wine and she takes a sip before flashing me that smile I love.

It was her smile I first noticed when I met her. That, and her huge, cocoa-brown eyes which match her long hair. She used to turn up to art classes wearing some of those over-the-knee socks and a pinafore (only one side fastened), revealing a tight T-shirt underneath. Helen was quick-witted and wore bright make-up which highlighted her features. She was different back then, more of a free spirit. She had a wildness about her and I identified her as being on my wavelength, something which is important as a young eighteen-year-old, struggling to find your place in the world.

We were friends for months before anything happened. Best friends. We were never apart, me, Helen and Cal. We could always be found in either the art studio or the pub directly next to it. Helen and I finally got together at a sweaty Britpop night in Camden, drunk on cheap cider, dancing to Pulp's 'Common People'. As students at Saint Martins, the irony was not lost on us. But the three of us laughed, talked, lived and breathed art. It was our passion. Three completely different characters, but art glued us all together.

Now we couldn't be more different. Helen rejected all romantic fantasies of exhibiting, instead going into the commercial sector, working as a designer at an advertising firm in Manchester. Cal is an artist and designs incredible leather pieces of clothing and accessories.

And there's me, an art teacher and a big fat disappointment to Helen. I work too many hours, I worry about my students more than I should, and I don't get paid enough for any of it. But I love it. The kids are there because they have a passion they need to nurture. You can see it when they come into class. They throw their bags down and can't wait to get started. They work through breaks and stay after the bell goes. They demonstrate true dedication, reminding me of how *I* used to be. They're at that stage where they're starving for inspiration, their minds ready to absorb art and be blown away by it. The school I work at is in a fairly rundown area and these kids don't have much hope, but I feel like I make a difference – especially on days like today.

'So, how was your day?' I ask, shovelling sausages on to Helen's plate for her.

'Oh, all right!' she replies. 'Well, bloody Grotbags laid into my presentation.'

'Jesus, she never lets up, does she? Daft hag!'

'Everyone else thought it was a great concept, then she piped up "Yeah, mmm, I do like it …'" she says, doing a brilliantly affected impression of the fake-accented Lisha (who we only ever refer to as Grotbags). "'… but I feel it's not quite hitting the core audience that we are aiming at" and then she slagged the entire thing off for five minutes.'

'Was any of it remotely justified?'

'Was it hell!' she says. 'It was signed off in the end, but she just likes to watch me under pressure.'

'She's got some nerve.'

'I know.' She shrugs. 'Sarah came up to me afterwards and said not to worry about it.'

She's putting a brave face on, but I can tell she's down about it. Grotbags – aka Helen's new boss – has been making Helen's life difficult for about six months now.

'I know it's hard, but it's likely she's only being a bitch because she knows how brilliant you are. She's just jealous and intimidated by you. You're obviously doing something right.'

'I suppose. Can't wait for the weekend. I thought we could perhaps drive to Liverpool on Saturday? There's a food festival on,' she says, chomping into her sausage bun. 'And on Sunday, maybe lunch at The Lowry overlooking the Quay?'

Helen is a very organised person and always likes to have things to do. She gets so many recommendations and freebies with her job that we spend most of our weekends eating out, drinking at new bars or seeing the latest up-and-coming band. I'm more laid back with my time; I'd quite happily sit and just enjoy being in the house sometimes, but Helen likes to be out and about.

'Sounds good. How's the food?' I ask. 'There's more on the grill if you want some.'

'No, I think this will do me,' Helen says, wiping her mouth with a blue napkin.

'Well, I'll put the rest of this in the fridge. I can pop some of it in a Tupperware thing for your lunch tomorrow, if you like?'

'No, you're OK. I'm in London tomorrow, remember. I'm on the seven o'clock train.'

'Ah, right, I forgot. What's that for?'

'All to do with plans for the company expansion.'

'Yeah, you mentioned that.' I nod, stuffing a burger into my mouth.

'They're on a real drive for talented designers, illustrators,' she says, pushing some salad around her plate. 'Great money if you fancy it?'

I look up at her, mid-chomp, and laugh.

'Never in a million years!' I tell her, reaching for my beer.

'Oh yes, I forgot,' she looks up. 'God forbid you become a big corporate sell-out like me!'

'Shut it, you!' I tease, leaning over to give her a kiss. She wraps her arms around my shoulders, pulling me closer to her.

'Besides,' I say, when we finally break apart. 'Someone has got to be the house husband around here. We can't both be hotshots. Have you seen how immaculate this bloody house is?'

This is the perk of being a teacher. Thirteen weeks off a year. Well, I still have stuff to do, but it means I can do things to the house and – when the time comes – look after our children. Helen works such long hours and, thinking ahead, I'd love to take on as much childcare as I can. And I love making sure she comes home to a nice, tidy house in the holidays. Dinner is always made and she never has to worry about the food shop. We're a good team.

'I suppose you're right.' she laughs. 'You still do that weird thing with the towels, though.'

She's told me this many times and I never understand it. Something to do with how I fold them.

'Well, you can't have everything,' I joke.

The kids who live next door are larking about in the garden. I can hear squealing and shouting amid intermittent splashes so they must be in the paddling pool. You're never without background noise when you live in a semi-detached house.

The room is dark, but for the flicker of the TV in the corner. Helen always goes to bed much earlier than me. We're not one of those couples who synchronise bedtime. In the early days, we'd go to bed together and talk for ages, before having sex pretty much every night. That's pretty standard at the beginning, though. It changes as you get further into a relationship – not worse, just different. But now I like to stay up late reading, watching TV, drawing, thinking. Helen loves to sleep, which is fine; everyone is different.

I glance at the photo on the mantelpiece – our wedding photo. I love that picture. You can just about see me and Helen through the shower of confetti which has been thrown over us. We looked so happy, and we were.

'We *are*,' I whisper to myself, barely audible as a shard of guilt punctures through my chest.

But, it just felt *right*, us being together. I never yearned to be with anyone else. I mean, yes, we have the odd argument like any other couple. Who doesn't? But generally, we have a very content relationship. We respect each other, love each other. We have lives independent from one another; we each understand the importance of having time and friends away from each other. She has weekends away with the girls, I'll go away with the guys.

We're a good match and know each other inside and out. We're best friends.

I've never, ever been tempted to cheat.

I don't even think I can put into words what it is about Stephanie. I could probably paint it better than I could describe it.

Something dark, unique, captivating.

Beautifully melancholic. That's it.

She's a naturally stunning woman. But that wasn't it. That wouldn't be enough to make me do what I did. It would never be enough.

I found myself thinking about her every now and again. She kept cropping up, no matter how hard I tried. Sometimes when I saw a girl with blonde hair, I'd think it might be her. Whenever I was talking to a girl with green eyes, I'd think of the time I gazed into hers. Then, Helen would snap me out of it, asking what was going on with me. Why had I been so 'distant' lately? I knew, then, I had to get a grip on it. I mean, what the hell am I doing? I'm happy with Helen. And, yet, I can't *not* see Stephanie.

And now I have to send her this message. I have to see her.

CHAPTER 6

Thursday 21 August 2008

Stephanie

It always took pride of place in the middle of the mantelpiece, as it now does on mine.

The frame is thick, embossed with pearls. The photo has a grain to it in that way old photos do. Ebony and I adored looking at it when we were kids.

It doesn't matter how dated her dress looks, or how awful my dad's suit is – it's a gorgeous photo of their wedding day.

'What was it like, Mummy? Did you feel like a princess?' I asked her one day. I couldn't have been much older than about eight.

A big smile appeared on her face.

'Perfect. And yes, I did. I felt like the luckiest girl in the world. I still do,' she said, gazing fondly at the photo.

'Did your mummy and daddy go?' Ebony asked.

Her smile dropped for a moment.

'No, darling, they didn't,' she said, looking away at the floor briefly.

'Were they busy?' I asked.

'Kind of. Your daddy is a wonderful man, you know. He always finds the best in people,' she said, brushing the hair out of her face and gently touching the scar on her right eyebrow. She did that sometimes.

'Steph! Can you bring the salad out?' Ebony yells from the kitchen. Tearing my eyes away from the photo on the mantlepiece, I head in there and do as she says.

We've only been in the new house two months, but it's slowly coming together. Matt found it and insisted we came for a viewing, saying it wouldn't be on the market long. He was right. Three other couples viewed it the same day we did, and all made offers. It's a three-hundred-year-old detached house in Poppybrook, the next village along from Dad and Ebony, not far from Cambridge. Exposed wooden beams adorn the ceilings, an Aga warms the kitchen and a welcoming porch is out front. It's everything Matt and I wanted in a house: traditional, old features but modernised throughout. It didn't need anything doing to it but I was prickling with excitement, walking around, thinking about how I'd put my stamp on it. Matt kept squeezing my hand at the best bits – the kitchen, the study, the huge garden!

'That's the one,' he said, the second we got back in the car. 'I'll make sure we get it.'

This is why he's so good at his job, I guess. What Matt wants, he gets. He quickly ensured we offered the most – with help from both sets of our parents – and it was ours. Our 'forever' home.

Ebony has really gone to town on the decorations for my birthday meal, which we're eating outside as a result of this beautiful weather. Bunting hangs from the trees, balloons float on the lawn and the table is set in pastel shades. She completely takes over whenever she comes around and it's always funny watching her boss Matt about. Flouncing in an hour ago, she shoved a huge oven dish of chilli con carne (my favourite) at Matt the second she was through the door.

'Pop it in a pan and let it simmer with the lid on. You *do* have a pan large enough, don't you?'

He looked at her, bewildered, not daring to refuse her demands.

Ebony is currently in the throws of enjoying new motherhood. Well, it's more like her new project. She spends all her time finding the newest baby fad and becoming obsessed with it. She was all about hypnobirthing and 'breathing the baby out' for the entire pregnancy, then fifteen minutes into the labour she told the midwife to 'turn that fucking CD off and give me an epidural!' She *loves* baby topics. But why she thinks I need to hear a twenty-minute rant about 'baby-led weaning', I don't know, because I still have no idea what that is. Her gorgeous baby, Jude, is only one month old but she's already ahead of the game and researching how best to feed him real food just so she's prepared. She's very particular about things. Everyone has to wash their hands before they touch him and she carries sanitising gel around in her handbag in case anyone within a five-mile radius gets near him without having degermed.

She frogmarches everyone outside, giving them jobs and things to carry. Will, Ebony's husband, does it without a second thought. He's used to it after so many years. Standing back to admire the beautiful banquet she's put on, he puts his arm around her and kisses her on the side of the head.

'Great job, Ebs,' he says. 'You always pull it out of the bag on birthdays.'

Her broad grin says everything; she's brimming with delight with Will's praise, and she should be praised. I don't even know how she's managed to find the time to do all this being a mother of a one-month-old baby.

'Yes, thanks so much. It's really appreciated.' I smile as I delicately place the salad in the centre of the table and then stand awkwardly behind one of the wooden chairs, feeling lazy and inadequate.

'Well, come on then! Sit down and tuck in,' Ebony demands, flapping her hand around in the direction of the food.

'So sorry I'm late, everyone!' Dad's voice echoes through the hallway before he rushes into the garden, clutching a huge bouquet of brightly-coloured flowers in one arm and a bottle of champagne in the other. As always, he's wearing some horribly mismatched ensemble consisting of cream linen trousers and a black shirt. A bizarre straw trilby hat is on his head, which I stare up at and have no words for. He doesn't have a natural flair for fashion and Mum always used to make sure he looked smart for occasions.

'I got tied up talking to Ian Wagstaff in the village,' he goes on. 'Proud as punch, he was. His twin girls just got their GCSE results today and they got ten As across the board – both of them! He insisted I went to the pub with him for a pint ...'

I knew it was GCSE results day because I've been thinking of Jamie. I hope his students did well and made him proud. I bet he's a wonderful teacher.

'Doesn't seem two minutes since you two got your GCSE results,' Dad says, laughing, taking a glass of wine off Will. 'And look at you both now!'

Yes, look at me now.

Twenty-eight years old and working for my dad with no career motivation whatsoever. Brilliant.

'School days, best days of my life!' Matt tells us all. I've heard this before. He was the popular kid at school; had all the girls he wanted, captain of the football team, well-liked but fairly average academically. It hasn't held him back, though. His school photos show a good-looking boy, blond floppy hair and a cheeky smile.

'How come you didn't go to university, Matt?' Dad had asked when they'd first met.

'Didn't see the point, really. Learned everything I needed on the job. Far more useful in the long run. Besides my brother and sister came back so smug, I didn't want to turn out like them.'

Matt's brother and sister are a doctor and a scientist of some sort, both very bright and successful at what they do. Matt calls them 'arrogant' and 'smug' about their lives. I've only met them a handful of times, one of which was at the wedding. They've always been perfectly pleasant to me.

'Fair enough, best way in many cases,' Dad had said, nodding in agreement. Well, of course he would. Dad is a self-made, successful businessman and left school with five O levels.

Now Jude murmurs momentarily in his car seat beside the table. He looks like a baby angel. So perfect. His legs scrawny and yet delicious, poking out of a little white Babygro.

'So, big sis,' Ebony teases, 'twenty-eight!'

'Less of the big, thank you very much. You're only three years behind me.'

'So, when are you thinking of ...?' she said, gesturing towards Jude.

'Not for a while,' I reply. Christ, does she have to bring this up now? 'Both of us are happy with our careers at the moment. We don't want a huge interruption to that. When are you going to go back? Isn't nine months standard?'

'Hmm. Well, I'm not sure if I will. I've been reading all these articles and reports about how your children end up brighter and more nourished if they have one parent staying at home with them, so I'm thinking I might just … not. Well, not for a while.'

My mouth drops open in shock. Ebony is a solicitor and started working at a prestigious law firm only two years ago. I look at Dad to see what he makes of this.

'Her decision,' he states, raising his eyebrows, whilst simultaneously shoving some garlic bread into his face. He's obviously known about this before today.

'We've talked about it,' Will interjects, sensing the shock around the table. 'I'm more than happy to support Ebony in this decision. She can always go back to the law if she wants to in the future.'

I've no doubt they can afford it. Will earns a six-figure salary doing something 'banker-y' in London, so I'm sure money isn't an option, but that's not the point.

'Are you sure?' I ask, rather taken aback. Ebony has always been the more career-motivated out of the pair of us.

'Stephanie,' she says calmly, 'I want to be there for them in their early years. That's what Mum did. I want Jude to have that. Remember how lovely it was when she was there at the school gate every day, waiting for us?'

Of course I remember. She'd be there whether it was sunny or snowing. You don't really appreciate that until you're older. Walking out of the classroom, we'd scan the playground for her face amongst the sea of others. She was always at the front, waiting to collect us, ready to greet our little thrilled faces as we ran out of school to cuddle her. She'd appropriately 'Oooh!' and 'Ahhh!' when we launched our crafts in her arms in the school yard: space rockets, igloos and castles. In reality, they'd be a mishmash of Fairy Liquid bottles, loo rolls and tissue boxes.

'Yes, of course,' I smile. 'And you're right. No child needs a distant parent who isn't there most of the time because they're at work. They need love and nurturing.'

Dad stops eating for a second and places his knife and fork down with an overly loud clanging noise, reaching over to take a sip of his wine. Ebony shoots me a glare from across the table. My gaze bounces between the two of them like a metronome.

'She's got the right idea,' Matt rather helpfully intervenes. 'I mean, she doesn't have to work, so what's the point?'

'What's the point?' I utter. 'She's not a baby-making machine, Matt. She has a life, too.'

'But, my God, who on earth would work if they don't have to? She should count herself lucky.'

'Some people love what they do. They have a passion for it. Ebony has always loved practising law and she worked hard to get where she is. I just don't want her to make a rash decision. It's not about whether she *needs* to work or not,' I reply, making a little hill out of rice on my plate.

'These people who work for the "love of it",' he says, rolling his eyes. 'Because they "have a passion for their craft" and all that shite. I don't believe them. Worthy buggers.'

I instantly think of Jamie and how he spoke so excitedly and intensely about his work as an art teacher.

'I do. I think some people are genuinely that amazing,' I uncharacteristically shoot back at him.

'Well, I think you'd be lucky to find one.'

Yes, wouldn't I?

'I know what you meant, Steph,' Ebony says, smiling. 'And I appreciate the concern, honestly. But I'll be fine. I'm happy about this!'

'But what if you go ... mental?'

'Don't be silly, Steph! Of course I won't. I'll keep myself busy! I've already signed up for baby massage, Little Swimmers and Tiny Tots this week ... and there'll be more to do as he gets older. And I'll probably just knock another couple out anyway.'

'Sounds like you have it all planned out,' I said, taken aback. Ebony and Will have been married for four years, but she was always going to get married first. She was planning her wedding from the age of fifteen and the actual thing hardly deviated from that original idea.

She met Will at university and they really are perfect for each other. They're one of these couples who bounce off each other really well, but you know she wears the trousers and has the final say on absolutely every decision in their house, from where to go on holiday, down to which shower gel to buy. Ebony went through many boyfriends in the past, and not many were able to put up with 'her ways'. Some would call her a control freak. She would describe herself as 'organised'.

'Look, can I give you my advice?' Her long liquorice-black mane of hair is tied loosely in a bun on top of her head, which bobbles up and down as she talks. 'I know you've only been married, like, a year,' she whispered, and an image of Jamie flashed up in my mind as she did, which I quickly removed. 'But just remember ... it's so much easier to snap back into your figure the younger you are. I'm back into my size ten jeans now and you're older than me, so don't leave it too long.' She raises her eyebrows, as if this is a perfectly acceptable point to make.

Yes, you can always count on your little sister to make you feel better about yourself.

People have already started asking. It's the natural progression, isn't it? 'Oh, you're married now, can you tell us when you plan on making some humans, please?' And you can't really say 'Well, it's none of your business, actually', so you just have to politely laugh and mumble 'we'll see' or some other such bollocks. God help the women who don't even want children. What the hell do *they* say?

Except I *do* want children. Just not yet.

'How's work, Matt?' Dad asks. 'Did the Farrington deal go through?'

'The presentation went like an absolute dream. I'm pretty sure it's in the bag.'

'Great news! You've got that magic touch, Matt. I don't know what it is, but you've got it,' Dad gushes.

'Thanks, Michael. Dedication and a good work ethic shines through and gets results, I find. I can work on it this weekend if you want me to put pressure on them? I'll go in early on Monday morning and get it tied up.'

Dad shakes his head. 'No, best not push it. Let them think about it. I'm sure they'll come back.'

'Oh, yes, of course. I didn't mean I'd pressure them. Just chase it up.' Matt is keen to stress the point.

'Oh, let's leave it for now,' Dad says, gently tapping the side of his glass with his fork. He's so clumsy, I worry for a second he'll smash it, which makes me laugh. He glances at me, knowing that's what's cracked me up and we share a lovely little moment before he speaks.

'Happiest of birthdays to my eldest daughter, Steph. Just wanted to say that we are all very proud of you. You've come a long way in the last year or so. Yeah. It's lovely that you've really turned a corner and you married the man of your dreams. I'm so pleased you've finally got everything you want.'

Everyone picks up their drinks and raises them. 'To Steph!' they all cheer.

I politely smile at everyone, inwardly feeling terribly guilty about the little dig towards Dad a few minutes earlier.

Jude then chooses this precise moment to start rocking in his car seat, demanding to be fed.

'You enjoy the rest of your meal, I'm finished anyway,' I say to Ebony, who is eating at a million miles per hour. 'I'll feed him upstairs.'

It was lovely to have a few minutes of quiet, feeding my nephew. I had no idea how to do it before he came along and at first I'd been worried I was holding him wrong, was scared I'd choke him. I cuddled into his little body afterwards until he fell asleep and stared at his perfect little face for an hour while everyone was downstairs, momentarily smelling his head. I don't know what it is about their heads, but they smell divine; it's comforting, beautiful, innocent. A twang of broodiness vibrated through my heart like a symphony.

And, yet, I don't want my own and I don't know why. I should, because I'm married, but it just doesn't feel right at the moment.

Matt falls asleep on the sofa when everyone leaves. Taking a glass of wine outside, I sit on one of the garden chairs and, letting out a large sigh, I reach for my iPod and press play on shuffle.

'Nothing's Gonna Stop Us Now' by Starship. Oh, I love this song! What an eighties classic.

There isn't a cloud in the sky. The stars shine like someone has scattered glitter all over it.

My phone lights up beside me on the table. An actual parade of fireworks shoot down my back when I see the message flash up on the screen:

Hi Stephanie! Hope you're well? Got some bad news. The course has been cancelled! Poor Bob is in really bad health. Just let me know what you want to do. Jamie. X

We booked the rooms months ago. One message between us to confirm we were still going. That was it. But, now, the only reason for us to be there is each other.

No art workshops, nobody else, no distractions – just us.

Staring at the screen, I think about that weekend last year and the time I shared with him. The laughs we had and that kiss. He made me feel so alive and happy, just being in the same room with him was a delight. But that was different. I had a reason to be there. This time, I wouldn't.

I'd have to lie to Matt. I'm a terrible liar.

I wait until the song finishes and pick up the phone to reply, wondering if I'm about to make the worst decision of my life.

PART TWO

Only Love Can Hurt Like This

CHAPTER 7

Saturday 12 October 2008

Stephanie

'I'm so sorry, Mr Dobson,' the receptionist says, tapping away at the computer in front of her, 'but your room reservation was automatically cancelled when the course was. It was the same for all tutors.'

With both hands resting on the reception desk, Jamie bows his head and steps away for a second.

'Can I book another one?'

'I'm afraid we are fully booked tonight,' she says. The name badge on her burgundy blouse informs us her name is Avril; a middle-aged lady with red-rimmed glasses on one of those chains around her neck, her auburn hair styled in a wispy long bob, her fringe dancing about in her eyes.

'Oh! Hold on a second ... we do have one room left. But it's the Paisley Suite, £275?'

Jamie takes a sharp breath at this information.

'Can you just give us a second, please?' I smile at Avril, pulling Jamie away from the reception desk for a moment. We walk past the fireplace, both glancing up at the sign above it without saying anything.

'Look, you can't pay that,' I tell him. I know Jamie doesn't earn a lot and I'm not sure how he'd explain that to his wife.

'What do you want to do?' he asks in a lowered voice as people walk past us. 'You've paid for your room. I'm so sorry ...'

'Please don't apologise! It's not your fault, just a terrible mix-up.'

One of us has to suggest it, or neither of us could. It's the obvious solution.

'Why don't you stay in my room? It's got a sofa in there. You can sleep on it, if you want.'

He looks at me for a moment, those shiny blue eyes, right into mine.

'You sure?' he asks, without breaking his gaze.

'Yes.'

He walks back to the desk where Avril is waiting patiently to see this drama played out.

'I don't need that room, but thank you for your help,' he tells her.

'Of course, Mr Dobson. I'll get you two keys.'

I've thought of little else but this moment for the last few weeks. On the one hand, I can't believe I'm doing this. On the other, it's the only thing that's actually kept me going. In general, I've been happier, funnier, sparklier – everyone has noticed, not least Ebony, who asked '*What* is making you feel like this?' in a suspicious tone only last week as we were at the spa getting our nails done. I mumbled something about how I was embracing life and practising yoga, which was exactly the right thing to say, as it set her off on a rant about how good endorphins are for you which she knew all about because she read it in an article only last week.

But coming here had meant lying to Matt, at least on some level. I didn't want to tell a complete lie and say I was going somewhere else because it felt too … deceitful. Nor did I want to say I was attending the art course because he could easily find out that was a lie. So, I said I'd decided to come back to Heathwood Hall and catch up with a friend for the weekend.

Which is 100 per cent true. Ish.

A lie wrapped up in a truth. Of course, if it was completely innocent I'd tell him who that friend was, but I can't do that because the friend is a man I've only met twice before.

Walking into the room where we shared that kiss a year ago, I fling the keys on the bed. It's silent. The room looks exactly the same – it hasn't changed since I first came here two years ago.

Jamie walks over to the grey sofa on the other side of the room.

'Shall we get changed and go for drinks before we eat?' I ask, at the exact same time Jamie starts to say something.

We both start laughing nervously.

'Sorry,' I smile, taking my coat off. 'What did you say?'

'I was just saying the same. I could do with a drink after the long drive. How do you want to …?' He trails off, doing a weird motioning thing with his hands I cannot fathom. I look at him, utterly confused.

'You know, erm, getting changed,' he manages to get out. 'You're a woman …'

'Yes, I am,' I say, amused.

'… you'll want space and time to – to do what you do.'

I start giggling at how embarrassed and awkward he is.

'I'll just get ready in the bathroom. Will take me twenty minutes and I'll go downstairs and wait for you,' he offers.

'Yeah, great!'

Well, this is all very polite, isn't it?

Getting ready for dinner with Jamie is surreal. What do you even wear for such an occasion? Something nice but not too pretty or inappropriate. His scent fills the bathroom as I walk in after he's been in it. Later as I head downstairs I feel sick. Nervous, excited … guilty. Guilty because I've lied to Matt to be here. But I feel even guiltier over the fact I don't regret coming. Not one bit.

He's in the bar, and I love it here. It's full of shiny leather sofas and discreet lamps, while regal red wallpaper covers the high walls.

I see him before he sees me. He sits on the sofa in the corner, next to the massive window which overlooks the terrace and fountain outside where we had that first proper chat. His arm outstretched along the back of the sofa, he's looking at some of the art on the wall next to him: portraits, landscapes – all done in that way you see at these places. He looks so unbelievably handsome when he's dressed up. He's in a white shirt and dark blazer and, gazing intently at the paintings on the wall, he doesn't see me watching him. I take a second before I walk over, just to drink this moment up.

Then I make my way over to him, weaving through the chairs, tables and other couples.

'Wow! You look … beautiful,' he says as he stands up and glances at my pillar-box-red fitted dress. I wear my long hair swept around my right shoulder, which complements the Bardot neckline of the dress.

'Thank you. Shall we eat?'

We spend hours talking about the most random subjects. Both being huge Bond fans, we discuss the new film, *Quantum of Solace*, which is out in a few weeks. A debate ensues regarding which actor is the best Bond.

I say Brosnan, he reckons Moore and he laughs when I inform him that if he'd said Connery I'd have walked out immediately.

'Best Bond girl?' I ask, narrowing my eyes.

'Solitaire. Jane Seymour. Any day of the week,' he says, without any hesitation whatsoever.

'Good choice!'

'Best film?' he asks.

'*The Spy Who Loved Me*. First one I ever saw,' I confirm. 'Mind you ...'

'Nope. You only get one. No indecision. It's final,' he says in a super-serious voice.

'What? I have different favourite ones for various reasons,' I plead.

'Take it up with the Bond adjudicators,' he laughs, taking a sip of his wine without breaking my gaze.

We somehow end up reminiscing about our favourite childhood films. I thought he was going to declare I was actually mental when I said I watched *Back To The Future* every single day in the six weeks holidays when I was a kid, until he told me that not only was he also obsessed with it, he did the same with *Star Wars*.

'Isn't it weird how you get so engrossed with films?' I ask him.

'I think they're an escape, aren't they?' He shrugs. 'You get lost in them. Like anything creative.'

I realise, far too late, that I'm smiling at him far too high up there on the swoon scale.

'Art, innit?' he declares proudly, like I'm falling into his world.

'Why do you love art so much?' I whisper, leaning forward slightly. I think I'm a bit tipsy.

'Why do you love music so much?'

'It says what I want without me saying it,' I reveal to him, without hesitation.

'And that's exactly what art does for me.'

I smile, but feel suddenly embarrassed. Like we've shared some kind of secret.

Changing the subject, he asks how my therapy sessions are going and I tell him they're going well. I see Jane once a month now.

'Has your life been made easier, better from seeing her?' he asks.

'Yes.' I nod. 'I mean, it's definitely a process. Much of it is her answering things with more questions and coming to unhelpful conclusions with no suggestions on how to improve the situation.'

'In what way?'

'Well, I have a self-destructive nature, apparently,' I admit. 'I am drawn to things which aren't good for me.'

'Is she right?'

'Yes,' I say reluctantly, slowly twiddling the base of my wine glass. 'I have done in the past.'

'Do you know why that is? Has she told you why?'

'Nope!' I laugh. 'That's not Jane's style. She'll make me find out myself, even if it takes ages. She likes leaving things on cliffhangers, but she knows about all my flaws and demon.'

'Wow, and you pay this woman to point them out to you?' he laughs.

'Better I show them to her and nobody else,' I say, reaching for my wine. 'So what are yours?'

'Some people say I don't take enough risks. That I'm too safe,' he says, not looking at me when he does.

'In relation to what?'

'Oh, just life. You know, my job and stuff.'

'Really?' I ask, genuinely confused. One of the things I really love hearing Jamie talk about is his passion for his job. The dedication he ploughs into looking after his students really is incredible. The way he talks about them, how he loves watching them being inspired by art at an age where they're just about to find out who they are – you can tell he lives for his craft.

'But you're so passionate about your job. I can see you love it. Having said that, you do need to get your own work out there. You really are so very talented.'

'Thank you, but I can't see it happening now unless an amazing opportunity was thrown in my path. Life kinds of gets in the way of these things, doesn't it?' He shrugs.

'This, coming from the big fate-believer? I don't believe it,' I say, with mild mock outrage in my voice.

'Well, what's meant to be will be,' he says, laughing.

'Do you really think that?'

'Yeah, I do.'

'So where do we ... where do I fit into this?' I ask, tilting my head and definitely crossing over the flirty line.

'Well, the course was cancelled, but here we are ...'

'So, what does that mean?' I tease him.

'You're the one thing I just don't get.'

I smile, ignoring the fact that I'm blushing. Thank goodness the room is darkish. I tuck my hair behind my ear before taking a sip of wine, clinking it back on the table a bit harder than I needed to. His gaze hasn't diverted away from me.

'What?' I ask, embarrassed.

'You're adorable, you know that?'

'Not really,' I reply.

'I think you are.'

'Why?'

'You just are.'

I suddenly feel shy, something I have never done when a guy has complimented me. But, then again, he is something else.

I need and want to kiss him. I want to kiss him so slowly and tenderly that I feel the world around me fall away. That's pretty much how I feel just talking to him and I can't imagine how I'll survive anything else. I'm worried I might not come back from it.

'Do you want to go?' I whisper, looking into his eyes, which are focused on mine.

'Yes,' he replies without hesitating.

I smile as he stands up and takes my hand. We walk out of the bar towards the huge, sweeping staircase. We don't fully hold hands, but our fingers loosely interlock as we walk close to each other. My heart is racing. I don't think I've ever been so excited and nervous at the same time before.

'Oh, I think I've left my wallet on the table,' Jamie says, patting down his jacket. 'I'll just go and get it. Don't go anywhere.'

'I won't.' I'm smiling.

He walks off back towards the restaurant and I stand, smiling like a goon, biting my lower lip. My head is light, my whole body is ignited with something I haven't felt before. It's *alive*.

Clutching my handbag, I'm waiting patiently for him to come back when I feel a hand rest on my shoulder. Still smiling, thinking he's sneaked up behind me, I turn around.

'Stephanie? We thought it was you! How are you?'

My only hope is that Sam Chaplin and his wife, Liz, are so drunk that they don't see the sheer panic on my face.

'Oh! Erm, hi!' I say. 'I'm great, thanks. You?'

'Lovely! It's our anniversary, so here for the weekend,' Liz gushes. Her enormous coiffed brunette hair is the centrepiece of her appearance. That's the problem with growing up in the countryside; everyone knows each other and everyone else's business.

'Is Matt treating you to a weekend away? He's a romantic, that one!' she says, winking.

'No, actually.' I fake a laugh. 'I'm here with a friend.'

Liz cocks her head to the side, doing a very overexaggerated 'Oh! I see!'

'Girls weekend,' I reiterate.

At this point I see Jamie walking back towards me. *Oh God, please don't talk to me.* My heart starts to pound, faster and harder by the second to the point where it actually interferes with what I'm trying to do and say.

'So, Liz,' I say, loud enough so that Jamie can hear me. 'How long have you been married now? You must have known my dad for at least twenty years!'

I glance at Jamie out of the corner of my eye as he sweeps straight past us and heads upstairs, not even looking at us. Breathing a tiny sigh of relief, I switch off as Liz goes on a five-minute monologue about how she came to live in our village.

'Well, my friend must be wondering where I am, so must dash! Got an early start at the spa tomorrow! Lovely to see you both,' I tell them as I head upstairs.

'You OK?' Jamie asks as I walk through the door. 'I figured it was better if I skipped the introductions.'

'Yes. Thanks for that. Much appreciated,' I say, walking over to the leaded window and swinging it open. I have a thing about windows being open, even when it's freezing. I only open it a centimetre or so, but

95

it's enough to let a bit of the autumn breeze in through the curtains.

'Well, we're alone now,' he says.

Yes, we are. Completely alone. I've thought about this for a whole year; fantasised about it, dreamed about it, spent nights in bed thinking about what I'd do if it ever happened and hating myself for it. We could do anything and nobody would know.

But I would, and I'd have to live with it.

I give a half-smile, walking over to the bed and sitting on my hands, a throwback from my teenage years. Jamie walks over and places himself right next to me.

'It's thrown you, hasn't it? Seeing them,' he says.

I daren't look at him, for fear of falling into his eyes. 'Seeing people outside that bubble reminds you of what you're doing, the people you're ...'

I turn to look at him. I don't need to finish my sentence. What's the right way to finish it anyway? 'Lying to'? 'Betraying'? We both know it's heading that way. Or it *was* before I bumped into Mr and Mrs Chaplin.

Jamie pulls my hand out from under my leg and holds it, softly.

'We don't have to do anything at all. I just love seeing you. We planned to come and catch up over dinner and that's exactly what we've done,' he says, smiling. 'This is probably for the best.'

'Yeah, I guess it is,' I say, both proud of myself and hating myself at the same time.

We let the moment rest, allowing the decision we've made to sink in. We can't go back on it now.

'So,' Jamie jumps up, 'I'm going to get ready for bed. Well, I mean, my sofa!'

I laugh, glancing over at Jamie's resting place for the night. Jamie is tall and the sofa is nowhere near long enough for him.

'Look, sleep in the bed. It'll be fine.'

His eyes dart over the huge king-size bed I'm sitting on. 'You absolutely sure?'

'Yes, it's big enough for both of us. We can stick some pillows down the middle if it makes you feel better,' I joke.

'It's OK; I trust you'll manage to keep your hands off me.'

The four-poster bed is quite something. Some are ugly and imposing. This one is simple but pretty. The four columns holding the canopy up are dark wood and beautifully ornate, matching the grand headboard. It would look so over the top in any other setting, but in this room – it works.

I thought I'd have my own room, so I brought a little dusky pink shorts and vest set. As I walk from the bathroom in it, Jamie desperately attempts to avert his eyes as he passes me to go in there himself. I would never usually wear a bra for bed, but I keep it on tonight. Jamie emerges from the bathroom after a few minutes wearing only boxer shorts. Standing in the doorway, he is obviously self-conscious, fiddling with his hands and not knowing where to put them.

My good God. I quite literally do not know where to look. I want to admire every part of him but daren't. I splutter out words which are complete gibberish.

'I'm so sorry, Steph. I've only got the jumper I came in or a shirt. I can put one of them on?'

'Ah, no! Please don't worry, it's fine!' I say, as if all this was completely normal. But my voice is higher than usual.

I lie on my back on the right side of the bed and he climbs in next to me. I turn off the table light and now it's pitch-black.

My mind whirls with thoughts along the lines of 'What the *hell* are you doing?' This is Jamie, why on earth aren't you jumping on him? And I don't know why I'm not. But it just doesn't feel right.

I feel his hand reaching out underneath the covers. It searches around for my hand, which is resting on my stomach, and he brings it down between us, so our hands are interlocked. Gently and slowly he strokes the top of my hand with his thumb. Our arms and shoulders are together and, even though it's dark, I know his head is tilted towards mine. His short breaths gently rush on to my face, gradually transforming into a deep, rhythmic breathing. I find myself adjusting mine to sync with his as we both drift into unconsciousness.

And that's how we fall asleep.

*

He's already in the shower when I wake up, which I'm thankful for. I don't think lounging about in bed would be good for either of us. I have no idea what time it is – late enough to be light outside because a tiny crack of bright light streams into the room through the curtain, just enough for me to see the outlines of most things in the room.

I'm slightly paranoid that maybe I cuddled Jamie in the night or did something embarrassing.

'Morning!' he booms, bursting out of the bathroom, fully dressed.

'Hi!' I beam at him. 'Did you sleep OK?'

'Like a log – even though you are a terrible duvet-hogger.'

'I am not!'

'Last time I share a bed with you,' he says and laughs. 'Right, it's almost eight. How about breakfast in the room so we don't bump into Mr and Mrs Nosy-Parkers then we'll get outside and take photos?'

'Sounds absolutely wonderful!'

Standing in the car park, with the best twenty hours together behind us, there doesn't seem to be enough words to express how great it's been. We both know it.

'Well, I'll see you next year.' I put it out there. It's a statement but actually a question. I'm utterly destroyed that I have to leave him at all.

He smiles. 'Same time next year.'

'Just one last thing,' I say, pulling out a small white envelope from my handbag. On the front is scrawled his initials – 'JD' – in black ink.

'What's this?' he asks, taking it off me.

'Just a little thing I wanted to give you. Don't worry, it's not all emotional. Just something you should read every now and again.'

He starts to peel back the corner of the envelope before I interrupt him.

'No,' I say, putting my hand over his. 'Do it after I'm gone.'

'All right.' He pops it in the pocket of his winter coat.

'Take care, Stephanie.' He wraps his arms around me and his hand sinks into my hair as I hold on to his waist. We stay here for a while, neither wanting to let go. Releasing from the embrace, he kisses my cheek while his hands delicately brush the sides of my neck. Our mouths are centimetres apart.

He pulls away, walks back to his car and drives off.

Stepping into my car, I don't even bother fighting against the torrent of tears which start to fall. It's better they come now than when I get home and have to explain them to Matt. I feel like I've been wrenched in half already. I whisper to myself, on repeat, 'You can't have him, he belongs to someone else', but it makes not one scrap of difference. Because for the last twenty hours, he *did* belong to me, and I belonged to him. In that parallel universe, we belonged to each other. Now, we're going to be thrown back into reality, and I hate it.

Returning home and pulling up on the driveway, I turn the ignition off. A veil of guilt descends over me. I don't want to go inside. What if he knows? I've spent the last hour rehearsing and going over what I'll say if he asks what we did … 'Oh, it was lovely to see her, we couldn't stop talking about the old university days. She has two children now, her eldest has just started nursery.'

All lies.

He's in the kitchen when I eventually go in.

I smile cheerfully. 'Hi!' My eyes are immediately drawn to a bunch of flowers in a glass vase on the island, a mixture of purple, red and pink carnations. They're still in the cellophane, leaning to one side.

'What have I done to deserve *them*?' I ask, nodding in their direction.

'I don't need an excuse to buy my wife flowers, do I?' he says and laughs, before coming over and giving me a hug. It feels different to the one I had only an hour ago. 'How was the girly weekend?'

'Great! Lovely to catch up. Never stopped talking. Anyway, I'm going to take my stuff upstairs,' I tell him.

'Well, I thought we could go out for a drive.'

'Lovely! I'll be two minutes,' I tell him, sloping upstairs, feeling like the worst wife in the world, and we spend the afternoon wandering around a nearby village.

It's a cold, blustery day so we nip into one of the pubs and sit by the fire. Matt tells me about last night which he spent with the boys playing poker. It's become their thing in recent times. They bought a proper set with all the chips and they really get into it. I try to remain upbeat and normal, but my mind is a million miles away. I feel as if I'm performing, although I'm not sure who for any more.

We arrive back home on the cusp of darkness and I treat myself to a bubble bath. Submerging myself into the water, surrounded by candles which release the sweet scent of vanilla into the bathroom, I think about the weekend; what it means and what I've done.

I can't do this to Matt. He's a good person and doesn't deserve this. I have to stop it before it goes any further. I'll have to do whatever it takes to get Jamie out of my head. Thank God I saw the Chaplins there last night.

It was the wake-up call I needed.

Sitting at my French dressing table, I glare into the three-way mirror. That self-destructive side of me I know so well stares back, the wet hair slicked back from my face, no make-up. Just me. There she is.

My phone pings in my handbag. Reaching for it, I see a message from Jamie. I hold my breath looking at it. I swipe right to open it and it takes me to the message which is a link to YouTube and one single 'x'. Quickly grabbing my earphones, I plug them in.

Clicking on the link takes me directly to a music video I've seen so many times. I've always loved it. Sexy, sensual, the twangy guitar, his haunting, unusual voice ... and the beautiful lyrics. Chris Isaak's 'Wicked Game' echoes through my head and I listen to every single word. I'm hypnotised watching him and Helena Christensen flirt about on a beach. All I want to do is call Jamie, text him, tell him how much I enjoyed the weekend and how I wish I could have kissed him.

But I can't.

I compose a message and link back, then press send. I have no idea if he likes that song, but I hope that over the next year, whenever he hears 'You Do Something To Me' by Paul Weller, he will think of me.

CHAPTER 8

Tuesday 6 January 2009

Jamie

I look at her sometimes, usually when she's doing something mundane like pouring a glass of wine and that's when I ask myself: what are you doing to her? She's so oblivious, has no idea that you've developed this inexplicable connection with someone else. Is that even possible? Is it real if you've only met someone three times? We're not doing anything physically wrong. But we're doing everything emotionally wrong.

I can't stop thinking about her. The guilt crushes down and I feel the weight of it suffocating me, like I can't breathe sometimes.

I always imagined the kind of men who do this as arrogant, tawdry, smug twats. They float around with not one thought for their poor unknowing, suffering wife. They brag about it to their equally-as-vile friends, sharing tales of their illicit hook ups, laughing about it. They book hotels, tell lies about where they're going, take their wedding ring off when they're with her. They revel in the excitement of it all.

Am I really any better than them? Is Stephanie? We are, but I guess we're not … not really.

We've not had sex. We've kissed once. We just love being with each other. Is that better? Or is it even worse? Does it really matter if you're a bit classier about it? If you keep it to yourself? Does it matter if you start having a few feelings? You're still lying. Being unfaithful.

Cheating.

It doesn't matter how you dress it up.

And, yet, I can't stop it.

Helen deserves better than this … than me. I can't begin to imagine what people would think of me if they knew. Our couples friends, who we've spent many nights down the pub with, laughing, doing pub quizzes, talking about serious subjects and daft ones. What would they think of me? Well, I *know* what they'd think of me. And, at the same time, I'm the last person they'd expect this from.

I know, more than anyone, the pain this kind of behaviour causes. I'll never forget the day my dad left home, leaving Mum for another woman. They'd been having an affair for eight months and the only reason he came clean and told Mum about it was because everyone on the estate knew about it and someone was about to tell her. That's how much of a coward he was.

I was only ten at the time. I sat on my bed, listening to them rowing for hours. This kind of thing was normal in our house. Dad was a plasterer and worked long hours, preferring to spend his time after work in the pub getting bladdered with his mates before coming home to us. We lived in a tiny terraced house on a rough estate in Manchester; the kind of place where everyone had a nickname and nobody had any hope of escaping. Mum worked as a dinner lady at my school and Dad always had a very cavalier attitude – even as a child I recognised it. He had a swagger about him, wound people up the wrong way. He irritated men, but women loved him. We never had a close relationship. He was never around long enough. But he used to draw pictures for me. He had a talent for illustration and could have done something with it, given half the chance.

I wasn't allowed to see him after he left. He lived locally for a few years with 'that woman' and he made half-hearted attempts to see me. Mum always said the same thing: it was for the best and he'd eventually let me down. She was right. It only took about two months before he stopped trying to see me altogether. I was disappointed he didn't try harder because I missed him and needed him at times. He wasn't the best dad but he was mine.

He moved away in the end, somewhere down south. That was the last I heard. Everyone said I was the spitting image of him – we had the same blue eyes.

It took my mum years to get over it. It knocked her confidence and she was exhausted having to work and look after me too. I was an angry arsehole over it for a while.

Now I'm doing exactly what he did. The thought I could end up inflicting the same amount of pain on Helen, as he did to Mum, kills me. And yet I feel powerless to stop it. That's why it's important to contain it. *Her.*

Once a year.

I just want her to be in my life.

As we pull up on the drive of Helen's parents' house, I remember the first time I came here. I was eighteen years old and, at the time, it was the most amazing house I'd ever been in. Posh was an understatement.

It was in a cul-de-sac where everyone had trimmed hedges and pristine gardens. There were no cars without wheels outside, no playgrounds with graffiti scrawled all over the slide, and definitely no lads drinking cans of Ace lager with their feet in a paddling pool. When Helen picked me up from the bus station, I attempted to hide my nerves by chatting about our exam results but she saw straight through it.

'Don't worry,' she said, 'they can't wait to meet you.'

Her parents' house was like a museum. Everything was shiny, standing up straight, and it smelled of Shake n' Vac or something clean. It was completely immaculate. There were vases of fake flowers all over the place. It was nothing like my mum's house. We didn't have the money for anything like this. Our house was a bit shabby, messy and all over the place.

I remember telling Mum that, after having our meal at Helen's house, her mum immediately removed the table cover – table cover! – and polished the mahogany table underneath with a duster and special spray. Mum, who bought some dust polish and kept it under the sink, only using it on special occasions, pulled a face of absolute bewilderment and asked if they had a tumble dryer too.

I still feel a bit uneasy when I visit. I'll always be that slightly awkward eighteen-year-old who isn't good enough for their daughter.

'It's a great stroganoff, Judy!' I gush now.

'Thank you, Jamie. I picked the meat up from the local butcher yesterday. They have some great cuts. I must get you some,' she offers.

I wouldn't have the slightest clue what to do with it but I appreciate the sentiment. Helen glances at me from the across the table and laughs, which I return. I can cook basic things but I think I'd struggle with a stroganoff.

'How was the cruise, David? Helen said you had an amazing time,' I ask. David, Helen's dad, is a retired GP and is now into sailing and boats. That kind of thing. He's a nice fellow, but one of those people you never quite know how to take. Like you're talking to him and he glares straight through you. I have never seen him in casual wear. He's always wearing a shirt and V-neck of some sort and sensible trousers.

'Oh, it was magnificent, wasn't it, Judy?' he reveals, putting his knife and fork down to properly get into this. Judy nods enthusiastically. 'The Italian Riviera is truly stunning. Just stunning. You two should go.'

'I quite fancy a cruise actually, honey,' Helen says.

'Not sure it's my thing, to be honest,' I inform the table, which was quite obviously the wrong thing to say.

'What's not your thing?' David scoffs. 'Stunning sunsets? Visiting beautiful places?'

Everyone looks at me. I walked straight into that one.

'No, that sounds great! I just wouldn't like being stuck on a boat for that long. I think I'd get cabin fever.'

David shakes his head, laughing in a mocking way. 'Did you hear that, Judy? Cabin fever!'

'Dad!' Helen, says in a stern voice. 'It's not everyone's cup of tea. We haven't decided where we're going on holiday this year.'

'I read an article, actually, about how more people are staying here for their holidays. There are some beautiful places in the UK. I'd love to visit Cornwall, it's supposed to be stunning,' I say. I've been meaning to mention it to Helen anyway.

'Cornwall?' Helen laughs. 'Baby, I don't work fifty-hour weeks to stay in this country for my annual holiday!'

David nods at Helen in agreement, almost as if I've just suggested we visit a war zone for a fortnight.

'You need to get away, go abroad, Jamie!' Judy coos.

'I'm just thinking of money and things we've got to pay for this year, that's all,' I say. That's about as tactful as I can be in front of her parents without screaming out 'Aren't we supposed to be saving up to have a baby?'

'Well, I think I'm owed a proper holiday,' Helen says. 'I certainly wouldn't turn down sitting by a pool on a ship for two weeks.'

'Not saying I'd turn it down,' I say, defending myself. 'Just that it's not really my thing.'

I spend the rest of the meal listening to the three of them chattering on about stuff which doesn't concern me. I offer to polish the table afterwards, thinking of my mum when I do it. Both Helen and I have things to do before work tomorrow so we head back fairly early.

The car journey home starts off silent. That's never a good sign.

'What's up?' Helen says.

'Nothing. What do you mean?' I ask, pulling out on to the dual carriageway.

'You were being weird. All that stuff about holidays.'

'I wasn't. I genuinely would like to go to Cornwall. Why is that so weird?' I ask.

'Really?'

'I thought you wanted a baby, Helen? We can't afford that if we're going on fancy holidays. And you were on about putting the extension on the back of the house. We don't have the money for everything. We need to prioritise what we want most and go from there. I feel like you want everything at once and I can't give you that. I'm sorry, Helen, but you just can't have it all.'

'We could if we had more money coming in.'

'But we don't,' I reply in a clipped tone, knowing exactly where this is going.

'Well, I told you about the opportunities at my place. All you have to do is say the word and you'd be in with your talent. Really well-paid job, brilliant benefits, great exposure ...'

'No, Helen.'

She pauses, staring straight ahead out of the window. 'Why not?'

'Because I already have a job. Which is the answer I gave you last time you asked.'

'I know you do, honey. And it's only because you're so talented that I want you to be properly appreciated and earn proper money from it with so many more benefits—'

'I teach children, I love it, I get six weeks off in the summer! What more benefits do I need?' I laugh.

'I mean *proper* benefits, for the future, Jamie,' she says, placing particular emphasis on the word 'proper'.

'Like what?' I reply, irritated.

'If we are thinking about kids, we need to think ahead. You've been working at the school since we graduated and you've got so much out of it, but your earning capacity could be so much higher ...'

Hearing Helen talk about my skills and passion in such a clinical way makes me feel so depressed. Do I have a say in this at all?

'What about my ability to provide childcare when we do have kids with all the time off I get in a year? Isn't that a benefit? Besides, I couldn't work at your company, Helen. I'd hate it,' I tell her. 'It's just not what I want in life.'

'Well, sorry for trying to help,' she says in an obvious huff, turning her head towards the passenger side window. I can't bear silences or leaving things on an argument.

'Look, I'm sorry. I didn't mean to snap. It's been a long week,' I say, stretching over for her hand and holding it.

'I'm sorry too,' she says, reaching into the footwell for her handbag. A stab of guilt shoots through me when she does, and I return my hand to the steering wheel.

I bought that bag for Helen at Christmas. It was expensive and I did it for two reasons. Firstly, because I knew she'd love it (she did). Secondly, it was a pure guilt purchase and I thought it would somehow make me feel a bit better about meeting Stephanie a few months earlier (it didn't). She ran her fingers over the dulled black leather exterior of the designer bag, caressing the studs on the front and shiny silver clasp.

'Thank you so much, baby! I absolutely adore it!' she'd squealed on Christmas Day, kissing me on the cheek before going back to admiring her new gift. She immediately took pictures of it from various angles, posting them on Facebook with the caption 'Look what my *amazing* hubby bought me for Christmas! Aren't I lucky?! Feeling very loved right now. X'. It got 154 'likes'.

There's something about Christmas which makes you appreciate your other half. Maybe it's because you spend so much time with each other. Maybe it's because you spend hours walking around shops, thinking of things they like and enjoy, so you can buy them the perfect gift. Or, maybe, it's because you listen to sentimental songs as you drink mulled wine around twinkly Christmas trees and wonder how the hell you could do this to them.

'You're right,' I say. 'You do work hard and deserve a nice holiday. I'm just worried about money if we want to try for a baby.'

'We both deserve a nice holiday. But, listen, let's look into the Cornwall thing. There must be some nice hotels down there. I absolutely draw the line at camping!' Helen says and laughs.

I smile. 'As if I'd make you do that! Sorry for being distant and snippy. January is always stressful at school.'

'About the job thing ...' she says seriously. 'I hope you know it's only because I want the best for you. For us. For our family.'

'Yeah, I know.'

'And while I appreciate that you love your job, we all owe it to ourselves to grab any opportunity to make the best life for ourselves. There's nowhere left to go in your current place so unless you're going to stay there forever, this is the furthest you'll go. You could start climbing a ladder elsewhere.'

'I know what you're saying, Helen, but I just feel like I'm selling out.'

'Well, I think you need to accept you're not going to be a full-time artist,' she says, confidently, 'but you should absolutely continue it as a hobby.'

Something hits me in the pit of my stomach when Helen says this. Is she right? I've always had this 'never give up' attitude, probably because of where I'm from. But this is my wife telling me I should forget it. Perhaps she's right.

I don't say anything. She's said her piece and we drive the rest of the way in silence. It's only a few minutes until we're home. The house is cold and in darkness when we get back. Helen heads upstairs to prepare for a presentation tomorrow. Giving her a kiss and a hug, I tell her I love her but that I need to get some stuff sorted for my class.

The garage is freezing in winter. I pull the light cord and the strip lighting flickers on. The heaters are plugged in and the hot air starts to blast out, filling the ice-cold space. I glance around my 'studio' and the pieces I've made in recent months. Are they even any good? I don't know any more. Canvases are strewn around, shelves are packed out with paints and brushes. This is my space. A place where I keep the dream alive. My outlet.

I walk over to a box in the corner where I keep all the stuff from the art weekends at Heathwood Hall. Crouching down on the floor, I rummage through it; it's full of admin forms and students' pictures. I don't like to throw them away – they spent a lot of time creating them. The paper is cold to touch, I should really keep it in the loft.

Buried in the middle of all the paper is exactly what I'm looking for. I hid it there in October last year and now I pull out the card Stephanie gave me last time I saw her.

On the front is a chaotic depiction of an artist's studio. In the middle, an artist is painting on an easel.

'Never give up on your dream' it says inside. Nothing else.

I think about sending her a message but I don't know what to say.

Turning my phone off, I turn the heaters up and start to draw.

CHAPTER 9

Saturday 20 June 2009

Stephanie

'What first attracted you to Matt?' Jane asks in the thick Liverpudlian lilt I've come to know so well over the years.

I didn't know what to make of her at first. She always looks chic and yet I can't pinpoint her style at all. One day she'll be wearing a masculine-looking shirt and slimline trousers with extremely high heels. The next month she'll be wearing a floaty wraparound dress. She reminds me of the women from an era of years gone by, perhaps the '50s; she has that kind of captivating air about her.

I would love to know more about her personal life. Is she married? Does she have children? What are her friends like? Is her house messy or tidy? Does she drink coffee or tea? She knows all of my secrets and I don't even know how old she is.

Today, she's sitting in a new tall black chair which freaks me out. I can't take my eyes off it. The back of it is way too tall and extends far beyond her head, like something out of a surreal horror film. Leaning to the right side of the chair, her elbow hangs off the side.

'When I first met Matt, he seemed so ...' I glance around the room, searching for the right word. 'Enthusiastic,' I eventually settle on.

'In what way?'

'We were at a party in London. I didn't want to go but my flatmate made me on this particular night. Matt came over to chat and he seemed really interested in me, I suppose. I needed that at the time.'

'At the time?'

'You know, when you've just graduated from university and don't really know who you are. When you like anyone who takes an interest in you. You feel lost,' I reply, smoothing out my tangerine-orange, silky dress.

'Right,' she says, nodding.

'And, he was a bit older than me. I think I needed looking after at that point.' I smile. 'He made me feel safe.'

'OK ...' she says slowly, sweeping some strands of cherry-red hair out of her face.

'And as it happened he worked in software sales and was looking to move to another firm, so we were chatting about Dad's company. I was saying how I could introduce him and maybe get him an interview ...'

'Right,' she says abruptly. I always know there's a point to be made when she clips something in that harsh manner.

'Is Matt like your dad in any way, do you think?'

This is obviously a loaded question and I'm not really sure how to answer it. There'll be a reason why she's asking but I have no idea what it is. I've become so suspicious of her questions.

'Like my dad? How do you mean?'

'Do they share any characteristics?' she asks.

'I don't think so,' I say, frowning. 'Well, they both get on. But Matt is very charming like that. He makes it his business for people to like him. He always said his charm would make him rich one day.'

'Hmm,' Jane says, nodding momentarily with her eyes closed. I take the brief opportunity to stare at her amazing coiffed hair, which has been pinned up in the same black butterfly clip for every session I've seen her for.

'And I suppose they're both very work-orientated,' I go on. 'Dad's always admired that about him.'

'Anything else?' she asks. 'What would you say about them, emotionally?'

'Emotionally? I've never thought of Matt being an emotional person. Or Dad. He used to be, but not since … well, you know. Matt's quite closed with his emotions,' I say, quietly.

'Has he always been like that?' she asks.

'Yes. Well, I mean, not in the beginning. He was a bit open like most guys, I suppose. Said the stuff you need them to say …'

118

'What kind of stuff?'

'You know – "You're different to other girls" – and it didn't take long before "I like you" turned into "I love you",' I tell her, remembering the euphoria of that honeymoon stage of a new relationship. The one where you stay up talking every night, desperate to learn everything about each other, a smile erupting across your face when you look at him, when he's the first thing you think of when you wake up. The problem with this stage is that it isn't real. In Matt's case it lasted for about six months. By that time we were sharing a flat and he was working for my dad. We used to joke that he was the son Dad never had because they get on better than Matt and I do a lot of the time.

'It moved quite quickly, I guess,' I tell her.

'How did he make you feel in the beginning?'

'Wanted. Secure. Safe,' I fire out.

'And how does he make you feel now?'

'I try to be a good wife, fulfil his expectations ... but it never seems to be enough.'

'Enough in what way?' Jane asks.

'Something's always my fault, or he speaks to me as if I'm a child. I don't really feel like it's an equal partnership. We're not really like a team. We're sometimes more like ...'

'... father and daughter?' Jane says.

'Yes ...' I say, sighing. 'You think I went for Matt as part of some kind of weird Freudian attraction because he was like my dad, don't you?'

Jane smiles. 'Is that what you think I think?' This has become a game between us now. I second-guess what she thinks but I suspect she gains far more in terms of what's going on in my head from what I suggest, so she wins either way. I laugh, because we both know this.

'I think it's highly likely there's a relational pattern at play here, certainly,' she says, shifting in her seat.

'Relational pattern?'

'When we are attracted to someone, there's always a reason for it. It's primarily physical, but there's something subconscious too, like a radar that attracts you to that person.'

I'm captivated listening to this explanation, but at the same time, even as she's explaining it, I'm wondering where the hell Jamie fits into it all.

'So, where does the pattern bit fit in?' I ask.

'We all get into patterns, some more than others,' Jane explains. 'But you'll probably find that all of your main relationship partners have something in common – and I wouldn't be surprised if they share similarities with a parent. Your dad.'

This is all getting a bit too weird for me now.

'Errm. OK … But why? How? What?'

'You're seeking approval from intimate partners who are similar to your dad, or who your father approves of. You think if you can get them to love you, approve of you, then, by proxy, your relationship with your father will be better, or healed. You had a very close relationship with your dad up until your mother died, didn't you?'

'Yes,' I reply, swallowing hard. Just acknowledging the fact of it physically hurts.

'And then he closed himself off emotionally and has never been the same since,' she points out. 'But you crave that close relationship back, don't you?'

I sigh, looking up to the ceiling briefly in an attempt to stop the tears coming out.

'More than anything,' I admit.

'So, you subconsciously chose a partner who is incapable of intimacy to effectively rewrite history.'

'What? That's ridiculous. Why on earth would anyone choose to be with someone who wasn't good for them? Who rejected them, or was cold towards them or anything like that?'

Jane laughs. 'Because it happens every day, Stephanie! And it keeps me in a job! It's subconscious. Think of it as a blind spot. People can't help it. But it happens, it's called "repetition compulsion". It's the same reason women stay with men who abuse them – because it's familiar to them. They're usually acting out behaviour from the past, their childhoods, trying to get their partners to love them.'

I feel sick.

'In your case, you believe the breakdown in the relationship between you and your dad resides with you, so you have coupled with Matt, a stand-in. But it won't work because, ultimately, you have to repair the relationship with your dad directly.'

Jane lets this information sink in. She always delivers the killer lines delicately but with firmness. There's always a brief silence afterwards which allows me time to gaze around the room and think about it for a few moments. It sounds uncomfortable, but it's actually not. I suppose that's the sign of a good relationship: being comfortable in each other's silences.

'And, Stephanie,' she goes on, 'that's not your fault.'

I remain silent. I hear the words being spoken and they make sense – but, of course, I don't believe them.

'You were a child. You lost your mother, and in many ways you lost your father too. You were left to fend for yourself and your sister on your own. You are not responsible for the breakdown in your relationship. *He* was the adult. Don't carry this on your shoulders. You've done it for long enough and you've more than paid the price.'

'But I don't know how to get that relationship back,' I say, quietly.

'You'll find a way,' she says confidently. 'No relationship is ever damaged beyond repair. You just have to find that thing which brings you back together. There's always something. You'll find it.'

I hope she's right.

When Matt picks me up my thoughts are all over the place, so I could really have done without him bringing up the baby topic. After Jane's bombshell revelation that I've somehow married my dad, I'm just not really in the mood for it.

'I thought you'd fall pregnant really quickly,' Matt says. 'Do you think it's because you drink? Maybe you should cut it out for a while.'

These conversations have become more frequent in the last six months. Matt's frustration is becoming more present with every monthly period I have. It's not like I'm doing anything to *not* get pregnant and I've been off the pill for ages, I take folic acid and regular-ish exercise, and I don't actually drink excessively. At the age of twenty-eight I am not yet considered geriatric.

We have sex at the right time of the month, even if it is a little mechanical sometimes, with the intention to produce a child. We used to have quite good sex – it was passionate, the kind of sex which would be had in a car, at night, by the side of the road, or on the stairs of our flat in London, the second we walked through the door. There was an element of spontaneity about it. I liked that.

'I don't think that's the problem, Matt. These things just take time. They can't be rushed,' I reply, firing out all the clichés.

'Your sister fell pregnant inside three months of trying, didn't she? Maybe there's something wrong with you?' he says. 'Do you think we should see a specialist?'

123

'There's nothing wrong with me, Matt,' I reply, as we park on Ebony's road. 'Just be patient. These things can't be rushed.'

He goes to say something else, but I get out of the car and wander away from him into my sister's house. It's Ebony's twenty-sixth birthday party and she's having quite the celebration. Because it's Ebony, she isn't content with it being a small, intimate family affair, and she has to ensure everyone knows how much money she has (or rather, how much her husband makes) so they've really pushed the boat out.

This garden party is all I've heard about for months. She was terrified it would rain (it hasn't), or people wouldn't turn up (they have) and she's even hired a professional photographer to take 'natural' photographs of everyone having a great (presumably, natural-looking) time. There are games laid out for the kids on the lawn and a huge drinks table in the shade (staffed, of course). A DJ sets up under the gazebo, playing all the party classics. God knows where she got him from – he's terrible.

'Matty!' Dad yells in Matt's direction. They embrace in that kind of hug men do where they whack each other on the back, almost breaking each other's spines in the process. I watch the pair of them in a completely different light now.

'Hey, how did that deal with the firm in Birmingham go?' Dad asks. 'I heard you did a phenomenal presentation, as usual.'

There's nothing I can really add to the gush-fest between these two so I just keep quiet. It's like this all the bloody time. Nothing I say can ever compete with the shop talk or how marvellous Matt is. He's like the son Dad never had. Clearly, Jane *is* right about this. I feel as if I spend my life trying to please both of them but constantly let both of them down.

'Steph, your sister was looking for you. Something about blowing some balloons up ...?'

Ahh. Right, yes.

By 6 p.m., the garden is heaving with Ebony's friends. They're all having a great time. Mind you, who wouldn't? Free booze, fabulous hosts and an amazing setting in the countryside. The entire garden swells with the sound of chatter and occasional roaring laughter. The terrible DJ continues to play a selection of the greatest hits from the last thirty years. Women regret wearing heels, constantly having to yank themselves out of sinking into the grass. It's easier to take their shoes off. I wore my wedges for this very reason.

I've never been any good at day drinking. It always goes straight to my head and I'm envious of people who can do it. The idea of drinking champagne in the sun appeals to me greatly, but it's like pouring poison down my throat. However, on this occasion, it feels like a good idea. I think it was Matt stressing me out with his pregnancy questions.

There are loads of people I don't know from Ebony's new social circle. In other words, the parents she's trying to get in with from the local private school. Despite the fact that Jude is only one, she's wasting no time in diving head first into this entire scene. We both went to the school Jude will be going to and have seen, first-hand, the power one can wield from being in the right circle. Mum was never interested in any of it. Everyone loved her and wanted her in their circle, but she was just lovely to everyone and never participated in any of the bitching. She had far too much class for any of that.

Ebony introduces me to various parents, all of whom are jiggling infants on their hips, trying to bribe them into stop screaming bloody murder with organic sugar-free treats or wiping gooey crap off their faces. It's not the most encouraging advert for parenthood. I absolutely adore my nephew, but other people's babies are not as cute to me.

It's a beautiful hot day. The music has everyone in a good mood. It even gets me jigging at one point. I've never been able to resist 'Crazy in Love' by Beyonce, so can't resist swinging my hips and singing the chorus when it comes on.

'Steph, calm down,' Matt whispers, placing a firm hand on the small of my back.

'What? I'm only having fun.'

'People are looking ...'

'So? It's a bloody party, Matt!' And I sigh, suddenly feeling embarrassed and stupid even though I know I shouldn't.

'How long do we have to stay here anyway?' he asks, swigging back the dregs of his champagne glass.

'Well it's Ebony's party, so until it's finished, I'd imagine.'

Matt sighs, looking at his watch. He made a great fuss before coming out because it was so hot and he didn't want to wear anything smart.

'Right, I'm gonna have to get pissed then,' he declares walking off to get a beer, leaving me alone.

Casting my eyes around the garden and watching everyone laughing, having a brilliant time, my mind suddenly turns to Jamie. I can't help but think that he probably doesn't have to get drunk to spend time with his wife's family.

CHAPTER 10

Saturday 10 October 2009

Jamie

It's uncharacteristically sunny and warm for an October weekend. It's more like a day in May, when you can *just* get away with a T-shirt and wear sunglasses without looking like a dick. But the light gives it away as being autumn and it's like looking at the world through an orange filter.

I think about Stephanie on the way down to Heathwood Hall in the car. I also think about Helen and our plans for the future. The two are so tragically incompatible and I know I have to end this before it goes any further. The lies have already started. 'I'm just going to see friends from university' proved to be a complex web of anxiety, having to think of people she has heard me mention before but doesn't know well enough to talk to.

I shouldn't be doing this. And I *am* going to stop.

We meet mid-afternoon. We booked our rooms way in advance so there was absolutely no chance of a repeat of last time. Stephanie is staying in her usual room and I have a single.

'Good afternoon, Mr Dobson! Lovely to see you here again,' Avril the receptionist sings at me as I approach the desk.

'Hello! Thank you, hope you're well?' I ask, not sure whether to be alarmed that she recognises me.

'Fabulous,' she trills, handing my key over. 'Room Thirty-three. Up the stairs, turn right.'

'Thank you so much,' I reply, picking my black weekend bag up and turning around to head off to my room.

'Miss Carpenter is already here,' she announces as I walk off.

'Well, hello you!' Stephanie says, opening the door.

I can't help but lunge towards her with the biggest hug. I wrap my arms around her waist and she grips on to my shoulders with such force that I don't want to let go. My face sinks into her hair, the faint scent of which I breathe in. We don't say a word. By the time we let go all we can do is look at each other and giggle, like two schoolkids who have just had a first snog.

'So great to see you, Steph!' I gush. And it is. She looks beautiful. I think about her so much throughout the year that it hardly seems real when we're in the same room.

She fiddles with the sleeves of her jumper before putting her hands on her hips as we chat about the journey here. In contrast to the intimate embrace we had only moments ago, we now stand metres apart, like people who barely know each other.

And that's the problem.

We *don't* know what we are. We're not actually anything.

'Listen,' I say, like an excited child, 'I had an idea. Let's do something different. It's a gorgeous day. Let's go for a walk to the next village and find a proper pub for some food and drinks then come back here later. What do you think?'

'Sounds great to me,' she says. 'Let me just change into my flat boots.'

'You brought more than one kind of boot?' I ask, aghast.

'I'm a woman, Jamie,' she says, laughing.

Hours later, we've walked miles, built up an appetite and are sitting in the corner of a beautiful country pub in the village of Busby Hawkton. I've never been here before but it's very quaint, the kind of place people come for a weekend lunch or to have a wander around the village pond, feeding the ducks with their kids. The views from the benches outside are alone worth the trek here. I do like places like this but I don't think I could live in one. Stephanie lives in a village like this and she loves it, but I'd find it too claustrophobic and I don't know … perfect? I quite like my world slightly chaotic and messy; I don't think I could handle the perfectly trimmed hedges and flower beds, village politics and gossip.

The level of enthusiasm the pair of us are on at the prospect of some proper pub grub as opposed to a posh dinner at Heathwood Hall is completely off the scale. Steph is getting lasagne and I'm having steak and ale pie. Both with chunky chips, because what's the point if you don't have chunky chips?

All the time I'm aware that this is different to all the other times we've met. It feels more casual, like we're in a different world. A parallel universe, perhaps. One where we are on some kind of date. It would be a bloody brilliant one if it was because we haven't stopped laughing and talking since we left the Hall. Walking through the fields and down the country lanes with her was a complete joy. Catching up with her and hearing about her year is always my favourite part.

She loved hearing about my students and some of the stuff they come out with.

'"Sir, did art GCSEs exist when you were at school?" they ask me. How old do they think I am?' I said, laughing, and showed her some of their artwork on my phone.

'Ooh! What's that one?' she said, placing her hand over my finger to stop me scrolling through for a second.

'Oh, just a project I set for them this year. I told them to write down the lyrics to a song they liked and illustrate their interpretation of them.'

She studied the picture, pinching the screen to zoom in.

'That one was Lisa's. She's recently discovered the Beatles and loves "Lucy In The Sky With Diamonds".'

'Sounds like my kind of project,' she said, smiling.

We talked about Michael Jackson dying in June then had a very heated debate about what his best song was.

'"Billie Jean",' I said, without a second of hesitation.

'Shut up. "Beat It".'

'Arguably a better video. But still no.'

Topics then moved on to 'important current affairs', which was mainly just me not having a clue who anyone was.

'Did you hear about Jordan and Peter Andre getting divorced?'

'Who?'

'You know! Her with the boobs. She's on everything. And him – he's got all the muscles. Sang about a mysterious girl in the nineties?'

'Vaguely. Terrible shame.'

'Yes. I won't even bother going into the whole Keisha leaving the Sugababes drama,' she went on, as if she knew these people personally. I could listen to her going on about anything all night and be entertained.

She seems spikier than normal, smilier, as if something has shifted for her. I don't know what it is but maybe she will tell me later. God, I hope she's happy. I wish I didn't have to do this.

'Erm, what the hell is this?' I utter in her direction when I see what she's bringing back from the bar.

'Snakebite and black. Diesel. Come on, you must have drunk this when you were a student?' she says, proudly, clutching two pint glasses with blood-red liquid in, foaming at the top, like something out of a chemistry class.

'Yes, you drink it when you're a student for a reason,' I say slowly. 'You have no money and it gets you smashed.'

'It's delish! And come on, you have to have it when you're in a country pub in autumn. It's the law.'

She shoves the glass in front of my face and I take it and we clink.

'Jesus Christ! That is *sweet*,' I hiss, screwing my face up.

'Oh. just drink it!'

Tell her. Tell her now.

Placing the glass down on the table, I put my hands on my legs and sit up straight. Automatically taking a deep breath, I turn to face her.

'So, erm, how are things with Matt?'

Oh great, delaying it. That will help you.

Stephanie smiles in a way I haven't seen before. I've never really seen her look happy when she talks about Matt. I can't deal with hearing about how happy they are together, and I know I've got no right to say that.

'Well, actually, I've been doing a lot—'

'Table Sixteen?' the waitress barks, hovering over us with two plates. She slings them down in front of us and marches off.

I can't put this off any longer.

'Steph, I need to talk to you about something …'

'What? What is it?' she replies, cutting into her steaming lasagne.

'I'm not sure I'll be able to do this again. I'm so sorry.' It takes me every bit of strength I have to say the words, but I know I have to.

She stops what she's doing. Like something has completely punched the life out of her. Her face drops and she looks away for a moment. Turning back to face me, she doesn't say anything for what feels like forever.

'Helen's pregnant, isn't she?' she says eventually.

'No,' I say, honestly. 'But we are trying. And when it does happen, this has to stop.'

'Of course it does,' she agrees, quietly. 'I understand.'

I wonder what's going on in that head of hers. I've come to know her so well in the very short space of time I've known her, but there's this small corner of herself she never lets me into.

'I mean, I was a nice little escape for you for a while,' she says, grinding some black pepper on to her food. 'You don't need me any more. I get it.'

'Is that what you think you are to me? An escape from my marriage?' I ask, genuinely bewildered. 'Because you couldn't be further from the truth. I absolutely adore spending time with you, more than I can tell you, but I'm not unhappy in my marriage …'

She looks right through me with a hard stare for a few moments and I have absolutely no idea what she's thinking. She looks like she wants to kill me.

'Then why are you doing this?' she asks, in an irritated tone.

Well, I walked straight into that one. I think about it for a few seconds, aware that the atmosphere has turned colder than it was only minutes ago.

'Because I can't … not.' It's not the best answer, but it's true.

'That's not an answer,' she says.

Oh.

'Well it's the best one I can come up with, and it's true. Why do *you* do this?'

Stephanie looks genuinely taken aback when I ask this, as if it never occurred to her I ever would. Her big green eyes frown at me for a second. Given the atmosphere right now, I have no idea what she's going to say.

'For the longest time, I was so numb,' she says in a way that obviously doesn't come easily. It's like she has to force the words out. 'Even when I met Matt,' she goes on, 'it was very functional – going through the motions, really.'

I listen to what she says and wonder: how did she end up like this? This beautiful girl, so incredible but so lacking in realising how amazing she is.

'And it's kind of been like that ever since. Until I met you,' she says and smiles.

135

'What did I do?'

'You made me ...', she turns her gaze away from me for a second, taking a deep breath before answering, '... feel. For so long I didn't feel anything, and then I met you and, all of a sudden, I felt everything. And I know that's awful, because you belong to someone else and I'm being selfish, but ... well, there is no but ...' she says.

'I know this is doomed and can't go anywhere. All that,' she continues. 'But I'm addicted to the way you make me feel. Because nobody, and nothing, has ever made me feel like you do. *That's* why I do it.'

It feels as though we are standing on the edge of a cliff, holding hands, in the middle of a storm which is whipping up speed. Are we bad people? I don't think we are. But we must be.

'Why is it so complicated?' she asks.

'I honestly don't know.'

'So,' she says, '*is* this it, then? Really?'

There's an anxiety in her voice I can sense. Of course I don't want to end it, but I can't carry it on if Helen and I have a baby. There is no place to come back from there.

'I think it has to be,' I say, forcing the words out. I've considered asking if we can be friends, but I think we'd both be kidding ourselves. What we have is too close, too special to contain in a friendship.

What a bloody mess. I didn't ask for any of this. Not that I'd ask for or get much sympathy from anyone about any of it. I didn't ask to meet her. I didn't ask to

---

have these feelings for her – whatever they are. But I do. I can't stop them. That's the thing about feelings; you can't switch them off – I wish you could.

Even if I stop this now, I'll still think about her all the time. I'll continue to crave her in that way I shouldn't. I'll also continue to love my wife; that won't change. So, what's the answer? I'm fucked whatever I do.

We're determined not to let our last weekend together be depressing so we decide to let it go out with a bang.

The atmosphere is more relaxed here in the pub. It lacks the formality of Heathwood Hall which means we can act more like ourselves, like we're just down the local having a laugh. We're so stuffed that we can barely move, but as darkness begins to descend, we think about heading back to the Hall. There's something mysterious and elusive about dusk in the autumn, I think, so we decide to skip a taxi and walk back.

Setting off into the countryside, along the paths and trails, the sun quickly falls in the sky, casting all kinds of radiant shades of orange out on to the land. We are the only ones out here, which is both terrifying and liberating.

'You must be used to this?' I ask, nodding out across the landscape, nothing to be seen for at least half a mile but rolling countryside. Heathwood Hall is just visible in the distance.

'Yeah,' she answers. 'I love it. It's where I feel happy, out here. You know why?'

137

'Go on?'

She walks just ahead of me, spreads her arms out and smiles. Her red lipstick contrasts against the jet-black Ray-Bans shielding her eyes, although I have no idea why she's wearing them, given that's it's getting dark.

'Because there's nobody else here. You can do whatever you like and there's nobody to see you or judge you.'

'Really? And what do you like to do out here?'

'Oh, nothing. I just meant you can be on your own,' she says, shaking her head and returning to my side. She starts obsessively tucking her hair behind her ear.

'Steph,' I ask, playfully, 'what do you do out here?'

She sighs, turning away from me.

'I don't do it *now*!' she says, in an over-the-top manner.

'What is *it*?'

'I'm not telling you,' she says, the smallest smile creeping on to her face. She's trying so hard not to laugh.

'Steph, you have to tell me now.'

'After my mum died, I didn't really get much time to myself,' she says, walking slowly beside me. 'I was looking after Ebony, Dad was working all the time, I was dealing with the fact she was gone. It's a lot to take on when you're thirteen.'

'I can imagine,' I say. 'Well, I can't. But you know what I mean.'

'My mum loved musicals. Me, her and Ebony always used to listen to them around the house. *Phantom, Miss*

Saigon, Grease, Joseph, all of them. We knew all the words and we'd sing at the top of our voices.'

'OK ...'

'Then, when she died, that all stopped.'

I reach out for her hand. Our fingers touch, acknowledging each other for the briefest of seconds.

'So, that was my release. I'd go out for long walks on my own in the fields where I lived with my Walkman, wait until I was alone and sing those bloody showtunes at the top of my voice. It made me feel weirdly closer to her and somehow made me feel less, I don't know, stressed?'

'This is the most brilliant thing I've ever heard!'

'What? Don't you think it's ... odd?' she asks, suspiciously.

'I love it! So dramatic!' I laugh. 'That's the thing you refused to tell me isn't it? Last year?' It makes sense, now.

She coyly shrugs her shoulders. 'Maybe!' she says.

'When was the last time you did it?'

'God! Outside? Probably when I was about sixteen or something. Although ...' she teases, looking at me bashfully, '... I *may* still do it in the house when I'm alone.'

'*Yes!* There it is,' I yell, punching the air. 'How did you feel when you did it?'

She laughs. 'What? You mean apart from completely mental? Well, brave. Alive. Like I was a teeny person on a huge stage. Just not giving a shit. I didn't care what anyone thought of me. I was lost in that moment. It was great!'

She sparkles telling me about this, like the feeling runs through her body as she recounts the experience.

'Well, Stephanie, this is your stage and I am your audience.'

'What?' She looks at me. 'No.'

'Oh, yes. Why not?'

'I've never done it in front of anyone. I'll die of embarrassment.'

'Well, this is the last time I'll see you,' I remind both of us. It comes out more brutally than I intended. I lighten the mood by telling her we are both on the wrong side of tipsy and I probably won't remember it tomorrow anyway.

'I haven't got my iPod anyway,' she lies.

I walk over to her, grabbing her handbag off her shoulder as she laughs, attempting to tear it away from me.

'Oh, come on! I know you carry that thing everywhere with you. You just never know when you'll need to belt out a showtune!' I say, rummaging through her handbag. 'Ah! Here it is.'

She's laughing so much she can barely talk. It's so lovely to see her in this state. Christ, I'm going to miss her.

'OK, OK,' she says seriously, straightening herself up and taking the iPod from me. 'What do you want?'

You. I want you.

'You choose,' I tell her.

'Hmmm. Right, Let. Me. See.' Stephanie scrolls through her iPod muttering to herself: 'No. No. God, no! Don't have the strength for that one!' A broad grin sweeps across her face when she finds the one she wants.

'Right. You have to sit over there. But put your sunglasses on because you'll put me off otherwise,' she demands. 'And I'm no singer. I'm only doing this because I'm drunk.'

'Yep. Sure. I'm ready,' I tell her, sitting on the grass waiting for this performance to start.

'This is a song my mum and I loved. I hope you love it too, Jamie. It's from the musical *Dreamgirls*. This is "And I Am Telling You I'm Not Going".'

She clears her throat. It's otherwise quiet, there's nobody else around. She stands about ten feet away from me with her earbuds in. I've never heard of the song she's about to sing.

It starts quietly, squeaking out the first few lines. She looks shy, holding on to the iPod in one hand, while the other fiddles with her coat pocket. Her ankles flick in and out in that way children do. I can't hear any music – just her – so I encourage her to get into it a bit more, knowing she can hear the music.

'Wooooo! Turn the music up!!' I shout, waving my arms in an 'up' motion.

Slowly, she starts moving around the space in front of me, her voice gaining strength and volume. Sass and attitude are added to the performance and she starts doing that wavy hand thing big singers do.

'*Yes*! Go Mariah!' I scream.

'What?!' she yells back, removing an earbud.

'*Go Mariah*!!'

'It'sNotMariahIt'sJenniferHudson!' she screams, quickly, mid-song, before getting back to the epic tune.

She's not a great singer and she's screeching it out at the top of her lungs. But it doesn't matter one little bit. Because she's absolutely lost herself in the moment and she's claimed a little bit of herself back.

'You're gonna love me …' she sings.

No need for the future tense. I already do. That's the problem.

She knows every word to this song. Every groove, quiver, rise and change. She doesn't hit every note, but it's clear she's sung it many times and lost herself in it. Music makes her feel alive. She punctuates every sentence with her hands, her arms flailing wildly by the end of the song, the shyness of only a few minutes ago completely gone. Halfway through she even starts using the iPod as a microphone. I give her an extra cheer for that.

She sings these lyrics to me, carefully chosen, knowing her, ever more profound in the circumstances. This girl I can't have and can never see again. It's a lovely, cute, sexy, endearing, beautiful, heartbreaking performance all rolled into one.

As the song rolls into a crescendo, I stand up and give her the biggest round of applause because she deserves it. Every time I see her she reveals a little bit more of herself and I'm going to miss that.

Finishing the final note, she pulls her earbuds out and breathlessly puts them back in her bag. She's visibly exhausted, but clearly thrilled. I walk over to her.

'Well, it sounded great in my head!' she says, still panting from her exquisite performance.

'Not as brilliant as it looked, trust me,' I reply.

Then I take her face in my hands and place my mouth on hers. It's an urgent, passionate kiss. She wraps her arms around my waist and we melt into a place we've both yearned to be in for three years. I'm never going to see her again. The guilt will come and I will deal with that. But not tonight.

Tonight is about us.

She's beautiful when she sleeps. Lying on her front, half of her face on the pillow, the other half exposed to the world. Strewn around her face, her blonde hair looks simultaneously wild and delicate.

I could watch her sleep for hours. The room is so quiet, the only thing I can hear is the sound of her breathing. It's a little heavier than it would be if she was awake. The sound of pure contentment. I could lose myself in its rhythm and go to sleep myself, but I don't. I prefer to stay awake and watch her. I'll never do it again.

Swinging my arm around her waist, I pull her close to me. Her body is beautifully warm and I love it next to mine. Her skin smells and feels even more incredible than I imagined. Everyone goes through this stage at the beginning of a new thing; the one where you find everything absolutely captivating about the other person and you want to know everything about them, you love the way they do everything, you just want to talk to them all the time. I had all that with Helen.

But this is different. A level up from that.

I'm sure it's because I only see her once a year, but I find her truly hypnotic. She isn't even one of these women who you could describe as being so full of life she's infectious, or 'bubbly' or any shit like that. Her beauty is actually quite dark.

Beautifully melancholic.

There's so much going on under the surface, simmering away. She's real and honest and flawed.

Steph wriggles under the covers, so I take the opportunity to cuddle into her. I hope she isn't freaked out by the naked Jamie in her bed. We were both drunk but very much wanted last night to happen.

'Morning, you!' a little voice squeaks out from nowhere.

'Morning! How's your head?'

'A little delicate. Yours?'

'Same,' I reply. She's facing away from me so I can't guage where things are between us.

'No regrets though,' she says, as if reading my mind and pushes back further into me as I wrap my arms tighter around her.

'Nor me,' I say, kissing her shoulder. I'd often thought about what having sex with Stephanie would be like. I'd tried convincing myself that perhaps it would help get rid of my 'ridiculous infatuation' with her. All rubbish, of course. Because I'm in love with her. If anything, all it's done is make it harder to leave.

'I'll miss you, more than I can ever tell you,' she says.

'I know. Me too …'

This is so horrible, I'm almost convinced it's causing me physical pain.

'But I know why you're doing it. Ending it, I mean. Especially now.'

'There's no other way,' I whisper. 'I care too much for you. It's better to let you go than get in deeper.'

She doesn't say anything to that, or move.

'I guess so,' she says, reaching over to check the time on her phone. 'We've got three hours before we have to check out. Let's make the most of it, shall we?'

The car park farewell comes far too quickly.

'I'm so sorry,' I say. It doesn't even brush the surface of what I want to express.

'I know why you're doing it. Doesn't mean I have to like it,' she replies.

'You and Matt?' I ask. 'You're OK? You were going to say something about him yesterday, just as I blurted all this out.'

She half smiles and looks away.

'Don't you worry about me. I'll be fine.'

I hug her, briefly: I know the longer this takes the worse it will be. After kissing her one last time, I pull back and look into those big green eyes I adore so much.

'You take care, Stephanie.'

'And you, Jamie.'

I turn around, walk away, get in my car and drive away.

At 10.24 p.m. my phone pings and there's a text from Stephanie.

A YouTube link takes me straight to the video for Robbie Williams's song, 'Feel'. I watch the video, which tells the story of a borderline illicit relationship. Stolen moments and fleeting glances are depicted throughout and the lyrics to the song, and the video, are perfect. But they make me want to cry for her, for this woman who I can no longer be near.

Uncharacteristically, she sends another message a few minutes later. It simply says:

Thank you for making me feel. Xx

I put a link into the text message with three kisses and press send. I hope she likes it. It was very carefully selected. The lyrics sum up exactly how I feel about her, right now, and probably how I will forever.

Paul McCartney's 'Maybe I'm Amazed'.

I watch the video four times before I start to feel traumatised and slam the laptop shut. I wonder how she feels watching it and hope I haven't upset her. I suddenly feel vulnerable, as if I've shared too much. But it's over now. She'll like the gesture. And it's all true anyway.

CHAPTER 11

Thursday 6 May 2010

Stephanie

'Wow! Where's that come from? I only saw you last week!' I squeal at Ebony, gawping at her rapidly growing baby bump.

I'm delighted at the prospect of another little nephew or niece to cuddle, but the news that Ebony is pregnant again only frustrates Matt even further. She's thrilled about it, if not a little apprehensive about having a newborn and a toddler, but since she's abandoned any desire of going back to work in the near future, I don't think she's that bothered.

'Steph, it'll be absolutely fine,' she says, reaching for an antiseptic wipe out of her bag and rubbing it all over Jude's face, which is caked in 'organic' crumbs from his healthy bag of some kind of carrot sticks. They just look like orange crisps to me.

'I mean, it'll be hard, but apparently it's better to have them close together – get all the sleep deprivation out the way at once and then they can start playing together and bonding. They really will be the best of friends, you know,' she announces, sending Jude off to play. It's lovely here in the park at this time of year, when all the flowers are coming out and the smell of freshly cut grass fills the air. The sound of giggling children is everywhere. I love it.

I look at Ebony as if she's mad. 'You remember how much we used to fight, right? Like, all the time?'

'Well, yes, but once we got past that we were great, weren't we?'

'Ebony, let me be clear,' I say in a stern voice. 'I have never forgiven you for the Game Boy incident.'

Gasping in a dramatic manner, her mouth drops open as she turns to face me.

I was ten years old, Ebony was seven. She didn't do it on purpose, but, my God, I *hated* her for it.

I still believed in Father Christmas and, that year, all I'd wanted was a Nintendo Game Boy. I was the happiest girl on the planet to actually find one waiting for me on Christmas morning. After playing with it non-stop all day, I was horrified to emerge from a bath on Boxing Day to find Ebony playing with it. Being typical siblings, an enormous row ensued: she refused to give it back to me and I chased her around the house. To cut a long story short, it ended up falling in the bath and it never worked again.

I refused to speak to her for three days, after which, Mum intervened. Dragging us into her bedroom, she sat us both on the bed.

'Listen, you two,' she said firmly, 'life is far too short for falling out with people you love. So, you need to end this silly feud right now.'

'But—' I interrupted.

'Nope,' she said, putting her hand up to stop me. 'I won't have it. You two work far better together, not apart. You're wasting the Christmas holidays not speaking to each other when you could be having fun and making memories.'

Ebony and I glanced at each other sheepishly.

'Nothing good ever comes from falling out with those who love you,' she went on. 'Trust me, I know. It's a waste of everyone's time. End this now and let's go and make some Christmas cookies.'

Mum spread her arms out, inviting us in a group hug, which we accepted.

'I want you both to promise me,' she whispered into our hair, 'you'll always think twice before falling out with people you love. It will only make you miserable and you will always regret it, always …'

'Stephanie, that is *harsh*! It's been twenty years!' Ebony squeals.

'And it will be another twenty,' I say firmly and then giggle, unpacking the picnic I've brought. 'So, I suppose you want a girl next?'

'Honestly, I'm not bothered. I would love a brother for Jude, actually. I think same sex siblings have a special relationship,' she says, casting a lovely little smile my way, which I return. 'But I can't deny I'd love a girl too. Would be nice to complete the set.'

'Perhaps you'll have twins, one of each!' I laugh.

'I hope not! Don't think even I could handle that!'

I've no doubt she could handle it. Ebony might have her funny ways about her, but she is tenacious. She's my baby sister but she's much stronger than me in many ways. She's always been so much more *with it*. I often thought it would hit her at a later time, perhaps even years down the road, but it never has. Well, not as far as I'm aware, anyway. Maybe she's in denial. Perhaps she's a mess behind closed doors and I just don't know about it. I'd like to think she'd tell me if she was.

We sprawl out on the red tartan picnic blanket I brought for the afternoon. I've taken a few days off work to spend time with Ebony and Jude and I promised him we could have a teddy bears' picnic, so the entire thing is child-orientated: ham and cheese sandwiches, crisps, sausage rolls, cookies, and fruit juices with far too much sugar in. I watch Ebony eyeing everything up as I unpack it. She brings her anxious voice out, the one which is about three octaves higher than normal.

'Oh! Don't you have any hummus? Or cucumber? He loves cucumber sticks!' she shrills. I gaze at her, cocking my head to one side.

'Ebony, I am not bringing my nephew rabbit food on a fun day out. He gets enough of that at home. What's the point of having a rebellious auntie if she can't even bring you crisps, for God's sake?'

'Well, I suppose one day won't harm. I just don't want him getting a taste for it.'

'Look, if he eats this, he doesn't have to have the crack cocaine I brought for dessert,' I say, deadpan. She bursts out laughing, putting her head in her hands.

'Non-alcoholic wine?' I ask, shoving a plastic wine glass in her face.

I miss my sister. I don't see enough of her these days and it's something she's obviously picked up on.

'I was starting to get a complex. Whenever we invite you both round you always have plans,' she says.

I smile. 'Oh, don't be silly. It's the summer, there's just so much stuff going on. That's why I took a few days off, to see you and Jude … just the three of us.'

I don't tell her that most of the time, we don't have plans. It's just Matt not wanting to go. He's got some kind of issue with Will, Ebony's husband and Ebony has never really clicked with Matt either, so I'd rather have time with them separately.

Jude runs over and lunges at me, throwing his little arms around my neck. He has long hair for a boy, a mass of dark curls which contrast against his pale white skin. I cuddle him up with all the strength I have and sit him on my knee, giving him a ham sandwich to chomp on.

'You're a natural,' Ebony says, looking on proudly.

I pop a little kiss on the top of Jude's head, smoothing his hair down afterwards. He really is the cutest thing.

'I don't think it's going to happen for me, Ebs,' I say without looking up. 'I've been trying to get pregnant for ages.'

'Do you really want a baby now?' she asks.

'What do you mean?'

'Because your body won't give you something you're not ready for, or don't want yet,' she says, quite astutely. Since when did my sister become so wise?

'But it happened so easily for you! All you have to do is stand next to Will and you get pregnant. Matt thinks I should be the same.'

'He's not putting pressure on you, is he? Because that certainly won't help.' Ebony bristles as she speaks.

'No, no,' I respond quickly. 'It's just frustrating because it feels like having a baby is the last piece of the puzzle and I can't get it. I can't even get that right.'

'You will. When the time is right,' Ebony smiles at me. 'You're only twenty-nine.'

'But what kind of wife am I if I can't even have a kid?'

'Steph, you're not defined by your ability to have children,' she says delicately. 'You have a million other amazing qualities. I know you've had a tough time and we all want you to find yourself in a great place, but you need to find that without children.'

I nod my head with a slightly confused face.

'You *are* happy, aren't you? With everything? Matt, I mean?'

'Yes, I just want to make him happy, be a wife he's proud of.'

'Well, I hope he's proud of you no matter what,' she says.

'Mmm ... yeah,' I shrug.

'Steph? Are things OK? With Matt? You know you can talk to me.'

'I don't know,' I say, stroking Jude's little leg as he eats his sandwich. 'I just feel like we're not really a team. Like we're not as tight as we should be, perhaps. I'm sure I'm just being silly.'

'Have you talked to him about it?'

'What can I say? It's not like he mistreats me in any way. I'm sure I'm just being awkward and overanalysing everything. Maybe my expectations are too high. I've probably just watched too many romcoms,' I say, laughing it off. I wish I hadn't said anything now.

'Well, we know more than most that life is too short to not make the most of it,' she says with a delicate smile. 'Talk to him. Don't bottle things up.'

We stay at the park until late afternoon, hanging out, chasing Jude about on the grass, laughing, playing, just being sisters. Jude is shattered for the walk home and collapses in his buggy. Naturally, Ebony panics that he's sleeping far too late in the day which means that he won't sleep tonight. He slumps in his stroller, limbs hanging out of the sides and mouth wide open. Long black eyelashes rest on his cheeks as he sleeps. His skin looks so soft and white. I always feel so broody when I look at him.

By the time we reach my house after walking home in the late afternoon sun, we've had such a great day. Ebony leaves me at the gate. It's a lovely evening – that kind of bright, sunny, yellow light which bears down on everything at this time of day, but as soon as you get into the shade, the temperature drops dramatically.

As I walk up the path to the house, I text Ebony:

Had a great day with you and Jude. Love you. Xxx

I smile as I put my phone back in my shorts pocket. What a lovely day I've had. As I rummage around my handbag for my front door keys, my phone beeps. This is going to turn into a sister slush-fest.

Grabbing my phone out of my pocket, I catch my breath when I see the banner across the middle of the screen. It's Jamie: why the hell is he messaging me in May? Or at all? Without thinking anything else, I swipe across the screen to open it, exhaling deeply as I do so.

Sebastian Dobson came very quickly – and suddenly! – into the world a month early, this afternoon, 6 May, at 2.03 p.m. Baby and Mum doing really well. Helen was absolutely amazing and I couldn't love them both more.

'*I couldn't love them both more.*'

I couldn't love *her* more.

Too. Much. To. Take. In.

I immediately reach out and grab on to the outdoor porch column to steady myself. I feel sick. Staring at the ground for a few moments, processing what I've just read, I take a few deep breaths before looking at it again. I need to approach this with a clear head.

Right.

I knew they were trying for a baby. Was she pregnant when we last met? 'A month early'? I do all kinds of mental gymnastics trying to work out if it's possible he would have known in October. At the very least she would have been in very early pregnancy. I have no idea how early you know because I never get to that stage.

Why the hell has he even sent me this?

Thankfully, Matt is at work so I don't have to hide anywhere in the house and cry about this. I close the message down and put the phone in my bag. But it plays around on loop in my head. I can't see anything else.

Grabbing a glass of water, I open a window in the lounge. A soft breeze runs in and I sit in the armchair next to it, allowing it to sweep over me. It's quiet, but for the sound of a lawnmower roaring in the distance somewhere.

The past seven months have been awful. No, not awful.

Crucifying.

There is nothing more torturous than having to get on with your normal, everyday life when you're dying inside because you know you'll never see someone you care so much for again. What do you do when they're all you think about?

And, to make it worse, you can't tell anybody else about it. No long rants to your friends on the phone, no crying on their shoulder, none of those inspirational chats where they tell you you're better off without them because they're a dick, nobody cheering you through the heartache, pain, anger, devastation.

You have to deal with this on your own.

Everyone wonders why you're so miserable and eventually you run out of excuses. You can only blame hormones, work, life, for so long. Weeks turn into months. It's no wonder I'm not getting pregnant. People think my recent weight loss (not that I needed to lose weight but it's definitely noticeable) is because I'm preparing for a baby. It's actually just grief-induced stress. The only person who came close to guessing something drastic had happened was Jane who asked once, 'Is there anything you want to tell me?'

I loathe myself for even being in this state. What did I expect when I met him last October? Oh yes, my big plan: tell him I didn't think I was actually happy with my husband any more so did he want to consider this information in view of his own situation? Did I actually expect him to do anything about it? Oh, the humiliation. Thank God he stopped me before I said anything. It was a blessing in disguise, especially in light of this news.

I torture myself thinking about Jamie and Helen's perfect birthing experience. The post-birth glow she probably had, him taking photos of the stunning wife and child (which was obviously placed on her perfect breasts immediately), her immaculate make-up, both unable to stop beaming at this perfect creation. All the 'I love yous'. Eugh. I bet the pictures are all over Facebook already.

As my imagination really starts to run away with me, my phone beeps again.

> *Stephanie. I'm so sorry. I didn't mean to send you that message. I automatically sent it to all the contacts in my phone and only realised after I'd sent it you'd receive it. I'm so sorry X*

I think about not replying, pretending I've not seen it. But I decide to send this, after composing and then deleting the text about a hundred times:

> *It's OK. Didn't expect to hear from you again but glad you're well. I know it wasn't intentional. Many congratulations! Xx*

There was so much more I wanted to say. I wanted to say that I missed him. I wanted to say that I'd been thinking about him a lot.

When he told me he couldn't see me any more, I was devastated. I wanted to beg him to reconsider. But I knew there was no other way. He's trying to do the right thing. And, ultimately, whatever it was we had together was doomed anyway.

It's so very hard, doing this. But I don't have a bad life and I need to appreciate that. You can't always get what you want. I'm financially comfortable, I have a supportive family, a good job, a beautiful house, a nice car and go on lovely holidays.

So why is it that when Jamie Dobson told me he didn't want to see me again it felt as if I was having my soul ripped out? And I'd give up everything I have to see him as I have done, just one tiny weekend a year. That's all. Is that really too much to ask? Yes, of course it is, because he's moved on, and so must I.

CHAPTER 12

Friday 20 August 2010

Jamie

The first night in a new house always prompts a mixture of emotions: sheer exhaustion from moving day, sadness at leaving one chapter behind, excitement to start a new one.

And in this particular case, an anxious thrill I can't quite compute – or rather, daren't.

Switching the 'big light' on in what will be Seb's nursery when we get it sorted, I scan the room looking at the vast amount of boxes piled up in Tetris-like shapes with NURSERY and SEB scrawled on in black permanent marker.

I've come to realise that relationships are all about compromise. How big those compromises are depends very much on individual couples. Some people sacrifice more than others. I never, ever imagined I would move down south, far away from where I grew up. I also never thought I'd leave my job. The things you do for love, hey?

*

People warn you all the time about how hard having a baby is. They love telling you about how tiring it is, as though they get a sick satisfaction out of it. Parents of newborns, babies and toddlers actively seek out expectant dads and about-to-drop pregnant mums simply to inform them just how hard their lives are about to become. 'Make the most of the sleep you have now!' they crow, dramatically jiggling a whinging infant on their knee. 'You won't sleep again until they're sixteen!' Right, yes. 'Enjoy the peace and quiet! Be spontaneous and just go out because you feel like it – the cinema, shopping, anywhere. Just because you can.' Honestly, anyone would think you're signing up for a prison sentence.

Before Seb came along, Helen and I would roll our eyes at these people the second their backs were turned. Oh, heard this one before, mate. Yeah, thanks for that. Haven't you got anything original to say?

And then he was born and, three months down the line, I laugh at how right they all were. Because, it's not that I didn't hear them, I just didn't listen.

Becoming a parent is so huge, so life-changing, so enormous, you can't even begin to comprehend the job you're about to undertake – not really. Not even when you're painting the nursery or lovingly gazing at that black-and-white scan photo. It's still all pretend. Sure, you think, 'Yep, I'm so ready for this. Look at me now, all grown up, about to become a parent and shit,' but

161

it's laughable how unprepared you are. You read the parenting books, you buy the (wrong size) romper suits and all the crap from Mamas & Papas they con you into thinking you need and you kid yourself into thinking you're ready. But you're not. You're nowhere near.

All that stuff only becomes real when you're in the delivery room and you see that little human being coming into the world.

That moment.

That's the second you grow up. That's the minute you become a parent and you're responsible for another tiny little person.

I'd prepared myself for the ultimate cliché of Helen gripping on to my hand while screaming her head off – it actually became a joke between us. But, when the time came, there was no actual screaming, nor did she need me or my hand. She just zoned out and listened to the midwife. I was just standing there, looking and feeling like I was getting in the way.

When he was born with a little funny-shaped head because of the suction thing they used to get him out, they straight away took him for oxygen and I hugged Helen, who looked like she'd run a marathon.

'Is he OK?' she panted. 'Is Sebby OK?'

We knew from the twenty-week scan it was a boy. We weren't one of these couples who could wait. We wanted to create a little personality for him and give him a name. It felt like we knew him already.

'He's going to be fine. You did so well and I love you so much,' I whispered, grinning from ear to ear.

She smiled, wrapping her arms around my neck and pulled me close to her.

'I love you too,' she said, as the midwife brought our son over and handed him to us.

The whirlwind of having a newborn is a bit like when someone dies, I've decided. There's an initial period of hysteria: everyone comes around to see you, the house is always busy, people constantly ask if there's anything they can do – yeah, tidy up, make the tea and do the food shopping. Family bring flowers and cards and the house smells delicious. There are random balloons, teddy bears, and the kitchen is full of baked goods. It's lovely … but it's not real life. This period lasts for about a week before it starts to tail off and you realise *this* is real life. Then you're left to deal with it on your own.

All of a sudden, it's just the three of you.

Your previously always-tidy house is now like a tornado has gone through it, throwing off all kinds of baby paraphernalia. Helen has always been an immaculately tidy person and I'm not that bad but not a slob either. However, you don't get a choice about these things once a baby is thrown into the mix. Before you know it, your house is a bombsite and you don't really know how it's happened. There's a load of washing-up that needs doing, you live on microwave meals, you don't sleep, you don't get dressed or shower. How is this even possible? This baby is tiny and I absolutely love him to bits, but how can one small person change our lives so much?

The reality properly kicked in when I went back to work after my paternity leave. Nothing prepares you for the levels of tiredness you reach. You know you're living on the edge when you consider it a triumph to get three hours of unbroken sleep a night. It turns you into a monster.

Then the rows start. The classic who-has-the-hardest-job one is the most frequent and explosive. *I* have the hardest job because I have to work on no sleep. But Helen has the hardest job because she has lost her identity and social standing and at least I can get dressed and go and talk to people all day. It's a battle nobody ever wins. We're both suffering.

The sex stopped, not that this was a surprise; we were far too knackered to even contemplate it. But the intimacy stopped too, which was sad. We were both so wrapped up in the baby we neglected each other – and ourselves. I'd settle down for an evening on the sofa with Helen when Seb was asleep in his little Moses basket, bring her a glass of wine and put my arm around her, which she'd remove, saying she just wanted some space of her own. Fair enough, seeing as she spent most of her time with an infant practically Velcroed to her body. But I wanted to reconnect with her.

*

How on earth does a three-month-old have this much stuff? I glance at the cot which is unassembled, waiting for me to put it together tomorrow, the art I made for him leaning against the wall. I can't wait to make this room special for him. Opening one of the boxes, I smile as I pull out a fluffy white cuddly rabbit. Running my hands over the fur, I remember exactly when I bought it for him. My smile slowly fades as the events of that day return to me.

Eight months after last seeing Stephanie, it was a hot June weekend. Sebby was a month old and slept most of the time. But he was the most adorable thing I'd ever seen.

Helen had arranged for us to go on this family picnic day with some of her work colleagues in the park. It involved all kinds of intricate planning just to leave the house for more than four hours (including a forty-five minute drive, there and back). Nappies, bottles, bottle warmers, nineteen spare changes of clothes, baby hats, parasols, blankets, baby toys, baby wipes, dummies, nappy sacks ... the boot was practically full when we left the house. I mean, it's just ridiculous. Sebby cried all the way there which stressed us both out. The car was hot and traffic was slow. The atmosphere in the car became even hotter as a result of the constant bickering between me and Helen the entire journey.

'The car's too hot', 'open the window', 'he needs feeding', 'no, he doesn't', 'turn the air con off', 'give him a dummy', 'turn the radio down', 'you're driving too fast' … the whole journey was mega-stressful. By the time we arrived at the National Heritage middle-class fest that was this Teddy Bears' Picnic, which cost twenty pounds just to enter, we were already wanting to murder each other.

The entire site had been draped in streamers and helium balloons. They blew about in the breeze, enchanting the infants nearby who reached out to grab them. All of Helen's friends are ahead of us in the parenting stakes. We are the newbies. They spend most of the time talking about their offspring – mainly about how advanced they are, and how they reached all their milestones months ahead of when they were supposed to. There wasn't really much we could add to the conversation apart from doing amazed, 'wow!' faces and, in my case, trying not to look as bored as I was. I would have much preferred to be at home with just Helen and Seb, enjoying the weather, but I knew she liked these sorts of things.

As we all sprawled out on the grass, everyone unloaded the boxes and baskets of food they'd brought. It occurred to me how different picnics are now to when I was a kid. I used to love a proper scraggy picnic at the seaside or at the park, sitting on the grass, devouring soggy sausage rolls and squashed ham sandwiches on – God forbid! – white bread, then tucking into some Space Raider crisps and a Trio biscuit. It would all be washed down with a can of sugary pop, obviously. It always tasted so much nicer when you ate it outside, then Mum would fuss around, gathering all the rubbish.

These days, it's all carrot sticks, brown pitta bread, hummus, cucumber slices – seriously, what kid has ever eaten a cucumber slice and enjoyed it? – and smoothie drinks, it's all militantly laid out in compartmentalised Tupperware boxes. I couldn't believe my eyes. There I was, just trying to get dressed and feel like I've survived the day, and these people had time to make tomato and cucumber pinwheels for their three-year-olds.

Thankfully, Seb had worn himself out screaming the car down on the journey there, so he was fast asleep in his pram, giving me and Helen time to actually eat our lunch in peace. Well, I say lunch but it was 11.15 a.m. which counts as lunch when you've been up since 5.40 a.m. As I was stuffing my mouth with sandwiches, constantly on edge that the calmness could be interrupted by the baby at any second, one of the little girls in our group started acting up, getting grouchy in the heat. She was about four years old with long blonde hair, wearing a little pink summer dress. She wasn't being naughty, just a bit bored.

'Isabella! For goodness' sake! Will you sit down and stop messing about?' yelled her mother, a work colleague of Helen's.

'I'm not messing about, Mummy!' She started to cry, holding her rabbit cuddly toy by the leg.

'Everyone else is trying to eat their lunch in peace, so stop acting like a baby and sit down!' this woman snarled at her. Jesus Christ, calm down.

The little girl just stood there on her own, crying, and I thought – why would you do that?

Reaching into the changing bag, I pulled out my drawing pad and pens – I take them everywhere, it's like a comfort blanket for me.

'That's a very cute bunny,' I said to Isabella. 'Shall we draw him?'

'She's a *girl!*' Isabella said, as if it were perfectly obviously from its all-over pale-grey exterior.

'Oh! Of course she is!' I replied. 'Let's draw her with a nice pink bow in her hair, shall we?'

She nodded excitedly and I set to work. It didn't take long to knock a quick bunny up and it kept her entertained for fifteen minutes or so. After proudly drawing her own dress and bow on the bunny, she was proud as punch and hopped off to show her mummy.

'Oooh, baby! That's so clever!' her mother cooed, cuddling her now angelic girl. 'Did Jamie help you with that?'

'Yep! He did the ears,' she said, proudly. Everyone laughed.

'What is it you do, Jamie?' asked the mother, making me the centre of attention, which I hated.

'I'm an art teacher at the local secondary school.'

'You're wasted there,' the mother's husband said. 'You've got a talent. Have you thought about moving into the commercial world? You'd earn a fortune. Far more than you do now and for much less work—'

'I keep telling him that but he won't have it!' Helen interrupted.

'I enjoy what I do now, thanks,' I said to all of them, generally.

'Eugh, I don't know how you do it,' offered some guy in an oversized straw hat which was both ridiculous and unnecessary. 'All those kids screaming and shouting all day.'

'Well, they're between eleven and eighteen so they don't tend to scream or shout, really,' I explained.

'Oh, well, yeah. It's just not very ... you know? Sanitised, is it?' he said.

'Sanitised?'

'Oh, it's very worthwhile and selfless and all that,' he went on. 'But you're not going to ever really make any money, or progress, are you?'

'It's hardly selfless; I get a lot out of it,' I replied, irritated. How do these people think it's OK to say such things? I'd never be so fucking rude.

'Well, maybe when Hels gets the promotion she could put a word in for you. There will be loads of new opportunities in the new place,' he said.

'What?' I replied, completely confused. I looked at Helen who was shaking her head at the guy, who now obviously realised he'd said something he shouldn't have.

'What new place and promotion?' I asked Helen. Everyone else on the picnic turned back to their own business, clearly knowing that there was an issue about to begin between us. They all knew something I didn't. The wife of the guy who'd let this piece of information slip started giving him grief about it in that way wives do.

'I meant to tell you about it but wanted to decide if I even wanted it first,' Helen said quietly.

'Wanted what? What the hell is this?'

'I've been offered a promotion. A big one. They've asked me to be creative director of the London office,' she told me, nervously.

'London?' I spluttered.

'Yes.'

'From when?'

'In three months.'

'But Seb will only be four months old. I thought you wanted nine months off with him?'

'Well, I did. But this opportunity came up and they asked me to go for it and I did and I got it and I can't quite believe it!' she said without pausing for breath.

'When did you get it and why didn't you tell me?'

'Last week ...'

'And when do you have to give them an answer?'

She paused and looked at me, stuck for something to say.

'You've already told them you'll take it, haven't you?'

'Erm, well, not exactly. But I've said I'd love to …'

'Jesus Christ, Helen. Without even properly discussing it with me? And everyone else knows?!'

'I haven't said I'll take it!'

'It sounds like you've made your mind up without even speaking to me about it'

'That's not true, I'd never do that!'

'I mean … London! I don't want to move to London.'

She went to say something, but stopped herself, giving me a careful look instead. It was loaded with irritation but also the knowledge that she has to tread carefully here if she wants to get anywhere with this.

'I know you don't like the idea of it, but can you just try to keep an open mind so we can talk about it, please?'

'Oh!' I laughed. 'NOW you want to talk about it?'

'It doesn't have to be *in* London,' she suggested. 'I'd be prepared to consider somewhere within the commuter belt.'

'Oh, would you? And where does my job and career fit into this? Has that even crossed your mind in all this? Or am I simply an afterthought?'

'Of course it has. You can get a job in a school anywhere. I can't do my job anywhere. London is the next natural step for me.'

'Yes. For you. What if I don't want to leave my school?'

'Oh, come on, Jamie. Don't be awkward about this. You're not tied to that school,' she said, screwing her face up as she took a gulp of her Pinot Grigio out of a plastic wine glass. I was regretting agreeing to be the designated driver by this point.

'No, but I love working there. I love my students and I enjoy working with everyone. Maybe I don't want to just up and leave to work at a random place in London.'

At that point Seb started making noises. What started as a gentle cry swelled until it burst into a full-on bellow, letting us know he was hungry and wanted feeding *now*! I was grateful for the interruption. Things were about to escalate into a full-on row if we carried on and I didn't fancy doing it in front of Helen's work colleagues.

Scooping him out of his pram and snuggling him into my shoulder, I retrieved his bottle from the changing bag with one hand. I love the moment when a baby is crying and you start feeding them. It's so honest and blatant. The switch between screaming their heads off one second and being utterly content and quiet the next is so satisfying to watch. I wish adults could be like that – that it was that simple. Maybe it is, and we just complicate it all. Perhaps we all just need the basics; food, water and love.

So, what do you do when your wife gets this worldly professional opportunity? Do you stand in her way because you don't want to move? Do you kick off because you don't want to leave your job? Or, do you make huge changes in your life because compromise is what marriage is all about? Because you love her?

Because you owe it to her because you've cheated on her?

I expressed my concern that we'd be completely alone there. Both of our families were in Manchester so we would lose any help with Seb and further children. Not to mention that we'd be leaving our friends too. But after many long chats about it, she still wanted to take the job.

So, I handed my notice in and here we are.

We both agreed that living in London wouldn't be good for any of us. Helen could handle an hour's commute, so that gave us more to play with. Helen's new role paid very well and offered a relocation package, so we had a bit of financial slack.

She was the first to mention Cambridge.

'It's within commutable distance, pretty, family friendly, very arty. It's perfect!' she said, almost as if she'd had a eureka moment.

My heart began to race the second she suggested it.

Could I live that close to *her*?

No. Too dangerous.

But ... the thought of being that close to her all the time filled me with such happiness.

Should I tell Stephanie? What if I bump into her? What if I'm with Helen and I see her with Matt? I should warn her. But that would mean contacting her, and if I do that, I'm done for because I can't resist her.

So, here I am, surrounded by boxes with furniture stacked up everywhere. My wife and son sleep in the other room, ready for the chaos of unpacking which will start tomorrow. Our new life in Little Lyton, a small market town on the outskirts of Cambridge is about to begin. The house is nice, not much bigger than the one we had in Manchester because you get less for your money down here, but it's a lovely three-bedroomed semi-detached house with a decent garden and a garage which I can use as a work space.

I'll miss the old house. I prefer old houses to the new builds, like this one. They live and breathe; make noises in the middle of the night and have floorboards that creak when you stand on them. I became accustomed to, and eventually rather fond of, the ones I knew to avoid stepping on when Seb was a sleeping newborn. The new house seems a bit characterless. But I suppose you have to just roll with what you've got.

I don't know why this has happened. Is it coincidence that we are moving less than twenty miles away from Stephanie? So much for me always banging on about fate and the universe always knowing what it's doing. Well, that backfired, didn't it? Because I have no idea what this all means. Why am I being moved closer to the one woman I never thought I'd see again?

CHAPTER 13

Saturday 16 October 2010

Stephanie

The train clanks and wobbles as it approaches King's Cross. As it slows down, it dawns on me that I have become one of those people who stands up before it comes to a full stop – I hate these people.

Stepping off the train and walking to the end of the platform, my heart starts to gallop and my pace quickens.

I couldn't believe it when he contacted me last month. Staring at the notification on my phone, I left it there for several minutes before opening it. I had to mentally prepare myself because I genuinely never expected to hear from him again, let alone be asked if I wanted to meet in October.

But I was even more shocked to hear he was moving to Cambridge. Well, gobsmacked is a more accurate description. Text messages went back and forth. They remained 'friendly', never once descending into an emotional place. But he said he would like to meet this month and, now he lived close by, we could try to be friends.

Is that even possible? It seemed so when we were hundreds of miles apart, but something happens when we are in the same room.

We agreed to meet, just for the day, in London. As friends.

More specifically, he said he had something to show me. It sounded very intriguing and I'm sure, being Jamie, it'll be brilliant.

I've felt sick all morning with nerves.

There he is, standing outside the station, next to the steps, just as we agreed. He's already looking at me by the time I spot him, smiling in that way which makes me feel like I could collapse if he did it for more than ten seconds.

Walking towards one another, we immediately melt into an embrace without saying a word. It's the kind of hug I wouldn't give a friend – my hand grips on to his hair as I plunge my face into it. He holds me closer and tighter than he would his other female friends, I imagine. But that's as far as either of us take it today.

'So lovely to see you, Stephanie,' he says, breaking away from me.

I smile. 'And you ... Can't believe you've moved.'

Jamie rolls his eyes and we both burst out laughing.

'I did it under duress, obviously,' he says, doing a gun-to-his-head motion. 'You look great. Really great.'

'Thank you, so do you,' I say, genuinely. He really is so classically tall, dark and handsome

'So, are you excited about our day of fun?' he teases, popping his sunglasses on.

'Very! I have no idea what to expect. Something ... arty?'

'Oh, Steph, you know me too well! Come on, let's go ...'

'The National Portrait Gallery?' I ask, gazing up at the magnificent entrance to the building.

'The very one.'

'Oooh! I'm intrigued ...'

'I told you I'd introduce you to some proper *kul-chorrr*,' he replies in his broadest Mancunian accent.

'I can't wait!' I tell him, genuinely. 'Ah! Portraits? That's your thing, isn't it?'

'It's my favourite thing to paint, yes,' he says as we walk into the foyer of the grand building. 'I come here this time every year to see the finalists in the Portrait of the Year competition. This year I wanted to bring you and it's the final day it's exhibiting.'

I look around to see banners advertising what he's talking about. I've heard of this prestigious annual painting competition – arguably the best in the world.

Jamie is the best person to go to an art gallery with. He's so knowledgeable and I love listening to him talking about the artwork, seeing his expressions as he studies the exhibits. It's inspiring. His passion for art radiates out of him. I don't know much about it but he goes out of his way to explain things to me in an easy, engaging way.

The gallery is busy, bustling with people. It echoes with voices and footsteps, the occasional shrieking of children. Everything in it looks very 'classical'. Huge portraits in elaborate gold frames hang on the walls. It's like being in one of those period dramas you see on BBC2.

By the time we get to the Portrait of the Year finalists, Jamie looks positively giddy, darting about examining each of the portraits. He studies each one intently, commenting on the paints, technique, and overall effect.

The winner is a painting called *Last Portrait of Mother* by an artist called Daphne Todd. I'm taken aback when I see it.

It depicts a one-hundred-year-old woman who has just died. It's raw and vulnerable, exposing and harsh. The elderly woman slumps on a pillow, her yellow skin sallow, her mouth sags and eyes remain open. It is undeniably a corpse. The artist painted it – her own mother – over three days, after she'd passed away.

My jovial mood of moments ago switches when we stop to look at it. It's too much.

Jamie marvels at it, talking about how shocking and disturbing it is. But I'm unable to take my eyes off it. From nowhere, nausea stirs in my stomach and surges up my throat. I feel strangely lightheaded all of a sudden. The room starts spinning and I stumble backwards slightly, clutching on to Jamie's arm as I go.

'Steph? Are you OK?' he says, holding me upright.

'No,' I say, exhaling deeply. 'It's just a bit hot in here, actually. Can we go?'

Jamie quickly glances at the picture, then back to me.

'Yes, of course we can,' he replies, taking hold of my hand and leading me out of the gallery. 'It's lunchtime anyway.'

We head to Soho for lunch. I adore it there. I came all the time when I lived in London, I loved how eclectic and vibrant it was. It's a world away from my life now. Not better, just different.

Settling in a little trendy bar and ordering overpriced wraps – 'Posh sandwiches that don't fill you up,' according to Jamie – and skinny chips he thinks ridiculous, we throw caution to the wind and order a bottle of wine.

'Look, I'm sorry about that picture,' he says when the food arrives. 'It was shocking. Some art is. I suppose I take that for granted and didn't think to warn you. I didn't know that portrait won.'

'It's fine, not your fault. It was just a bit gruesome, that's all. Don't worry about it.'

I really don't want to waste the time we have talking about why it upset me. That is not for today.

'Tell me about you. So much has changed – new house, new job, new baby. How's it all going?' I ask, taking a big gulp of wine. I suspect I'll need it for the answer I'm about to receive.

'Yes,' he laughs, running his hand through his hair. 'It's all … good. I've settled in the new school although it's very different to my old one; it's in a much more privileged area. Sebby is wonderful, but exhausting!'

'And how're things with Helen?' I ask without even thinking. I regret it as soon as it's out.

'Fine. I'm happy,' he says, without hesitation. His answer has the same effect on me as a million bee stings; a short, sharp pain shoots through my body. I can't dwell on it. This is how it is.

'So, why are we here?' I ask, boldly. 'I thought we weren't doing this again?'

He nods. 'So did I. But it's hard not to see you when you effectively live down the road.'

'That's the only reason you contacted me? Because you moved down south?'

'I care for you, Stephanie,' Jamie says. 'I don't regret what happened last time at all. And while it can't be repeated, I would love to still see you as a friend.'

'What happens if I see you in Cambridge? Now that we're "friends"? If I'm with Matt and you're with Helen?'

His face tenses; he's obviously thought about this and the very thought of the scenario causes him anxiety.

'What do you think should happen?' he throws back at me.

'I don't think we can acknowledge each other. Too much.' I smile, gently.

'I agree.'

'And that's why we can never be real friends,' I reply.

He knows I'm right and reluctantly nods in agreement with me. Our eyes meet as we take a drink and I have to look away to stop myself sinking into them.

We discuss everything that's happened in the last year. The recent international news story involving the thirty-three men trapped down a mine in Chile has completely gripped us. They've been there for sixty-nine days and there's just been a fabulous rescue mission which involved bringing them to the surface in a metal vessel which travels really fast, like something out of a space film.

'Imagine, not knowing if you'd ever see me again?' I put to him as we wait for the bill to arrive.

'Well, I really did think that last year,' he says putting his coat back on.

'I don't mean like that. You could always change your mind and see me in those circumstances. I mean, if you thought I was going to vanish forever.'

'Like if you were going to die?' he asks dramatically, raising his eyebrows.

'I suppose so, yes,'

He thinks about it for a few moments.

'One of the most tragic parts of that, aside from the fact I'd lose you and would be devastated beyond all belief, is that I wouldn't be able to come to your funeral,' he says, looking at me with a strange sense of sadness in his eyes.

'What?'

'How would I explain who I was? To everyone in your life, I'm nobody. Another person on the street. I couldn't just turn up.'

I've never thought of this, but now he mentions it, it makes me feel so terribly sad, because it's true. And it works the other way too. I couldn't go to his funeral either.

'You know you'd be one of the most important people there, right? I'd want you there. So, I'm insisting you come,' I laugh.

'You thinking of popping your clogs anytime soon, Missy?'

'Nah, just important to clarify these things,' I reply in a mock-serious tone. 'So, where now?'

'I've got something to show you,' he says, smiling. 'You'll love it.'

The Tate Modern doesn't look like an art gallery from the outside. It looks like an industrial factory and actually used to be a power station. Jamie loves this, and adores the building. As we walk over Millennium Bridge towards the imposing structure, taking in the sweeping London skyline, he asks what I think of it. I think my squinty-not-impressed-face says it all. He laughs at me, declaring 'wait until you get inside'.

It's all skewed angles, sweeping block staircases and huge bright spaces – a complete contrast to the more traditional gallery we visited this morning. He loves playing the tour guide, pointing out things I wouldn't even notice if I was alone.

It's busy. The moderately noisy hum of chattering and footsteps echoes throughout the building. The whispers follow you everywhere you go.

He leads me into a space which hosts a large, white marble sculpture. The enormous window nearby shines a natural light on to it, transforming it into a translucent glimmer.

Jamie excitedly beckons me over with a nod of the head, as I follow. There's a gathering of people looking in its direction. A few teenagers giggle at its naughtiness. A group of very arty-looking people point and gesticulate wildly towards it.

'What do you think of it?' Jamie asks.

I raise my eyebrows. He's brought me to look at this for a reason. I walk over to the plaque next to the sculpture to find out more about it.

Auguste Rodin
The Kiss
1901–4

The Tate's *The Kiss* is one of three full-scale versions made in Rodin's lifetime. Its blend of eroticism and idealism makes it one of the great images of sexual love.

The sculpture is two naked lovers embracing, about to kiss. It's a very sensual image.

'Erm ... it's very sexual, isn't it?'

'Yes,' he whispers. 'There's more going on than that, though. Look closer.'

'Jamie, they're naked, I'll look like a right perv if I get any closer!'

He smiles and, taking my hand, slowly walks me around the piece.

'It was sculpted in such a way that it would be viewable from 360 degrees. Look at the bodies, the way they're holding each other ...'

Even as an art novice, I can see what an incredible piece it is. To think it's been carved out of marble is amazing. It's visually stunning from all angles.

'Do you want to know the story of who the lovers are?' Jamie asks, returning to the front of the statue.

'There's a story?'

'Oh yes. It's a scene from Dante's *Inferno*. They're Francesca and Paulo. Francesca was married to Paulo's brother, but she fell in love with her brother-in-law after reading the love story of Guinevere and Lancelot. Look, you can see the book slipping out of his hand on the statue ...'

I quickly look to see if he's right, and there it is, the book in his left hand.

'They're ultimately doomed lovers, but the sculpture perfectly encapsulates the passion and romance between them. It's thought that Francesca's husband killed them both immediately after this kiss,' he says.

I gasp. 'Oh, well, that puts a different spin on it.'

'So, what do you see?' he asks again.

'What do you mean?'

'Well, now you know the story, look at it and tell me what you see.'

I'm no good at this – interpreting art and all that kind of stuff. I just say what's there. Jamie places his hands on my shoulders and spins me round so I'm facing *The Kiss*.

'Come on,' he says. 'Let's hear it.'

I want to say something meaningful, but I can't. Especially not after what he's just said about doomed lovers and passion. I can't think straight. It's noisy in here. High ceilings and lots of people chattering make me feel like I'm back in the dinner hall at school. It's too loud to concentrate.

I gaze at the statue, trying to dissect it. Cocking my head to one side, I can feel Jamie standing behind me.

To my immediate right is a group of tourists who are having some kind of art lesson by the sound of things. Their tour guide spouts out all kinds of arty jargon: 'The lovers, fused in passion, the sleek and supple bodies provide a striking contrast to the roughly chiselled rock on which they sit ...'

I laugh and copy the sentence, word for word, in a faux-intense voice. I hear Jamie chuckle behind my right ear, momentarily resting his face on my shoulder.

185

'Nope, sorry, you're not getting out of it that easily,' he says. I feel his hands rest upon my shoulder, before sliding gently up the sides of my neck. Tingles and fireworks shoot through my whole body and I freeze.

'Look at it, block everything else out, and tell me what you see,' he whispers, before moving his hands up and firmly placing them over my ears.

Everything goes quiet. A muffled sound drowns out the sound of my heartbeat which is rising by the second. I can barely concentrate, with this much physical contact from him. Taking a deep breath, I look at the intertwined lovers.

Who are they?

I think about me and Jamie as I scan my eyes over the smooth marble bodies. *Doomed lovers.* The whole time, I feel his body right behind me. It feels so good to be this close to him. After about a minute, Jamie removes his hands.

'So, what do you see now?' he asks, moving around to stand beside me.

Unable to remove my gaze from *The Kiss*, I deliver my verdict.

'They've completely lost themselves in each other. They're so involved in the kiss, it's like the world has fallen away – they're oblivious to anyone else. It's raw emotion. They're entwined, infatuated with each other, becoming one. The kiss is so intimate, you can barely even see their faces. It just makes the fact they can't be with each other even more tragic.'

I suddenly look at Jamie, snapping myself out of this art trance I've weirdly found myself in. He looks so proud, smiling at me.

'About that kiss, though, you've missed something,' he says, walking me around to the part of the sculpture where the heads are. 'They don't actually kiss. Despite being called *The Kiss*, it actually captures the moment seconds *before*. It's said that their forbidden love is symbolised by the lack of touch between their lips.'

'So, it's actually a non-kiss?'

'Yes,' he replies. 'And I love that. It doesn't detract from the piece; if anything, it makes it stronger. Sometimes there's far more passion, meaning and sensuality in what *isn't* there, than what is. Very often, the most beautiful, sensual moments are actually when nothing happens. This piece is far more romantic, and says more, than one showing them having sex, for example.'

'Like the drawing?' I add. He looks puzzled, clearly forgetting that was one of the first things he taught me in that art workshop years ago.

'You know, "Sometimes it's what's around the lines you draw which is important, in the shadows", or something?' I remind him.

'Yes,' he smiles. 'That.'

We stand facing each other, next to this beautiful piece of art depicting doomed lovers and sexual infatuation, and I'm unsure how much longer we can stay here and make reference to how their struggles mirror our own.

It's not easy for either of us. I'm also aware that the day is wearing on and we will have to be heading back to the train station soon. Neither of us want it to end, though.

'Right,' he says, snapping us out of the place neither of us can afford to be in. 'A drink before we get the train?'

'Sure!' I reply. I *need* a fucking drink after all that.

Sitting next to each other in a crowded bar, we talk non-stop about everything else apart from the elephant in the room – *us*. It's busy, so we have to sit close enough that our legs and arms touch. Darkness falls outside and it's bustling with tourists in the bars around the train station. We decide I should get the first train back and Jamie will get the one after.

I'm tempted to ask if we can stay longer, but I know I can't.

We enter King's Cross station and locate my train on the departure boards. It leaves in twelve minutes.

Walking over to the platform, I try to think of the right words to say which sum up how grateful I am that he came to meet me today. I need to pitch this right. I can't be overemotional about it. I feel sick. There are people running about all around us which is probably a good thing. I think I'd crumble if we were alone. I dare not even think about him returning home to his wife and child.

Stopping just before the platform, he turns to face me.

'Thank you for such a wonderful day, Stephanie.'

'No, thank *you*. It's been truly amazing. I've loved every minute. Especially the art chat!' I say, forcing a smile.

He doesn't reply. Instead, he edges closer towards me, sliding his right hand around my waist, as his left hand reaches up into the back of my hair. His face moves closer to mine so that our noses brush against each other. His eyes remain open, gazing straight into mine. The tension between us crackles as I place my hands delicately on his chest. He very gently takes a handful of my hair and pulls it downwards, so that my head lifts up ever so slightly. He doesn't break my gaze the entire time, but places his mouth millimetres away from mine and keeps it there for what must only be a few seconds, but it feels like minutes.

A non-kiss.

The world falls away and nobody else matters. I don't see, hear or care about them. When he slowly breaks away, neither of us say anything. It's the perfect goodbye: words would ruin it.

I'm only minutes out of the capital on the whooshing train when I see my phone light up. It's Jamie.

A sweep of excitement rushes over me. I didn't expect anything from him, that non-kiss was enough. It says simply:

What we have ... it's this. Thank you for a beautiful day. Xx

As always, there's a link to YouTube. It takes me to a black and white video. Two people sit on stools playing guitars, singing ... and that's it. No grand orchestra or hitting the big notes. Just two voices with great harmonies. Extreme's 'More Than Words'.

I have the perfect song to send to him. I pop the video into a text message and add:

I understand. I enjoyed every second. Xxx

The lyrics are beautiful.

The video is ghostly and grainy. I love those ones, from the '60s; they're so atmospheric. It's dramatic and moving. Her haunting tones echo throughout the studio she's in, hypnotising everyone there.

Her voice has a sadness to it; I've always found it rather melancholic.

Dusty Springfield's 'You Don't Have To Say You Love Me'. As the song goes on, I realise that if I want to keep him as part of my life, I need to get on with my own.

Can it even work? I've no idea. I just need to remain detached, not get jealous and just be happy that we have what we have.

But I've had one of the best days of my life today. No, scratch that – probably *the* best. I want that feeling *all* the time. Do people actually have that? Am I expecting too much? His wife has that, I bet. I get eight hours of bliss a year.

The Day We Met

And now I have to go home to my husband and pretend everything is fine. I can't even remember the last time Matt and I went out and had fun – not that it would even be on the same scale as Jamie and I. Oh, yes, it was the Charity Gala night with work about six weeks ago. I got drunk on all the free booze and Matt dragged me home early, feeling frisky. The entire sexual experience lasted less than two minutes.

Six weeks ago.

And I haven't had a period since ...

CHAPTER 14

Wednesday 15 December 2010

Jamie

'Welcome to the exhibition of Cal Mendez. May I see your invitation, please?'

Helen and I throw a glance towards each other. In the chaos which ensued before I left to meet her in London, which included getting ready at lightning speed, calming a screaming Seb, ensuring all the bottles were made up and the baby food was defrosted for the babysitter, it never entered my mind that I'd need an invitation.

Helen laughs at the surly woman, peeking over her shoulder through the doorway to the exhibition. 'Oh! We don't need an invitation. We're his best friends.'

'Invitation only, I'm afraid,' she snaps. Her slicked-back hair and heavy eye-shadow make her look as if she got lost on the way to Robert Palmer's 'Addicted To Love' video.

'Don't let them in! Bloody riff-raff!' yells a familiar voice. Cal parts the crowd, charismatic as ever, insisting we are allowed in – minus an invitation.

'So pleased you could make it!' God, it's good to see him. 'And Helen, looking radiant!' he says, leaping towards her.

'Cal, charming as ever!' she says, beaming. The three of us back together. Like the old days.

Cal's speciality is leatherwork. He designs and creates exquisite accessories, footwear and couture. I hear him asking Helen about Seb as my eyes flit around the room.

All of his items are carefully and beautifully displayed under delicate lighting, intended to show the pieces off. I recognise some of them from pictures he's sent me over the past few months. They were half-finished at that point; a leather outline of a shoulder cape, the external skeleton of a headpiece, both of which are now covered in ornate and intricate decoration. Rich berry-reds, browns and golds adorn the pieces. It's amazing to see what they've been transformed into. That's the thing I love with art: transforming raw materials into things of exceptional beauty. They are stunning to look at. He's obviously worked so incredibly hard for this. I'm stupidly proud of him. The room is full of people admiring his work, and rightly so.

'Mate, what do you think?' he asks as Helen goes off for drinks.

'I'm actually speechless,' I say. 'Unbelievably good.'

Cal smiles, bashfully. He is probably the most confident person I know, but he still gets nervous before an exhibition. Only I know that, though. He's a larger-than-life character and I was drawn to him on my first day of university. He sashayed into class wearing shades, tight jeans, heeled boots and a shirt pretty much undone to the waist. He wanted to be Prince back in the day – didn't we all? His dad is Spanish, so he's blessed with olive skin and jet-black hair with a slight curl. Needless to say, absolutely every single girl fancied the arse off him, and lots of boys too. Loads of people thought he was gay. He started getting tattoos and wearing eyeliner the further into art school we got, which just made his fan club even bigger. This is a guy who has absolutely no issue with his sexuality – he's just an infectious, assured character who charms everyone he comes into contact with.

Cal, Helen and I hung out together for three years. We went to gigs, created stuff in the art studio, went drinking, visited art galleries and talked about our dreams.

'So, how's fatherhood? I really, really appreciate you coming tonight. I know you can't stay long. School night and everything,' Cal says.

I smile. 'Wouldn't miss it for the world. But yeah, it's knackering! We're getting through it though. Can't complain.'

Helen returns with three glasses of champagne for us, and we all clink.

'To the triumvirate!' she says.

'Jamie! Helen!' a Geordie voice screeches from behind us. Helen and I smile, turning around.

'Vicky! Brilliant to see you!' I say, reaching out to hug her.

Vicky – Cal's wife – is a tiny blonde woman, who looks even smaller when she stands next to him. She is stunningly beautiful, with big blue eyes and big blonde hair. I don't think I've ever seen her not looking like a '60s bombshell – that's her look. You'd look at her and assume she's some kind of model, but she's actually some kind of shit-hot corporate lawyer in Canary Wharf.

Helen and I couldn't believe it when he said he'd met The One. Given his tendency to have a different girlfriend every other week, we were sceptical. No girl had ever held his interest before ... until Vicky came along. I remember the weekend he came to visit us in Manchester, saying he'd fallen for some girl ... a *lawyer!* They'd met at a Prince night at a club in East London. He'd spotted her during 'U Got The Look' and went over to talk to her, using the song as an intro. They chatted all night and he knew there and then she was the girl he was going to spend the rest of his life with. We tried gently telling him it might not work, given that they were from different worlds. That she might be too straight-laced for him and he was ... well ... very 'Cal'. But they proved everyone wrong by buggering off to get married in Las Vegas without telling a soul. That was three years ago.

Vicky and Cal are a great match.

'How are you both?' she says, and kisses Helen. 'How's the bairn?'

'He's really good, thank you! How's things with you?' Helen asks.

'Oh, you know. Boring work! I'll be glad to get this one back,' Vicky says, nodding at Cal and tenderly holding on to his arm. 'He's put so much work into this, I've barely seen him! Couldn't be prouder though, obviously.'

'It's incredible, Cal,' Helen says. 'All those years paid off.'

'How's work, Helen? Must be hard with the little one?' Vicky asks.

'Yeah, it's tough on both of us,' she admits, quite rightly. 'I went back to work after four months because of the new promotion so it's been really full-on. Think we are both pretty much sleepwalking through the days at the moment!'

'I can imagine!'

'You look incredible!' Helen says. 'I feel so fat and haggard next to you!'

'Don't be silly,' I say, reaching out and putting my arm around Helen's waist. 'You look beautiful.' And she does. She was worried about tonight, what to wear, how to do her hair. She thinks she's gained loads of weight, which she hasn't. She's doing remarkably well considering she's working full-time and being a mum *and* we've just relocated to another part of the country.

At that point Cal and Vicky get dragged away by some people so we take the opportunity to have a mooch around and get another drink.

Helen messages the babysitter to make sure Seb is OK, which he is, and we discuss whether we've got him enough Christmas presents.

'Are you picking him up from nursery at normal time on Monday or will he have to stay longer because I'll be back late?' she asks.

'No, I should be fine for Monday. Thursday I may have a problem …'

'Right, I'll sort that,' she says, typing something into the calendar on her phone.

'Will he be walking soon?! What age do they start walking at?' I ask out of the blue.

'Not yet!' Helen laughs. 'Maybe in about four or five months! God, can you imagine when he's properly mobile, though? God help us!'

'I know!' Just the very thought of him brings a smile to my face.

'Is this the first time we've been Seb-less since he was born?' Helen asks, like it's just dawned on her.

'Yep!' I reply without hesitation. I know it is because this was my worry when we moved down here, how we'd do anything together without help around the corner.

'Well, now Daisy can babysit we can do it more often,' she says. Daisy is one of the girls from Seb's nursery who does babysitting outside of work. It's a relief knowing it's there if we want it. Both of us have been living in an exhausting cycle of work, Seb and home for the past seven months and have had no time for each other.

Later, I sneak off to find the man of the moment as people start drifting away. He's been surrounded by people all night.

'You've done all right, Cal Mendez,' I say and smile, holding my beer out to clink his bottle, as we finally get a moment alone together.

'Yeah, took blood, sweat and tears, though,' he says, clinking it back and sitting down beside me, facing one of his finest pieces – a headpiece he created for an international dance company. It's like something out of a fantasy film. A colourful burst of gold, pink and shiny brown feathers. 'Don't tell anyone about the tears, though.'

'Wouldn't dare!'

'You could have all this,' he says, looking around the exhibition space.

'That's kind. But I don't have your talent, Cal.'

'Oh, shut up! Are you serious?' He raises his voice, turning to face me. 'You're one of the best artists I've ever seen.'

'No, I'm not!'

'You think you couldn't do this? *Get* this? Are you kidding me? I'm no more talented than you,' he goes on, animating his speech with his hands. God, he's had too much to drink. 'What's happened to you?'

'Life! We can't all be artists like you, Cal.'

He looks at me, confused. Anger flashes across his face and he shakes his head.

'Do you even remember how good you are? That fire you've got inside you? Your stuff used to blow me away,' he says, intently. 'This,' he says, looking around, 'is all risk. It's about putting yourself out there at the right time. Showing it to the right people. Hard work at the right time. That's it.'

Taking a drink of my beer, he can see I'm not sold. There's a world between me and achieving anything like this.

'Do you remember what you were doing in the summer of 1999?' he asks, randomly.

'What?'

'Do you remember?'

'Erm,' I murmur, raising my eyebrows, desperately trying to recollect that timeline, 'I think I was doing the summer internship with Russell Harris.'

'Yep,' he says. 'How did you get that?'

'We had to submit a portfolio, like, the spring beforehand,' I tell him. What on earth is he going on about?

'How many people applied for that?'

'Christ, I dunno!'

'Eighty-seven,' he says, with absolute certainty.

199

'OK ...'

'And you won it.'

'Right.'

'I know eighty-seven people applied for that because I was one of them. I really wanted that internship, Jamie. I loved that artist. We *all* wanted it.'

'I'm sorry,' I say, slightly embarrassed.

'I never told you this,' he says, picking at the label on his bottle of beer, 'but before we had to submit our portfolio, I looked at yours. I saw it in the art studio one day and took a peek.'

'Really?'

'Yep.'

'And?'

'It proper pissed me off, Jamie,' he says like he's actually pissed off with me right here and now. 'Because I knew you were better than me. That shit was effortless to you. You were streets ahead of me – and everyone else. Your interpretation of things the rest of us even mildly struggle with is mind-blowing sometimes.'

I can't look at him. I've never been any good with praise. Hearing it from someone as talented as him makes me feel embarrassed, so I just stare at his exhibition piece.

'You took risks in your art. You won that internship – of course you did, you deserved it. But I went home after seeing that and I was angry because I knew I had to up my game. Because I knew I had to make myself stand out. Because, in this life, you don't get anywhere without taking risks.'

An image of Stephanie flashes through my mind when he says this. I turn to face him again, almost as if to knock it out of my head.

'You could still have all this. You just need to remember how good you are and keep the dream alive. Art is about making yourself vulnerable, but people have to see it. They won't if it's stuck in your garage, mate.'

'I'm an art teacher at a school. Am I wasting away there? Helen thinks I am ...'

'It's an amazing thing that you do,' he says. 'Kids get an unbelievable art education because of you. Imagine having a teacher like you when you were sixteen ... eighteen. You'd have your mind blown. Not to mention all the teenage crushes you're fulfilling.'

I laugh, shaking my head.

'Helen thinks I should leave. That I should stop arsing about there and get a proper career.'

'Like what?' he frowns.

'A job with her, at the ad company.'

'Fuck that for a laugh!' he spits out, pulling a face. 'You'd drown there. I don't think that's the answer. If you go there, you really won't escape. Look, if you're happy at the school, then stay there. But you can't hide there forever. Don't keep your talent locked up, Jamie.'

201

'Well, it's not going to happen anytime soon. Not with a new baby,' I tell him.

'Doesn't have to happen immediately,' he says optimistically. 'Trust me, you'll know when the time is right. But just have faith it will happen and be open to it.'

'Here they are, H!' Vicky announces, strutting in holding my wife's hand in that way girls do.

'Think we'd better be heading off, babe,' Helen says.

'Yes, last train back, I'm afraid. Been so great to see you both,' I tell them, diving into the hugfest which inevitably begins between the four of us.

As we head towards the door, Cal shouts out to me, 'Jamie, don't forget what I said, mate. I'll be in touch soon.'

'Yeah, appreciate it. Have a great night.'

'What was that about?' Helen asks as we walk outside into the freezing cold December night.

'Oh, nothing. Just something about a piece he's working on.'

I don't know why I don't tell her what Cal said. Maybe it's because I know she would rather I abandoned all those 'daft dreams' and go to work with her. But, tonight, for now, I'm keeping the dream alive and thinking that, one day, that could be me in there.

'It's been lovely to get you on your own, baby,' Helen whispers into my ear, resting her head on my shoulder as the train leaves the station. She's a bit tipsy.

'I know,' I tell her, kissing the top of her head and gently moving her long hair out of her face. She's exhausted at the moment, doing her best. I put my arm around her and she snuggles into me.

'I know we don't do it enough and it's hard without any help …'

'We do our best. We'll get through.'

'Jamie, maybe you were right?' she says, lazily, drifting off to sleep.

'About what?' I frown.

'Maybe it was too much, coming down here on our own. No help. Me working full-time. It's just too much, isn't it? We're just so knackered all the fucking time. I'm sorry.'

'Nothing to be sorry about. We'll cope. We always do,' I tell her, pulling her towards me.

She's asleep within seconds. Rummaging about in my inside coat pocket, I get my iPod out. Predicting this exact scenario would happen, I knew I'd need something to keep me awake. We're usually asleep by 9 p.m. these days, so this is an exceptionally late night for both of us.

Inspired by seeing Cal tonight, I transport back to my Britpop days and ignite the nostalgia from the '90s. Back when we had no worries, New Labour was going to save us all, election fever gripped the nation, we read *FHM* and watched *The Big Breakfast*.

Just hearing the guitar intro, followed by symphonic strings makes me smile and gives me unexpected

Roxie Cooper

shivers down my back. My God! Was it really that long ago?! The distinctive, whiny but utterly genius voice kicks in. It was always them over Blur for me. No competition.

'Whatever' by Oasis.

CHAPTER 15

Wednesday 1 June 2011

Stephanie

It's funny how you spend the first three or four months after finding out, scrutinising yourself in the mirror every single day. You spend hours looking at yourself from different angles, pushing your pelvis out, convinced your jeans are getting tighter. You feel a little self-conscious the first time you step out in maternity wear, declaring to the world, '*I am pregnant*', worrying that your bump isn't quite big enough to wear it. Will other pregnant women much further down the line judge you and laugh?

Then, out of nowhere, you're nine months pregnant, with a bump so big you can barely walk.

I want to sit down and cry with the amount of energy it requires to do anything now. That, or just be carried everywhere. I haven't gained much weight, despite Ebony's stark warning years ago.

Sitting in Jane's waiting room, I pick up a leaflet and fan myself with it. I've nervous for this session. I don't know why – Jane has heard far worse from me. But saying things out loud makes them real, and I'm not sure I'm even ready to confront this.

My right hand rests on my bump, which is swathed in a black tent-like jersey dress. My hair is up in a bun and I'm wearing flip-flops. Everything about me is screaming: 'Please God make me less hot and more comfortable.'

The door clicks and Jane appears, as put-together as ever, wearing a red and white gingham summer dress.

'Well, look at you! Come on through,' she smiles.

As far as results go, there was no ambiguity. I have to admit, I felt a bit cheated out of the experience. When it comes to revelations such as these, I feel like you ought to see your fate being revealed in a slow, easy-to-process way, giving your brain the chance to get used to the idea. I much prefer the idea of seeing two pink lines racing up a piece of litmus paper as opposed to the new-fangled digital tests, which give you no warning before flashing up the brutal 'PREGNANT 4–6 WEEKS' declaration. They could at least put a countdown on before showing the result.

I did the test the day after my London trip to see Jamie. How had I not realised before then? Having felt a constant excitement and nausea at the very thought of seeing him again, I'd naturally presumed that was the reason for it. I'd been trying (and failing) to get pregnant for so long, I'd stopped attributing possible symptoms to that. But there it was. A little digital test telling me I was carrying Matt's child and I quickly worked out I'd be due around June. I am so happy that I'm going to become a mum. I'd love to know what my own mum would make of it. She'd have made a lovely grandma and I'm so sad I can't share this with her. I immediately called Ebony, who screeched at me down the phone and drove round with both kids within ten minutes.

'I'm so happy for you, Steph,' she said, getting all glassy-eyed. 'You'll make a brilliant mum. And ours would be proud of you.'

'So, how have you been? Jane asks now, watching my woeful attempt to get comfortable on her rock-hard sofa.

'Not great, to be honest,' I say, diving straight in.

'OK ...'

'Look, there's something I want to tell you which has been on my mind and I need to talk to you about it and I should have told you before now but I didn't so I'm telling you now OK?' I mumble, without pausing for any kind of breath.

'OK,' she replies, again, calmly.

'I've had an affair. Kind of. Well, not really.' I wince, as tears well up in my eyes. 'Oh, Jane, I don't know. Everything is a mess.'

'Take a deep breath,' she says, handing me a tissue from the box on her desk. 'And let's unpack this ...'

I start at the beginning and don't leave anything out. I don't know why I'm surprised when her response is 'I suspected something had happened with someone. Your presence changed.'

Midway through this revelation, she stands up to turn the fan on in the corner of the room which starts whirling cool air into my face. It's constantly warm in here at the best of times; it's one of those rooms which always feels stuffy and claustrophobic no matter how many windows you open. It's south-facing so the blinds are necessary, which means that it's stifling in the summer.

'I knew *something* significant had happened in your life – something positive – and something to do with a man. Yes.' Jane says, very matter-of-fact.

'But why didn't you say anything? Or ask about it?'

'You know the answer to that, Stephanie! I had to let you tell me yourself. The question is, *why* are you telling me *now*?'

I instinctively place my right hand on my baby bump, which has undergone a huge growth spurt in the last few weeks.

'I guess pregnancy forces you to reassess things ...'

'It absolutely does do that,' she says. 'It puts your relationship under a magnifying glass.' I can't quite work out if Jane knows this from experience, or whether she read it in a textbook.

I remember being weirdly nervous about telling Matt about the baby, God only knows why, considering he's wanted this for so long. It was as if I felt immediate pressure to do it in the right way, to make it super-special for him. I considered all kinds of original ways of doing it, but in the end I blurted it out the second he walked through the door.

'I'm pregnant!' I screamed, waving the pregnancy test in his face.

He looked at me like he'd misheard what I'd just said, or dared not believe it.

'What?'

'It's true! We're having a baby! Look!' And I laughed, nervously.

Dropping his kitbag on the hall floor, he grabbed the test out of my hand and looked at it for a few seconds. A massive grin spread across his face and he swept me up in the biggest hug.

'It finally happened!' he yelled into my ear. 'Brilliant news! I can't wait to tell everyone! When can we tell everyone? Who have you told?' he quizzed, standing back, putting his hands over his mouth in disbelief.

'Erm, I did tell Ebony. But I think it's normal to wait three months …'

'Well, we can tell close family, obviously! Oh, Steph, I'm thrilled, I'm going to be a dad! You *are* happy, aren't you?' he asks.

'Yes,' I replied. 'Of course!'

He came to all of my scans, never complained more than a tiny bit when I dragged him shopping for yet more baby stuff we didn't really need and agreed, in theory, to change half the dirty nappies.

'I suppose I had this idea that pregnancy – a baby – would bring us closer together,' I say to Jane. 'Everything would suddenly click into place. We'd have that family unit and everything would be perfect.'

'And …?'

I pause for a second, staring at the plant in the corner of the room.

'And all I can think about is *him*.'

I looked up Jamie's wife on Facebook and saw pictures of them on their holiday to Majorca with Sebastian. I know I shouldn't look. I *know*. But I can't help it.

The perfect family.

Except they're not.

There they sit, in a Spanish restaurant on an evening, all done up, sunburnt from playing on the beach all day. Laughing, smiling, living a happy life. Their friends don't know that he's got feelings for another woman.

For me.

I've found myself doing it more often in recent months. As soon as I type in 'H' on the search function she's the first person who comes up because I've searched her so frequently.

Her profile picture is currently a photo of her smiling, her long dark hair cascading over both shoulders. She's wearing a pretty, floral, floaty dress, obviously at a wedding or something. It's like nothing I would wear and she couldn't look more different to me. Jamie is next to her with his arm around her shoulder, wearing a suit and tie. He looks smart and handsome, smiling at the camera. She looks thrilled, and why wouldn't she? If he were mine, I'd be showing him off too. I'd be as happy as that.

Every time I look at it, it's like a car crash. I know I shouldn't, but I can't look away.

'How does Jamie make you feel?' Jane asks, propping her chin up on her hand.

I involuntarily smile. Well, *that* ... for starters.

'Happy, alive, electric, like I can do anything, vibrant, appreciated, wanted ... loved,' I reel off.

'And how does Matt make you feel?'

I pause for a second before answering. I don't want to do him a disservice, because as much as he might not be perfect, he's still my husband and I have to respect that. I gaze at the blinds for a few seconds, which are tilted, shutting out the hot June sun. The gaze of Jane, and heat in the room, burns down upon me.

'Not like that.'

'OK,' she says, nodding. 'Put it another way. If you could have anything now – any life – what would it be? Who would you be with?'

She's put me completely on the spot. But, there's no point in lying to her.

'Jamie,' I say quickly, as if that makes the betrayal to my husband somehow less treacherous.

'Now is that because Jamie is so special or because Matt isn't actually right for you?'

God, she has a way of wording things and slamming things home.

'Both,' I say, surprising myself.

'Do you think you and Matt will be together forever?'

'I don't think I will ever be the partner Matt wants me to be ...'

'And who is that?'

'He wants the girl he fell in love with.'

'And who is she?'

'She's not there any more. I didn't like her and I don't really want her back.'

I see the faintest, tiniest smile flash on Jane's face. It was there for a second, then vanishes.

'Why is that?'

'She's grown since then,' I tell her. 'She was ...' I look around the room, searching for the right word. 'Lost, weak, vulnerable, scared.'

'And who is she now?'

'Still all of those things, I guess.' I laugh, gently. 'But less so. She's grown up.'

'Is she growing on her own, or is she growing with Matt?'

'What do you mean?'

'For a relationship to thrive, both people grow and evolve together – as well as independently.'

Coming into Jane's therapy room is like walking into a truth vortex. She forces you to look at your life through a prism, stripping everything back, and lays everything bare in front of you.

'We are not growing together,' I say, shaking my head.

'OK.' She changes tack. 'How do you feel about what you're doing with Jamie?'

'It brings out a side of me I really don't like,' I say, unable to look her in the face. I pick at the red nail varnish which I really ought to take off, it's so chipped.

'Which side is that?'

'Well, would you believe me if I said I really wasn't prepared for the jealousy when this started? Or the guilt?' I tell her, laughing at my own naivety as I say it.

'Yes, I would. Very much so.'

'It was much easier to compartmentalise all that in the beginning. Then that all goes out the window the deeper in you get. Before you know it, you're on Instagram, seeing what Helen made Jamie for dinner on their "hashtag date night" and what an amazing husband he is because he bought her a fancy handbag for Christmas. And I'm getting irrationally angry and jealous about it because he's with her and not me.'

'It's a complex situation, Stephanie.'

'But I hate feeling like this, Jane!' I raise my voice at her. 'And the next minute I feel crushing guilt over it all. Because she has no idea I even exist. I've completely screwed her over *and* my own husband, and I deserve to feel like shit. We are both awful people. But I can't switch it off. It's ugly and destructive and I hate feeling like this.'

I throw my head in my hands, wailing and crying as Jane hands me more tissues. It's a relief to get it out.

'Bloody baby hormones,' I whimper, reaching for the tissues.

'Look, Stephanie,' Jane says, getting back into business mode. 'If there's one thing I can tell you about the human psyche, it is that we are a very complicated breed. Wouldn't it be so easy to pitch all issues as being black and white? When, actually, there's a whole load of grey in the middle.'

I dab at my eyes with a tissue, staining it with black mascara in the process. I probably look a right mess now.

'And I'll tell you something else, 99 per cent of people exist in that grey area, no matter what they say or like to believe. Emotions are complicated and complex. There are no right or wrong decisions, because they're wildly subjective. Ultimately, you can't help how you feel – but you can control how you deal with it.'

'But *how*?' I plead. 'I don't know how to deal with it. Look at me. I'm pregnant with my husband's child. I'm in love with another man, who's also married and I'm pretty sure he feels the same. We can't ever be together. How does anyone deal with that? Tell me, how?'

It's terrifying saying the words out loud.

I wipe the tissue across my eyes again – the floodgates are intent on staying open today. Jane waits until I've composed myself before speaking. The room is silent, but for the whirring of the fan.

'Why can't you be together?' she asks.

I look at her as if she's mad. Has she not heard anything I've just said? What the hell am I paying her for?

'What?'

'You said you can't be together,' she repeats, shrugging. 'Why not, exactly?'

'Well,' I burst out, 'for starters, it would be so messy for both of us.'

'Love *is* a messy business, I'm afraid. It's not a Disney film.'

'We're both married ...'

'You could both get divorced.'

'We'd both end up hurting so many people ...'

'It would be painful for all four of you, there's no question about it, but is that a reason to miss out on a lifetime of happiness if you're meant to be together?'

'But there are kids involved ...'

'Stephanie, the point is, if you truly are meant to be together, you will find a way to be together and you'll find a way to make it work.'

I fold the moist tissue up into a neat little square, ironing it out with my fingers.

'You know, my mum always said the universe sends the perfect person to you. Fate will actually put them in front of you. That's what happened with my dad. They were so perfect for each other,' I tell her and Jane smiles. 'And I always thought that would happen for me at some point. They'd come into my life and I'd be wowed, sorted. Everything would be perfect. I didn't expect this perfect guy to come into my life *with his wife*. So he *can't* be my "one", can he?'

'That's where we disagree, Stephanie. I don't think fate or destiny or whatever it is you believe in is that tidy. They may well be placed in front of you, as you say, but you might have to do the rest of the work.'

'Do you *really* believe that?' I ask, baffled as to how she can. For a second, she looks slightly uncomfortable; this conversation is clearly straying outside the remit of the professional guidance she can offer, but I really am keen to know what she thinks. She shuffles in her chair, readjusting her crossed legs.

'Look at some of the greatest love affairs in history,' she says. 'Johnny Cash and June Carter. Richard Burton and Elizabeth Taylor. John Lennon and Yoko Ono. What do they all have in common?'

'Yeah, all deeply in love,' I say, rolling my eyes. 'Good for them.'

'All of them were affairs. A lot of people got hurt as the result of those unions coming together, but we all know them as being some of the biggest love stories. And, more interestingly, the infidelity somehow becomes socially acceptable, because they're famous and it's glamorous and involves these larger-than-life characters ...'

I hang on to every word she says, unable to take my eyes off her as she talks.

'Look, I'm not here to judge you,' she says. 'That isn't my function. I'm not here to tell you whether infidelity is right or wrong. But it certainly isn't black or white, either. You really think anyone would want to deprive Johnny and June of the happiness they had for thirty-odd years, just so that he could remain in his unhappy marriage?'

She looks at me, and I don't know what to say. Obviously, the answer is no.

'I don't think anyone would want that. That would be ridiculous and stupid, wouldn't it?' I reply.

'Yes. Yes, it would.' She smiles then. 'And I'm obviously not saying you're deeply unhappy in *your* marriage. I was just making a point.'

'Oh, yes. Of course.'

Glancing at the clock in the corner of the room, she gives me the now-familiar nod indicating that's enough for today. Of all the sessions I've had with her, this is the one I really don't want to end. I want to stay and chat to her for longer.

'OK, Stephanie. That was a good session. I'll see you next month, if you're not too busy with the baby. Good luck with everything,' she says, smiling at me in that way she always does.

I think about what she said all the way home while listening to Johnny Cash's 'Walk The Line' at full volume. I drive back the long way, down the winding country roads, enjoying the early evening sunshine as it pours in. This is one of my favourite things to do, and I do it often. There's nothing quite like the freedom of taking off in your wheels and going for a long drive.

As I feel the familiar kick against my ribs, a noticeable limb pokes out of my right side, and then a tidal wave of movement shudders over to my left; she's woken up.

My little girl, who I've only seen on grainy black-and-white scan pictures. I've spent hours staring at them; the rounded shape of her little head, the tiny button nose, her curved spine ... and I marvel. How did I make such a beautiful, perfect thing? I mean, I know I didn't do it on my own – Matt did a tiny bit in the beginning but, let's be honest, his part was over the second he yanked his penis out of me and *I'm* growing an actual human being.

I didn't think I'd be the maternal type, actually. I thought pregnancy would be something to be endured, not enjoyed. How wrong I was. From the second I saw my girl on that screen in the scanning room at the twelve-week appointment, I embraced every single ailment and milestone. I'd lie in bed on a Sunday morning, stroking my bump, watching her move, giggling at how cute it was. I sang to her. I talked to her about her about my mum – her grandma. I imagined all the things she would have done with her: baking fairy cakes, painting in her art studio and chasing her around the garden.

It's also brought me a bit closer to Dad. He started crying when I told him. I think, after everything I've been through, he just wants to see me settled and happy. He took us all out for dinner to celebrate and his face beamed throughout the entire meal.

'I'm so pleased you get to experience this,' he said, enveloping me in a huge cuddle.

'Me too, Dad,' I replied.

Every Wednesday marked the next week in the pregnancy, so I'd excitedly turn to that stage in the baby book, eager to see what my baby was doing, and growing, now. I thought I'd hate getting bigger, but I love it. And for the first time in my adult life, I don't care about not drinking.

She has become the most important thing in my life, the only thing I've ever done right. Right now, the only thing I care about is being a good mother. I want my daughter to feel about me the way I felt about my own mum. That unconditional love, paralleled by no other; nurtured and loved no matter what happens. I hope I can do it right, because I know how it feels to have that ripped away from you, to have your emotional core shattered apart overnight. I might not be perfect, by anyone's standards, but I will never, ever let my child down.

I love it when she does this. She reacts quite well to music, jigging about, stretching her limbs and rolling around.

She likes Johnny Cash, it would seem.

CHAPTER 16

Saturday 15 October 2011

Jamie

I didn't quite compute what it was at first. Doing the food shop with Seb on a sunny July morning, he was kicking off in the ice cream aisle because he wanted an ice pop, so I opened a box and gave him one.

There was no message with it, just a picture of a baby girl, identifiable only by her little pink babygro. My heart ached a bit. I don't know why, and I know I have absolutely no right to say that, but it did. Probably in the same way hers did when she found out about Sebby. It's a weird situation. About a minute later, she sent another message:

Evie Elaine Bywater. Born 9 June. I wanted to tell you but didn't know if I should. Hope you're well. X

And it went from there.

Stephanie said she still wanted to meet in October, back at Heathwood Hall this year. Being a newbie to the newborn biz, she said a night away would be a welcome break from the sleepless nights, so if we could arrive late and leave early, that would be great. We've booked one room because we both agreed it was pointless to pay for two when, never in all these years, have we ever stayed in them both, so it made sense.

I don't think either of us believed it.

I arrive first. The staff recognise us now and I'm pretty sure they know what the score is. They must have all kinds of shenanigans going on here.

Waiting for her to arrive in 'our' room, I think back to the last time I saw her. The very last time I held her, touched her, was that non-kiss at King's Cross Station. It wasn't something I'd planned, it just happened. I'm glad she saw the sculpture, though. It's a lovely piece, which parallels our own situation in many ways. I wanted to let her know how I felt without telling her directly. As the time came to say goodbye, I panicked about how to say it, being wrenched away from her at the platform. The non-kiss just seemed perfect.

Now, here we are. Back at Heathwood Hall.

Doing OK, so far. She came in, beaming, looking thrilled to see me. We hugged, smiled a lot. Her hair is shorter and it suits her.

Sitting on the sofa as we open a bottle of wine, we do the usual round-up of news and I love her take on things.

She becomes all animated when telling me about the party she had with Ebony to celebrate the wedding of Kate Middleton and Prince William in April.

'I was obviously heavily pregnant, so Ebs brought a tonne of food around and we just sat and ate all day, watching the entire thing on TV,' she tells me. 'I mean, for twelve hours all we did was cry, bitch about outfits and swoon over the princes. It was the best day ever! You must have watched it?'

'I took Seb to the park,' I say, rolling my eyes. 'His mum got into it, but it wasn't really my thing.'

'Ah, I just loved it. The whole thing was like a dream. They looked so happy, I couldn't stop crying! The way he looked at her, kissed her, everything ...' She drifts off into her own world.

I love how she's been affected by motherhood. She seems to have a new layer to her, like she's more complete in some way. She speaks of her daughter with such fondness and love. Her sister has Evie tonight.

She asks if I went on holiday this year and I briefly mention I went to Majorca for a week. Asking if I had a good time I tell her it was great. I don't say Helen and I rowed for most of it because a holiday with a one-year-old is not a holiday for anyone – apart from the baby.

'So, how are you?' I ask.

'Knackered! You have a baby, so you know the drill.'

'No,' I say, stroking her hair. 'How are *you*?'

223

'I'm all right, really. It's such a huge, life-changing thing, isn't it?' She sighs. 'She's given me so much love and purpose in life. I've never really had that before she came along.'

'How can you say that? You have people who love you. You're an incredible person,' I tell her. I hate that she can't see this herself.

She shrugs, taking a drink of white wine from the glass she's cradling in her right hand.

'You're always so hard on yourself,' I tell her. 'Look at you.'

She screws her face up, clearly uncomfortable with this level of praise. I don't think she hears it too often, which pisses me off.

'I don't feel amazing at the moment, to be honest.'

'What? You've just had a baby and you still manage to look beautiful.'

Stephanie tucks her hair behind her ears and rearranges the cushions on her lap.

'No, I'm not beautiful,' she says and laughs.

'Well, I think you are,' I reply, in all seriousness.

A moment of silence falls between us before she jumps up and walks over to her overnight bag which is on the cream chaise-longue underneath the window. Retrieving some kind of black pyjama things, she walks off towards the bathroom.

'What are you doing?' I ask her.

'Oh, umm, just going to get changed. I'm not really comfortable in this dress,' she replies, sheepishly, twiddling the garments around in her hands as she does so, smoothing them out. She looks at them – not me. 'I don't like my body since I had the baby. I don't feel very attractive. Sorry. I mean, I know I'm not what I used to be,' she says, glancing up, almost embarrassed.

Probably the most beautiful girl I've ever seen in my life – inside and out – standing there, looking awkward, feeling terrible because she's put on a few pounds after producing a human.

I walk over to her, removing the pyjama set (or whatever it is) from her hands and throw it on the floor. Placing my hands on her waist, I pull her close to me so that our faces are right up against each other. Sliding them up her back, and gently past her neck on to her face, I run them slowly down the curves of her body through her dress, not taking my eyes off hers the entire time.

'I remember this body,' I whisper to her.

She tenses slightly as my hands skim over her breasts, which have grown since last year. Her waist and hips have become more defined. As my hands sweep over her tummy, I kiss her softly. She pushes herself into me, grabbing my hair. I firmly move my hands around to her arse, scrunching her dress up as I do and peeling it up and off her body. I throw it on the floor and she stands in front of me wearing only a black bra and knickers.

Delicately running my fingers from the top of her legs to her breasts, which makes her giggle, I hold her face in my hands. Brushing her lips with my thumbs, I rest my face close to hers so that her bright green eyes are lost with mine.

'I don't think I've ever seen you more beautiful,' I tell her. And I mean it.

She smiles in the way she does which makes her eyes light up. They crinkle at the edges, taking on a personality of their own. Usually, whenever I give her a compliment she looks away; gazes at the ground or glances uncomfortably out the window. But this time, she doesn't. She looks straight back at me.

'Thank you,' she says, softly.

By 11.30 we've sloped into bed after having a glass of wine each and one cup of tea and we're chatting in bed with the curtains open. The moon has settled right outside the window so it shines in just enough light to negate the pitch-black brutality.

This is actually perfect.

'You know, it would, of course, be possible to see each other more often now,' Stephanie says, her sweet voice cutting through the darkness.

My body tenses slightly.

'It would. But it's probably better we keep it as it is. It works, don't you think?' I say, forcing the words out. I'm grateful for the fact it's dark and she can't see how much it pains me to say this, as I lie on my side, facing her. Our fingers intertwined, resting on the space between us.

'Wouldn't you want to see me more often?' she asks.

Christ, yes. All the time.

I take a second to consider my answer, not because I don't know what it is, but because it's physically hard to say.

'Stephanie,' I say then, 'the time I spend with you is so, so special and I love it so much ... I can't allow it to be more than what we have now.'

She doesn't say anything, which is never a good sign.

'But we can still have what we have, just ... more often.'

I run my hand up her arm and up into her hair. Shuffling closer to her, I have to say this, knowing it's going to hurt.

'It would make it harder,' I tell her. 'I'd see you for a few hours, then I'd want to spend the night with you. Then I'd want to spend the weekend with you. Then I'd want to spend the week with you, then I'd want to start calling you to ask how your week's been, or texting you on a morning, then meeting up through the week just to see your face ...'

She remains quiet and her breathing gets a little heavier.

'Do you know how many times I've almost called you? Had my finger over the call button? Wanted to phone on the off-chance that I'd get your voicemail, just to hear your voice?' I ask. 'More than you can imagine.'

'So, what stopped you?'

'I can only see you if I have strict boundaries in place. It gets too complex if I see you more than what we have.'

'Well, if you feel like that and it's so complex, that – in itself – raises questions you may need to think about ...'

'Steph, you've always known the score, that I'm not going anywhere—'

'I know, but—'

'No, I need to say this. My life would be so much easier if I didn't love my wife, or if I was thoroughly miserable. But it's just not the case.' I have no idea how she's taking it – but she needs to hear it. 'And that's what's so difficult to get my head around. The anxiety of it all makes my heart feel like it's being torn in two different directions and it fucks me up, Stephanie.'

Rolling over on to my back, I run my hands through my hair. What am I doing to these women? I don't deserve either of them.

The silence is heavy between us for what feels like a lifetime. She needs to know this, but saying it feels like a deliberate betrayal of her.

'I know it's hard – for both of us,' she says, cuddling into me. 'So let's just keep it the way things are. You're right, it's simpler that way.'

I wrap my arms around her, giving her an extra squeeze as I kiss the top of her head. She smells divine. I couldn't tell you what of – some sort of girly shampoo – but it's gorgeous.

'Thank you for being honest,' she whispers through the darkness. 'I know, even though it's not always easy. But I appreciate it. It helps me understand who you are.'

'What are you doing tomorrow?' I ask, in an attempt to lighten the mood.

'I'm actually going straight to work from here.'

'Work? Aren't you on maternity leave?'

'Well, technically, yes,' she says, 'but something needs doing for the art award competition and it's quicker if I do it rather than leaving it to everyone else.'

'Art award?'

'It's a thing we do every year. In memory of my mum.'

'Oh, OK. Well, that sounds lovely. What exactly is it?'

'Well, my mum was a local artist and after she died, we set up an art award in her name. Every year we run a competition for local artists.'

'Ah, really?'

'Yes. In, fact, you'd be eligible to enter now. Now you're local, I mean.'

'I suppose I would. Don't think it would be right, though.'

'Well, you're good enough. Brilliant enough, obviously. But I understand.'

229

'But, more to the point,' I go on. 'Your mum was an artist?! How did I not know this?'

I've known Steph for five years now and we know each other so well, in some respects, and not at all in others. Her eyes light up when she mentions her mum. They sparkle whenever she talks about her and her smile spreads right across her face, the kind of smile which you have no control over. But then she'll stop and change the subject, as though a searing pain spreads throughout her body, preventing her from carrying on.

'I don't really talk about her very much,' she says.

'Why not?'

'Because losing her was the worst thing that happened to me.'

'Do you want to tell me about it?'

I feel her body tense. Her fingers stop caressing me and she lays her palm flat on my chest. I take hold of her hand, kissing her knuckles before returning it to its original spot on my torso.

'About what?' she asks.

'I'd just like to understand you a little more and this is the one part I have no knowledge of,' I explain. I remember the pain I saw on her face that day at the National Portrait Gallery last year in London when she was looking at the winning piece.

'But ... there are parts of it that you might not like,' she says. 'About me ...'

'Impossible. There's nothing you could tell me about you which could alter my opinion of you,' I tell her. And it's true. 'I know it's scary, telling me stuff,' I say, looking out towards the darkness outside, stroking her hair with my right hand. 'But I want to know everything about you.'

'She was so, so wonderful, my mum,' she starts. 'She had an infectious presence about her that everyone loved. You noticed her when she walked into a room. When I was little, I thought she was the prettiest woman in the world and I wanted to be just like her.'

'I bet she looked just like you when she was younger.'

'Yes, I'm the spitting image of her. That's what Dad always says.'

'Sorry, go on …'

'She was the mum everyone loved. The one who always invited our friends around after school, made them yummy dinners and they always wanted to come back. She loved giggles, fun, singing, cuddles, kindness. She never said a bad word about anybody.'

'She sounds like a lovely woman.'

'And she was really creative. When Dad bought the house when they got married, Mum made it her own. She loved interior design and was always at junk yards and second-hand shops. She'd drag knackered old coffee tables and wardrobes home and spend hours in the garden painting them and making them look fabulous. "You can't buy class or style" she used to say.'

231

'And she was absolutely right! My friend Cal lives by that!'

'She and Ebony and I used to pick flowers and put them in vases all over the house in summer and, in the winter, the whole house was dressed in fairy lights. She was the heart of the house, the soul – she breathed life into it,' Steph tells me, excitedly.

'Dad had an art studio built in the garden for her thirtieth birthday, just after Ebony was born. It was a brick outbuilding with huge sash windows all around to let lots of natural light in, stacked with easels, paints and art supplies. She'd stay in there for hours, listening to her music and creating art. She was really good, selling some of it at the gallery in town. She became a pretty famous artist locally. Ebony and I used to go in there and paint sometimes. She'd set up a station for us with that really thick kids' paint you get and we'd always paint her: two green blobs for eyes, a big cherry-red smile and loads of yellow hair.'

'Ms Bywater, I can't believe you hid the fact you're actually an experienced artist!'

'Hardly! After all these years my skills have not improved!' she laughs. 'The studio always had an acrylic, plastic smell to it. Whenever I smell it now, I'm immediately transported back to that room.'

'You've just described the sort of place I spend 80 per cent of my time – though it's not nearly as posh. And I love that smell. It's home to me.'

Hearing her open up and talk about her mum is so wonderful. We lie in the darkness, laughing and getting to know each other more.

It's bittersweet. Because although it's beautiful to hear about Stephanie's mum and the relationship they had, I know what's coming because this story doesn't end well. When she gets to this part her voice cracks; it takes her a while to get the words out and she breaks down. She was nestled into my neck and I had to struggle at times to hold it together because I've never heard anyone speak so honestly and tragically about losing someone.

By the time she falls asleep in my arms, she's bared her soul to me. She's showed me the true side of her, the honest side, the beautiful side ... and the ugly. And I don't think I've loved her more.

Everything now makes so much sense: why she married Matt, why she needs this – *me* – in her life, why she is the way she is. This girl just needs to be loved.

By the time the sun comes up, I've been drifting in and out of sleep. The good thing about sleeping with the curtains open is that the natural light shines straight on to the bed.

The morning feels as though we are in a time lapse video, everything going far too quickly, and before we know it it's time to check out and leave. We try to be upbeat, but there's no getting around the fact we won't see each other for another 364 days. This situation gets more messed-up every year.

Stephanie seems a little on edge after last night. She's talking ten to the dozen about work, winding herself up like one of those mechanical toys.

'Yeah, so I've got to go to work and deal with the art award and the One More Chance charity intake …'

'What's that, then?'

'Oh, six people who basically need a break in life – drug addicts or alcoholics or people like that, you know? They work on basic wage for six months to get a good reference and virtually all go on to jobs afterwards. Some stay on with us and it's really great for them. God, I'm going to be busy this week. Are you?'

Walking over to her, I scoop her up into a cuddle.

'I'm so sorry for last night,' she says.

'Why? I don't mind you speaking to me like that,' I tell her honestly.

'It was a bit – a bit much though, wasn't it?' she says, visibly cringing.

'Don't be silly. I loved that you felt you could open up to me.'

'I don't really talk to anybody about that kind of stuff.'

'I know.'

'And I don't want to leave,' she says sticking her bottom lip out.

'Me neither. But we have to. There's no other way around it.'

She goes to say something, then stops herself. Probably for the best.

It only takes me forty minutes to drive home. It's not long enough. Switching from Stephanie-mode to Family-mode requires more time, but it's time I don't have. I'm making things harder for myself, seeing her like this. It's becoming more difficult to wrench myself away. Not to mention how much of an utter bastard I feel for doing this to Helen and Seb. Something has to give eventually.

Pulling up on our road, I stay there for a few minutes, getting my head into place before I go in and see my wife and son. Compartmentalise. That's the key. So I'll do this first and then go in.

I'm going all out with this song. It's dramatic and epic. I don't know if it's too much, but it seems so apt for how I feel right now, at this moment, and I want her to know. No message, the song says enough.

Press send and that's it for another year. I hope she loves it. It conveys absolutely everything I want and need to say right now about this girl. When I listen to it, I think about her face, her skin, her hair, how I feel when I'm with her, how nothing has ever made me feel like that before.

There's something so old school about the whole production of this song. The singer's voice sounds like velvet and it's astonishing how good it is, sung in front of a live audience,.

'Unchained Melody' by The Righteous Brothers says everything I need to.

Turning my phone off, I get out of the car and go into the house.

CHAPTER 17

Tuesday 25 September 2012

Stephanie

'"She's dead, isn't she?" That's the bit I always wake up on. The sequence is always the same. It never changes,' I say, staring at Jane's high-heeled ankle boots. 'What scares me most is how accurate it is to what actually happened. It's as if my brain recorded every single detail of what occurred in those twenty minutes and recorded them.'

'Recurring nightmares are unpleasant, but common.'

'This was real, though,' I tell her. 'It happened. I relive it all the time. Finding out your mum is dead in the headmaster's office after being dragged out of French on a Friday afternoon. Just ... well, there aren't any words for that.'

'No,' she agrees. 'There aren't.'

You're just not equipped to deal with losing your mum at the age of thirteen. When it happens on the cusp of puberty you're asking for all kinds of bother.

Drinking, smoking, boys – I indulged in them all over the next few years. And I didn't care, nor did I listen to Dad who tried talking sense into me. 'What would your mum think of this behaviour?' he'd say, which just made me even worse.

'Do you think you'd have coped better if you'd had a better relationship with your dad?' Jane asks.

'Yes, I caused such a wedge between us.'

'Go easy on yourself there,' she says, frowning. 'You were a child. You had no idea how to cope.'

'I didn't make it easy for him, though. Ebony dealt with things way better than I did.'

'Everyone has their own ways of dealing with trauma, and that belongs to them,' she states.

'I guess I just feel bad for putting him through that. Now I have my own child, I see things differently, I suppose.'

It's hard to properly grasp that perspective before you have children; the worry, anxiety and concern you cause your parents. You know you're doing it, but you can't stop. On my eighteenth birthday, I was presented with a letter my mum had written for me just before she died. It was so full of love and hope for my future and the overwhelming sentiment of it only served to remind me how much I'd fucked everything up.

I *lived* for hovering my finger over the self-destruct button and I had enough self-awareness to know what was happening. I expected it to last maybe a year, but one year bled into another. The drinking continued; in fact, it just got heavier, a serious emotional crutch. I was the party girl, always the one wanting to go out, always the girl with a drink in her hand.

The girl who's always up for a good time. She's up for anything, Steph.

The parties became wilder and the destruction became more heightened and dangerous. I don't know how I managed to survive university, let alone scrape a 2:1. It was inevitable I'd stay in London after I graduated, ignoring Dad and Ebony's pleas that I move back home to 'calm down a bit'. Why would I do that when I could spiral a bit more out of control? And that's exactly what I did.

I remember so vividly the moment I knew I needed help. It wasn't when I got sacked from my marketing job for turning up at work, drunk. Nor was it when I was doing lines of cocaine in the toilets on my breaks, just because that was the only way I could get through the rest of the day (Ebony was more horrified that I did it off the toilet seat without cleaning it first with an antibacterial wipe, than the actual act).

No.

It was one cold night in April when I was twenty-five, in a pub with Matt in central London. Something inside me just snapped and I had a panic attack. I couldn't breathe. I felt like something was squeezing every bit of life and breath out of me at a rapid pace and there was nothing I could do to stop it. I was going to die.

I somehow staggered out of the pub and collapsed on the street outside while Matt called my dad. He came to pick me up and I moved back home. There were lots of stern talks after that.

'You can't go on like this,' he'd say. 'Matt wants to look after you, let him.'

How do you repay someone who has put up with you being so troublesome for so many years? When they look at you with so much despair in their eyes, willing you to just … *stop*. After everything he'd been through with Mum, and over ten years of me carrying on. What do you do? Well, I suppose you marry the guy he wants you to. Which is asking for trouble. But, then again, life is full of bad decisions, isn't it? Like Mum said, none of us are perfect. We all make mistakes.

I agreed to go and see a therapist and stop all the drinking and drugs and everything that wasn't good for me. Essentially, it was time to grow up and start facing everything which had been following me around all these years.

'How do you see things now you're a mother yourself?' Jane asks now.

'I feel like I'm grieving for her all over again,' I admit, quietly. 'Having Evie has made me appreciate what she did for us, the sacrifices she made, the responsibilities she had in making sure we grew up well-rounded, making us feel so very loved.'

I still think of her every single day.

It stings when my friends talk about meeting their mum for coffee and it makes me want to cry when I see proud grandmas pushing their grandchildren in prams. I wish I could just call her and ask her to nip round sometimes. I want to ask her all the silly things: 'Is this how you give them a bath?' 'Which is the best way to make them burp?' 'Am I doing any of this fucking right?'

'And how are you feeling about motherhood?'

'I love it. I love Evie more than I could ever say, but ... it's hard,' I confess. 'There's so much pressure, isn't there? Matt wants me to go to work so she goes to nursery three days a week and I feel so guilty about it. But you're fucked whatever you do as a woman, aren't you? If you work, you're neglecting your kid. If you stay at home, you're letting yourself and your career down. You can't win either way.'

'It's hard to be a woman, Stephanie,' she says, dryly. I wonder what sacrifices and hurdles Jane has had to overcome to get to where she is. 'You have to do what ultimately feels right.'

I've now been promoted to Marketing Director at work. In reality, all it means is that I have a new title and get a bit more money for doing the same job. Dad dragged me in his office one day and said I deserved it because of all my hard work. And I *do* work hard, but I've just come back from maternity leave so I think it was more about boosting my self-esteem to ensure I don't fall down some kind of post-pregnancy depression rabbit hole than anything else.

I'm not actually sure I want to work at all. I'd much rather stay at home with Evie, watching her grow and learn. My mind wanders back to that conversation I had with Ebony years ago, when she told me she was leaving law to look after Jude. I couldn't believe she wanted to give that up to look after her baby. But I get it now. Because I want to see Evie do everything for the first time, cuddle her, watch her little face change. She's just started to walk. Grabbing on to the sofa to steady herself, she sets off at speed across the room, with only the momentum to carry her through. I whoop, holler and clap, watching her run. We both squeal and clap and she falls into my lap. I cry every time. *My little girl.* She's so proud of herself.

'I just feel like I can't please anyone at the moment – I'm either a bad mother who isn't at home with her child, or a bad wife who isn't contributing financially. Not actually excelling at anything.'

'Well, what a load of absolute rubbish!' Jane says, abruptly. 'Now, I really am going to get cross with you if you carry on like that.'

'It's true!'

'No, it isn't. You're spinning many plates at the moment and doing a brilliant job. Stop giving yourself a hard time. Now, we don't have long left out of this session and I want to ask about Jamie. Are you seeing him next month?'

I'm quite unprepared for such a direct question about him. It's exposing and makes me feel guilty and bad. Shameful. But what I'm doing is wrong, so I suppose I deserve to feel like that.

'Yes, I am.'

'And how do you feel about that?'

'Excited.' I say and smile. Jane knows this smile, she's seen me do it so many times. I know she's clocked it so I get in there first to point it out.

'I literally can't help but smile when I think about him. Even after all these years. That never goes away. That's what he does to me,' I burst out, feeling I have to justify myself.

'You have a special relationship, that's the effect you have on each other. I'm sure he is the same,' she offers, clasping her hands together.

'Yes, well, I hope so. But you know what I mean. I feel bad for saying that, obviously,' I mumble.

'I know you do.'

'But, yes, I am seeing him next month. Same place. I'm just looking forward to feeling ...' I look around the room, searching for the right word which might even come close to describing how a night with Jamie feels '... special,' I finally settle on.

'The whole basis of your relationship with Jamie relies upon you seeing each other once a year. You say that he makes you incredibly happy for various reasons, but for other reasons, you can't be together – and I understand that.'

I watch her as she explains this, not giving anything away in my face. My body tenses as she talks about it, though. Having someone analyse our relationship feels wrong, and I suddenly feel as if I've betrayed Jamie by telling her about him.

'But I'd like to know why you settle for only being that happy once a year?'

'What?' I look at her blankly. 'I thought you had a question about my relationship with Jamie?'

'Yes, that's it,' she says.

'I'm not sure I understand the question, Jane ...'

'How long has this been going on now, Stephanie? Six years?'

I nod.

'Why have you settled for not feeling loved for so many years?' she asks, carefully.

I don't say anything.

'Why do you settle for being so blissfully happy only one weekend out of fifty-two in a year? Because you should be that happy *every* weekend, Stephanie.'

I'm silent for a good minute. I don't have an answer. Not one. She knows the answer, of course. She won't tell me, though. Any second now she'll pull the bloody triangle diagrams out and get me to talk through what I think the answer is. I'm flummoxed with this one.

'I don't know,' I reply, finally.

'Yes, you do,' she says. 'Deep down, you know. You always do.'

'Yes, OK, I'm not blissfully happy with Matt, but that's the choice I've made,' I reply like a sulky teenager.

'You know it runs deeper than that,' she says. 'You could leave Matt tomorrow if you really wanted, find somebody else who appreciates you and makes you feel as special as Jamie does. Except you'd feel like that all the time, not just one weekend a year.'

'But it wouldn't be like that!' I sigh in frustration. 'It's not that simple ...'

'No, it isn't. So, tell me why you really do it?' Jane has this way of talking to me sometimes, which is stern and authoritative, but also kind and caring. I've absolutely no idea how she manages it, but it's almost impossible to hate her for it because I know she's only looking out for me. Well, in a professional sense, anyway.

I've got no idea.

I glance at the clock in the middle of the pale grey wall. The ticks echo loudly around the room when neither of us speak. Jane is comfortable with silences, whereas I hate them. I think she uses them as some kind of tactic to stress me out, or maybe I just crack easily under pressure. Either way, I don't like it and she knows it.

'This is just my life, OK? You make the best of what you're given, don't you? Some people are meant to have these happy, loving, perfect lives. They just *do*, don't they? Everything just seems to go right for them.'

'And you don't have that?'

I try to keep it together, but the tears well in my eyes far quicker than I would have liked.

'I ended up marrying a guy, basically out of loyalty, but also because I felt as if I owed it to my family because of everything I'd put them through. I work for my dad in a job which doesn't challenge me and I didn't enjoy my wedding day. I had an emergency C-section for my daughter, so I couldn't even do *that* right. I'm pretty sure I irritate my husband most of the time. And I'm in love with another man.'

'So you've consigned yourself to a life of unhappiness because of this? Because you think you're, what? Unlucky?'

'No ... yes ... look, I don't *know!*' I raise my hands up in exasperation, gazing out the window at the rain which is now slamming down outside.

Then calmly Jane asks me, 'Stephanie, why are you content only being happy one weekend a year?'

CHAPTER 18

Saturday 13 October 2012

Jamie

I'm so sorry, Steph. Going to be a bit late. H has to work and won't be back until early evening. I'll get there as soon as I can and will keep you updated. Really looking forward to seeing you. X

I look at the text I sent this afternoon. She still hasn't replied and it's now just gone 6 p.m. I really hope she's not pissed off. Helen hardly ever has to go into work on a weekend, but she's in the middle of this lucrative job and her team are having to work all hours. Obviously, it falls on this date.

'I'm sorry, it looks like it'll be a late one. I'll hopefully be back for about six or seven. You'll still be able to get away for your night out, won't you?' she asked. An enormous bolt of guilt shook through me when she said it.

'Erm, yeah. It'll be fine. Peterborough isn't far and it's only the lads. They won't even be going out until about ten. You know what they're like!' I lied.

I didn't feel right the rest of the afternoon. I took Sebby to the park, made Play-Doh animals with him, but something felt off.

By 6.45 my bag is packed and in the hallway. Seb is, uncharacteristically, wide awake and not wanting to go to sleep, rampaging around the living room and throwing every toy on to the floor. Attempting to tidy up after him is like trying to shovel snow in a blizzard. He's been bathed, fed and is ready for bed, but he quite clearly has other ideas. Chasing around after him, I'm now checking my phone every two minutes for a message from either Stephanie or Helen.

He's overtired – he gets like this sometimes. Chucking himself dramatically on to the floor with his limbs wriggling all over the place like an octopus, he whinges for no other reason than because he can. I pick him up and his body goes rigid, his whining transforming into high-pitched screams. I could really do without this tonight.

My phone beeps and I pull it out of my pocket, still wrestling Seb in my other arm. It's Stephanie:

Can you let me know if you're still coming tonight? It's getting quite late and might not be worth your while.

Oh crap. I can tell she's pissed off. It's a balancing act between the two of them and I don't want to upset either. I call Helen as I pop Seb on to the sofa; he immediately climbs off, runs to the bookshelf and starts pulling books off.

'Hi!' I say, rubbing my forehead. 'How are you getting on?'

'Yeah, shouldn't be too long now.'

'Ah, OK,' I say, trying to sound absolutely chilled and not at all stressed by the situation. 'Any idea what kind of time I should expect you back?'

'Think about eight now. Aim to set off about that time.'

'You sure? If it will be later, just say. I just need to tell … the lads. They might head out now, that's all, so they need to know whether to go ahead or wait for me,' I say, cringing as I wrap myself up in lies to my wife on the phone.

'No, I'll be back home for eight. Don't worry. Tell them to get you some shots in as you'll be playing catch up.'

'Yes.' I fake a laugh. 'Will do. See you soon.'

Straight after ending the call I immediately compose a text to Stephanie:

I'm so, so sorry about this! She will be back at about 8 which means I should hopefully be with you around 9. Better late than never! Can't wait to see you. X

Maybe I should have called her. What else could I say, though? I appreciate it's a special evening but there's nothing else I can do. Just as Sebby starts demolishing another bookshelf, my phone pings and I check the message:

Fine. I'll be in the bar.

I don't think an hour has ever gone more slowly. Every time I hear a car go past the window I pull the curtains back to see if it's Helen, who has miraculously got back early. Thankfully, after half an hour of wrecking the house, Sebby appears to have finally worn himself out, so I give him some warm milk and he falls asleep in my arms. Wrapping his arms around my neck as I carry him up the stairs to bed, his little head full of dark hair teeters on the edge of my shoulder. I think about what I'm about to go and do, who I'm going to see as I feel the warmth of his little body cuddling into me, and hold on to him a bit tighter.

I. Am. A. Terrible. Person.

As I gently lay him down on his cot bed, pulling the duvet up to his chin, I hear the front door close. Kissing his forehead, I whisper into his ear, 'See you tomorrow, buddy. Love you.'

Running down the stairs, quick enough so that I can leave the house as soon as possible but not so quick that it looks like I'm dying to get away, I ask Helen how her day was.

'Christ, I'm glad that's over!' she says and sighs.

'Grab yourself a glass of wine and order a pizza.'

'I will!' she replies, looking knackered. Her hair is piled up on the top of her head, her glasses shield her tired brown eyes.

'Go on, off you pop,' she demands. 'Have fun!'

Picking my bag up in the hallway, I give her a hug, kissing her forehead.

'Love you,' she says.

'Love you, too,' I smile, closing the door.

9.12 p.m.

That's the time on the car clock as I pull into Heathwood Hall car park.

Leaving my bag in the car, I run to the entrance. I'm so looking forward to seeing her, even if we only have a fraction of the time we usually would. But this is getting harder to do every year. Harder to lie to Helen, harder to leave Seb, the guilt and anxiety over it weighs down more heavily every year. And, yet, I still do it, because I have to see her.

The stress of today and not being able to get here earlier definitely made it more difficult; I tortured myself all the way here over what I was doing. It seemed 'more wrong' this year, somehow. I questioned all day whether I should come; something just seemed off kilter with it all.

A woman sits on a stool at the bar with her back to me. She's in a sexy black fitted sleeveless dress, her long blonde hair is wavy and swept around her right shoulder.

There she is. I can't help but burst into a huge smile as I walk up behind her.

'Stephanie?'

She swings around, slightly off balance, and just looks at me.

'Oh,' she sighs. 'Hi Jamie.'

I frown at her in a mildly amused way and lean in to hug her, but she's so unwelcoming; all she does is very lightly place her hands on my back as I sink my face into her hair.

'So sorry I'm late,' I tell her. 'What are you up to?'

'Nothing,' she snaps. 'Just chatting to my friend Greg,' she says proudly, delicately slurring her words, turning her head towards the very young bartender, who clearly wants no part of this.

'It's Craig,' he says awkwardly, walking off to the other end of the bar.

'Okaaayy,' I say, raising my eyebrows. Going by her almost empty wine glass and the empty bottle next to it – and the fact she's quite clearly drunk – I'm guessing she's been here for a while. 'Right, well, shall we go upstairs?'

'Hmmm ... nope!' she says, holding on to the bar for support.

'Why not?'

'You think it's OK to keep me waiting here for hours on end while you play happy families?'

'I wasn't playing "happy families"—'

'And then just waltz in expecting me to cruise upstairs with you for a fuck?' she spits at me. Some of the other hotel guests' ears prick up at this point.

'I meant so we could talk and so I could get changed to come back down for something to eat.'

'Why can't we talk down here?' she says, spreading her arms out dramatically.

Gently placing my hand on the bottom of her back, I usher her away from the bar. The reception area has people milling about in it, so we step outside.

Because it's a cold October evening, it's absolutely freezing. It's the kind of cold snap which feels like a film of ice is being placed over your body.

We stand opposite each other, just outside the entrance to the Hall. She's in her lovely dress, shivering, folding her arms to keep warm. I hate to think she's been ready for hours, waiting for me to get here. She's gone to so much effort, looks beautiful.

'Here,' I say, taking my coat off, 'take this.'

'I don't want your coat. I don't need it.'

'What's going on, Stephanie? I've just driven all the way here to see you. We've both waited a year for this. Don't ruin it. Please.'

'I'm not the one ruining it. You're the one who's late.'

'Yes, and I've apologised for that. Can we move on? I'm here now.'

'No! We can't "move on".'

253

'Well, can you explain to me what the problem is, because I don't understand.'

She moves closer to me, so that she's inches away from my face.

'Do I mean *so* little to you that on our one night of the year, you couldn't make other arrangements? Make a bit of an effort? To get here on time?'

'Look, I'm sorry. There was no way around it. Helen got called into work all day, then she had to stay late and I had to watch Seb. He's my son – what was I supposed to do?'

'Oh yep, of course,' she mocks. 'Your perfect family. Your perfect marriage, I forgot.'

'Steph, don't—'

'Don't what?'

'My marriage is my marriage and it's not up for discussion.'

'Oh Christ, don't I know it! Yeah, you're just *so* happy, aren't you? You just can't stop pointing that out to me, can you? Lucky you!'

'I don't point anything out to you. But, on the whole, I am happy, yes.'

'Bullshit, Jamie! Utter bullshit!' She laughs, throwing her arms up in the air. 'If you were that happy you wouldn't be doing this with me. Fact!'

'I didn't plan to do this with you, Stephanie. It's not like you fill a gap I'm missing in my relationship with Helen. You're something beautiful and special, I …'

She looks at me blankly, like she can't believe the words I'm saying.

'Oh, so I'm basically like a hobby?' she scoffs, getting more wound up by the second. She's shouting now, in that way you do when you're drunk but don't realise how loud you're being. 'Something you do on the side of your marriage?'

'What? No! I didn't mean it like that.'

'I mean, what the fuck are we even doing?' she screams at me.

'I don't know how it's got to this point,' I reply, honestly. 'We try to be just friends, but—'

'And *that's* the problem,' she says, laughing and waving her finger drunkenly in my face.

'I just want to be around you, I can't explain it … I'm sorry,' I plead with her.

She's no longer shivering. Almost as if all the angry dancing about and shouting has warmed her up. I don't know if there's anything else I can say to make this better. She's obviously wanted to say this for a long time.

'Do you even know how much you mean to me?' I tell her. 'I don't even need to have sex with you. I just want to be around you. To see you. And I don't know what the fuck this is either, but all I know is I need to see you.'

'Oh yes, you need to see me so much you can't even get here on time the only time I see you a year—'

'Please, Stephanie, don't do this.'

'It's always on your terms, isn't it?'

'Steph …' I whisper, moving closer to her. Cuddling up to her, my hand rests in her hair as I feel her arms wrap around my waist. She pushes me away, her face swelling with rage.

'You know something?' she says. 'I don't think I can do this any more. I need you to *want* me, not *need* me. I need to know I give you something she doesn't. If she's so damned perfect, then you don't want me …'

Oh Steph, please don't. I can't lose you.

'… so why don't you go straight back home and fuck her instead?'

Every word is loaded and delivered with anger. The only sound cutting through the silence is the muffled voices coming from the reception area.

'Do you think I don't know what you're doing?' I say, softly.

'What?' she asks, confused.

'I know you're pushing me away because that's what you feel comfortable doing. I might only see you once a year, Stephanie, but you forget how well I know you.'

'Oh give up the psychoanalysis crap, please. I get enough of that with Jane.'

'Unless you tell me you want me to stay, I'm going to go over there, get in my car, and drive home. I won't contact you again.'

'I don't take kindly to threats, Jamie. Go home and be the perfect husband you *think* you are. I can't be bothered with you any more.'

'That's how you want to end this? Please, Stephanie, don't. I—'

'Jamie, all you do is toy with me,' she interrupts. 'You either want me properly or you don't.'

'It's not that simple, Stephanie. Please …'

She stands, looking at me, shaking her head, wearing a face of sheer indignation. She's made her mind up.

'Do you know what, Jamie? I wish I'd never met you,' she says. And right here, in this moment, she means it. Her eyes are filled with hurt.

I take the words in. It's brutal, making someone feel like that. I take one last glimpse at her, this girl I'm in love with. I know I'll regret not telling her how I feel, but I've done enough damage. I turn around, walk back to my car, get in and drive away.

PART THREE

Nothing Compares 2U

CHAPTER 19

Wednesday 22 May 2013

Jamie

'Ten years!' Helen remarks, almost as if she can't believe it. The air con drifts across my skin as I glance out over the panoramic view from our dining table. The burning heat from the Nevada desert lashes down on to the garish buildings outside. I've never known anything like it.

'Feels like less,' I say, yawning, struggling to stay conscious. I've been awake for so long now, I've no idea what time of day it is. Knocking back the espresso in front of me like it was a shot of tequila, I hope it has the desired effect on me in less than two minutes. 'How come you're so perky, anyway?'

'I slept on the plane, which is what you should have done,' she says.

'You know I can't sleep on planes. I get too nervous.'

'Well, I don't think throwing all those vodka and cokes down your throat helped but it got you here, I suppose.'

She's right, I guess. I certainly don't feel better for it now. It's like some kind of weird drunk-but-simultaneously-hungover jet-lagged state and it feels like nothing is real. All I want to do is go to bed.

'No sleeping, though,' Helen barks at me, poking my arm with her finger. 'It will bugger everything up for the next few days. Trust me, you'll thank me for it! Now, what do you fancy for breakfast?'

There's a little boy a few tables down, about the same age as Sebby. He's sitting with his parents and wearing a little blue cowboy hat, eating pancakes. My heart aches a bit; I've never been away from my boy for this long before.

'Do you think Sebby will be OK?' I ask Helen.

'Yes, of course he will! You know how much my parents absolutely spoil him rotten.' She smiles. 'As long as we bring him presents back he won't care we've gone!'

'You're right. Let's enjoy the next five days. Can't believe we've actually got some time to ourselves,' I gush, gently sliding my hand down her arm as she studies the menu. 'And that you planned all this without me knowing.'

'Well, we both deserve it, Jamie,' she says, before going back to selecting her breakfast.

'Sorry we're late!' Cal says, appearing from nowhere, with his arm draped around Vicky's shoulder.

'Don't worry, mate!' I reassured him. 'We've only just got here.'

'I thought you'd both gone to sleep. I was about to turn into the jet-lag police and run up to your room,' Helen tells them.

'No way!' Vicky says, outraged at the mere suggestion, and sitting down. 'You don't come to Las Vegas to sleep. Sorry, we just got, erm … distracted.'

She throws a cheeky glance at Cal, who then turns to me and Helen.

'What?' he says and laughs. 'Oh, come *on*! You're here without your kid – you're the same, surely?'

I take a sip of my orange juice to release the awkwardness, knowing Helen feels it too.

There was no suggestion of any of that when we got into our room. We looked around the mini-suite we had, admired the view and Helen unpacked a few of her dresses while I messaged her parents to let them know we had arrived, asking how Seb was. No kissing, no hugging, and definitely no sex. But we were beyond knackered from the jet lag so I thought it would probably take a few days for us to settle in anyway.

Up until I arrived at the airport, I thought Helen and I were going to Rome for a romantic wedding anniversary trip away, the first since Seb was born. She insisted on arranging it all and I was totally confused when we arrived at the airport in the middle of the night to see Cal and Vicky waiting for us.

263

'Well, seeing as it's a big one, I thought we'd celebrate in style and invite Cal and Vicky too!' Helen squealed to my shocked face.

'God! Well, I'm thrilled you're here! Can't imagine anything better than discovering Rome with you lot!'

'Well, that's the last surprise,' Helen said, proudly. 'We're not going to Rome. We're going to—'

'*Las Vegas!*' they all screamed and whooped.

Twenty-four hours later I'm lying on a sunlounger by a pool, loud music blasting out, surrounded by scantily clad women in bikinis clutching cocktails in plastic cups. The entire scene is sponsored by the faint aroma of sun cream and fries. People wade into the enormous pool to cool off. It's not a regular pool here; it mimics the sea so you can sit in a few inches of it. Because, of course, there is no sea when you're in the middle of the Nevada Desert. And it's *hot*. I've never known a heat like it; it's all-consuming, oppressive, like being in a cooker. Too hot to walk anywhere, no sea to cool off in. It's mental when you think about it.

The girls love it all. They spent an age getting ready, running between rooms trying on bikinis, shoes, some kind of over-bikini dress things. I dared to ask if it really mattered at one point, which was met by both of them shooting me incredulous looks. Apparently, when you're in Vegas, it definitely matters what you wear around the pool.

They finally emerge about an hour later, done up to the nines like something out of *Dallas*.

'Bloody hell! Aren't we the luckiest men here!' I say to Cal.

Helen and Vicky sashay over to our sunloungers, dumping their day bags on the floor. Christ only knows what's in them – they look big enough to carry an entire weekend's worth of clothes and they're full to the brim. Helen looks different. She's always veered more towards a tomboy kind of look, or certainly a more masculine vibe. But seeing her today is different to any other time I've seen her. I don't think I've ever seen her wear heels like that, certainly not with a swimsuit, and she wears them with a confidence I've not seen before. Her long hair hangs down one of her shoulders and has bit of a kink to it in contrast to how straight it usually is. She's gone all out on the glamour, even wearing more make-up than usual by the look of things. She looks amazing.

'Whaddya think, fellas?' Helen says, popping her hands on her hips. 'Vicky dressed me and gave me a bit of a makeover.'

'Yeah, I did!' Vicky beams, like a proud mother, softly clapping her hands. 'Doesn't she look fab? Can't believe you've had a baby, sweets.'

Vicky reminds me of a tiny little pixie doll. She wears a sparkly USA flag bikini and aviator sunglasses. Her massive blonde hair partially covers the huge dragon tattoo on her back which is already causing people walking past to admire it.

265

'You both look great! You show us up, though,' I say.

'Oi! Speak for yourself – I'm always stylish, thank you very much,' Cal says, laughing, as Vicky skips over and sits on his knee, crossing her legs. He grabs her arse as she wraps her arms around his neck. Leaning in close, she whispers something to him which makes him laugh louder and he kisses her.

'Do you want a drink, baby?' I ask Helen, reaching over and running my finger down the outside of her leg.

'It's OK,' she says, heading off towards the bar. 'I'll go and get them.'

I thought that having had a baby might prepare me for dealing with jet lag. It did not. By teatime I was desperate to go to sleep, but Cal was forcing me to stay awake by throwing water from the pool on my face and ordering more margaritas. Booze, extreme heat, jet lag – it's like some kind of mad endurance test you see on TV.

The girls take selfies on their phones, squealing at each one: 'No! Take another one! Jesus. Not that one. That could be all right if you pop a filter on. Yes. Oh, I don't know – you're the bloody designer!' They force me and Cal take photos of them in the pool, out of the pool, on loungers, by palm trees, looking at the camera, laughing at each other, looking away from the camera – it's basically turned into a fashion shoot.

At one point when the girls go over to the pool bar to get more drinks, I watch as they strike up conversation with two guys. Everyone at this hotel has perfect bodies. They're toned, tanned and wear skimpy outfits, even the men. Thank God I've been hitting the gym for the last few months. I watch Helen as she talks to them. I don't feel jealous, it's not that. Helen has lots of male friends and I've never had a problem with it and Vegas is a place where everyone talks to each other. It's the way she's smiling, laughing. They're saying something so funny, she's proper belly laughing, her smile huge and genuine.

Why can't I make her smile like that any more?

I used to be able to do that.

They say that having a baby brings you much closer together. Well, yes and no. It strips away everything gluing you together in many ways and forces you to look at who you are, what your relationship really is. Conversations become much more businesslike and transactional. We no longer ask about each other's day, but discuss whose turn it is to do the nursery run, bath time or the food shop. Everything revolves around the baby, it's all you talk about. Days which would once be spent wandering around food markets and spontaneous day-drinking have been replaced with baby-friendly days out.

You start to wonder: what did we used to talk about? Stuff we did, places we went, things we saw. But now we don't do those things, so it's not an option. It's stripped back, stripped bare.

Having a baby truly tests whether you're right for each other, because if you're not, you'll find out.

Sink or swim.

Flaws and irritating habits which previously lay dormant for years rise to the surface once you have children. Since having Seb, Helen has identified a host of annoying things I do. We both keep a mental scoreboard of what we've done for him and use it against the other whenever rows come up: 'I got up with him on Saturday morning so you could have a lie in.' 'Well I took him out for a few hours on Sunday afternoon so you could go to the gym.'

Nobody tells you about this bit.

Of course, it doesn't help when you're also in love with another woman. That also fucks things up a bit, especially when it all goes horribly wrong and ends one freezing cold October night in the middle of the countryside.

Those first few months after she broke it off were really tough. All I could think about was her, and I mean *all* the time. It affected my work. I'd find myself drifting off thinking about her at school, in assemblies and classes. I kept seeing her face – how angry it was. What a complete bastard I was to be killing these two women simultaneously, one aware of it, the other oblivious, and I couldn't decide which was worse. I saw the pain in Stephanie's eyes that night, the anger, frustration, sadness, resentment and jealousy of knowing she wouldn't ever have the man she loves. I did that to her. There was no 'It's for the best, take care', or 'I wish you well'. It was pure, bitter pain which had built up for months, if not years. I'd never led her on, she'd always known the score, always known I was happy with Helen and would never leave her. But I still did that to her.

Then there's Helen. She has no idea her husband has fucked another woman. Well, except it's not just 'fucked'. I love her. My God, she'd never understand that. Why the hell would she? But I didn't plan it. I didn't plan any of this. You just can't help your feelings. Not that this explanation is at all valid in the real world.

But I just had to keep telling myself it was for the best. Perhaps me and Stephanie were just not meant to be. The hurt burned inside me, but it was one I deserved. I simply had to live with it and rebuild my relationship with Helen.

That's what I intend to do on this trip ...

On day three, Helen and I go out for lunch on our own – on our actual anniversary. It's nice to get her to myself. We order champagne and almost feel carefree again.

'Who'd have thought we'd last this long!' Helen exclaims and laughs, guzzling the bubbles out of her glass.

'I didn't doubt it.' I lean over, clinking her champagne flute and admiring the spectacular view. She's pulled a blinder, but then again, she's brilliant at finding the best restaurants in town. We sit next to a glass balcony

269

overlooking the Bellagio fountains, which are stunning. As they launch towards the sky with immense force, their gentlest spray blow towards us – a welcome break in the heat.

'This is lovely,' I say.

She smiles at me. It's great to see her like this, relaxing. The bright orange dress she wears brings out her tan.

'I just can't believe we're on our own with no Seb!' she says, leaning forward excitedly. 'Obviously, I miss him, but you know ...'

'Yeah, I know,' I sympathise, reaching out for her hand across the table.

'You didn't mind coming here, did you?' she asks. 'I know you were really looking forward to visiting Rome and I felt terrible, lying to you!'

'Don't be daft!' I tell her. 'I'd have loved Rome too, but it's just nice to spend time on our own together anywhere. It's been such a long time since we've done that.'

She glances over to the fountains, which are dancing about in some kind of musical formation.

'It's like going on honeymoon with a couple of newlyweds being with Cal and Vicky, isn't it?' she says, with a rather forced, mock laugh.

'What do you mean?'

'Well, they're all over each other, aren't they?' she says, removing her hand from mine and going to take a sip of her champagne. 'I don't know where to look half the time.'

'They're just in a different place to us, that's all.' I shrug. 'We used to be like that.'

She stops, just before the glass touches her lips. 'Jamie, you've *never* looked at me the way Cal looks at Vicky.'

I'm not quite sure how to take that.

'What are you on about?' I scoff. 'Of course I did. I do!'

Her eyes stare at me all the way down the champagne flute as she slowly takes a sip out of it. I look away, choosing instead to straighten up the cutlery on the pristine white tablecloth.

'That's just what they're like with each other. Always have been,' I remind her. 'Why did you invite them if you didn't want to be around that?'

'I'm not saying I don't want to be around them,' she says defensively.

'But we'd talked about going away on our own for our anniversary, somewhere romantic,' I point out. 'Then you go and invite Cal and Vicky. I'm having a great time with them, but I'm just not sure why you did it.'

Helen sighs and leans back in her chair. She fiddles with the neck of the champagne flute for a few moments, which suggests she either has no answer, or one she doesn't want to give.

'I don't know. I suppose it just highlights ...'

'What?'

'Have we become the couple who never has sex and only ever talks about their kid?'

Wow. Well, someone just woke *that* elephant up.

I guess the day of our tenth wedding anniversary is as good a time as any to broach this issue.

'Can we not be so hard on ourselves?' I say. 'We're juggling a two-year-old and two careers. It's been a tough couple of years and we will get through this, if we both want to.'

'I suppose so. Just … seeing them together makes me wonder if we can ever get that back.'

'Look, we'll be OK. We've lasted ten years. We can't give up now,' I say, reaching over and stroking her cheek.

'I guess so. It's just hard. Harder than I thought it'd be, you know? To balance everything.'

'It certainly would have been better with a handbook.' I laugh. 'But we'll get there.'

We enjoy the rest of the lunch, getting a bit tipsy and talking about when we first met. She remembers how excited she was when I proposed to her on a weekend away in Edinburgh. I remember how thrilled I was when I found out she was pregnant. And all the memories in between.

I'm glad we had the chat. It cements my intentions and priorities to my wife. It also reaffirms that my relationship with Stephanie is over. Well and truly.

Except, whenever I try to do this, it seems like fate, the universe, or some other bastard cosmic force shoves Stephanie in my face. Later on in the day, the girls come back from a wander to tell me and Cal they have a 'treat' for us.

'Guess what we're doing tonight?' Helen teases.

'Going to see a load of strippers?' Cal replies, excitedly.

'Ha! Nice try,' Vicky says. 'That's tomorrow, baby!'

'We're going to see a musical!' Helen squeals.

Cal and I couldn't possibly be less impressed.

'What? I'm not going to see a musical in Vegas. You two can go,' he says.

'I'm with him. I don't do spontaneous singing or dancing or any of that,' I say, laying it on the line.

'Oh, come on! This has famous people in! An ex-Destiny's Child member and someone from American *X Factor*,' Helen points out, as if this would make any difference whatsoever.

'Jesus Christ. What is it?' I ask, grimacing.

'*Dreamgirls!*'

I've never seen this show, I've never heard of it. But I know one song from it – the song Stephanie sang to me on that warm October day.

Annoyingly, Cal starts to come around to the idea only because he's interested from a costume point of view.

I couldn't be the only one not going, so now here I am, third row in, watching Effie White sing about how she isn't giving up on the man she loves: 'And I Am Telling You I'm Not Going'…

It's nice to put the song into context. It's a song of defiance and strength from a woman who's been through a lot, allowing her vulnerability to pour out of her skin with no shame.

Watching the actress takes me back to that day and I feel a bittersweet smile spread across my face. God, I'd love to know how she is, what she's doing today. I hope she's OK.

This woman is incredible. She belts the tune out, hits every single note, and it's spectacular to watch and hear. But it's still not as good as the version I heard that night.

Things always happen for a reason, and usually for the best. We are obviously not meant to be together. If I was meant to be with her, I would be.

CHAPTER 20

Saturday 26 October 2013

Stephanie

'Hang on! Ten more seconds, I swear it's coming!' I promise him.

We both go quiet, not moving an inch. His hands, spread out over my huge bump, waiting for the tidal wave of movement I know is imminent. I'm in the final few weeks of pregnancy now and I love this part; they move, lash out, kick and writhe about, wanting to break free.

As predicted, a limb pokes right out of my belly and jabs Matt's right hand.

'Woah!' he yells. 'That is some freaky shit!'

'That freaky shit is your daughter,' I tell him, protectively placing my hands over my bump. 'And shhh! She'll hear you.'

'And I can't wait to meet her,' he says, kissing my forehead. 'You ready?'

'Yes, how do I look?' I ask, peering at myself in the mirror.

'Lovely!'

'Thank you!' I smile gratefully. 'You sure it's not, you know, too much?'

'What do you mean?' he asks, frowning.

'This …' I say, gazing down at the incredible cleavage I've spawned in the past few months. It's just about contained in a crossover black jersey dress tonight, but I'm already looking forward to putting my pyjamas on later.

'Steph, that is *never* too much,' he says and laughs. 'You're definitely the sexiest pregnant woman here.'

'Let's hope I don't go into labour – you promised you wouldn't drink,' I say seriously. 'I'm due in two weeks, Matt, it could happen anytime.'

'Let's just stuff ourselves with food then!'

It was Matt's idea to do this. A little night away before the new baby arrives. I arranged it, as I couldn't chance him booking Heathwood Hall. I'm not sure my hormones could have handled that. Ebony said she'd have Evie so we dropped her off and arrived here at dusk.

We finally go in to eat, which is great; because, being almost nine months pregnant and mother of a two-year-old, I'm absolutely shattered and pretty sure I'll be in bed by ten o'clock.

Matt mildly irritates me by doing the same thing he does every single time we make it out the house on our own. All he does is criticise everything. *Everything*.

Whether it's 'Why would you wear that?', 'This food isn't very good', or 'I don't like the music in here', everything has to be so negative. It's draining. Tonight, he's complaining that the couple on the next table are obviously pissed and being a bit loud. They're about mid-twenties, I'd say, clearly on some kind of sexy weekend away. They keep hooting with laughter, generally just having a great time.

'They should vet people before allowing them to stay here,' he says, sounding bitter and ungracious. 'I'm sure people don't pay a fortune to eat here only to be surrounded by people like that.'

'People like what?' I challenge him. 'People having fun?'

'Rowdy. Probably got a cheap deal off the internet and thought they could mingle with people who could afford to actually be here.'

I'm taken aback by his blatant, shameless snobbery.

'Do you hear yourself?'

'What?' he asks, shocked I'm even questioning it as he shoves a piece of overpriced steak into his mouth.

'Why does it matter how anyone came to be here?'

'Oh, come on, Steph,' he scoffs. 'Don't be so worthy. Look at them.'

I discreetly look over at them to see what he's on about. Yes, she's in a very skimpy dress. It's white, tight and nothing I would wear – especially in my current state. She's brunette, it looks like she's wearing extensions and her face is slapped with make-up. But, so what? The guy she's with looks tickled pink to be with her. He's gone out of his way to look smart, choosing a blazer jacket, white shirt and his dark hair has been groomed within an inch of its life. I don't really get this current trend of styled men. I prefer the more rugged look, but that's just me.

'So, what? They're having a good time. We were like that once, you know,' I say, reaching for my water and taking a drink.

'I was never all over you like that!'

'No,' I say, looking over at them, 'I suppose you weren't. We were different, back then, though.'

'Of course we were. We didn't have a kid, you were a completely different person ...'

'Yes, I was,' I say, guardedly. 'But that's not a bad thing. People and relationships have to grow, evolve and change. You can't stay the same. Nothing can stay the same or it dies.'

Having this kind of conversation is always frustrating because Matt simply doesn't believe in concepts like these. He finds them difficult to grasp. Everything is black or white to him. He calls this kind of stuff my 'hippy shit'. I call it a basic understanding of life and human beings.

I watch him contemplate what I've just said. Surely he can get it? It's not difficult.

'Nah, I don't think I've changed at all,' he says, matter-of-fact.

'In ten years since we've been together, having a child, growing older, being married to me, you don't think you've changed, or grown? At all?'

He shrugs. 'No, not really. This is where you and me differ, Stephanie. You're obsessed with all the growing and changing,' he says, rolling his eyes. 'But you don't see that you were great to start with. Yeah, you had some issues but you sorted them. You were fun, carefree, wild, didn't give a shit when I met you. That's who you need to get back to. You do too much thinking these days.'

I sit opposite him – this man – and I don't think I've despised anyone more.

'If I'm being honest, I'm not sure all this therapy is more of a hindrance than a help,' he says, almost as a throwaway comment.

Jane immediately flashes into my head. I see her doing one of her 'unimpressed' faces, the ones that don't require any words. They're usually accompanied by a delicate but pronounced intake of breath.

Why are you content only being happy one weekend a year?

One question. Eleven words.

That blew my world apart. Why *don't* I search for happiness the other three hundred and sixty-three days of the year? It must exist somewhere. But, where? Why don't I leave him and go looking for it? Well, the huge bump in front of me prevents me from doing it now. We didn't plan it but I'm so glad it happened, even though it's double-edged.

On the one hand, it's a sister for Evie, something which will bring immense joy into our lives and a reason to be utterly thankful for every single day I wake up.

On the other, it's part of the iron cage I made for myself with this marriage and this baby is the lock turning.

I can't leave now.

Sleep escapes me when we eventually head back upstairs. I toss and turn for hours, thinking.

Sliding out of bed, I pop the fluffy hotel dressing gown on and the Ugg boots I arrived in and head downstairs. Thank God Matt is asleep: he'd have kittens if he knew I was lowering the tone.

There's something calming about being up in the dead of night. Being in the middle of nowhere, nobody is up, except the night porter and receptionist. Dim lighting illuminates the rooms as I make my way to reception.

'Can I help you? Are you OK?' the receptionist asks, alarmed, gazing straight at my baby bump.

'Oh, I'm just having trouble sleeping. Would it be OK if I sat in the drawing room? I can't get comfortable in bed.'

'Yes, of course,' she says. 'I can get the porter to bring you a hot chocolate if you'd like? Marshmallows?'

'That would be lovely – thank you.'

I park myself on the comfy sofa in the corner by the window and the receptionist comes in with the hot chocolate. I don't feel guilty for thinking this is the best part of the trip away.

Tightening the knot of the dressing gown above my bump, I feel a tsunami of movement from the baby. She must have clocked the abnormal nocturnal activity.

'Sorry, Adelaide,' I whisper, 'didn't mean to wake you up.'

Reaching into the pocket of the dressing gown, I get my iPod out, pop the earbuds in and press shuffle.

The piano intro gives it away. It always makes me cry at the best of times, but given the current hormonal situation, I've got no chance of getting through it dry-eyed so I might as well just go with it.

As the melody and vocals swell – a song about letting go and everything turning out how it's meant to be – I take a sip of my hot chocolate as something catches my eye in the corner of the room.

I've never seen it before, but there's something familiar about the painting on the wall. It's messy and chaotic in style, a palette of greys, whites and neutral colours. I'm surprised my eyes were drawn to it. It's not bold in any way.

Pulling myself up, I walk towards it to get a better look.

As I edge closer, it becomes clear. I smile, and then cry.

Rodin's *The Kiss* in spectacular art form, on the wall. The two lovers embrace, just like they did on that day in London at Tate Modern, when I saw it with Jamie.

Taking some deep breaths, I alternate between laughing and sobbing.

Let It Be.

Indeed.

CHAPTER 21

Saturday 2 August 2014

Jamie

Mum's been down visiting all week, so on her final day with us we all head off to this funfair gala day at Rotherton House, one of those stately home type affairs I love, but this year, they've got an exhibition on, showing the photos of local photographer Richard Horlock which I quite fancy seeing.

It's all the usual stuff: fair rides, helium balloons, and a huge bouncy castle. Seb insists on having his face painted as Spiderman. The weather has turned out lovely and it's scorching hot. Naturally, Seb wants to go on absolutely everything so we spend the first hour there making our way around the fair.

'Ah! Look at his little face!' Mum says, watching Seb going crazy on the bouncy castle. She's absolutely loved spending time with him this week, just hanging out, being granny. It's also been nice for me to have some company. Since I moved down here I've found it hard to make new friends. There are some decent people at the school and we go out for the odd pint, but that's as far as it goes. It can get quite lonely.

'He's a right little rascal,' Helen replies, waving at him from the sidelines. He doesn't seem at all troubled by the fact he's surrounded by older kids. He can clearly hold his own.

'Do you think you'll have any more?' Mum asks us, out of the blue.

Helen looks at me, clearly a bit startled by the bluntness of it.

'I doubt it, Heather,' she says, confidently. 'Not now. I'm flying at work and I think we are both just getting over the exhaustion of Seb's early years!'

'I wish you'd had a sibling,' Mum says to me. 'I think you missed that growing up.'

'Nah, I did all right, didn't I?'

She smiles. 'You did, love. I'm very proud of you.'

'I'm glad you got a day off today, Helen,' Mum says. 'You've been working so hard, getting back late ...'

'I know. We're just so busy at the moment. I'm sorry I've barely seen you this week.'

'I was hoping I could have babysat for you both,' Mum goes on. 'Must be so hard for you and Jamie to get out on your own. Maybe next time.'

Helen waves at Sebby on the bouncy castle before turning back to Mum.

'Yes, that would be lovely, Heather. Thank you, so lovely of you to come and see us. And Seb has adored it.'

Mum waits until Helen takes Seb on the huge ferris wheel to say something that's clearly been on her mind all week. She's no good at subtlety so she says it how it is.

'Jamie, is everything OK?' she asks, leaning into me. Her dark brown hair brushes against my face.

'Yeah, why wouldn't it be? What do you mean?'

'It's just that the last week I've been with you, you don't seem … right. You and Helen seem very distant with each other.'

I frown, acting as if I don't know what she's talking about.

'I think we're both just knackered, and she travels a lot with work and everything.'

'Are you happy?' she asks bluntly.

Am I happy? Well, that's a very broad question. I suppose so. Kind of. I can't complain. Well, I could. Could I be *happier?*

Yes. Best not to go there though.

'Yes!' I reply, completely over the top. 'Of course I am. And I've loved having you here this week. You've probably just caught us on an over-the-top week, Mum.'

She looks at me thoughtfully. 'You know you can talk to me whenever you want? I *am* only a phone call away.'

I hug her and she holds on tight. I think she misses me not being around the corner.

When Seb and Helen return, I take him off to do this treasure hunt paper trail thing around the grounds.

You find clues and it takes you to the next point and at the end you get a prize. They wave me off, laughing. 'Have fun, boys!'

It's actually a right laugh. I love doing stuff with my boy. He copies little things I do, like turning his baseball cap around to be like me today. He's adorable. It's so busy, there must be thirty other families also doing this trail. I grip tightly to Seb's hand so he doesn't wander off – I get paranoid about that kind of thing. The next clue is a butterfly around the back of this mansion-like house, so off we go to find it. Looks like every other family is also on this step. The sun beats down on us, the grounds bustling with the noise of families, fed-up children and even more fed-up parents.

And that's when I see her.

Standing in the middle of it all, with her husband and children.

Children, plural. There's a beautiful little blonde girl next to her – that must be Evie. But she's also pushing a pram with a baby in. It looks to be about eight months old and, going by the colour scheme, it's another girl.

Seb attempts to drag me away but I can't move. I can't be more than twenty feet away from her. I feel like my stomach has been yanked out of me. My heart aches. She's smiling and talking to Evie, looking at something she's drawn on the treasure hunt map. Her long blonde hair contrasts against the red dress she's wearing. That must be Matt, next to her, the blond guy on his phone. A stab of jealousy shoots through me just watching him. I want to stand and watch her. God, that sounds creepy.

'Daddy! There it is!' Sebby shouts, pointing to a big plastic butterfly atop the fountain a short walk away. Taking one last glance at her, I take my boy and walk away.

'How was the trail?' Helen asks.

'See for yourself!' I reply, pointing to Seb, who is devouring a huge chocolate lollipop. My mind is still doing somersaults over seeing Stephanie. Is she still here? Where is she?

'Oooh!' she congratulates him. 'What a clever boy!'

'Why don't you two head inside and see that exhibition you wanted to take a look at? I'll watch Seb,' Mum volunteers.

'You sure you don't mind, Heather?'

'Not at all! Nice for you both to get a bit of time together, that's what I'm here for!'

It's nice to jump into a bit of tranquillity. That's what I love about galleries. The quietness. I like photography exhibitions, they're different to art ones in so many ways; the arrangement, spacing, lighting. Going to these things with Helen takes us back to what we love, where we came from. We don't have long but it's nice to have time to breathe. Especially after just seeing Stephanie. I need a second to think on my own.

The photography is spread out over several rooms, each one fairly dark, with strategically placed lighting to show the photography off at its best.

We wander into the main room, walking past a gentle whispering of voices. Helen is drawn to a selection of photos next to the entrance, so I have a look around the other side of the partition in the middle of the room.

I catch my breath when I see Stephanie again, from the back this time. She's standing in front of one of the photos. The red dress and hair give her away.

My beautiful girl. Except she's not mine any more.

All I want to do is reach out and touch her. I have no idea if she's alone. I can see she's got her iPod earbuds in, which makes a small smile break out on to my face. I'd love to know what she's listening to.

Aware Helen is around the corner and could quite literally come around at any second, I walk towards her. I don't think. I just have to make her see me. Jesus, it's a risk.

I stand just behind her right shoulder and my reflection in the photo frame she's looking at slowly glides into view. She glances at my reflection once, and then twice. A double take, not quite believing it's me. She quickly reaches up to take her earbuds out but I shake my head and she stops. We gaze at one another through the glass.

A few seconds pass. I'm inches away from her and I'd do anything to kiss this neck, the perfume from which floats in the air. But I don't. I smile at her and she smiles back.

As I step away from her my reflection disappears, just as I hear Helen's voice coming around the corner. I turn around to face it and I watch Stephanie leave the gallery out of the corner of my eye.

CHAPTER 22

Saturday 17 October 2015

Stephanie

The thick duvet weighs down on the pair of us like a million feathers; a kind of light, gentle, cosy hug. I can tell what time it is by the clanking of the radiator which has just sprung into action under the sash window at the bottom of the bed. It's one of those enormous, heavy, period beds. The house has loads of them. Being in the countryside, there's no glare from outside. Only stars illuminate the sky. The only light is that which sneaks in from Adelaide's night lamp in her room.

It's 5.30 a.m. A little blonde-haired angel sleeps beside me. It's amazing how much space a two-year-old takes up. She starfishes every single night, pushing me to the edge of the bed, clutching on to her Belle princess soft toy, out for the count. She always gets too hot in my room, so I pull the duvet back and tuck her hair behind her ear. I can't help but smile at her – my beautiful little Adelaide.

Seconds later I hear the other one skipping across the landing. A silhouette bounds towards the bed; she can't possibly see where she is going, but she's been doing it every night for the past year so has developed a sixth sense for it. Evie jumps up and I wrap her next to us. Their warm little bodies radiate love and snuggle into me.

Everyone tells me I shouldn't do this. I've had all the lectures. 'Co-sleeping is a *terrible* idea', 'They're too old for this' and 'You're making a rod for your own back'. The horrified faces I encounter when I dare to tell people I bring Adelaide into my bed in the early hours because I'm simply too tired to get into a battle of wills at 2 a.m. when I need to get up at 6.30 a.m. on the days I work. Or because I let Evie come in for an hour before we get up. You'd think I beat them.

It's our time together and I treasure it. They love it.

But it also keeps Matt out. He couldn't sleep when the girls were in, so he took it upon himself to sleep in the spare room. He's been there ever since. It's dysfunctional and odd and neither of us mention it even though we both know it's not right. He sees it as me choosing them over him, which I suppose I am.

I've invited Ebony and the kids around for breakfast today. Jude and Jett are proper tinkers now. At seven and five they're keeping Ebony busy and she's not thinking about having more anytime soon. The kids play with each other as we have coffee and chat about all sorts of rubbish. Well, it's mainly Ebony Topics, really. She's a fully signed-up member of the yummy mummy set at the local private school now; officially a member of the cool gang.

'I mean, you would not *believe* the scandal that goes on within that circle, Steph,' she whispers, wide-eyed.

'Oh, I can imagine,' I reply.

'No. Seriously. I'm talking *all* the drama,' she says, leaning closer. I laugh at how into this she is. She's loving it. And a bit of comic relief is exactly what I need right now.

We set the kids up in the living room to watch *Beauty and the Beast* for the umpty-first time. Ebony's fed up to death of it, but I love this film. I insist on singing all the songs and always cry at the end.

I use this movie to explain to Evie that beauty isn't everything. She was born with a little strawberry birthmark on the side of her face and she's at the stage now where she asks why she's different to other kids. We tell her that she was kissed by a fairy – that's what Mum used to say happened to her. Mum had a few scars on her body and would tell us that's how she got them; one on her eyebrow where the hair no longer grew, and a silvery one on her lower back. I never found out how she got them but it was probably doing something fun, knowing my mum.

Ebony asks if I've been for my hospital check-up – she went for hers last month. I say I have, so as not to worry her, and make a mental note to make another appointment first thing on Monday for the one I missed.

'Did you get the results back? Mine were clear.' She does a sigh of relief.

'Oh, yes,' I stumble. 'Mine too. It's such a relief to get the letter, isn't it?'

I feel terrible lying to her, but I'm just all over the place at the moment. Must sort it ASAP.

'And how are your therapy sessions going? You still go, don't you?'

'Yeah,' I lie. 'But they're less frequent now, more of an ad hoc thing, when I need a bit of support.'

I haven't actually been since the night I fell out with Jamie.

I deliberately asked Ebony around today to distract myself from mooning around because of today's date. Our weekend.

God, I just feel so ... empty today. Sitting on the huge white armchair, cuddling into Adelaide watching the DVD, I feel so bereft. Like a piece of the jigsaw is missing.

Matt pops his head into the lounge and the kids run to him for a hug. Sweeping them up, he smothers their faces in kisses.

'I'm going out,' he says abruptly. He looks pasty, his eyes puffy and glassy. He's hungover. I heard him come upstairs at about 1 a.m., after drinking alone in the living room.

I nod. 'Will you want some lunch?'

'Not sure when I'll be back. Don't worry about dinner either. Don't know what I'm doing.'

'OK,' I say. 'See you.'

He dives back out and Ebony looks aghast.

'What the *hell?*' she whispers, her green eyes wild with outrage.

'Don't, Ebs. Just how we are.'

I'm actually relieved when Matt calls to say he's decided to go out for the night, so it's just me and the girls. After I've popped them to bed, I have a glass of wine and sit in the lounge with the TV off, enjoying the silence.

I replay those few moments at Rotherton House so often. In reality, it lasted no more than about fifteen seconds, but it felt like minutes. I should have said something, but of course I couldn't. He was the last person I expected to see. I was completely unprepared, and it shook me to my core. Not even being able to turn around, look at him, speak to him – probably for the best.

I justify the fact that he is no longer in my life by telling myself he's an inconsiderate, confusing, infuriating twat. But I know this isn't true. The worst part about it all is that the reason he isn't in my life is because I'm jealous. That's it. The only reason. Plain, old green-eyed jealousy. Not of *her*, particularly. But because she has him and I don't. She gets to say he's her husband, but I know that a little part of him belongs to me and always will. I didn't plan on this taking over when I got into it. I thought I could contain it, it wouldn't matter.

I could box it off. I was so special to him and he was risking everything doing it, so why would I get jealous? My God, how naïve of me. Days and weeks were spent obsessing over this man I saw once a year. The man I'd pretended to myself I wasn't having an affair with.

'It's harmless' we told ourselves in the beginning. It would have probably been less harmful if we'd had a six-month intense fling in which we'd fucked every week and it fizzled out. This is actually far more destructive. When you deliberately have to make a conscious decision to stay away from each other, with no contact, you really should know that what you're doing is dangerous. Emotions have got involved in the game and you're basically screwed.

Why were we ever so stupid?

Ultimately, you have to make a choice about what you can tolerate and balance it up with what your life is like without someone there. We all do it to some extent. Everyone has habits, behaviours and quirks their partners don't like, don't they? It's a matter of degree how much you can put up with it.

How can I miss someone I barely saw?

Looking around the room, it dawns on me how untidy the house is these days. I've always had a well-kept home – well, as much as you can with kids. I took pride in keeping it nice for everyone. But lately, I just don't have the motivation to do it. I glance around the room and don't even flinch at the sight of glasses the girls had bedtime drinks out of, chewed straws sticking out of remnants of warm milk. Dolls are scattered all over the floor, as are whole farmyards of plastic animals. No point in clearing them up, they'll be playing with them tomorrow.

It was the house which gave it away when my mum became ill. Looking back, it was obvious. She'd always kept the house so clean and tidy. She hadn't worked since she married Dad – she didn't need to. She was proud to be a housewife and her family was her life. She looked after us and made our home a lovely place. Then, all of a sudden, the house began to get messy. My bed still hadn't been made when I got home from school and the cushions in the lounge were all squashed in the corner of the sofa. Mum usually wouldn't stand for this. What was going on?

'Your mum's not feeling very well,' Dad said. 'She just needs some rest.'

'Will she be OK?' I asked.

He looked at me, worry in his face. Even as a thirteen-year-old I could see it. Adults try to hide things from kids but they aren't stupid, they pick up on things far quicker than adults.

'She just needs to rest, love,' he'd say.

Then all of a sudden someone called Granny Moira started picking us up from school. I didn't even know I had a Granny Moira until Mum became ill. She was introduced to us by Dad, who told us she was Mum's mum. A kind-looking woman with a soft grey bob which curled up at the ends, she had bright green eyes like Mum's and wore pale pink lipstick and her perfume stuck to me even after she cuddled me. She started coming to the house a lot after Mum became ill. I asked Dad why we hadn't met her before, to which he replied, 'It's a long story.' Apparently, my grandad had died a few years ago. It was all weird.

Mum started disappearing for days at a time, with no explanation as to where. She'd come back looking less like herself, almost as if the soul had been sucked out of her. Her sparkle was gone. Every time she left the house after that a part of her didn't come back. Even though she was obviously very ill, she still tried to make an effort to look normal for us. She'd wear her usual clothes and brush her hair but it wasn't the same. Her complexion was grey, she was skinnier. I was old enough to know something was drastically wrong, but also naïve enough to think it might get better. I just needed someone to tell me the truth. But nobody did.

It wasn't long before she could no longer walk and she didn't even have the energy to speak. Just watching her attempt to muster the energy to smile broke my heart. This woman – my mum – who used to be so full of life, now crippled with ... something.

Over the next few weeks, she was at the house less and less, until one day she didn't return.

She just left the house one day and didn't come back. It wasn't until after she'd gone we were told it was breast cancer. All I could feel was a crushing weight of missing something – like I couldn't breathe with the very loss of her. And it's so weird when you're a kid and your mum dies. Everyone wants to comfort and protect you, but they fuck it up and say the wrong thing.

'You've got to be a grown-up now, Steph. You're the woman of the house. Look after your daddy,' they'd say, which struck me as weird because I was a child. Shouldn't *he* be looking after me and Ebony? Why did I need to look after an adult?

Why am I always the woman of the house and looking after everyone else?

Finishing off my wine and making my way upstairs, I briefly remember when Leanne came to work for us. Dad hired a nanny just after Mum died as he didn't have a clue how to handle everything. We used to hear him crying at night, shut away in his bedroom. He stayed at work most of the time and left us with Leanne. She was very kind but Ebony and I did not want her in our house. Ebony refused to get dressed for school or eat anything she cooked for us, so in the end, I told Dad to let Leanne go and I'd sort everything; homework, meals, getting us ready for school, getting us to bed.

That's a lot to take on when you're thirteen and grieving for the person you've effectively replaced.

Lying in bed now, cocooned in the duvet and listening to my music, I make a promise to myself to confront what I'm hiding from. That's what my mum would have wanted and I owe it to her to sort this out. As the iPod switches on to the next song, I can't help but think how apt it is, and in a knee-jerk moment of madness I start composing a text to Jamie, linking the song from YouTube to the message.

Shall I do it? Hovering my finger over the send button, the lyrics could not express any better how I feel at this moment. Listening to the bluesy voice of Solomon Burke crooning out 'Don't Give Up On Me', I suddenly have a brainwave. Why have I not thought of this before? Smiling, I delete the message. I've got a better idea.

They say you've got to hit rock bottom before you can start healing again. I know this is true because I've been there before. But I'm my own worst enemy sometimes. I hopped on to this emotional rollercoaster when I was thirteen and never really got off it until I met *him*.

He's the only thing which made me feel secure enough to get off it.

CHAPTER 23

Friday 6 November 2015

Jamie

Helen and I are going out with her work friends tonight. We occasionally organise couples' nights where we get together with assembled friends and their other halves. They're always Helen's friends. She wouldn't really get on with my teacher friends; they're nowhere near trendy enough. I'm not massively into her advertising crew; they're OK but I wouldn't choose to hang out with them unless I had to. They're all a bit, well, into everything I'm not. They buy all kinds of posh foods I've never heard of from Waitrose and go to Pilates three times a week. That kind of thing. I used to make more of an effort with them, but they're all so up their own arses, I can't be bothered now. They take the piss out of me being such a 'working-class hero' but I'd rather be that than a stuck-up wanker.

They're always talking about politics and topical subjects – even Helen gets involved, which is strange, because she's never been that interested. And her accent has also changed a bit, which irritates me: a slight inflection at the end of every sentence. Like a posh telephone voice, but only when she's in their company. I tease her about it, but she gets cross whenever I mention it.

We're going to a dinner party at John and Lucy's. They live in an enormous, minimalistic house, like something off *Grand Designs* in a village about twenty minutes away. After spending a fortune on a taxi to get there, we are greeted by Lucy who ushers us in, giving us a brief tour before we sit down for dinner.

Most of the chat is limited to work-related topics I can't really join in with. But then the topic of conversation turns to the seven-year itch as a result of one of the couples having just celebrated their seven-year anniversary. They then start gossiping about one of their colleagues, a man who's been caught out having an affair with one of the junior writers. The guy, who is fairly senior, was married (no children), and had apparently completely fallen head over heels for this young girl and it was all a bit of a mess, not to mention the scandal of the year.

'I feel so sorry for poor Gemma. Imagine finding out that your husband is a complete bastard!' says Claudia, as I shuffle uncomfortably in my chair. Naturally, everyone agrees, nodding their heads and echoing the words 'Complete bastard!' and 'What a twat!'.

'What the hell was he thinking, anyway? Have you *seen* Gemma?' John says, screwing his face up before

301

shaking his head. 'You wouldn't be playing away if you had *that* at home, would you?'

'Exactly! She's such a gorgeous girl! And a lovely personality too,' Lucy chimes in. 'These fucking men, thinking they can just get away with all sorts.'

'Absolutely!' Helen agrees. 'He just never looked the type to do it, did he? He always seemed so ... nice.'

'Nice?' I ask. Everyone looks at me.

'Oh, Jamie, honestly, he's the most unlikely person to do something like this. And now he's leaving his wife for this slag! After only two years of marriage! Unbelievable!' John outrages.

I don't know if it's the fact I've drunk the best part of two bottles of wine, or that I'm in the company of these judgemental arseholes, but someone needs to play devil's advocate here. Or maybe I'm just fucking stupid because this is far too close to the bone.

'Maybe there's more to it than that, John,' I reply in an irritated tone. Helen shoots me a stern look.

'More to it? Like what? He's in love with her or something? Give me a break! He's in love with her twenty-six-year-old pert tits, more like!' John says and laughs, as does everyone else around the table.

'Well, I think anyone who is prepared to leave their marriage and cause that much pain to their wife has probably thought long and hard about it, actually. You don't do that on a whim,' I say, aware that everyone is staring at me. 'If anything, he's probably quite brave. If they think they're in love, good luck to them. Hope it works out.'

I lean back in my chair and finish off the last gulp of wine from my glass. I'm fed up with people constantly judging others for daring to have feelings they shouldn't. Is this how they'd talk about me if they found out what I'd done? This guy at least had the balls to do something about it. I don't.

Talk about a conversation-killer. The chat awkwardly moves on to monthly sales targets and client demands and Helen was frosty with me for the rest of the meal. Every time I spoke to her all I got was monosyllabic answers and no eye contact. I kept attempting to put my arm around her, only to have her wriggle away. As soon as we got into the taxi home, I couldn't bear it any longer.

'Can you just tell me what I've done wrong this time?' I ask, as she sits as far away from me as she possibly can in the back of the cab.

'Was there really any need for that?' she snaps at me.

'What?' I ask, knowing full well what she's referring to.

'All that stuff about how "brave" it is to have an affair.'

'Helen, that's not what I said and you know it,' I reply. 'Don't twist it.'

'Did you really have to act like such a smart-arse in front of my work friends?'

'Ah, so *that's* why you're really pissed off. I've embarrassed you!' The taxi driver must be cringing at this. Or perhaps he's loving it.

'This is all about you and your precious work friends. As usual,' I say, rather uncharacteristically. There's a sadness in my voice; she can deny it all she wants – she knows I'm right. 'Everything about you lately comes back to your work. You spend more time there, with that lot, than you do at home with me and Seb.'

'I'm earning a living, Jamie,' she snarls back at me.

'Until ten most nights? Drinking with clients? Colleagues? Anyone would think you don't want to come home.'

'You know I have to do that, it's just part of my job. And besides, is it any wonder I don't want to come home when you say shit like that? I'm sorry, Jamie, but when you start standing up for guys who cheat on their wives you come across as a bit of a dick!'

This is very un-Helen-like behaviour but she's had quite a bit to drink so she isn't remotely bothered about speaking like this in front of anyone. She's usually the kind of person who tells you to lower your voice if you so much as have the slightest issue in public.

'I wasn't standing up for him, Helen. I was simply saying things aren't black and white when it comes to marriage or emotions, that's all. And I don't think people should be so judgemental, which your friends quite clearly are. Admit it – you're embarrassed what they think of me and I reflect badly on you.'

'Oh, give it a rest! What absolute bollocks, Jamie!'

'I don't know what's happened to you, Helen. I really don't—'

'You can talk! I don't know what's got into you,' she throws back at me. 'Ever since we moved down here you've been like a different person. Not interested in things, we aren't as close, we never have sex any more ...'

Hearing your wife say these things is mortifying. Not because they're not true (they are), but because it's as though someone notes your most private, intimate details and flaws and points them out. It's so much easier to ignore them and pretend everything is OK. But we both know it's not. And the fact is, I can't say with 100 per cent truth that it's all down to Stephanie either.

Helen and I have been together for so long now, since we were eighteen. We were such different people then. Kids, really. How can you decide who to spend the rest of your life with when you're a teenager? You grow in so many ways. You're not the same people you were nearly twenty years before. So, what's the answer? What do you do? Do you stick it out and work at it because you have so many years under your belt? Or do you cut it loose and restart your life again?

'We've had a tough few years,' I whisper. 'You've been settling into your new job, we've got Sebby, I've been busy in the art department. It's just how things are.'

'Well, it's worrying, Jamie,' she says, ignoring the last part of what I've said. 'Especially when you start defending men having affairs—' She cuts off. Then it dawns on me where she's going with it.

Please don't ask me.

'I'm just going to ask you once, Jamie,' Helen says. And I realise she's obviously wanted to ask me this for some time. I'm completely on the spot and my heart starts to race. I'm very aware of my body language and start randomly thinking about how women are so good at reading such things.

A million things rush through my head before she asks me the question I've been dreading coming for years.

I don't want to lie to her but the truth is just too awful to admit.

'Are you having an affair, Jamie?'

She stares straight at me, looking at me for any indication that I might be lying. *Do I blink too many times? Should I look straight at her? Should I pause before I answer? Will that make it worse?* I feel the weight of her eyes on me, desperate for an answer.

'No,' I say immediately. 'I am not.'

It's the truth. But I also feel like I'm telling a big, fat lie. Being asked this question goes to the core of the betrayal I have inflicted upon our marriage over the past nine years. It's much easier to lie when you're not being directly asked about your infidelity by the one person you've betrayed. Littering your everyday life with little white lies seems much less devilish than one big black lie to your loved one's face, even though it all amounts to the exact same thing. And it's nothing less than I deserve. The pain Helen would feel if she knew the extent of my actions – no, I cannot bear to think of it.

We stare at each other for what seems like minutes. I don't know if it makes me look more or less guilty. The lights of passing headlights and lampposts flash on to her face. She eventually turns her head to look out of the window and spends the rest of the journey like that.

When we arrive home, Helen storms out of the cab, slamming the car door. I apologise to the driver for the drama and he replies 'Good luck, mate', raising his eyebrows. She heads straight upstairs to bed and I pay the babysitter.

Going to the kitchen, I pour myself a glass of whisky. Kicking my shoes off, I take it into the living room and switch the lamps on. All of Sebby's toys are still strewn about the room. Half-built Lego structures, remote-controlled cars and random gadget toys lie dormant, in the same place they were abandoned before bedtime, ready to be activated early morning tomorrow.

I get up and mooch into the study for my art pad and pencil, picking up the post I brought home from school earlier today. Returning to the living room, I sink into the sofa and start doodling, whilst spinning 'Stop Me If You Heard This Before' by The Smiths on the record player I treated myself to for my thirtieth birthday. I love the hissing, crackle sound as you place the needle on to the vinyl – it takes me back to being a child. There are some things you lose with modern technology.

As the pencil glides over the smooth white paper, my mind flashes back to the early days of meeting my wife. We were so different then. She was funny and quirky and I loved her creativity. We'd get lost together in a locker of art, beauty and visual heaven. I adored her passion for it all, which was equal to my own. I hadn't met anyone like that before. I loved her free spirit and wildness. She loved my dedication and ambition. I guess we fell in love with very different people to what we are now. People change.

Remembering I'm waiting for a cheque from a teaching course I did, I start going through my post from school. Most of it is just alumni stuff from Saint Martins. Except the last one.

It's a white A4 envelope marked 'Private'. The school address has been handwritten. I open it and pull out an information pack of some sort.

Dear Mr Dobson

Thank you for your recent application to be considered for the 2016 annual Elaine Carpenter Art Award. Please read the attached information and consider the process carefully. You must submit three pieces of original work to be considered by our panel by 15

March. You will be informed by 1 April as to whether you have been shortlisted as a finalist.

The three finalists will have the opportunity to showcase a selection of their work in an exhibition in Cambridge, in December 2016. This exhibition attracts national press and a number of well-known art critics and collectors from London. Many of our previous finalists have gone on to forge prestigious careers through entry to this competition. Should you become a finalist, your main piece will be an original painting and you are free to interpret the theme as you wish. You must also provide a statement of intent detailing why you chose the subject. The theme this year is 'The Perfection of Beauty in a Broken World'.

The finalists' exhibitions will be assessed by three independent judges from within the relevant field, including the well-known artist David Nelson. The winner of the award will win £10,000 to assist in launching their art career, an internship with David Nelson and can expect significant media exposure.

The panel for the first stage of the process this year consists of:

Michael Carpenter – late husband of Elaine Carpenter and CEO of Carpenter Software Solutions

Hannah Thornton – Lecturer in Art History from Cambridge University

Roxie Cooper

Dominic Jervis – Arts Editor from The Cambridge
Arts Review *newspaper*

I didn't apply for this competition, so I'm momentarily
confused. It's obviously the award Stephanie's dad runs
every year because I recognise her mum and dad's
names. *Michael and Elaine Carpenter.*

Then, it suddenly makes sense. I laugh at the sheer
irony of it, wishing I could tell him why. But I can't, so
I text him this instead:

> *Cal, thanks for the kick up the arse and entering me*
> *for the art award mate! Maybe this is my time to get*
> *my stuff out there!*

I wait for a reply, laughing at Cal – my best friend who
always has my back. He always said I'd know when the
time was right. I'm just not sure this is the right way.
My phone pings seconds later.

> *No idea what you're on about?*

Staring at the text, it dawns on me there's only one
other person who could have sent this to me.

CHAPTER 24

Tuesday 5 April 2016

Stephanie

'Stop at the road!' I yell at Evie, who is hurtling towards the country lane at alarming speed. It's the quietest road in the world, but it doesn't stop me worrying every single time. It only takes a second for someone you love to be taken away from you. One minute they're there, laughing, breathing, chatting and the next they're gone, forever. Matt calls me over-protective. I think I'm cautious. I'd protect my girls with my life.

I love walking the girls to school and nursery. It's my favourite part of the day. I could take them in the car, but it's a fifteen-minute walk and I love chatting to them on the journey. Evie witters about all kinds of random, cute things, pointing out butterflies, bees and birds. She picks daisies and tenderly gives them to Adelaide, giggling as she does. I enjoy watching her skip along in her cute little school uniform, her bright white ankle socks contrasting sharply against her black shiny shoes. The royal-blue tartan pinafore bounces up and down as she proudly walks by her sister in the buggy. She insists on wearing ribbons in her hair every single day. She's such a glamour puss. I think Adelaide will be the same.

As we head down the country lanes and through the bluebell wood, Evie tells me about the Easter egg hunt she's looking forward to at school. I used to love Easter as a kid. Ebony and I would wake up on Easter Sunday to find little baskets hanging on our bedroom doors and then we'd have to search the house for little chocolate eggs and bunnies. In the garden, Mum hung treats from bushes and by the time we woke up it had been transformed into a kaleidoscope of sugar-coated bliss. Our baskets brimmed with goodies.

I'm so pleased it's spring. Daffodils are all over the village now, along with other lovely little flowers I don't know the names of. They're very pretty, though, in fuchsia pink, violet, yellow, bright orange, lime green and red. It's like something out of a TV show: the classic sleepy English village where nothing ever happens. Pristine gardens and perfect lives. Well, they're not, but that's how it looks.

After dropping the kids off, I start to feel that butterflies feeling in my tummy you get when you know something big is going to happen. I've tried putting it out of my mind all morning, concentrating on the kids and getting them ready. But now they've been safely delivered, I can't avoid it any more.

I sprint back home and get changed for work. Except it's not a normal day at work today and I wanted to get ready properly after the girls had gone, so I shower and put my make-up on in peace, when I get back.

I have no idea what to wear. I don't want to look too formal, or as though I've made too much of an effort. But, at the same time, I need to look nice. No, not nice. *Special.*

It's typical that the one day I need to be early for work the traffic is terrible. I'm stuck on the dual carriageway for thirty minutes with no sign of going anywhere. Every cell in my body is shaking with absolute rage.

I call Georgia, our receptionist, to let her know I'll be late.

'OK, Stephanie. They've gone in to the presentation now, but hopefully you'll make it for the coffee afterward,' she says, breezily.

'Yes, yes. Obviously, I'd like to meet them. Please don't let them leave before I get there!' I reply, hoping she can't sense the sheer desperation in my voice. It's now 10.46 a.m.

The lift pings at the second floor and I rush out. I don't run, more of a very quick walk, which suggests I'm very late for something, which I am. It's 11.25 a.m.

I shoot past reception as Georgia deals with a delivery guy, signing for some documents.

Oh God, please let them still be here.

Picking up pace as I walk down the corridor to our main function room, the anxiety returns to my stomach, taking residence there like a lump of concrete. I take a few deep breaths in an attempt to calm down, but I'm walking so fast it has no effect at all. My heels drag on the carpet and I'm convinced that at any second I'll fall over.

Thinking about it, I should have looked through the windows of the room before barging in. I should have stopped for a second to compose myself before clumsily pushing the handle of the door down and exploding in the room at a hundred miles an hour.

But I don't.

Straight in I go – and the first person I see is Jamie Dobson. Not my dad, or the other finalists, or panellists. No, Jamie Dobson.

It takes me a second to catch my breath. He's standing talking to my dad. Three years of no contact, hidden feelings and a big need to apologise (from me) standing between us, and we have to act like we don't know each other.

Turning to face me, a smile sweeps across his face, like he's happy to see me. *Thank God!*

'Ah, Jamie, can I introduce you to my daughter, Stephanie? She's also our marketing director,' Dad says.

Oh my God.

'Steph, this is Jamie.' Dad gestures towards the man I've been hopelessly in love with for the past ten years. 'He's one of our art award finalists.'

And Jamie extends his hand for me to shake. I look at his face when our hands touch, and the familiar sparks of electricity that only he's capable of stirring, fly through me. It's as if he plugs me in to an electrical switchboard.

'Really pleased to meet you,' he says. The eye contact is brief, a second or two at most. Dad then launches into telling Jamie about last year's competition and how successful the winner went on to become. I stand awkwardly, not knowing what to do with my hands. Jamie puts his in his pockets. Our eyes flicker towards each other as Dad talks, and we smile. I don't think either of us are listening.

He looks thinner than he did last time I saw him, but not in a bad way. Leaner, like he's been going to the gym. His hair is still long and untamed in that way I always adored, combed back just enough to be off his face, but still has a soft look about it.

I need to get him on his own without it looking suspicious.

'Actually, Jamie, I need some more details off you before you leave, if you wouldn't mind? Don't leave without seeing me first,' I say, casually, in front of Dad.

Jamie nods. 'Yes, of course.'

I smile at both of them before heading off to meet the other finalists, constantly aware that Jamie is watching me in the room. I can feel his eyes on me wherever I am.

After thirty minutes I simply can't take any more and have to interrupt him chatting to one of the other finalists.

'Jamie, would you mind nipping to my office, please? I just need you to fill some forms in,' I ask, a little louder than I need to.

'Sure, no problem,' he replies.

Jamie shakes hands with everyone in the function room as they all say goodbye. I'm not in the slightest bit surprised to see that he's charmed them all already. I hope that bodes well for him in the final.

Leaving the room, we walk down the corridor in silence, side by side, closer than we would if we were business associates. Our arms occasionally brush against each other. We don't look at each other when it happens. Reaching the lift area, I press the button and the big arrow illuminates red as the machinery can be heard clunking into action.

'It's two floors up,' I explain. 'I'm not running up the stairs in these heels.'

In the ten seconds or so it takes for the lift to arrive, we look around awkwardly. I just want to stare at his face because I've missed it so very much over the past three years.

The lift pings and the doors open. I walk in and Jamie follows behind me. I press two and after a few seconds, the doors shut.

The lift clanks as it pushes through the floors. We stand not more than a couple of feet from each other, not speaking. I don't know what to do or say. Jamie looks at me and doesn't break my gaze. It's not an angry face, more like he's just looking at me because he hasn't seen me for so long – I can relate to that.

I'm relieved when the lift pings.

The one thing I insisted on when I started working for Dad is that I had a nice office. I am not one of these people who can concentrate in a bland, grey space. I need to put my own stamp on it, while retaining professionalism, obviously. So I have artwork on the walls, a sofa in the corner and strategically-placed lamps. I also have photos of the girls in frames on my desk. I only work part-time, but I still like to see them when I'm here.

Jamie looks around my office as I close the door. I'd love to hug him, but it doesn't feel right … yet. I sit on the sofa and he joins me. He's not too close and I don't think either of us know how this is going to go. Sitting on the edge of the sofa, bolt upright, I have no idea where to even start. It should be me.

A huge smile bursts on to his face. 'It's fucking amazing to see you, Steph!'

'I thought you hated me,' I whisper, doing a cringe face.

'I could never hate you,' he replies, immediately.

'I'm so, so sorry for that night,' I blurt out. 'Everything I said was completely uncalled for.'

'Some of it was. Some of it, I needed to hear,' he admits. 'I think it was probably building up for a while, for both of us.'

317

'I didn't know how you'd respond to me sending the letter about the competition to your school. After that day I saw you, I just had to contact you.'

'I was pleased you reached out to me. That you believed in me. You've always done that. That is ...' He trails off.

'What?'

'Look, I don't mean to sound ungrateful for this opportunity, but I just need to know. Given that it's you – your dad. Well, I'm so thrilled to get into the final but I don't want any part of this if you'll fix it for me to win,' he says, uncomfortably.

'No, absolutely not,' I assure him. 'I have no influence whatsoever over who is selected to be a finalist, Jamie, or who wins. I sent you the application form, but anyone can get them. That was it. I'm purely the marketing girl. I deal with the publicity around it, that's all.'

It's important he believes me, because it's true. All I ever wanted was for him to believe in himself.

'I thought that would be the case, I just wanted to make sure.'

'This is your chance, Jamie. Your chance to show everyone how talented you are. You're so close now! I've seen the successes finalists and winners have had with this competition. I've seen what you're capable of and you have the talent to make it. What are you going to do for your exhibition? Have you decided on a subject yet?' I'm so giddy and excited for him.

'I've only just started to think about it, not decided on anything yet. The exhibition isn't until December so I have plenty of time.'

I nod, trying to calm myself down.

'So,' I change the subject. 'How is ... everything else?'

'Yeah, good. The same, really. Seb is six next month and he's such a little rascal, keeps us busy.'

'I can imagine. Have you had any more?' I ask. I know I'm being nosy but I can't help myself.

'No. And I don't think we will,' Jamie says, gazing down at the floor. 'Well, I'd like another one but Helen wants to concentrate on her career, doesn't want any more. Especially given that she's doing so well, heading up the London office. Her choice.' He shrugs.

I do a half-hearted smile. I bet Jamie is such a great hands-on dad.

'And what about you?' he asks.

'Oh, another girl! Evie is four, Adelaide is two.' I smile as I tell him.

'Bet they both look like you,' he says.

'They do. I didn't think I'd have any more. But after ...' I pause, looking at my lap for a moment. 'After you, I went through a bit of a hard time. I thought maybe I should try and make things work with Matt and then I had another baby ...'

Jamie reaches out for my hand, which I take hold of and squeeze.

'My world just went into a spin. I spiralled for a bit. But, actually, Adelaide saved me in a lot of ways,' I say and smile. 'She gave me something to focus on. I love my girls, I reached out to you with this competition, I'm back in therapy – I'm going through massive, healthy life changes at the moment.'

'It sounds like it! Soooo,' he asks, tentatively, 'why have you contacted me now?'

I take a deep breath, ready to deliver the speech I've been practising for weeks.

'I've done a lot of thinking in the past few months. Well, years, really. One thing I know is that I need you in my life. It's better when you're in it. And I know I can't have you in the way I want you. I've finally accepted that now,' I say.

'But—'

'No, please,' I interrupt, placing my hand on his knee. 'I need to finish this. I've rehearsed it enough times and it's hard enough already.'

He reluctantly remains quiet, allowing me to finish.

'For the longest time, I held on to that glimmer of hope that you'd finally realise what we had was so special, so beautiful, so amazing, you'd wake up one day and realise you needed it – me – more than your wife. The last few years have made me see that's never going to happen. I suppose I've grown up and become less selfish. I know you've struggled with the guilt, more so than me if we're being honest. And if the only way I can have you in my life is as a friend, then so be it.'

'Is it even possible? Us being friends? Proper friends?' he asks. 'I thought you said we could never be friends?'

'That's what I always thought. Honestly, I did,' I admit, shaking my head. 'But maybe you're right about all this fate stuff.'

'What do you mean?' he says, confused.

'It's been ten years, Jamie. How many times have we tried to stop seeing each other?'

'I've lost count.'

'Every time we try to move away from each other, something drags us back together. I didn't expect to ever see you again after that scene at Heathwood Hall, let alone pop up behind me in an art gallery in the remote countryside like a bloody ghost.'

He laughs, looking around the room.

'Yes, sorry about that. Was a difficult situation.'

'It was. But it happened. And it shook me up. I'm trying to be a better person and I realised I couldn't do that without sorting out the one thing which mattered most to me. You.'

Jamie reaches over and hugs me. It's the kind of cuddle you give a friend: not too close, not too long.

'The alternative – not seeing you – was too hard. So, I'll have to make it work. *We* can make it work.'

He nods. 'Yes, we can. I missed you terribly. My world was certainly duller without you in it. It'll be nice to have you back. I've missed your annual news round-ups.'

'Well, you can have an extra dose next time!' I laugh. 'Listen, I'd better get you back to my dad before he thinks I've stolen you.'

I walk him back to the lift and as it pings open, he walks in alone and stands facing me.

For the past ten years, every time I've said goodbye to him, it felt like my world was crushing down on me. Like the ground just fell away and I started falling to the centre of the earth. I'd be suffocated with sadness just watching him drive away from me, every single time.

But this time, it's different. This is the first time I'm smiling as he walks away from me, because something has changed. I'm not sure why, or what, or how. But it has.

As I walk back into my office, I see my mobile make the tri-chime it does when I receive a text message. I pick it up to see who it's from but it's from an unknown number.

I deleted Jamie's number the night of our row so I wouldn't be tempted to contact him again, and his name doesn't come up – but I know it's from him. Opening up the message, it simply says:

That second verse ... Xx

The link to YouTube takes me to Prince singing 'Purple Rain'. The opening twang of his guitar, the distinctive chords, a second verse which could have been written for us. I listen to the way his delectable voice swells and the eye-watering guitar solo comes in. Sitting on the sofa where we'd been only moments before, I'm drowned with goosebumps. By the time the time Prince is roaring those final notes out, I'm smiling and I feel weirdly happy.

There is absolutely nothing I can do about this situation. It's not about whether he's happy enough with his wife or if he loves me enough. It's far more complicated than that; it always has been with us.

I watch it until the end, turn it off, and get on with my day.

CHAPTER 25

Saturday 20 August 2016

Jamie

The Perfection of Beauty in a Broken World.

That's the theme for the art competition.

I've thought long and hard about it. Paintings aren't just pictures, they really do speak a thousand words and I communicate so much better through my art than with words. I always have done. It's important to get this right.

I'm very aware who will be seeing this piece – critics and influential artists who could start my career if they're impressed with it. This is my chance to show them all who I am and what I can do. I've always had a unique style. I'm not what people would describe as a classical fine artist. I mean, I can do all that, but my own personal style is more colourful, bold and daring. That is what this portrait is going to be. Throughout my life I've held back and been safe with my art in public, saving my personal style for myself. Not any more. It's now or never.

She gave me the courage to do that.

But I sometimes think I must be absolutely mad doing this. All it will take is the wrong person to see it, at the wrong time, and I'm absolutely screwed.

Helen sees it as my hobby, just a little competition I've entered. She doesn't understand this is potentially my big break. She knows I have to produce a key piece and suggested a stand-out modern landscape. I listened to her suggestion but kindly rejected it, guilt swelling. There's only one piece I can do and have any chance of winning with. It's a portrait – and I know exactly of whom.

Last month, Helen started talking about going on holiday next year.

'I'll have to see what happens with this competition before booking anything,' I said

'What do you mean?' she replied, looking confused.

'Well, part of the prize is an internship,' I tell her. 'I'd have to give up my job and go to London every day. The money is minimal and I wouldn't be able to just ask for time off for a holiday.'

She looked at me like I was crazy for a second.

'Jamie, you have a child to support and house to pay for. I appreciate you want to fulfil your dream, but I don't think this is the way to do it.'

I remember, in that moment, feeling that I'd never heard anything so selfish.

'Helen, I've supported you throughout your career since we've been together. That's almost twenty years.

I've supported every decision you've made, often to my own detriment. I think I'm owed something,' I told her. 'And besides, I might not even win.'

'How are we supposed to survive, financially, if you win?'

'We'd manage. Fewer luxuries, no holidays for a few years, cut down on things we don't need,' I pointed out. 'I want this so much, Helen.'

She was tidying the living room and started throwing toys into Seb's toy box with more force than was necessary.

'What made you apply for it now anyway?' she asked, without looking at me.

'I guess I just realised I was good enough,' I said.

She used to love the bohemian artist in me. I used to love her feisty nature. I suppose the things you're initially attracted to are the things you eventually end up disliking about each other.

We are completely different people now. She has a new group of friends from work, and it's obvious she'd prefer to spend time with them than with me. She goes out with them every Friday after work, getting back in the early hours. I hear her staggering in, kicking her shoes off in the hall then going into the kitchen for a pint of water and some food. We never do anything together. What would we even talk about? It's got to come to a head at some point, and we both know this, but neither of us wants to bring it up. It's just too much trauma.

And I take responsibility for that. Did we ever stand a chance, when Stephanie was in my life? No. But I do think Helen has changed too. The Helen of now would not have married the Jamie I am today; we are simply too different and want different things in life. People change a lot in twenty years together. The one thing we are agreed on, however, is the love we feel for our son. And that's the one thing keeping us together. Yes, that old cliché.

I often wonder how different things would have been if I'd been brave enough earlier on. If I'd left Helen and been honest with Stephanie – and myself – about how I'd felt. It would have been painful for us, yes – but we'd have all moved on. This isn't a good way to live. Now we're both miserable, waiting for the other to end it.

Putting things into words is a nightmare for me. Especially when I have to minutely analyse my own work. I'm an artist, not a writer. If I was any good with words I wouldn't have to paint. It's how I make sense of the world.

I waited until the summer holidays were in full swing before I started the painting. I need to properly dedicate my time to such things without any distractions, so even thinking about starting it while I was still teaching was a no-go. Don't get me wrong, I'm not one of these arty, 'needing to be in the zone' people in order to create. If a job needs doing, I'll get it done. But I need to be free of distraction and completely unrushed. I identified days when I had a set amount of time to myself, usually when Helen was taking Seb to her parents for the night, or for a day out meeting friends with all the kids. The house needed to be quiet so I could go into the garage and get started.

I've finished the piece and I'm happy with it. Really happy. I was anxious to start it, staring nervously at the canvas for quite some time before I applied the first smear of paint, a pale-grey shade which would form the background. As the oil moved around the canvas, it began to take shape. That's what I love about using oil paint – the fluidity. The lengthy drying times means it can be manipulated over a longer period. I thought it looked crap for ages, as usual. Portraits don't tend to look good until you start adding the finer detail. It helps to leave it for a week or two and come back to it with a fresh pair of eyes. I wanted lots of rich textures and multi-layers – *just like the subject matter*. Portraits are so much more interesting if they invite people in to look at them more closely – the finer detail, beyond the surface. I used a brush and palette knife, bringing out the texture of the paint, moving some of it around with my fingers on parts of the face, bringing it to life. I wanted it to have a personal feel, and in order to do that you have to get in close, touch it, caress the canvas.

All artists have their quirks and what works for them. Some work better in silence – I work best listening to old-skool hip-hop blasting out on the stereo. I'll have two coffees before I start but then I have to switch to water or I start throwing crazy things on the canvas and it's best not to spend more than a few hours on it at a time. The last thing you want is to become tired or frustrated and do something daft you can't erase. After five sessions, the strokes became fewer; finer and more delicate. It was like seeing a person slowly coming to life, imprinting a soul on to the canvas.

Standing back, once it was complete, I admired it from all angles. I don't think I've ever been so pleased with a piece before. It's my finest work but also the hardest thing I've ever had to create.

And now I have to write this bloody statement. It's obviously massively important to get it right. Art folk place significance on these things.

Helen takes Seb away for the weekend to her parents' house so I can work on it. Standing in the hallway as the sun streams in through the front door, Sebby tells me he'll miss me. 'I'll miss you too, Sebstar!' Helen stands a few feet away from me, watching. I love it when he wraps his little legs around my waist: he reminds me of a baby monkey.

'We'll be back tomorrow at about five,' Helen says, walking out the door. 'Come on, Seb!'

He leaps out after his mum. How has it come to this?

Shuffling into the lounge, I pick up the notepad and pen to tackle this stupid thing. The limit is five hundred words.

Five hundred words! I think I'll struggle to get fifty. I stare at the paper, expecting something to come. Well, that's a lie, actually. I don't expect anything to come.

But maybe I'm reading too much into it. *Just say something. Anything.*

Placing the tip of the pen on the paper, I close my eyes and clear my mind. Thirty seconds or so pass. Nothing. I meander to the kitchen and grab a chilled beer from the fridge. That's got to help. It hisses as I pop the top off and take a swig. I walk back into the lounge and the pad and pen taunt me once more.

Just say what you think.

No, you can't say what you think. That's the whole fucking point.

How the fuck do you write the unwritable, though?

Oooh, that's not bad, actually. Well, without the 'fuck' in it, obviously. I could start it like that. I want to keep it as unemotional as possible. The painting speaks for itself because I put all of myself into it so I can't go overboard with this statement. Not that I could even if I wanted to. I'd sound ridiculous. As my mind drifts off, I realise I've started doodling in the top right-hand corner of the page. Ripping the piece of paper from the pad, I scrunch it up and throw it to the other side of the room.

Two hours, three bottles of beer and a football match later, I'm no further forward.

I really want to nail it this weekend while the painting is fresh in my mind and I have the house to myself. I don't think I'd be able to concentrate if Helen and Seb were here. Christ, though, it's difficult.

I scan the sandy-coloured carpet of our lounge floor, which is littered with balls of scrunched-up paper. Not much progress has been made today. I'm trying to sound clever and arty. I should just be basic and simple. But I fluctuate between trying to give them what they want to hear – which sounds utterly ridiculous – and sounding like a toddler: equally as daft. There is no in-between.

Right.

I'm doing it.

'The power and freedom of the brushstrokes evoke a passion within the subject's features …'

I'm unable to write any more because I'm laughing so much. I mean, this is *so* not me! I'm sure other artists buy into all this but I just can't get away with it. I'm too northern, perhaps?

Maybe I should just keep it more technical. Talk about the actual painting and keep all the arty bollocks out of it. Yep.

'The layers of texture on the canvas using brushstrokes and fingertips gives the painting a wonderfully intimate tangibility …'

Christ!

Why is it so hard to talk about a picture? It's a fucking painting.

I decide to call Cal for advice. He's done loads of these things and I'm hoping he will inspire me.

331

'Mate! I'm struggling with this statement,' I sigh, rubbing my forehead.

'Yeah, they're the worst. Fine line between giving them what they want and not sounding like a dick.'

I laugh and say, 'It's harder work than the painting!'

'Look, go back to basics. What are your immediate thoughts when you look at it? What do you feel? What do you see? Go back to your roots and take it from there. Don't overthink it.'

'You're right. Christ, I hate this shit.'

'And don't use any words like majestically or effervescent – you'll sound like a twat. Just keep it real.'

He's right. I need to look at it as I'm writing, even though I remember every brushstroke I did to create it, every time I used my fingers to spread the paint out on the canvas. I need some inspiration.

Flicking the lights on in the garage, I walk over to the competition piece. I take the cover sheet off and look at it. I can't help but smile. There's so much I could say. The words rattle around my head, but I can't put them into any kind of coherent order. Taking a few steps back, I admire it from various different angles.

Just write what you see.

The eyes.

They're the first things that you see. They immediately strike you down, without warning, blinding you with their intensity. I grab my pen and paper and scribble *'eyes that strike you down'*. Sitting on the battered old chair in the corner of the studio, I scan the painting, searching for words to describe it.

The mouth.

Voluptuous. Exciting.

But there's more behind it. There's more behind the entire thing. And that's why I can't put it into words. Because how do you write perfection? How do you explain it? It's not finite – just like the painting. I wanted it to have an unfinished, incomplete feel about it; to show that it was still evolving, growing, improving as the days, weeks and months went by ... *just like her.*

And then it hits me.

Taking a deep breath, I place the nib of the pen to the left-hand corner of a new page. I've been coming at this from the wrong angle, approaching it from the wrong direction. I've been trying far too hard. All I have to do is say it how it is ...

Several hours later, I'm sitting in the garden with a beer. The low, early evening sun creates a beautiful orange glow all across the sky.

I read over the statement I've perfected over the afternoon.

Nine sentences.

I've given it everything I have and I'm so happy with it. Reaching for my iPhone out of my shorts pocket, I compose and send a message to Steph.

Roxie Cooper

Thank you for believing in me. Just wanted to say I appreciate that. J x

Less than two minutes later, my phone pings. The reply makes me smile so hard. The end to a great day.

Always will. x

CHAPTER 26

Saturday 8 October 2016

Stephanie

'What's this?' he asks, taking the gift I've just given to him. He looks at it, wrapped in deep purple paper with silhouettes of spindly trees on. I chose it because it reminded me of autumn – our favourite season.

'Well, you're always illuminating my life with art,' I say. 'So, I thought I'd give you something from my world. Just open it. It won't bite!'

He delicately peels the paper back, slowly removing the Sellotape so as not to ruin the pattern. Pulling the book out, he glances at me quizzically.

'*Wuthering Heights*?' he asks.

'Yes,' I confirm. 'Have you read it?'

'I haven't!' he says, skimming through the pages. 'Why this book?'

'It's my favourite novel. I'll take your doomed lovers at the Tate and raise you Cathy and Heathcliff.'

'Is that why you love it?' he says, smiling.

'It's a beautiful love story about two very fiery, passionate people who can be dicks at times,' I say, raising my eyebrows. 'Give it a read.'

It was a good way to break the ice. We're not meeting at Heathwood Hall today. This is the new era and we're meeting at a beautiful country pub called the Haywood Arms in a village equidistant between us. We meet for lunch ... as friends.

'Oh God! What happens to them in the end?' he asks, panicked.

'You'll have to read it and find out, won't ya?' I tease, taking a drink of my Diet Coke.

It feels strange and yet completely normal to be in his presence again. We sit opposite each other, a contrast to previous occasions when we'd sit side by side. He wears a navy-blue sweater which matches his eyes.

'I'm glad we could, you know, do this,' I tell him.

'Me too. I didn't like being away from you,' he says. 'October was always hard when I knew I wouldn't be seeing you.'

Nodding in agreement, I pick up the lunch menus and hand one to him.

'How are things? At home?' I ask.

'Oh, erm, you know. Fine,' he says, burying his head into the menu.

'Good. I think I'll have the shepherd's pie,' I say, running my finger over the menu. 'It sounds delicious.'

'You're not wearing your wedding ring,' Jamie states, as his eyes flicker between my face and left hand.

I instinctively remove it from view by crossing my arms, which is ridiculous as he's already noticed.

'I haven't worn it for a few months now,' I tell him, unsure what his reaction will be.

'OK,' he replies. 'So … are you all right?'

I nod my head quickly. I hadn't really wanted to get into all this. I don't wear my ring as a matter of course now.

'Look, I'm absolutely fine,' I tell him. 'More than fine.'

Jamie looks at me, guarded. He knows there's something I'm not telling him.

'I'm going to leave Matt,' I blurt out.

'What?' he says, loudly, throwing the menu down on the table. The gesture, along with his face, makes me laugh, nervously.

'I haven't been happy with him for a very long time,' I say, tossing my hair out of my face. 'I don't want to waste my life with someone I don't want to be with. I need to be with someone who loves me.'

'Bloody hell!' he says, leaning back in his chair. 'Well, good for you.'

'Thanks,' I say and smile. 'Check me out, getting all my shit together. It's about time I injected some actual happiness into my life for the sake of my girls if nothing else. I owe it to them.'

'Yes, you do,' he says. 'And you're an amazing person, you deserve to be with someone who knows this and fully appreciates you.'

'Yes, I do.'

'Does Matt know yet?' he asks.

'No, not yet. I need to get it straight in my own head before I go full-on war with him, because he's going to fight me on everything,' I explain. 'I need to be completely prepared. It's hard with the girls but Dad and Ebony know I'm not entirely happy. I'll get the kids away for the night and talk to him.'

Jamie nods. 'Good plan. Just look after yourself.'

'So,' I say excitedly, not wanting to dwell on the subject, 'have you decided what you're going to do for your main piece in the art competition?'

'I've got some ideas, not decided on anything yet.'

'Very pretentious, isn't it? "The Perfection of Beauty in a Broken World"' I say, putting on an art critic voice.

'Very.' He laughs, then sits back in his chair and fiddles with his cutlery. I immediately feel bad in case he feels I was mocking it.

'How does the actual evening usually work? I'm stressing about it already,' he confesses. I've never seen him nervous before, but he does look it now.

'Well, all three candidates have an art space each and present their work to the judges and the press,' I explain.

'And the judges are entirely independent to the company? So, do you know them?'

'Well, we change them every year to keep it fresh and new. I've met them once but I've deliberately kept away from them because I know you feel uncomfortable about any kind of influence I might have,' I say in an attempt to reassure him.

'Look, I know this sounds ungrateful after everything you've done,' he says, gazing down at his food, 'but, I can't have you there on the gala evening. I'll obviously be there with Helen.'

'I know. I've thought of this, obviously,' I tell him. 'I'm OK with that. This is your night and I want you to feel as comfortable as you can.'

I see the massive relief in his face. That whole conversation made him so tense – I have no idea why.

'Christ, Matt won't be there, will he? I don't fancy bumping into him.' He laughs nervously.

'No way.' I shake my head. 'Matt hates the art award evening. You couldn't pay him enough to turn up. It bores him to tears.'

'Your dad seems lovely, a really nice guy,' Jamie says. 'He's not going to be at the gala though, is he? I read about how he's going to be in America on business that week or something?'

'Yes, he's usually a judge at the event but this year it's not possible. He's got to attend a conference in Portland which he's gutted about, but it's completely unavoidable. The company has been losing business lately so it's really important he goes.'

'Ah, really? Nothing to worry about, I hope?' he asks.

'I hope not. Quite a few customers have chosen not to renew their contracts with us, which has been a huge blow. They've taken their business elsewhere, which has really upset Dad. It's all very odd,' I say, frowning at him. 'To be honest, he shouldn't really be running the art award this year but he insisted on it because he's never *not* done it since Mum died. He felt it was important.'

'He sounds like a great man.' Jamie smiles.

'He is,' I say proudly. 'But, actually, the fact he won't be there should reassure you that the whole process is impartial. You'll know that – if you do win – you'll do so fair and square.'

'I can't even imagine that I'll win. I'm genuinely just honoured to get this far, that someone thinks I'm good enough to get through to the final. Well, not just anyone – experts in the field. You know …'

'I do know, yes!' I smile. I'm so happy for him. It's such a confidence boost. 'And it would kick-start your career. Even if you don't win, something might come from it.'

'I'm very excited either way,' he says, beaming. 'Thank you so much.'

'For what?'

'Coming back to me.'

I smile. 'Thanks for having me back.'

Bloody hell. This guy. This beautiful relationship – because that's what it is. It may no longer be an affair, but Jamie Dobson is still the love of my life.

I drive straight to Ebony's house and pick the girls up, before going home.

I've become used to this feeling now; a sick, swirling, anxious feeling in my gut. Knowing I'm going back there, to *him*. What kind of mood will he be in? What will I have done wrong now? How have I ended up here?

By the time we get home, Matt is there and in an absolutely foul mood. The girls run into the house, excited to see him, and burst straight into the study where Matt is on the phone. I hear him yelling at them to get out and they run straight to me, wrapping their arms around my legs for comfort, and crying. Bending down to hug them both, their little wet, hot cheeks stick to mine. Taking them to the kitchen I settle them by popping *Peppa Pig* on the TV. They're giggling within seconds.

I walk into the study where Matt is sitting at his desk.

'Was there any need for that? You really upset them.' He's leaning over the desk poring over some papers which he very quickly snatches from my sight as soon as I speak.

'Can't you knock?'

'I'm not knocking on a door in my own house. This isn't a school,' I reply, folding my arms.

'Well, I pay most of the bills.'

'And who pays your salary? My dad.'

'What's that supposed to mean?' he snarls at me.

'Nothing. I'm just not being told what to do in my own house,'

'Well, don't be so fucking difficult then, Stephanie! Jesus Christ! You push me and push me *all* the time,' he yells.

'No I don't.'

'Yes, you do,' he says, as if I'm a child. 'And then I snap and you make out like it's my fault. But you always drive me to it. I never look for trouble, but you always stir it up.'

'Oh, here we go.' I laugh, sarcastically. 'My favourite game – What Else Is Stephanie's Fault?'

'It always is,' he interrupts.

'I'm taking the girls out. I don't want them around you,' I say, blinking back tears.

'Good,' he says. 'Can't hear myself think when they're screeching around the house.'

We walk around the park for hours, kicking hardened brown autumn leaves. Evie holds Adelaide's hand all the way around and there's hardly any fighting (they're getting terrible for that now). Walking through the woods with them is so much fun; picking up sticks and seeing how far we can throw them, covering ourselves in golden leaves and squelching in mud in our wellies. They're exhausted by the time we get back.

I pop them to bed and climb into my own, lying awake for ages.

Thinking.

People say all the time: 'Why don't you leave if you're that unhappy?' But it's not so simple when you have kids. It's almost like you need something to force you into doing it. People rarely leave a situation unless they absolutely have to. I wish I could talk to my mum about all this. But, then again, I'm not even sure I would. I'd be so ashamed. What would she think of me? Doing this, for so long. A failed marriage with two kids. I've made such a mess of absolutely everything.

Why are you content to only be happy one weekend a year?

My phone lights up: a message from Jamie. I didn't expect one of these after today. I guess old habits die hard. A text with a YouTube link:

Never gonna stop sending these. Just 'Thinking Out Loud'... *X*

I fell in love with this song when I saw the video. I remember actually crying, as I did. I think it was a mixture of the song, the video and how happy and in love Ed Sheeran and the dancer looked – which is ridiculous, because they're just acting. But it got to me and I've adored it ever since.

That's what I want. *That*. Everything in this song. I want kisses under stars, growing old with someone I absolutely love, adoring every inch of them. All the time.

I compose a message back simply saying:

Enjoy the book. X

Attached is the YouTube link to Kate Bush's *Wuthering Heights*, in which she dances about like a beautiful white enchantress. I watch it through to the end myself, before getting out of bed and putting my dressing gown on. I check on the girls in their rooms and they're out for the count. Evie's leg hangs out the side of the bed so I tuck it back in, underneath her Princess Elsa duvet cover.

Downstairs, I calmly open the lounge door where Matt is watching a film. He's slouched on the sofa, one hand behind his neck. He doesn't look at me when I come in.

'Matt,' I tell him. 'I'm leaving you ...'

CHAPTER 27

Wednesday 16 November 2016

Stephanie

This is the session I've been waiting for with Jane. Arriving fifteen minutes early for the appointment, I sit in the waiting room, eager to get in there and spill all of my news. As November peaks and December is about to spring up from nowhere, it seems like 2016 is determined to go out with a bang.

'Start at the beginning, let's unpack it,' Jane says, typically.

'I told him I wanted a divorce and he agreed to it. Just like that. No rowing. It was very calm, like releasing a pressure valve for both of us, I think.'

'Good for you,' she says. 'A very brave thing to do. And it sounds like you handled it with grace and maturity.'

It didn't feel like it at the time. I sat cross-legged on the sofa opposite him, the TV on mute. My heart galloped and my body shook uncontrollably. I always knew the day would come, but I thought it would be more explosive. I didn't want an argument, there was no point.

We just didn't work any more. I'm not sure we ever did.

But something had been bugging me about Matt's strange behaviour in the past few months – lots of meetings in the work diary which didn't add up to where he was, acting very secretively at home and that kind of thing. So I did some digging. I genuinely expected to find out he was having an affair and, to be honest, I couldn't blame him.

The truth was far worse.

We'd agreed that we'd stay in the house for a few weeks until we told the girls. So, I waited until one day when he was away on a business trip to have a snoop in his study. I checked though his personal diary and one thing kept coming up: golf days with a guy called Simon Grayson. Now, everyone in our industry knows Grayson – he's a dodgy character, not to be trusted.

But the most disturbing thing about this information was that Simon Grayson is the Managing Director of our rival company. I wasn't aware that Matt even knew him and he'd certainly never worked with him – so what was he up to? Matt's good at his job, but nowhere near senior enough to be headhunted by a top dog. And then it all made sense.

How Carpenter Software Solutions had been losing business to our rivals for the last year or so.

'Matt had been selling details of our price list to our main competitors,' I tell Jane, the anger in my stomach whipping up as the words left my mouth.

The first Matt knew he'd been caught out was when he was called into a board meeting with all the shareholders – and me. With his bank statements and personal diary placed in front of him, he looked straight at me, knowing I they could only have come from me. I have never seen anyone look more furious.

'I suppose you're happy now?' he growled, walking into my office after he'd been sacked.

'No, Matt. Just sad,' I replied, honestly. 'But I think we're done now, on all fronts.'

'Yes, we are. I want you, and your mental family, out of my life for good.'

Tears welled in my eyes, which I didn't want him to see. Inhaling deeply to compose myself, I walked around to the front of my desk, leaning on it to face him.

'Why, Matt? Just tell me why? What did you need that you didn't have?'

He stood a few feet away from me in the navy-blue suit I've always loved him in. The red tie looked so lovely against it. His blond hair had darkened in recent years, but he's still got that Scandinavian look about him.

'You, Stephanie,' he said, without an ounce of hesitation. 'We've been together fourteen years and you've never let me in. You always held yourself back. Steph, the Ice Queen. Well, look where it got you—'

Roxie Cooper

'Oh, come on, Matt,' I interrupted. 'All you ever wanted was the girl who existed when she was twenty-two. There's a reason you haven't seen her for all these years, and that's because she's dead. For good reason. She was a mess and I don't want her back.'

'At least she talked to me!' he cried, in exasperation. 'She shared stuff with me.'

'Matt, we were a fun relationship which served us both well at the time but we should not have stayed together for this long. We haven't grown together. We brought each other down.'

'Don't even start to put this on me,' he snarled. 'I put everything into this marriage. It could have worked but nothing was ever perfect enough for poor Steph, the perpetual victim.'

He was right in one sense, yet so very wrong in others. But none of it mattered. Not any more.

'We both married the wrong person, Matt. I learned more about myself and what I do and don't want from life from being with you, than I ever will with therapy.'

'Good grief!' Jane exclaims now, wide-eyed with all this drama. 'This is significant news. How do you feel about it?'

'Free. Wonderful. Happy … I think.'

'So: where does this leave you with Jamie?' she asks.

I look at her, confused, knitting my eyebrows together.

'Why would me and Matt getting divorced make any difference to me and Jamie?'

348

'Well, it means you're free now ...'

'But he's not.' I point out the obvious.

'No,' she says. 'But regardless of whether it's Jamie or someone else ... you can finally go out there and find happiness. It may not happen for a while, but you deserve to be in a relationship where you're happy all the time, not just one weekend a year.'

Whenever Jane gets on to this topic, I get edgy. I don't like it.

It's like an albatross around my neck, weighing me down. I know she's always going on about it and there's a reason for it, but I don't want to know, quite frankly.

'Well, I'm happy with the situation with Jamie at the moment. It suits me perfectly,' I lie.

'No, it doesn't,' she says. 'You meet up with a man you're in love with, masquerading as friends. You're not happy with that at all.'

I look at her, stubbornly, in the same way a toddler glares at her mother when she's told she can't have a doll in a toy shop. It's pointless, because Jane always wins these stand-offs.

'What do you think your mum would say about that if she was here?' she asks, completely out of the blue.

'I'd prefer to keep my mum out of this, if you don't mind!'

'Well, yes, I do mind. Because she's the key to all of this – your marriage, for example,' she says, very matter-of-fact.

'What?'

'You haven't worked this out yet?'

I look at her with a blank expression. She's completely lost me now.

'What the hell has my mum got to do with my relationship with Matt?'

'Not just Matt, Jamie too,' she says in a way which suggests it's so obvious even a toddler could work this out.

'Jane, I know you're good at what you do, but I really think you're clutching at straws with this one.'

'It's classic textbook, actually. More common than you think. Even Matt worked it out.'

'What?'

'He's absolutely right in what he said.'

'You're agreeing with Matt now?'

Either Jane is on crack or she's about to sort my entire life out, because my head is spinning.

'Stephanie,' she says, very calmly. 'When your mum died you were a toddler and it ripped away the core of unconditional love you had experienced in your life up until that point. Your dad was badly grief-stricken and he disconnected from you. So, throughout your teenage, formative years, and beyond, you had a huge emotional void that wasn't being filled.'

'So?' I ask, raising my eyebrows.

'You don't think you're worthy of real love.'

My God, it's raw to hear the words out loud, coming from someone else.

'You don't know *how* to be loved,' she goes on. 'And even if you did, you wouldn't allow it because the thought of allowing yourself to be emotionally intimate with someone is too terrifying for you to contemplate.'

'Why is it terrifying?' I ask her, folding my arms tightly round myself. My eyes feel heavy and the stinging sensation swells at the front. I do everything I can to try and hold the tears back.

'Because they might see the real you, and *that* terrifies you,' she says softly, as if it will lessen the blow. 'Matt never saw the real you and he was with you for fourteen years. You never let him.'

Nausea rises up into my throat. My breathing becomes deeper. This woman is running around my mind and saying all of my thoughts out loud and I don't like it one little bit.

'Well, that's not right, because how do you explain my relationship with Jamie if that's the case?' I ask, defensively, even though I know she'll have an answer for it.

'Jamie is married,' she says and smiles. 'Unavailable. He is safe – you can be intimate with him but not give yourself to him fully – because that would be far too scary. To a large extent, Jamie provides you with the kind of nurturing, unconditional love you're missing from your mum. There's no doubt you have a deep, incredible connection and love for him but you allowed yourself to be loved by him because you felt safe.'

This is far too much to take in.

'So where does Matt come into it?' I ask. I can't wait to hear this bit.

'Matt is, psychologically speaking, a stand-in for your dad. We've been through this.'

Jesus Christ.

'Right! So Jamie is my mum and Matt is my dad!' I laugh, putting my head in my hands. 'Jane, this is not a bloody Greek tragedy!'

'Why is it so difficult to comprehend? It's quite simple when you think about it. I see it all the time,' she says. 'It was obvious from the outset you wouldn't be emotionally intimate with Matt. But he displayed similar traits to your dad – he was emotionally closed and distant, cold to some extent. In marrying Matt, you sought to mirror the relationship with your dad by making him love you, but you'd never become close to him because you never made yourself emotionally available to him. It was doomed to failure before it even got going.'

I don't even know what to say. There's far too much to take in.

And the freakiest part is that I know she's right. About all of it.

All of it.

I don't think I've consciously been holding myself back from people, but I guess the prospect of revealing who I am, with all my flaws, is just too scary. Because the one person who loved me despite all of them died. And the other one is married to someone else.

'So, what do I do?' I ask her, the tears in my eyes now teetering on the edge of spilling over on to my face. 'I don't know what to do.'

Jane sighs and smiles.

'If you want to be happy – truly happy – you need to be emotionally intimate with people. You have to let them in. Show them who you really are. And it's scary, but you're human … we all are.'

I'm entranced by what she's saying, and she knows it. She's hit a nerve.

'Allow yourself to be vulnerable, Stephanie,' she goes on. 'Allow yourself to love, and to be loved back … fully. Only then can you be truly happy.'

CHAPTER 28

Saturday 26 November 2016

Jamie

If anyone is going to tell me some hard truths I need to hear, it's Cal. Sensing something was up on the phone, he agreed to meet for drinks in Camden on the Saturday before the art final.

'You all right, mate?' he quizzed.

'Yeah, just thought it would be good to catch up.' We're both so busy – me with work and Seb, him with his business – he knows I wouldn't usually ask. We see each other a few times a year at most. I had something to say and he knew it. I felt bad even asking, knowing how busy he is, but I really need to talk to him.

'No worries, mate. Be good to see you,' he said, suggesting this weekend.

We meet in a pub we used to go in all the time when we lived here. It's a proper dive but radiates charm and character. It hasn't changed in all these years, nor have the customers. I still recognise some of the faces. They've aged significantly, but there they are, still sitting at the weathered bar, ordering the same drinks. There's a comfort to that.

Cal's already there when I arrive, looking as stylish as ever in a garish shirt he probably got from a charity shop. A cold pint waits for me next to his, so I sit opposite him and start drinking it immediately. Think I'll need to down it before I get into why I'm here.

We chat about some art he's recently sold to a huge popstar and I'm thrilled (but not surprised) to hear how well he's doing. Vicky's been promoted to partner at her work and I can see how proud he is. He beams the whole time he speaks of her.

'That's great news! Bet she's chuffed to bits.'

'She is. And she deserves it, too. You know?'

'Yeah, course she does.' I pick up my pint and take a drink. 'How long have you two been married now?'

He does a quick mental tally in his head before answering, 'Nine years, why?'

'Do you think Vicky has, you know ... changed since you've been together?' I ask, awkwardly.

Cal looks at me like I'm mad, screwing his face up and folding his arms as he leans forward on the table.

'What do you mean?'

'You know, like ... I suppose people change as they get older. Their interests, ambitions and all that. Has that affected your relationship?'

His confused face of moments ago softens and it's obvious he's sensed where I'm going.

'Only in a positive way. I think we still bring out the best in each other. We've both progressed in our careers at different rates and in very different ways – art and law are at completely opposite ends of the spectrum. But we've always had each other's backs, sacrificed what we needed to, to help each other along. If anything, we're probably more of a team now than ever before. If that's what you mean?'

I don't know what to say.

'What's going on, Jamie?'

'I'm not sure Helen and I should be together any more,' I say, bluntly.

He raises his eyebrows and exhales, slowly.

'It's just feels like we've completely grown apart in the last few years,' I go on.

'Have you spoken to her about it?' he asks after a long pause.

'Many times,' I tell him. 'We've had so many discussions about how things have changed, especially since having Seb. Not that it's his fault, obviously. But even though we've tried to make it work, we just don't seem to enjoy each other any more.'

'Are you possibly just in a rut?' he suggests. 'We've all been mates for, what? Nearly twenty years. I don't want to see either of you unhappy and I know Vicky would feel the same.'

'I think I've been feeling like this for quite a while,' I admit. 'There comes a point where you just have to accept you're different people now. We don't make each other happy any more. I don't know what to do, Cal.'

'It kills me to think of the pair of you going through this. But if you're not happy, then you can't stay. If you've both tried to make it work and it still doesn't, then you'll have to call it a day. I'm so sorry, mate.'

'I just feel like I'm holding on to things which aren't there – my marriage, my art. Everything. I've failed as a husband and an artist. Jesus, how did it come to this?'

'Woah! I'm not having that!' he interrupts. 'You haven't failed at either. Sometimes, things just don't work out, Jamie. I've been saying this for years. You don't take enough risks, that's your problem. Put everything you have out there. Your problem isn't that you've failed … your problem is that you're *afraid* to fail.'

He's right. This has always been my problem.

'Why did you marry Helen?' he asks.

'What do you mean?'

'There must have been a reason. What was it?'

I look at him, blankly. What an odd question. 'Why does anyone get married? You just … do, don't you?' I tell him.

'"You just do"? That was your reason?'

'No, I loved her, obviously.'

'You can love somebody without getting married. I want to know the *reason*.'

Christ! If I'd known I'd be cross-examined by my best mate I'd have stayed at home.

'It seemed like the right thing to do,' I confess.

'Sounds like you're doing your tax return,' he says dryly. 'Do you want to know why I married Vicky?'

'No, but I'm sure you're gonna tell me.'

'I couldn't stand the thought of not spending every goddamn day with her. The thought of being without her, at any point for the rest of my life, terrified me. We have something so special, it's like she switches me on. We're so different, but so the same. I feel like I can do anything when I'm with her.'

'It's obvious you feel like that about her, everyone can see it,' I tell him, thinking back to that trip to Vegas. Helen was right – I've never had that with her.

'I've never seen that with you and Helen. Don't get me wrong, I love you both to death, but I was surprised when you got together. Even more so when you got married.'

'Really?'

'Look, I'm not saying everyone has to have this amazing chemistry when they meet, and it always seemed really safe with you two. But I know this amazing electricity and happiness between two people exists because I have it. And I think you could have it too with someone. You just have to find it.'

An image of Stephanie flashes through my mind when he says it. I accidentally smile when it does.

'There's nobody else, is there?' he asks, narrowing his eyes at me, clocking the smile on my face. 'You'd tell me if there was, wouldn't you?'

I hesitate before answering. I've always promised myself I wouldn't tell a soul about Stephanie, but in the current circumstances I might have to. It still feels too big, too large to say out loud, though. Where do I start? How can I even describe our relationship?

'No, nobody else,' I tell him, soaking up my pint.

Being men, this level of emotional talk has drained us, so we move on swiftly. I can't go home in a complete state so I say goodbye to Cal at the train station and we part ways. He gives me a hug, saying that if the shit hits the fan, I'm more than welcome to go stay with him and Vicky for a bit. I appreciate it. They're obviously going to feel awkward in the event of a split.

I think about what Cal said all the way home. A split has so many implications in so many ways. Helen earns a decent salary but I don't. How would I afford a place of my own where Seb could come and visit? Would he hate me? I'd like to think Helen wouldn't turn nasty and turn Seb against me, but you just don't know. All it takes is Mum to say a few bad things about Dad and that's when the hate can set in. I don't want Seb feeling tormented about coming from a broken family in the same way I was. What if he feels like I've abandoned him? Or that I never tried hard enough? Yet, surely, staying in an unhappy marriage is worse for him?

What I know is that there *is* a girl like Vicky out there for me – and I've already met her.

CHAPTER 29

Saturday 3 December 2016

Stephanie

I nudge the door open slowly, barely able to bring myself to face the reality of what's in there. The spare room is stacked full of boxes. The bed is a sea of clothes on hangers, with nowhere to be hung. This kind of chaos reminds me of when I used to come home from university in the summer holidays, only I was nineteen then. I never dreamed my life would end up this way. Or, maybe I did. I was never really going to have one of these happy, perfect existences, so perhaps I'm not really surprised at all. But, at the age of thirty-six, I'm back at my dad's house, living here with my two young children.

Everyone says I should have kicked Matt out and stayed in our house, but I honestly didn't want to stay there. It was a house with no happy memories and I wanted a fresh start.

But my girls deserve more than this. More than what I've given them. I've failed spectacularly on every level.

It's twenty-three years today since my mum died. All I ever wanted was to be the kind of woman she would have been proud of – and look at me. Mother of two, mid-thirties, separated, in love with someone I can't have, living with Dad, in a job which doesn't challenge me.

What would she think?

Stepping over shoe boxes, bags and random lamps on the floor, I walk over to the box underneath the window titled 'EVIE AND ADELAIDE BABY'. Sliding the lid off, I see what I came in for. I was explaining to them this morning about my mum, but they couldn't quite grasp it.

'Was she your mummy like you're our mummy?' Evie asked.

'She was, darling. Yes,' I said, smiling.

'Where is she, then?'

Pausing for a second, not quite knowing how to answer it without scaring them, I answered, 'She went to heaven. She was very poorly, you see,'

'You're not going to go to heaven, are you?' she says, worry on her face.

'Not for a very long time, my precious girl.'

'Did you love her like we love you?'

My heart ached when she said it. My God, the love between a mother and child is just too immense for words sometimes.

'I did, and she would have loved you, too. So much.'

Picking the memory books out of the box, I run the palm of my hand over the front of Evie's; a beautifully ornate purple hardback book, embossed with gold swirls and intricate design. Flicking through, I see every black-and-white scan photo she ever had, all the little notes I wrote her when I was pregnant and little keepsakes I stuck in. Adelaide's is the same.

Popping the lid back on the box, I leave the room and close the door. The girls will love looking at the books and now feels like the right day to do it. I'll sort that room out at some point. Just not today.

By some strange twist of fate, Mum's anniversary has also fallen on the same day as the art competition exhibition. Dad has had to cancel the conference in Portland, which is terrible given the current circumstances with the firm, because he's reignited an old back injury chopping logs for the fire so has been instructed to lie down and not move and I'm running around after him all day. We really could have done with the potential deal from this trip, but there's no way he could go. And he starts getting twitchy mid-morning and going on about attending the art final.

'Can't you just drive me down, Steph?' he pleads, clutching his back in agony. 'I'll sit on a comfy chair and you can help me around.'

'No, Dad. The doctor said you had to stay reclined. You're not leaving this house,' I say in my very best mum voice. Even if he was able to get out, I can't go to the exhibition – I'd give Jamie a heart attack if I turned up.

It's a very low-key day. We have a nice lunch with all the kids at the house. Ebony and I cook a gorgeous baked apple crumble and the house smells divine afterwards. Will plays outside with the children, wearing them all out by running around, pretending to be a monster.

When they come back in, I unwrap them from their snowsuits, hats, scarves and gloves. The earthy scent follows them, sticking to their skin. Picking Adelaide up, I kiss her freezing cold cheek.

'I love you, Mama,' she says, wrapping her little arms around my neck.

'I love you too, baby girl,' I reply, nestling my face into her hair.

Ebs and Will leave at about 3.30 p.m., just as it's getting dark. We wave them off from the eggshell-blue, church-window-shaped porch door. I've always loved the entrance to this house: it's like something out of a fairy tale. It was candyfloss pink when Mum was here and we used to peek over the lower windows of it, waiting for Daddy to come back from work and walk up the swirly path to the house.

It's an arctic-cold December evening. Dad and I cuddle up on our favourite sofa in the lounge, which is next to the big window in the room that overlooks the back garden, to watch the snow fall outside. It's twilight, a violet, inky darkness that blanks out the sky.

The snowflakes look like drops of lace falling from a huge embroidery. Christmas tree lights are twinkling in the corner, and the fire is crackling. I pull the tartan blanket around my legs, clasping my hands around my cup of hot chocolate.

'So, how are you doing? Really?' Dad asks. 'And don't give me any of this "I'm doing OK" bullshit.'

'Dad!' I yelp, shocked. My dad does not swear. He says things like 'BS' and 'Fyou' but this kind of suits his current state. Because he's been laid up for a few days he hasn't shaved or been that bothered about his appearance, so he's got dark stubble on his face, and his usually slicked-back hair is less styled, with a wilder look about it.

'I'm not messing about,' he says, licking the tip off his hot chocolate's whipped cream topping.

I laugh. 'No, you're really not! Honestly? I'm really OK. I mean, it's weird. I know I've done the right thing because I feel happier than I have done in years, but ...'

I hesitate for a second. It's the fear of saying the words out loud again.

'Go on, love. You need to talk about this.'

'I'm scared,' I whisper.

'What of?'

'This. All of it. Being a single parent. I know I haven't made life easy for myself but I guess I always hoped that I'd sort it out eventually. Maybe I should have tried harder with Matt, for the girls? What if I was just being selfish? I just feel like such a—'

'Don't you dare say it, Stephanie,' he interrupts in his best stern-dad voice which I ignore.

'A failure. No, I am, Dad.'

'No, you're not. I'm not having it. You're human. You can't stay in a marriage if you're unhappy, even for the kids.'

'But I wanted to give the girls a perfect childhood, just like Ebony and I had.' I smile sadly. 'I can't give them that now.'

'Oh Steph! Nobody is perfect! Perfectly imperfect, yes—'

'That's one of Mum's phrases,' I say and smile.

'Well, she was the pure definition of that phrase,' he says, looking out of the window at the snow which is falling more heavily by the second.

'What do you mean?'

Dad sighs, putting his mug down on the windowsill.

'You know, you remind me so much of your mother,' he says, smiling briefly, before a veil of sadness descends over his face. 'There's some stuff about your mum I never told you, stuff I tried to protect you from, because some of it is painful to hear. But I think you need to hear it now.'

A tiny whirlpool of nausea starts in my stomach. It swells, slowly gathering force and starts to creep up my throat. I don't know what Dad is about to say, but I don't like the sound of it.

'Go on,' I say, puzzled.

365

'Steph, your mum came to work for me initially as part of the One More Chance charity—'

'As a member of staff, you mean?'

'No,' he says. 'She was on the programme. She had an alcohol and drug problem.'

He gives me time to allow this information to sink in because he knows it's a shock. *Fuck me, it's a shock!*

'She was one of the patients selected to come on to the programme. She had some secretarial skills so I gave her a role on one of the admin teams.'

'No! Mum? No way did she have a booze problem, let alone a drug problem. No!' I say again and laugh. Mum was all about eating healthily, exercise. She used to buy organic food, for God's sake! I mean, it's totally ridiculous. *My mum?*

'Steph, I know this is a shock, but it's true.'

How can this be true? And how could I have never known about it? Suddenly, it feels like everything I've ever known has been a lie.

'But … how?' I ask, utterly confused. 'Why? She had it all so … so *together.*'

Dad laughs nervously as he reaches for his drink before looking straight back at me.

'She wasn't always like that. You saw the best of her, after she sorted herself out. She was a remarkable woman.'

Dad has always said this, but I always just assumed that's because she was his wife and although she *was* bloody amazing, that's how some people think of their wives, isn't it? Those annoying couples who just love each other so much and stay together for years. It never really occurred to me that they had a life before Ebony and I came along, that they may have had to deal with issues or trauma or heartbreak.

'Dad, just tell me everything,' I plead. 'I need to know.'

He nods. I need to hear it all. No editing, no sugar-coating ... just the truth.

'When your mum came to us, she was twenty and married to a guy called Neil Pike—'

'What?' I interrupt so loudly Dad actually jumps. 'She was married before you two met?'

'Yes, and he was a real nasty piece of work,' he goes on, looking out for my reaction. He knows this is hard to hear. My gut tightens when Dad says it. The thought of my lovely mum being in an abusive relationship tears me to the core.

'She fell out with her mum and dad over him when she was eighteen. They disapproved of the relationship because they knew what he was like. He was a well-known charmer and they didn't want her getting involved with him. But your mum was stubborn and didn't like being told what to do,' he says, glancing at me down through his gold-rimmed glasses in a way which says 'I don't know where you get it from'. I return the look with the briefest of smiles.

'... so she told them she was going to marry him anyway and if they didn't approve of the relationship they'd never see her again.'

Suddenly, it all clicks.

'And that's why we never met Granny Moira until Mum became ill?' I say, my brain scrambling to put the pieces of the last thirty years together.

'Yes,' he replies, sadly. 'Even after that marriage ended they never healed the feud. She felt so awful about the way she'd treated them, she felt like she couldn't go back.'

'But that's terrible,' I gasp. As a mother, I can't comprehend severing that bond, that relationship you have with your own children over any issue. Nothing my children do would ever be enough to never want to speak to them again. *Nothing.*

He glances out at the quickening darkness which surrounds the house at alarming speed. 'I made her get in touch. I didn't want her to ... go, without contacting her. Life's too short for feuds, isn't it?'

Just thinking this went on without our knowledge makes my head spin. How did I not know about any of it? The very thought that my poor mum was dealing with it all in her final weeks wrenches me apart. I desperately want to cuddle her – not as a child, as an adult.

'OK,' I go on. 'So, back to this Neil Pike ...'

'Yes, right.' Dad shifts on the sofa, taking another gulp of hot chocolate before continuing. 'Life wasn't quite the fairy tale mum had imagined for them once they got married. He turned into quite the controlling, manipulative, abusive philanderer.'

I run my hand through my hair, resting my elbow on the back of the sofa. I think I need something stronger than hot chocolate to get through this.

'It wasn't long before she was showing bruises and wounds all over her body, unexplained broken bones; she stopped seeing her friends and became a recluse. She was terrified of him.'

I feel physically sick. I close my eyes momentarily just to deal with this information and the whirling feeling of sadness whipping up inside my stomach. My lower lip starts to wobble.

'Don't get upset, love' Dad says, patting my knee as I flap my hand in front of my eyes. I have no idea what this motion is supposed to do; it doesn't actually stop you crying, does it?

'No. I'm fine. C-carry on ...'

'Well, about a year before she came to work for me, she got pregnant. She was so happy about having a baby. It was the one good thing in her life she could have. She thought of it as a distraction from everything going on with Neil. You've got to remember there was no support for domestic violence victims back in the '70s, Steph. It was a case of "put up or shut up".'

I shudder, thinking of this.

'So, what happened?'

'One night, when she was a few months pregnant, Neil, fuelled up on booze, beat her black and blue,' he says. It kills me to see the pain in his face recounting this.

'What happened to the baby?'

'She lost it,' he says softly. 'And she really suffered afterwards. Went to a dark place, unsurprisingly.'

I can't quite believe what he's telling me. The tears are streaming down my face, I can't hold them back any longer.

'Dad, I ...'

'Steph, honestly, this is forty years ago. Let me finish the story,' he says.

I nod, inwardly mustering the courage to listen to whatever he has to say.

'Neil was prosecuted for the assault and had a short spell in prison, but naturally he blamed his issues on alcohol and said he'd never do anything like that again. Your mum felt she had no way out so started drinking very heavily herself. Then, when that didn't numb the pain, she started taking drugs,' he says.

'What kind of drugs?'

'Cocaine, heroin – anything to make the pain go away, really,' he said, matter-of-fact. 'It was only when she accidentally overdosed and ended up in hospital nearly dead that she realised she had a choice – she could die, or she could start living.'

'So, she ended up on the One Last Chance programme?'

'Yes. She registered herself on it. She had some secretarial skills and was keen to improve them. I'll never forget her first day,' he smiles. 'Even though she had all these issues and problems, she'd made such an effort to appear professional.'

'Sounds like Mum,' I say, smiling.

'She walked up to me and said, "Are you Michael Carpenter?". I said, "Yes, that's me." And she said, "Thank you for giving me a chance. Nobody has ever done that before and I won't let you down." And she never, ever did.'

'What happened after that?'

'The placement gave her the focus she needed to sort herself out. I mean, it was rocky for a while, but she got there. The most important part of it was that her self-esteem shot up and she realised she didn't need Neil any more,' he says, gazing at the fire. 'She and I grew closer; I was hypnotised by her energy and determination, her humour. She was beautiful … and I fell in love with her.'

Such a bittersweet story in so many ways.

'So, I'm guessing you got together and Neil found out?'

'Oh, yes. Well, she told him. She was strong and brave about it. Told him outright she was leaving him for me. I was there when she did. He got angry and kicked off, obviously. He insisted he'd only divorce her on the grounds of adultery and I'd have to be named. A small price to pay to be with the woman you love.'

'My God. I can't believe any of this,' I tell him, absolutely dumbfounded.

'Of course, everyone said it wouldn't work,' Dad says and laughs. '"She's a mess", they said. "She's just after your money, just wants a ticket out of her marriage". But I knew her. It was the real deal. We got married after her divorce came through and we had you and Ebs and were blissfully happy until the day she died. She truly appreciated life and loved you both to bits, you know she did.'

'We know. We all know,' I reiterate.

'I know I wasn't the best dad after she died,' he says, looking outside. The flakes have graduated to being the size of fifty-pence pieces. 'I just couldn't understand why, after everything she'd been through, she was taken away. It wasn't fair. It wasn't her time.'

This is the first time Dad's spoken so honestly about Mum dying. It's raw and honest and I don't really know what to say.

'It just wasn't her time,' he repeats, this time breaking down into tears, placing his hand over his eyes.

'Dad, please don't,' I plead, cuddling up to him. It feels like he's needed this hug for years. 'She'd be so proud of you. Of all of us.'

'Well, so am I. I really am. I know I don't show it a lot of the time, but you and Ebony mean the world to me and I want to see you both happy.'

'We are! Well, Ebony is. Not sure I'm destined for happiness – one failed marriage down before the age of forty and put off for life.'

'Matt was never really the one for you, though, was he?' he admits.

'I thought you loved Matt?' I squeal.

'I thought *you* loved Matt!' he yells back. 'I was only nice to him because I thought you loved him. Ebony hated him.'

We both laugh through the tears we've shed over the last few minutes. God, I've missed my dad.

'Seriously, though,' I say, 'I just don't think I'm meant to be like Ebony. She has it all worked out. I don't think I'll find anyone to be truly happy with.' I think of Jamie when I say it and my eyes dart towards the clock. The portrait gala will be starting in fifteen minutes.

'Steph, have you not listened to anything I've said?' he says. 'Your mum came close to ending it, so convinced she was she'd never find happiness. That was just before she found me. Yet she was the strongest, bravest woman I've ever known. She used to describe those early years as feeling hopeless, destined for years of unhappiness,' he says. It dawns on me now, listening to it, that it all sounds very familiar. 'But in later years she described it as actually standing at a crossroads. Steph, you have the power to go after what you want if you have the bravery and courage to want something enough. It won't be easy, and it might upset people on the way, but you have to be true to yourself. You don't need to be unhappy forever.'

'She was special, though, wasn't she? I'm all kinds of messed-up,' I say, sorrowfully.

'Do you know what I loved about your mum? Really loved? How vulnerable she was. She had flaws and she let me see them. She wouldn't have voluntarily allowed me to in any other situation, but because of how we came to meet through the programme, I saw her – warts and all. Well, not literally warts. Your mother would never have had warts. She'd have had them frozen off or however you get rid of them.'

I giggle at the thought of it.

'Really?'

'I never used to believe in fate, destiny and all that … until your mum came into my life. But I do now. I think you're sent to the people you're meant to be with and you just know. And it doesn't matter *what* you do, because you'll always end up where you're supposed to be,' he says.

I gaze into the fizzing fire as he talks, thinking of Jamie. Can this mean we are meant to be together?

'You meet your fate on the road you take to avoid it, Stephanie.'

I quickly look at Dad when he says this.

'What?'

'Look, I know you think I'm crazy …'

'No, it's not that,' I say, looking confused. 'Where did you hear that?'

'Your mum always used to say it. She lived by it. Why?'

A smile expands across my face as I think back to the first time I heard this. I remember it like it was yesterday.

The Day We Met

Friday 13 October 2006 … The first conversation I ever had with Jamie Dobson as we both looked up the plaque hanging on the wall of the hotel on the evening we met.

An involuntary laugh pops out of my mouth as I feel my heart begin to race.

'What?' Dad says, desperate to know what the joke is.

'Dad, can I call Ebony and ask her to come around and look after you? I've really got to be somewhere.'

CHAPTER 30

Jamie

Very rarely do I get nervous, but tonight I am.

Girls dressed in black walk around, handing out glasses of champagne, but I don't take one. I'd drain it and immediately grab another. Tonight is not the night for getting drunk.

The gallery has been divided into three sections, one for each of us. It felt terrifying walking in tonight. Of course, we've all spent the last few days in here, each setting our own individual exhibitions up. But tonight felt different. All three finalists stood in the foyer as the press took our picture, exchanging pleasantries, wishing each other good luck, shaking hands. But, make no mistake about it; we'd all do whatever it takes to win this. It's me and another guy from Cambridge, and a woman from one of the surrounding areas. We walked off into our own sections, just to spend a moment alone before people start piling in.

I stand in front of my main piece, studying it. The portrait I'd spent so long working on. It takes centre stage on the bright white wall. The dimensions of it are such that it's the first thing you see as you enter the room; 900 mm x 600 mm. That was the specification. I found it daunting at first. That's a whole lot of face for a portrait, but I loved it in the end. It allowed me to sink into it and work on every single feature.

I can't take my eyes off it. It sounds arrogant, I know. But it's the best piece of work I've ever done. It's certainly the bravest: honest, raw and beautiful. I'm obviously apprehensive about people seeing it. I don't know how people will react but I do know that I'm proud of myself. For not playing it safe, for taking a risk.

Sometimes you just have to take a chance, I guess. I know why Stephanie can't be here, but she's also the one person I wish could be. She's been so supportive over the years and I know for a fact I wouldn't even be standing here if it wasn't for her. Whatever happens, whether I win this or not, I've pushed myself further than I ever thought I could and I have her to thank for that.

I watch the guests weave through the gallery, eyeing up my work which is placed on the walls. They're mainly art critics, art lecturers, local artists. They meander around, stopping in front of each piece with a notepad in one hand, glass of champagne in the other, dissecting my work. I watch them from afar, desperately trying to look cool and casual, hiding the nerves tying my stomach in knots. I'm incapable of standing still, fidgeting with my blazer collar and continuously rubbing the back of my neck. It's December, but I'm feeling uncomfortably hot as I unbutton my blazer and adjust my polo neck to try and feel some fresh air.

Everyone looks animated in conversation, wildly gesticulating, nodding their heads in agreement but I can't tell whether that means they love it or hate it.

'Relax. You can't spend all night worrying about it,' a voice says from behind me. 'Have a drink.'

I turn around to see Helen pushing a glass of champagne into my face.

'No, thanks. I'd rather stay sober. It's an important night and I'm so nervous I think even one drink will go straight to my head,' I reply.

'Ah, well,' she says and shrugs, 'more for me.' She drains her glass and starts the other one. Her black, long-sleeved dress is embellished with silver sequins which sparkle under the bright lights.

'They're all a bit nerdy, aren't they?' she says a bit louder than I'd like, scanning her eyes around the room

'They're artists. Well, more like academics, really,' I reply. 'I know it's not your thing.'

'Oh, so I'm stupid?' she says sulkily, pulling a face.

I sigh. Christ, not now. Not tonight, please.

'No. I didn't mean that and you know I didn't. I just mean—'

'I'll be outside, I need to call Imogen anyway,' she says, glancing at the portrait which looms over us as she heads out of the room.

'Absolutely exquisite, mate. Well done!' Cal says, patting me on the back and grinning like a proud dad.

'Thanks, pal,' I reply, as we stand, studying the portrait. He's been an absolute rock tonight, taking up a permanent position in front of my piece, charming everyone (the women love him, as always) and talking in depth about the 'refined and majestic techniques and presentation' of the portrait.

'So,' he says, confidently, nodding towards the picture we're both staring at. 'Who is she? And don't say "nobody". You don't put that much passion into a made-up girl. I've read the statement that goes with it, mate.'

I stare down at the floor for a few moments, thinking about what I can say.

He knows.

'Later,' I say, finally turning to look at him. He nods his head, accompanied by a subtle smile. I should have told him before now.

As the evening wears on, I'm introduced to each of the judges and chat to them individually, and collectively, about my work. To speak so creatively and freely about something you feel so passionately about is so liberating. And, yes, I'm aware how twatty that makes me sound. But it's true. I love teaching my kids at the school, but this is what I ultimately want to be doing. I've had a taste of it now and I don't want to give it up, especially when it feels like I'm so close.

Everyone wants to speak to the artist. *What did you want to convey with the piece? What was the inspiration? Do you have a muse? Who is your favourite artist? What motivates you? Where do you see yourself in five years?*

I've seen the other candidates' work and they're very good but I'm trying to remain confident. We all have different styles, which is a good thing – their portraits are more polished than mine, more controlled. Mine has an unfinished feel about it – an energy, a rawness.

'It really is a stunning piece,' says one short, middle-aged, jolly-looking woman who has been deep in conversation with some of the art critics for a few minutes.

I glance up at the portrait before answering and those emerald-green eyes lock right back on mine for a moment.

'Thank you, I'm really pleased with it,' I say and smile.

'You should be. It's captivating,' says her male companion. 'You've really captured the mystery and intensity in her eyes. She looks striking.'

They don't know the half of it. It's an abstract style with smooth, beautiful brushstrokes that fit within the lines.

A bit like her, I guess.

'Mr Dobson, marvellous to meet you! I've been admiring your work!' a voice pipes up behind me. I swing around to see Dominic Jervis, arts editor of *The Cambridge Arts Review* holding his hand out for me to shake. Need to keep it cool for this one.

'Yes, hello! Great to meet you!' I say, a little too enthusiastically.

'This is a terrific exhibition, Jamie. Very impressive. And I love your portrait piece.' He nods towards it. There are a bunch of people standing in front of it, admiring it at the moment, so only the blonde hair is visible.

'Thank you very much.'

'I was particularly impressed at how you interpreted the theme,' he says. 'I can see a real emotion and connection to this portrait. The intensity in the face is really quite outstanding.'

'That really is the biggest compliment to receive. You've no idea how appreciated it is, Mr Jervis.'

'Good luck, Jamie. I'm sure, regardless of the result of this competition, we will see great things from you.' He nods again before walking off and getting accosted by a group of people.

God, I might need that drink after all.

'Jamie!'

Never has the sound of my own name caused me so much anxiety.

She's gliding through the crowd towards me with a huge smile on her face. She looks really happy in a way

I don't think I've ever seen her before, in all the years we've known each other.

And even though she's the only person I want to see right now, she's also the only person in the world I *don't* want to see right now.

'Erm, Stephanie! Hi!' I whisper as she hugs me, burying her head into my neck. I quickly, but subtly, move her round so that she's facing away from the wall.

'What are you doing here?' I ask, my heart racing.

'Jamie, I really need to talk to you. I know this is your big event and you didn't want me here, but I couldn't wait. *This* couldn't wait,' she says breathlessly, looking around.

'I'd love to talk, Steph,' I say in hushed tones. 'It's not a great time, though, can we please do it tomorrow?'

But it's too late. By the time I've finished asking the question, she's already staring at it.

CHAPTER 31

Stephanie

It's me.

I'm looking at a painting of a woman's face on the wall. She looks confident, determined, gazing right at me with shining green eyes. Her blonde hair is messy, haphazard around her face. I love the colours; it has a real vibrancy and warmth to it and I love how chaotic the style is. There are very few definite lines and they're made up with shadows and light, just like he showed me all those years ago. It's all a bit dishevelled, like me, I suppose. I can't drag my eyes away from the face; the textures and strokes he's used are beautiful. It's like he's actually captured the composition of every inch of my skin.

The cherry-red plump mouth, slightly parted, looks sumptuous, even though I've never, ever considered it to be, and yet, they're very clearly my lips. The eyes are stunning and cat-like, consumed with tenacity. The nose is neat and cute. Do I have a cute nose? It's like looking in a mirror … a magical mirror which makes you more beautiful than you've ever felt and everything you wish you were. But, somehow, it's still undeniably me.

I walk closer to the portrait to see the information next to it.

Title of piece: *More Than Words*
Oil on canvas
900 mm x 600 mm
Theme of Portrait: The Perfection of Beauty in a Broken World
Statement of Intent: How do you paint perfection? How do you fix the unfixable? Capturing the essence of the unbroken, which is no longer broken. Eyes like lightning, we are seized by their uncontrollability. The mouth, tainted with a blush of red lipstick, concealing a sensual tactility from within. A goddess draped in armour, vulnerability radiates from her ethereal skin, allowing only those she wishes to see it. How do you truly express perfection of beauty? They say a picture speaks a thousand words. Some things are more than that … they're more than words.

I am stunned, in the truest sense of the word.

Firstly, because of the portrait. He chose to paint *me*. Secondly, by the statement which accompanies it. Is this really what Jamie thinks of me? All those times

I wanted him to open up and tell me how he felt. All those years he remained closed off, unwilling to let me in, or explain what I meant to him. And now he's told the whole world before he's told me.

After a few moments of staring at it on the wall, I turn to look at him. He looks vulnerable, as if he's just exposed his soul. He looks down at the floor with his hands in his pockets, then straight at me, but can't hold my gaze. It's adorable in a way which reminds me of a child. His face flushes slightly red. My God, I want to hold him.

'I needed to …' he mumbles, looking straight at me. His smile is cautious, not knowing how I'm going to react to the gesture. All I want to do is kiss him – and, right now, I don't actually care who sees it. We are in the midst of people who have no idea what has just happened, the enormity of it. It doesn't look like anyone has clicked that I am her. They're transfixed by Jamie's artwork – I'm just captivated by him and never want to leave his side. I have to tell him how I feel.

'I need to talk to you, Jamie. Now. Please …' I whisper, gently touching his hand. He quickly glances down at it, before smiling at me.

'Yes, of course,' he replies.

But we're interrupted by someone just as we're about to walk off. A woman with long dark hair, wearing a black dress with silver sequins on. She looks a bit pissed off, not to mention drunk.

Jamie's wife.

So many times over the years I imagined meeting her. All those times I stared at her photo on Facebook. What would I say? What would she be like? Would I remain cool under the pressure of it? Never in a million years did I ever imagine it would be in circumstances such as these.

'Are you going to introduce me?' Helen says in a way which suggests that Jamie has absolutely no choice in the matter whatsoever.

Oh. My. Fucking. Good. God.

After ten years, wife and mistress meet … and it's every single bit as awful as you'd expect. And nothing less than I deserve.

He glances at me, obviously thinking the same thing I am: she's going to recognise me.

'Erm,' Jamie says, awkwardly. 'Helen, this is Stephanie Bywater …'

Helen extends her hand to shake mine and I return the gesture, albeit reluctantly. The entire time, I'm holding my breath, consumed by an overwhelming sense of dread. I try and think of ways to explain it. *Why me?* Nope, I'm stuck. There is, quite literally, no explanation for it.

As we conduct the briefest shaking of hands, I'm so very reluctant to meet her eye. I allow my hair to fall in front of my face, desperately hoping that will conceal my features, somehow. I'll say, politely, it was lovely to meet her and get out as quickly as possible.

As our hands part, Helen's eyes narrow and she looks momentarily puzzled.

'You look familiar to me, Stephanie. Have we met before?'

I glance nervously at Jamie as I casually touch my face, trying to obscure my mouth, nose … anything which will make it less obvious.

'Oh, err, no. I don't think so,' I say, in the most casual tone I can muster. The blood rushes around my body faster than I can cope with, making me feel lightheaded. 'I do live locally – perhaps you've seen me in Waitrose?'

My eyes dart around the room, frantically searching for the nearest exit. I need to leave … now. However, at this very moment, the slight gathering of people in front of the portrait disperses and moves on to the next piece, leaving the area exposed.

'So,' Helen says, 'how do you know my husband then?'

I try to remain cool, mumbling about how my father is Michael Carpenter and I work for the company but, predictably, she stops listening after about five seconds. That's when I see her eyes flicker over my shoulder. The first glance is very brief, a second, if that. Then she does a double take. And stops listening to what I'm saying to stare at the portrait on the wall.

I say nothing. What the hell can I say or do at this point? It's far too late. I just have to watch the scene unfold. The most excruciating part about it is that I'm forced to watch the realisation spread across her face.

This woman, who I've helped betray over the past ten years. Never did I ever imagine she'd find out; call it naivety or plain stupidity, but I genuinely thought we could get away with it. And we almost did. Are we really going to be caught out now? Like this? *Here?*

We don't say anything to her. No point.

'Ah, so *that's* how you know him?' Helen says to me, with a very deliberate sting in her voice.

This is fucking horrific.

She is very clearly not stupid. She knows.

Her eyes jump between the portrait, Jamie and I. Our facial expressions of guilt, shame and regret at this awful scene being played out give it all away. Jamie doesn't say anything – he knows this game is up.

'Which one of you is going to tell me "It's not what it looks like"?' she says, very calmly.

Jamie walks towards her in an attempt to calm things down.

'Helen, not here, please ...' He looks like he might faint. The colour has drained from his face and he has actually turned white. My heart beats so fast it hurts my chest. The chattering throng have absolutely no idea of the emotional turmoil going on between the three of us, none of us knowing what to say.

I look at Jamie. He's looking at Helen. She switches her gaze between the two of us as people gently push past us to examine the next art piece.

'I fucking knew it!' she spits at him.

CHAPTER 32

Monday 23 January 2017

Jamie

The house is deadly quiet. The only sound comes from the kitchen – the gentle buzz of the fridge and the leaky tap I never got fixed. It drips, slowly, into the ceramic sink. Everything is the same, but different.

Standing in the hallway, I note the differences that would be subtle to a regular visitor of this house. They might not even notice at all. But they leap out at me the second I come in. The photos on the sideboard which used to be of the three of us have been replaced with photos of just Helen and Seb. The artwork which used to hang in the hall has been taken down. The wall where it was is now a slightly darker colour than that which surrounds it.

The living room door is ajar, so I gently push it open. Poking my head around, I see that a few bits of furniture have been removed, other bits changed around. There's no redecoration, no grand purchases. But make no mistake about it: this is not my house any more. I do not belong here.

I can't bring myself to say it's been the worst few months of my life because I don't deserve to. Not after what Helen has been going through. But I never, ever wanted to hurt her ...

The night of the exhibition was beyond words horrific. Watching Helen find out that way, watching her connect Stephanie to the portrait – everything. Usually I can't even bear to think about it. Other times, when I'm lying in bed on my own, in the dark, I go through it over and over again. And again. After working out what was going on, she'd screamed, calling me a cheating bastard and Stephanie a fucking slut, then punched me in the face.

I momentarily shudder seeing the big armchair in the bay window. I remember how Helen curled up in it, listening to me telling her about Stephanie. She sat in her pyjamas, red-faced and puffy-eyed. In all my life, I'd never felt so full of self-loathing. There was nothing but me, her and the truth.

'Just tell me everything,' she said. 'Even if it hurts. You owe me the truth.'

I've never felt so awful, telling her how I fell in love with another woman more than ten years ago and tried not to, but couldn't help it. That I'd slept with her, once, at which she snorted in disbelief. That, even though I'd tried to ignore it, I thought of her a lot and had feelings that just wouldn't go away. That even though I barely saw her, I felt so connected to her. That she was the person who truly got me. That I loved her, Helen. That I loved Stephanie ...

'You can't love two people at the same time, Jamie!' she mocked, running her hands though her hair in desperation. 'It's just something men like you say to get out of shit like this.'

I understand why she thinks that. I wouldn't have believed it either unless it had happened to me.

Now, feeling like I'm invading someone else's space, I leave the living room and close the door. Creeping up the stairs, I'm scared to make a sound and let the house notice that I'm here, an unwelcome intruder. All of the doors leading off the upstairs landing, bar the spare room, are shut. Not ajar, shut. *No entry. Keep out.* A twinge of sadness leaves my heart aching.

The mural I painted on Sebby's door catches my eye as I walk past. He loves animals so I created a jungle scene with his name spelled out in bright red letters. Running my fingers over the 'S', I can't resist going in, just for a second, even though I have absolutely no right to do it.

It's been two months since I've been in here but it feels like years. The entire room is a place of nostalgia and love I will no longer access after today, and that's a bitter pill to swallow. I peer up at the glowing planets hanging above his bed that we put up together and used to gaze at as he fell asleep, the bookshelf we'd sit next to and read together, the desk with colouring pencils scattered about, half-finished pictures and doodlings.

Cal and Vicky offered me a room at theirs immediately after the blowout, which was enormously kind of them given the politics involved. They sent Helen some flowers and Vicky called her saying they were so very sorry and weren't taking sides, but they loved us both and wanted to help. Helen was pissed off they were housing me, but they're hoping she will come round eventually. I told Cal everything and he said he wished I told him years ago.

Telling Mum was the worst. It reopened all the old wounds from Dad leaving. She'd wanted better for me and this was just like history repeating itself. I called her a few nights after it happened from Cal's garden, feeling sick as the phone rang.

'Me and Helen have split up, Mum,' I said.

'Oh God, Jamie! I'm so sorry. What happened?'

I knew she'd ask and I knew I had to be honest, but the words wouldn't come out. The line went silent. The shame was too much to bear.

'Jamie?'

'I … I had an affair, Mum. I'm so sorry.'

She couldn't say anything at first. I thought she'd actually put the phone down on me.

'Why, love?' she sighed. So, I told her. She made me go home for Christmas but I felt as if I was being a burden to everyone. I cried, didn't say much, didn't sleep, couldn't stop thinking about the pain, misery and upset I'd caused everyone.

I've got myself a little place now, a small two-bed flat about fifteen minutes away from Helen's house. It's all I can afford to rent for now but I'll make it nice for Seb. I just want to get back to seeing him regularly. It's been torture not seeing him every night. I've seen him since I left, for limited periods. Helen drops him off somewhere so I can spend a few hours with him, but I never come to the house. I know it must be hard for her on her own with him, working and dealing with this.

Helen told me all my stuff has been put into the spare room. She's been kind to do that, to be fair. Most women would have put it all on the lawn or set fire to it. All of my belongings are in black bags, piled on the bed, on the floor, or in unlabelled boxes ready for collection. I've hired a van to collect it today. Seb is at school and we figured it was better he wasn't here when I came.

I start loading the van with my stuff. After the fifth trip, I'm gathering the next load to take down when I hear the front door click shut. I stop what I'm doing, fearing it's Helen's dad sent by her to keep an eye on me. But I recognise Helen's footsteps on the stairs. I turn around, suddenly panicked, feeling quite sick at the thought of seeing her. She knew I'd be here at this time, so she obviously wants to see me.

She walks across the landing and into the spare bedroom.

'Hi,' I mumble awkwardly. It seems woefully inadequate and disrespectfully casual. 'Sorry, I won't be long, I'm nearly done ...'

She stands in the doorway. She's lost weight in the weeks since I've seen her. I recognise the coat she wears, but it hangs differently on her frame, now it's too big. 'There's all your art stuff in the garage. You can take that today, too.'

I nod, unable to look her directly in the face. 'How's Seb? Is he OK?'

'Not really. He keeps asking why I made Daddy leave and believes that it's all my fault.'

My eyes sting; I take a deep breath to compose myself.

'"I want to go and live with Daddy", he tells me. "You made daddy go away. I hate you!" That's all I hear day in, day out, Jamie. Do you know how hard that is?'

I can't answer, so I shake my head.

'Don't worry, I don't tell him that you're a lying, cheating arsehole. You'll still be the perfect daddy in his eyes and I'll be the villain of the piece.'

'I don't want that, Helen. Of course I don't,' I say.

She looks at my face for a few moments, like she's looking straight through me.

'What the hell happened to you, Jamie?' she asks, her voice breaking. 'To us? Never in a million years did I imagine you'd hurt me like this. Why?'

'I never wanted to. Please ...' I try to explain, 'I know you don't believe it, but I didn't want to hurt you. I just couldn't help my feelings and it got fucked up. I loved you both. I never left you, I never wanted to. I loved you—'

'You wanted to keep both of us? Have your cake and eat it?' She laughs in disbelief. 'Can you *hear* yourself?'

'No, not like that! I ... I shouldn't have done it and I'm not saying it excuses it. I'm just trying to explain what happened. In my head, I'm not even sure what I thought at the time, but then it started happening every year and it became something I got used to, I suppose ...'

Helen stands, shaking her head, unable to even look at me. I'm willing myself to shut the hell up because I'm making it worse. It sounds so pathetic ...

'What did I do that was so terrible, so awful, that you felt the need to go and have sex ... oh, no ... have this "incredible connection" with another woman?' she asks. The way she says 'incredible connection' drips with disgust and disbelief and she stares at me in a way I have never seen before. Her face is covered with a steely veneer; her lips are pursed, eyes blank; there is no emotion. She's being brave about this, but I know she will be dying inside.

'I know you don't want to hear this, but it's nothing you or we did,' I plead with her, sitting down on the bed. 'I think it's a combination of things. We were different people when we got together, changed as we got older, wanted different things and then she came into the equation.'

'Please don't use all that as an excuse for fucking someone else for ten years,' she says and laughs harshly. 'It's honestly pathetic.'

'I'm not,' I say, putting my hands up, defensively. I also want to point out that I wasn't 'fucking her' for ten years but don't feel now is the time to get into semantics, nor is it particularly justified. 'We did stop seeing each other, for several years. We tried staying away from each other on numerous occasions, but something always threw us back into each other's paths.'

'Oh, how romantic,' she snaps, sarcastically. 'And yes, I've heard the same from her; at least your stories are consistent, I'll give you that.'

Stephanie called me to let me know Helen had been to see her. She'd agreed to meet her one morning in a nearby park about a month ago.

'"Jamie saved me",' Helen says, in a whiney voice, attempting to impersonate Stephanie. '"I was in a terrible place and he was just so lovely and made me feel less worthless about my own spoiled, bratty, shitty life!" Didn't stop her cheating on her own husband though, did it? Picked a winner there, Jamie!'

'Helen, stop. Please,' I beg her, putting my head in my hands. I can't take much more of this.

'Oh, sorry!' she says. 'Does it hurt, hearing me insult your mistress? When are you going to tell me "it wasn't like that"?'

I don't say anything. I can't.

'We could have been happy, and you gave it all up for that. Was it really worth it?' she asks.

'Look, Stephanie aside, and while what I did was 100 per cent wrong, I do think we'd grown into different people over the years. We hadn't been happy for a long time.'

'You think we would have split up without your bit on the side?'

I instinctively go to say something about the 'bit on the side' comment, but let it go.

'I just think we were more compatible when we were younger. We would have just carried on making each other more unhappy. I'm so sorry for the way it happened, but us separating is for the best. You need someone more ambitious, driven, maybe? I never felt I was good enough.'

'Well, you suddenly became more ambitious for her, didn't you? Look at you now, Mr Big Time Artist, winning your little competition. Finally left your safe job and work in London now,' she points out. 'All because of her. What an inspiration.'

'She encouraged me and supported me like you never did,' I confess. It feels like a betrayal saying it out loud, but it's the truth.

'Do you know what she said to me as she left?'

'No,' I reply, genuinely interested. Sitting on the edge of the bed, I lean forward, clasping my hands together.

'I suggested that she probably fixed her little competition for her boyfriend to win—'

'Well, that's not true,' I reply, certain of it.

'She said "He won that based on his own talents. You should have had more faith in him all these years."'

And in that moment, as inappropriate as it is, I love Stephanie a little bit harder. Believing in me until the bitter end.

'Is that what *you* think, Jamie? That I never had any faith in you? But I only ever wanted the best for you. I tried to get you so many good jobs over the years—'

'Jobs I didn't want or ask for!'

'You didn't have a bad life, Jamie. Most people would be thankful for those opportunities.'

'But that wasn't me, Helen!' I shout at her, which I instantly regret. She jumps slightly, clearly shocked at my outburst. 'You tried moulding me into something I wasn't. We have different interests, friends, careers; our only common ground is Sebby. People change.'

'Our whole marriage was a lie, Jamie. Do you know how that makes me feel? Used. Cheap ...'

'I know,' I say, without breaking her gaze, because it's important she understands.

'I don't think you do,' she says. 'You know what one of the worst things was? Going over the last ten years and putting things into place. All those weekends you went away and came back the next day a little bit weird. Going off sex for a few months and me worried I'd done something wrong.'

Helen breaks off to look out of the window, taking a sharp intake of breath to compose herself. I want to

398

interrupt and say how mortified I am I've done this to her, but I don't have that right, so I don't. She has to say this.

'All those times, you'd been with her. Ten years …'

I don't think it's possible for this to get worse.

'Do you know what it's like telling the tale to another relative, another friend? They can't believe it. "My God! You've got to be fucking kidding? Jamie? *Jamie*? He doesn't seem the type!" they say. But you are that type, aren't you? It's always the ones you never suspect,' she says, her voice breaking off at the end.

'I guess I am. But, Helen, I never wanted to hurt you and if it makes you feel better, I'm tormented by it every single day.'

I don't know what else to say. Nothing I can do will make this better.

'Well, it's not enough, but it'll have to do,' she replies. 'Anyway, I'm only here so you can sign this. It's about the divorce.'

Reaching into her handbag for some documents, she slings them on the bed with a pen.

'Sign where the tab is.'

I do as I'm told and hand it back to her.

'I'll be divorcing you on grounds of adultery which I can't imagine you'll contest,' she says, confidently.

I feel sick when she says it. It's entirely accurate, but it feels brutal and raw, hearing it out loud.

'No, of course not,' I tell her, shaking my head.

'I want to know, though ...' she goes on, putting the paperwork back into her bag. 'Are you together now? Are you living with her?' A sharp intake of breath punctuates the end of the sentence.

'No. That's the truth. I haven't seen her since the night of the gala. I've spoken to her on the phone a few times, but I'm a mess, Helen. I've just lost everything in my life. All my own doing, admittedly, but I've still lost everything – my wife, son, house, life as I knew it. I'm going to be on my own and sort myself out.'

She looks at me intently, hugging her coat around her. Usually standing confident and tall, today she looks like a shadow of the woman she was. Her shoulders hunch forward and appear heavy from carrying the burden of everything I've inflicted on her. The stress of the last two months has taken its toll on both of us it would seem.

'Let me know when you're settled and you can start having Seb overnight,' she says walking out the door.

'Helen,' I call out to her, 'I—'

'Don't. I don't want to hear you're sorry or you still love me or any of that,' she states, firmly.

'No, I know you don't want to hear that,' I say.

'What then?' she sighs, turning around to face me as she walks out the door.

'I hope you'll find someone who treats you better than I did.'

PART FOUR

It Ain't Over 'Til It's Over

CHAPTER 33

Saturday 22 July 2017

Stephanie

It's written in black biro on lilac paper, faded over the years. Folded in half, the crease still stands, but it remains immaculate. I've read it hundreds of times. On some occasions, crying. On most, despising myself.

But I feel different reading it today.

Dad presented it to me on my eighteenth birthday and I was initially terrified to read it. It was like she was alive again, hearing her say new things. Running to my room and shutting the door behind me, I perched on the end of my bed and opened the white envelope.

Wednesday 24 November 1993

To my beautiful girl, Stephanie
From the moment I first felt you kick, to the last glimpse I had of you as a funny, sweet girl, always full of kindness and laughter, I have loved you more than you will ever know. In the thirteen years I have

been your mum, you have made me prouder than I could ever say and I know you will go on to such wonderful things.

So, on your eighteenth birthday, I wanted to share with you some advice I have learned over the years, because I won't be there to give it to you myself.

Find someone who accepts you for who you are. Let them love you unconditionally. Let them love your quirks, your scars, let them love you when you're happy and when you're mad. Don't strive to be perfect, none of us are. Embrace your imperfections and make sure the person you fall in love with adores them.

Don't hold grudges, especially against those you love. They're a waste of everyone's time. Don't push people away because you're too stubborn, one day they might not come back.

Life isn't simple, it can get complicated. But always put yourself first. Don't put up with people who mistreat you. It's OK to walk away from them.

Be kind to yourself. Be brave, always.

Keep taking photos, you have a natural talent for it.

You're so very special, Stephanie. Go out into that world and be the absolute best you can be.

Hold on to the memories we have, my darling girl. They are precious. Remember me how I was – how you, me and Ebony used to love singing along to the Joseph and the Amazing Technicolour Dreamcoat *soundtrack, stargazing in the garden and painting in my art studio. Daddy will always be there for you. You all have to look after each other now.*

Never forget how much I love you – now, always and forever.

Mum
Xxx

All it did over the years was remind me how much I'd messed-up. Instead of taking her advice, I railed against everything she said and I felt worse because of it.

But that was the old Stephanie.

Only now, eighteen years later, can I read it and finally understand what it means and put it into context. Giving advice comes from experience, and my goodness, I can relate to this. I never knew Mum and I were so similar. Not until the night Dad told me about how they got together. Everything made sense when I found out.

Life is chaotic. The last six months have been a blur and the night of the art gala blew my world away. Apart from a few phone calls with Jamie since then, we've had no contact. His wife called me at work about a month after, asking if I'd meet her. I don't blame her – I'd have done the same. We met in a park and she demanded all kinds of explanations about our relationship, none of which she accepted or wanted to hear, which was fair enough. I didn't play anything down and I was truthful about everything. I owed her the truth and I figured the last thing she needed was more bullshit.

My priorities now are Evie and Adelaide. We've moved into a little cottage in a village not far from Dad. Ebony was upset I hadn't talked to her about it but Dad was surprisingly sympathetic and a great support through it all, having been through a similar thing with Mum.

'You can't help who you fall in love with,' he said, as I wept in his arms on many a cold evening.

Reading the letter, I remind myself of how far I've come. She'd be proud of me today. I smile, folding it up and sliding it back into the envelope.

Walking into the kitchen to pop the kettle on, I check the time. I've got about an hour before I need to leave the house. It's going to be scorching hot today, apparently. The sun streams in through the lounge windows, making glorious sun patterns on the carpet. I'm hoping I don't look too garish in my outfit: a pillarbox-red knee-length playsuit with spaghetti straps. I'm so nervous.

Suddenly, three faint taps on the front door, which I ignore. I'm not expecting anyone and don't have time for people selling anything, so I turn the radio up and ignore it. The '60s sounds of 'Be My Baby' by The Ronettes echoes around the kitchen which makes me smile. It makes me think of *Dirty Dancing*, one of my favourite films.

After fifteen seconds or so, they try again – louder this time – so I reluctantly go to answer it.

I am not mentally or emotionally prepared for who's on the other side of the door.

'Hello, Stephanie,' Jamie says, his face lighting up.

I'm so shocked to see him, I almost lose my breath, never mind my balance.

Quite literally speechless, I look at him for a few seconds before lunging towards him, giving him the biggest hug. He holds on to my waist and we stand, for what feels like minutes, not saying anything. Every now and then we squeeze each other, which makes us both giggle.

'How did you know where I lived?' I ask, confused, pulling back to face him.

'You told me you were moving to this village last time we spoke so I just knocked on everyone's doors asking if they knew you.'

'Oh my God! Are you serious?'

'Yeah. I think that old lady at number four thinks I'm mental. But I could have guessed this was your house just from the outside.'

'What do you mean?'

'Look at it!' he says, nodding to the little front garden which is filled with brightly coloured flowers. There's a cute candy-pink birdhouse sitting on the left side of the garden, next to wind chimes and other swirly ornaments that have a calm stillness about them in this searing heat, but kick into action when a breeze starts up. 'It's like something out of *Alice in Wonderland*. It's so very *you*!'

'Thank you!' I say and laugh. 'Would you like to come in?'

'That would be lovely. I'm not interrupting you, am I?' he asks.

'No. Well, I'll have to leave in about an hour or so. Kids are with Ebony. I'm going to a wedding.'

'Oh! Right, OK. Nice day for it. Close friend?' he asks.

'Not really. I'm the photographer,' I tell him with my biggest proud face.

'What?' he replies, raising his eyebrows and folding his arms. 'Really?'

'Yep. I started a photography course at the local college in January. I'm doing photos for next to nothing at the moment, just to build up a portfolio. This is my third one.' I beam at him. 'I love it.'

His eyes flash between all the photos in frames. They're on the windowsill, the fireplace, side table and mantelpiece. I've created photo galleries on the wall. None of the frames match. Some are very new-looking and contemporary, some are older and distressed – or *shabby chic*. Some of the frames have jewels on, which capture the sun streaming in through the windows, immediately bouncing it back off on to the cream sofa.

Jamie can't hide his curiosity as he creeps around the room, looking at them all, bending down to see a girl he barely recognises. I follow him around, laughing. He sees that I'm in virtually every single one: laughing, smiling, gazing away from the camera, in colour, in black and white, with the kids, on my own, with friends and with my family.

'Erm, what happened to the girl who would never allow herself to be in front of the camera?' he asks, puzzled.

'She learned to let people in,' I say, smiling.

He does a very over-exaggerated 'Oh right, yes ... I see', much to my amusement. 'And which wise soul told you that? He must be very clever?'

'Nah,' I shrug. 'He was all right. Just someone I used to know.'

'Cheeky, you!' he whispers, playfully wiggling the tip of my nose with his finger.

I sit down on the edge of the sofa, and he joins me.

'Jamie ... Why are you here? And why now?'

He smiles, briefly looking down at the floor, before turning back to me and shuffling to find a position he's comfortable in.

'I've needed the last six months to sort everything ... me ... out, Steph,' he says.

'Of course.' I nod.

'I'm so sorry I haven't been in touch,' he explains. 'There was just too much going on, and I needed to get my head straight. The amount of stuff I've had to deal with …'

'I can imagine. I've had it all too …'

'How are things with Matt?' he asks.

'Well, we're not on brilliant terms, put it that way. The divorce is ongoing and our only contact is for the girls, who are fine. I'm just glad I'm away from him.'

'Good,' he says. 'Good for you.'

'How about you?' I ask him.

'How can you expect your wife to understand that you loved two women at the same time? How can anyone make sense of that?'

'It's a tough one,' I say. 'Took me years to accept it, and I wasn't your wife.'

He nods and it seems impossible that a fleeting encounter which caused us to meet ten years ago has led to where we are today.

'Stephanie, I need to ask you something,' he says.

I uncross my legs and turn to face him a little more.

'OK,' I reply, nervously.

'Helen and I are in the middle of getting divorced. And, if I'm being brutally honest, I'm not sure that even if you weren't in the picture, we would have made it. The people we became are so, so different to who we were when we met. And we grew in different directions.'

I interrupt. 'I didn't help, though.'

'No,' he says, and takes a deep breath. 'That's true. You didn't help my marriage, but you showed me the person I wanted to be. You made me a better person. Overall, and despite all the awfulness of the past six months, my life is better because of you.'

I can't stop the smile which spreads across my face. Taking my hand, he kisses the top of it as he looks right into my eyes.

My love.

This feels different to all the other times we've met. It's not sordid or illicit. It's honest and legitimate – and true.

'Stephanie, I love you so much …'

This is the first time he's ever said these words, so explicitly.

'I've always loved you. It's *always* been you. And I know we haven't exactly had an easy route to get here, in fact, it's been pretty ridiculous, but you're the only one I want and so I wondered if you, you know, wanted to … erm … give it a go? With me?'

I don't think my smile can get any bigger. Tears form behind my eyes, because sitting in front of me is the man I love who loves me back.

Reaching out and tenderly laying my hands on the side of his neck, I bring his face to mine.

'Jamie Dobson, are you asking me out?' I whisper.

'Well, I feel like after ten years of messing about, I should probably take the plunge. What do you think? Should we give it a go? I mean, a proper go?'

'I'd love to,' I reply, leaning in for a kiss. 'And I love you too.'

I don't know why things happen the way they do. Maybe the universe does have a path set out for us all and we have to follow it to get where we are meant to be. I honestly don't know. I hate that people have got hurt along this particular path. But *this* feels right. No, more than right.

Perfect.

CHAPTER 34

Saturday 21 July 2018

Jamie

'Turn it up, Mummy! I love this one!' Evie shouts from the back of the car.

'She really is her mother's daughter, isn't she?' I turn and laugh at Steph, who sits in the passenger seat and requires absolutely no encouragement to increase the volume.

'Mummy, you have to do the Ana bit again and Jamie does the Hans bit,' Evie demands, clapping her hands as Adelaide joins in. I glance at Steph, rolling my eyes, pretending I want no part of this, but she knows I love it.

'You joining in, Seb?' I shout, peeking at him in the rear-view mirror.

'No!' he yells back, quickly attaching the headphones to his iPad.

When you live with two little girls, you've got to be OK with Disney films, and that means watching them on loop and learning the songs. It's unavoidable. It also means that on this long journey from Cambridgeshire to Cornwall, that's all we've listened to. We're on the final stretch now so we're doing anything just to get through it.

So, here we go – 'Love Is An Open Door', for the twentieth time in the last five hours. The girls love it when Steph and I do the different parts. Steph loves it too, gets really into it. But, then again, she's always loved belting out a tune. As I drive us through the country roads on a beautiful summer morning, I couldn't ask for more than being in a car full of singing and happiness.

I just love this little crew we've got.

The house we're staying in for the week is beautiful, just above the beach, with panoramic views from a stunning decked area. The kids are desperate to run out and explore when we arrive, so we dump our stuff and head straight to the beach.

The girls are overwhelmed with excitement. Adelaide, four and, as she insists on telling us, three-quarters, runs around copying everything Evie does. At seven years old, she likes to think of herself as the 'big sister'.

'Now, Adelaide! Don't go too close to the sea. You'll have to hold my hand, OK?' she chirps.

They waste no time in skipping around the beach collecting shells and placing them delicately in buckets they've brought. Steph walks around with them, celebrating appropriately whenever they find a new one.

Sebby is straight into building a massive sandcastle city.

'Dad! Can we do it so that the water comes in and goes around it like a moat?!' he asks, excitedly.

'It's not even a proper sandcastle if it doesn't have a moat, son!' I tell him, setting to work. The tide is out so we take our time. He's fairly quiet throughout the epic construction. It usually takes him half a day or so to settle into being with us whenever he comes from Helen's, as if he needs to adjust to the different dynamic. I waited a good six months of being with Steph properly before introducing her to Seb. And as it turns out, Helen now has a boyfriend Seb's just been introduced to, so it's hard for him. It's difficult knowing another man spends time with him when I don't. It's a challenging situation for all of us.

It's not long before we've created a city of sand. Crouching in front of it, with sand sticking to our knees and hands, we admire our creation.

'Proud of that! Are you?' I ask him.

'Yeah. It's all right,' he says, shrugging and sitting next to me, pushing his bare feet into the sand.

'Seb ... how are things going?'

'OK,' he grunts.

'Everything all right at school?'

'Yeah.'

Looking out to the shoreline for a second, I see Steph knee-deep in the sea hand-in-hand with both daughters. They're jumping over waves and screaming when they break over their bodies.

'Your mum told me that you're going to see your granny and grandad next week, son. That'll be nice,'

'Yeah, I suppose,' he replies, without looking at me as he draws patterns in the sand with his finger.

'What is it, Sebby? It's not like you to be so quiet,' I tell him, gently sweeping his dark, messy brown hair out of his eyes. 'You know you can talk to me.'

He pauses before answering. I don't want to push him. We've had many moments like this over the past eighteen months.

'Why can't you live with Mummy any more?'

I didn't think anything could get worse than my wife asking me why I cheated on her. But I was wrong. This is worse.

How do you simplify that enough for a child to understand?

'Because sometimes people are better off apart,' I tell him. It's the nicest way of saying it, but important to be honest. 'But one thing we do know is that we both love *you* very much. And you must never, ever doubt that.'

'But I miss you,' he says, finally looking up at me. His blue eyes are filled with confusion.

'I know, Sebby,' I say, putting my arm around his shoulder. 'I love you too, more than I can tell you. And that doesn't stop just because I don't live with you. But I see you all the time and Steph and the girls love you too.'

He nods his head, nestling it into my chest.

'You're so very loved, Sebby,' I whisper to him, struggling to hold back tears. 'Don't ever forget that.'

A shadow appears in front of us and water drips on to our legs. I look up to see Steph, who has been drenched by the sea.

'I really should have put my swimming costume on!' Steph says, laughing. 'I didn't expect the waves to be that big!'

'Mummy, you're soaking wet!' Adelaide giggles, reaching for a towel and drying Steph's leg with it.

'Thank you, my beauty!' she replies. Steph's eyes flit between me and Seb; it's obvious he's been a little subdued since we left this morning and his head is still buried into my chest. Shooting me a look and mouthing, 'Is he OK?', I give him a little squeeze and nod my head. She crouches down beside us both so that she's eye-level with him.

'Seb, I don't suppose you'd be able to come and help me get the fish and chips for lunch, would you? Only, after what your dad did with your birthday cake, I just don't trust him to do it,' she says, winking at Seb. 'You know what I'm talking about, don't you?'

'Yeah, Dad!' he jeers, pointing at me.

'Look, it wasn't my fault I dropped the cake. It was … erm … slippery,' I stutter.

'And who saved the day? I can't remember …' Steph ponders.

'Me!' Seb shouts, putting his hand up in the air. He really did. After the cake went on the floor, Seb – with the help of Ebony – knocked up an 'emergency cake' which consisted of half a gone-past-its-expiry-date lemon cake with KitKats stuck on the outside and strawberry yogurt poured over the entire thing with hundreds-and-thousands sprinkled on the top. He made me eat most of it, much to the hilarity of all of us.

'That's awesome!' Seb had said.

'That's disgusting!' Ebony muttered, absolutely horrified.

'Yuk!' Adelaide and Evie said in unison.

'I'm going to be sick!' I declared after three mouthfuls.

'Make him eat more!' Stephanie screamed.

'He's resourceful!' Michael laughed. 'Do you want to come and work for me when you're older?'

Now Seb jumps up, popping his baseball cap on. Stephanie leans down and gives me a kiss. 'Be back in a bit. Girls, stay with Jamie. Come on, Seb!'

We sit on the beach, eating fish and chips with our fingers. They're drenched in salt and vinegar and the smell takes me back to being a kid. We laugh at Adelaide, who drops hers on the floor (who's the butterfingers now?) but we all share ours with her. Evie throws some to the seagulls and Seb shares some facts he learned from school about aquatic life.

'Did you know that sharks have the best night vision and also have *no* bones?' he says, enthusiastically chomping into his fish.

Evie gazes suspiciously out to sea as he divulges this information and we hang about on the beach for hours before heading back to the house. Time doesn't matter. We run around and play games. We splash about in the sea, which is the most incredible aquamarine colour I've ever seen. I already know these memories will stay with us all for years to come. Even Seb is laughing as we pack up to leave.

Adelaide jumps on my back and I give her a piggyback. Her little arms hang around my neck and I grab on to her legs. I have flashbacks of doing this with Seb, as I watch him walking ahead with Evie, stopping occasionally to 'floss' which is apparently the latest 'thing'. They keep attempting to do it all the way up the hill, and Steph joins in but she keeps getting it wrong, which cracks them both up.

They're all absolutely worn out by dusk. They don't even protest too much about getting into bed with their iPads. Steph and I loiter outside their bedroom door, listening to them all chatting, so pleased they all get on. I then run to the fridge and grab the bottle of sauvignon blanc which has been chilling all day, and two glasses and take it all outside to Steph who has made her way on to the decking and is fiddling with the Bluetooth speaker she brought.

The view is sensational. A spectacular drop down into the bay, surrounded by cliffs, as the stars begin to come out. The sound of the waves crashing on to the beach is gentled by the distance.

'Gorgeous day,' she says, kissing me slowly on the lips as I hand her a glass of wine.

'Perfect,' I say, smiling, sitting next to her on the outdoor sofa and putting my arm around her. I seriously doubt the novelty of being able to do this will ever wear off.

'Kids were so good,' she says. 'I know it's hard for Seb ...'

'Yeah. Difficult going through a split when you're an only child. He'll get there, though. He loves you and the girls. And I think it's harder for boys, they bottle things up,' I admit, speaking from my own experience.

'Of course. We'll take it as slowly as he needs.' She takes a sip of her wine. 'Hey! Stars are out tonight!'

I look up to the sky to see she's right. They're brighter than usual, probably because we're at the coast.

'It's Orion.' I point out to the constellation directly in front of us, remembering that first night we ever spent together outside at Heathwood Hall all those years ago. 'Told you the stars have been following us all these years.'

'You did. Think I'm going to have to finally admit you were right on that one,' she concedes as the next song on the playlist comes on. 'Oh, well, would you believe it!'

I laugh, shaking my head.

'Come on then,' I say, putting my drink down and standing up.

'What?'

'Dance with me?' I ask, putting my hand out for her to take. She doesn't need convincing. Immediately placing her glass on the table, she stands up. Leaning close to me, so that our noses are just about touching, she places her right hand on to mine and her left arm around my shoulder.

'Go on, then,' she says.

She loves this song. She always says it reminds her of us. And if anyone knows a good, poignant song, it's Stephanie. So, we dance, under the stars to Shania Twain's 'You're Still The One' and I just know this is what my life is supposed to be.

This is my girl. This is my family. We might have taken a long while to get here, but we got there in the end.

CHAPTER 35

Thursday 18 October 2018

Stephanie

I set the tone for how it's to be, and so we wait in silence.

Sitting bolt upright on the red, hard sofa, I hold on to Jamie's hand but we don't speak. We don't need to. I fill the remaining seconds thinking about the past fifteen months. How insanely happy I've been, how I've laughed and smiled doing the most normal things – with him. Watching TV, cooking, going for evening walks, doing the food shop, walks along the coast in the sun, sitting in the garden, playing Twister with the girls – just living life with Jamie. How the girls have seen me in a loving relationship with someone, and they adore him too. How they laugh and giggle every time he gives me a kiss. How they insist on him drawing with them for hours. Me, him, Seb and the girls are a family now.

For the first time in my life I'm absolutely, blissfully happy.

Every. Single. Day.

As fast as these images flash through my head, I have to turn it slightly, closing my eyes, almost as if they were inflicting actual physical pain upon my body: memories burning into my brain. I can't bear to think about what might come.

But as soon as they come in, I know.

Dr Weldrake comes in first, followed by Melissa, the lovely nurse I've been dealing with over the past few weeks in the Breast Clinic. They both smile at me in that way people do when they're about to deliver terrible news. It's more to be polite than an actual communication of gladness, smiles which evoke sympathy, sadness and consolation, all rolled into one. Jamie squeezes my hand, but I can't look at him, can't face it.

Dr Weldrake sits opposite me, teetering right on the edge of her mint-coloured upholstered chair. She can't possibly be comfortable sitting like that. I wonder if that's how she sits when she's delivering bad news or whether she sits like that all the time. Her long blonde hair is tied up in a ponytail and she doesn't look that much older than me. The whole room is deadly quiet as she faffs around with some papers for a few moments before speaking to me, My eyes are drawn to Melissa, who sits next to her clutching a load of leaflets in one of those A5 plastic folders. Staring at it, all I can think is: they don't bring leaflets in if it's good news, do they?

I just know.

'Stephanie, unfortunately, we've found cancer cells in the tumour,' Dr Weldrake says.

No build-up to it. Straight in.

Cancer.

Cancer. Cancer. Cancer.

The word rattles around my head like a dice being shaken in a cup. I hear Jamie draw in a sharp breath as the word is said. A shiver runs through my body and doesn't go away. This word has haunted me for so long. It's the word that took my mum away. And now it's got me.

I don't know what to do or say as I stare at a poster on the wall telling people they should give blood or something.

'Stephanie,' Dr Weldrake asks, softly, but firmly, 'did you hear what I said?'

Cancer. Mum. My kids. Chemotherapy. I'm going to die. I can't die. I'm going to lose my hair. Which famous people had breast cancer and didn't die? I need to Google this as soon as I get home. Cancer. Why is this happening after everything I've been through? This isn't fucking fair. Haven't I been through enough? For fuck's sake.

There's a heaviness in my breathing. It feels like there's loads of bricks in my lungs that I'm trying to breathe out. I can hear blood rushing though my head. It's deafening. No, that's not even possible, is it? I feel the weight of everyone's eyes on me, waiting for a response.

'I've got two kids. I can't die. I can't leave them without a mum, so what are we going to do about this?' I say, almost as if this woman hasn't just bestowed a death sentence on me.

Dr Weldrake immediately sits up and gets a pen and paper out of from her file.

'Well, *this* is what we are going to do about it ...' she says.

She then draws a load of diagrams, outlining what the plan is, and says positive people tend to do well out of treatment. Jamie asks all the practical questions I'm incapable of and he holds my hand the entire time.

I don't cry. It's almost as if the news is far too big, too overwhelming, to cry over. Like you bypass the crying and proceed straight to shock. I'm sure the tears will come, but not now.

I actually knew this was coming, so it's not as much of a shock as it could have been. Sometimes you just know something is bad, don't you? That morning in August, when I was standing in front of the full-length mirror trying on a new bra, was the day I knew. I'd lost some weight, so I was admiring my new body; not bad for a late-thirties mother of two. Then, putting my arms above my head, I noticed that something wasn't right on my left breast. The skin was inverted and puckered. How had I not noticed before? And especially with it in my family? I suppose with the divorce and everything that's happened lately, it had slipped my mind, but still ... How could I have been so stupid?

A visit to the GP sent me straight through to a mammogram appointment and suddenly I'm feeling lost and isolated, my mind protesting, 'I shouldn't be here, this is not my time, I'm too young'. How is that fair? Is this what my mum had to go through?

Coming face-to-face with your cancer is a weird, strange thing. You don't really know what to expect, what it looks like. Mine looked like a spider; a large, white, evil spider with long spindly legs. A white mass with poisonous tentacles reaching out, hidden from everyday view but very active within me. I stared at the image on the screen, as my boob was pressed between the cold metal plates on the mammogram machine. Of course, that was before the official diagnosis, but I just knew and that image stayed with me. You can see it on the nurses' faces when something is wrong. They try to hide it, but you can tell.

After that came the biopsy, but I prepared myself for the worst. And the worst has come.

Jamie and I drive to Dad's house straight after the appointment.

'I can't do it, Jamie,' I say, turning to him, suddenly losing control of my breathing.

'I'm here,' he replies, taking hold of my hand and kissing my knuckles. 'You're the strongest person I've ever known and you'll get through this.'

There's no messing about. I tell them straight away. Dad breaks down and cries, putting his head in his hands. His shoulders shake uncontrollably as he sobs. I don't know what to do. I feel like that long-ago thirteen-year-old again, not knowing how to comfort her dad. How can we be going through this again?

The colour drains from Ebony's face.

'No. Just no. I can't lose my sister,' she declares, adamantly, gripping on to my hands and shaking her head.

'We're going to do everything we can, Ebs. I feel like I need to be positive about this. I'll fight it and I will win,' I tell her, not even sure what I'm coming out with. It's all the stuff you're supposed to say when people get cancer, isn't it? I'm in a daze.

'My God! Why wasn't it found earlier?' she rages, at nobody in particular.

'No point in going down that route, love,' Dad warns, putting his glasses back on after wiping his eyes. He sits on one side of me, Ebony on the other. Jamie is content to allow them this moment.

'I'll be having a mastectomy in three weeks and I'll start chemotherapy too,' I go on.

'Three weeks? Oh, Steph,' Ebony sobs, throwing her arms around me. 'I'm so sorry.'

'Ebony, it's going to be fine,' I insist.

'Well,' she declares grandly, 'when you start losing your hair, I will shave mine off too, to support you.'

Jamie, Dad and I all exchange confused glances when she says it, each knowing this will not happen.

'Can I get that in writing, please?' I say, laughing, running my hand through her long black ponytail.

'Well, I can definitely support you by getting a good shorter cut,' she says and smiles back.

The room goes quiet. There's only so much humour you can introduce into these situations before the sense of dread comes back, thick and clinging.

'Steph, we're all going to help you through this. You're not going anywhere,' she orders. Her tear-stained face gazes at me with her huge green eyes. 'I am not losing my sister and that is final.'

It's just horrible having to deliver bad news to people you care about and seeing the effect on them. Horrific. It reminds me of an interview with a doctor I once read, who observed that in his line of work his sympathies are always with the families who have to watch their loved ones die as opposed to the actual patients, because it is possibly the most painful thing to watch someone you love in pain, dying ... I can totally relate to this.

By the end of the conversation, the discussion, I am the only one keeping it together and comforting them. I suppose it's a survival thing.

Picking the girls up from school is when it hits me. Both girls run to me, almost knocking me over with the force of their affection.

'Mummy! Look! I made a princess castle!' Adelaide declares, proudly, shoving a tissue box with wet glue, glitter and tissue paper hanging off it at me.

'Wow!' I praise her. 'That's beautiful! Is there enough room for me in there?'

'Noooo!' she says. 'You're a queen, not a princess!'

Fighting back tears I grip on to their hands all the way home, promising myself to not think about this until later. I need to enjoy every second with them.

Later that night, after the girls are in bed, I stare at myself in the mirror. I'd felt so feminine in recent months, in good shape. Being happy agreed with me, it had seemed. But inside my body something nasty had been growing – and I wanted to know: Why is this happening? Is it karma for loving another woman's husband for so many years?

I crawl into bed and Jamie holds me tightly. No words, no talking, nothing.

The tears start to roll down my face and they don't stop. They just get bigger and fall harder. I wail, I sob, I bawl. I cry for me, for Jamie, for my girls, for my family.

I just can't believe this is happening.

CHAPTER 36

Friday 21 December 2018

Stephanie

'Steph,' Ebony whispers from the doorway of my bedroom. 'You've got a visitor, are you up to seeing her?'

'Who is it?' I ask, screwing my face up. Who on earth turns up, unannounced, this close to Christmas?

She walks in, and I start laughing immediately. I glance at the digital radio clock in my room, then at her, raising what would be my eyebrows if I had some.

'You've got an hour. Sit down on that chair over there and make yourself comfortable,' I say. 'Great to see you, Jane!'

I'm aware I look so very different to how she's seen me before; I always used to make such an effort when I went to see her, always wanting to look as if I had it together, swishing through the door in cute dresses in the summer, chic coats in winter. Now, I'm bloated and bald and it's a shock for anyone who knows me. You can see it on their faces when they see me now. They try to hide it, but they can't.

Jane rushes over to me and perches on the edge of my bed, giving me a huge hug. It's strange, but really comforting. As my therapist, we've obviously never had this kind of relationship, but I've known her for so long, she feels more like a very close friend. She squeezes me tightly.

'Jane, I think we're breaking all kinds of rules here ...'

'Rules are made to be broken, Stephanie,' she says. 'I thought you'd worked that out by now.'

Classic Jane, always so wise.

The day they told me the cancer had spread to my lungs was the worst day of my life. I didn't think anything could top the day Mum died, or the day I originally discovered they'd found the cancer. But that day was darker than both of them put together. Even when you're told that you've got cancer, you cling on to the hope that you can fight it, beat it, conquer it, somehow. You hear it every day. 'So-and-so lost/won a brave battle with cancer.' It's everywhere, the analogy is that cancer is a battle, and if you fight hard enough, you can win it. But that's not the case. Because sometimes you just can't. You can't fight against biology, even with all the drugs in the world. Trust me, I've tried.

And how do you come to terms with the anger? I could hear myself screaming inside my own head but no sound was coming out of my mouth when Dr Weldrake told me the news that the cancer had spread. I'd been putting myself through the torture of chemotherapy, I'd lost my hair, my left breast and barely even felt like a woman any more. And now this disease was going to get the better of me in spite of everything we'd done to stop it?

They asked if I wanted to continue with chemo but I told them I didn't. It was too hard on my body, this double-edged sword of using poison to cure you. Well, that's the plan in theory, except it doesn't always work. It was worse than I ever imagined it could be. Of course, in the beginning I was convinced I'd be tough enough to handle it, everybody is.

I'm different to everyone else, I thought. They're just weak. I am strong. I have to get through this. There's more at stake for me. I can do this.

And then it starts.

For the first few days, I felt fine. Well, that was OK. What do people complain about? Then the throwing up started, and the vertigo, the constant feeling of motion sickness, of having the world's worst hangover, the distinctive taste in my mouth that only a load of sherbet lemons could get rid of, the plastic-like 'chemo smell' that only I was aware of. It became part of my world and I could barely remember what my life was like before it.

Just under two weeks after the first round of chemo came the inevitable hair loss. My beautiful, long blonde hair, which had defined me as a woman for so many years, was being dragged out in clumps. That was what upset me the most. A breast, you can hide or get a new one. Your hair is part of you, visible to everyone. Suddenly I felt like I properly had cancer. Eyebrows literally just wiped off with a stroke of a finger and don't even get me started on how weird it was to not have eyelashes. You simply don't realise how much you take these things for granted when you have them. You worry about inconsequential stuff which doesn't mean anything at all in the grand scheme of things. You worry about whether or not you're going to look fat at the village summer fete next month, or whether you allow your kids to consume too much sugar because you bake with them too much. The next thing, some doctor is telling you you're probably going to be dead next month and you don't have eyelashes any more.

Did I really want to spend the rest of the time I had left throwing up and feeling absolutely shit? Nope.

Everyone tried to talk me into having more treatment, everyone except Jamie. He was the only one who understood. They saw it as me 'giving up'. I don't see it like that. I see it as me having some tiny bit of quality of life left before I go.

The hardest part was how to manage it with the kids. They're too young to understand what's happening, but at the same time, they say wildly inappropriate things at all the wrong times which I love. I managed to accompany them to a kids' birthday party in my brand-new brunette wig when I first got it. It was exhausting, but it was important to me that I remained involved in their life. However, halfway through the party, Evie decided to inform absolutely everyone in there that 'that brown hair isn't really my mummy's hair, it's only pretend. Mummy, would you mind taking it off so everyone can see your bald head'. I couldn't stop laughing amidst that sea of horrified and pitying faces. I hope she remembers that scene when she's older and how much I laughed at it.

Jane takes a seat on the chair in the corner in my room.

'Christ, Stephanie, are you trying to give me brittle bone disease?' she says, shifting about on the chair, then sitting bolt upright as I laugh hysterically.

'Consider it payback for years of uncomfortable chairs in your treatment room,' I reply. 'How did you know?'

'At our last session, after meeting Helen, you were in a really great place. You felt like you had closure and felt confident enough to see me in a year's time, but you never came back, so I checked up on you.'

'Oh,' I say, smiling.

'I'm so, so sorry, Stephanie …'

'That's what everyone says,' I reply, straightening the covers out over my legs.

'And you're with Jamie now? Properly?' she asks.

'Yes. Finally. I got there in the end. Your therapy finally got through.'

Jane narrows her eyes, tilting her head to the side. 'What do you mean?'

'You really helped me to see things in a new light. I finally realised it's OK to have feelings that you can't control. Because everyone does at some point or another.'

Jane smiles in that way she does before she drops a bombshell.

'Oh God. What? I've got it wrong, haven't I?' I ask, panicked.

Jane smiles. 'Not at all. What you've said is correct. But you've missed out one crucial point about all of this ...'

'What's that?' I ask, utterly confused, yet again.

'*I* wasn't the one who helped you change, Jamie was.'

'Eh?'

'He showed you that it's OK to need someone,' she says. 'That you, too, can be loved – and more importantly, you *deserve* to be loved. Not just once a year, but all the time. You neglected yourself for so many years after your mum died, Stephanie, deemed yourself unworthy of real love and refused to let anyone in ... until Jamie came along.'

I listen to what she says as the wind rattles on the widows. Every single thing makes sense.

'You know, you could have told me this, like years ago. Would have saved me a whole load of bother,' I say and laugh.

'Nah, you know you had to go through it all yourself. I've seen such a transformation in you. You've been my patient for, what? Twelve years?' she asks.

'Feels like longer,' I say, deadpan. Jane shoots me one of her scary looks.

'But, off the record, you've become very dear to me and that's why I'm here today. Not as a therapist, but as a friend,' she says.

'Well, that means a lot. And I agree,' I say, smiling. 'This isn't going to cost me the earth, is it?'

'No, pay for twelve years, get the last session free,' she laughs.

We talk about our relationship over the years. Jane is probably one of my closest friends now and what do you say when you know it's the very last time you will see someone? Jane knows absolutely everything about me. *Everything*. My hopes, dreams, sins, regrets, flaws and issues. She's seen me laugh, cry, smile and worry, supported me through things I couldn't tell anyone else, never judged me, called me out on things when I've been unreasonable and, my God, she's frustrated me at times … because she's always been right.

Every single time.

She's everything my mum would have been if she was still here.

'How are the kids?' she asks, straight to the point. I love that about her.

'Too young to understand, which is both a curse and a blessing,' I explain. 'I've let them in as much as I can. Cuddling them 24/7.'

Jane smiles and nods. 'Best thing you can do. They will remember you, the memories you've created for them. Leave them things they can look at. They won't ever be without you. What's going to happen to them when you die?'

It's a good job Ebony can't hear this conversation – she wouldn't get it. She wouldn't understand the relationship Jane and I have, the things we've shared and the way we talk to each other. I like the brutality and honesty of it.

'Well, they're going to live with Ebony. Matt will have contact with them as and when he can,' I tell her.

'He's quite happy working in Dubai now so they don't slot into his life out there. They will be more than happy surrounded by Ebony, Will and the boys, Dad ... and Jamie.'

'Jamie?'

'They've grown very <u>fond</u> of him over the past eighteen months,' I tell her. 'Even if ... *when* ... he meets someone else, I'd still like him to keep in touch with them. He was such an important part of my life.'

'Yes, he was,' Jane says. 'He brought you back to life.'

We smile at each other, just enjoying the moment, this friendship we have, forged over many years. I may have paid for her relationship, but what we've been left with is utterly priceless.

'Well, I'd better go,' she says. 'I can see you're exhausted and I don't want your crazy sister coming to haul me out.'

I forget how well she knows everyone in my life, despite never having met any of them before.

Jane stands up, sliding her tan Mulberry handbag on her right shoulder and adjusting her black woollen scarf. Her bright red hair, striking as ever, is all down today, marking a contrast to how I've seen her before. She's not in work mode.

I exhale deeply, knowing I'm about to cry. This is one of the first goodbyes I'll have to do and I don't think I can cope with them. Would be better if I died in my sleep?

'Jane?'

'Yes, darling?'

'You'll come to the funeral, won't you?'

'Wouldn't miss it.' She winks.

'Make sure it's good, won't you? Don't let it be crap,' I say and laugh, softly.

'The best,' she says, smiling.

She sits on the bed and envelops me with love and the biggest cuddle. It lasts for a least a minute. Her perfume – the same one she's worn for all these years – comforts me more than I could ever tell her. She squeezes me so hard, it almost hurts in my fragile state, but I don't care.

'I've never been prouder of anyone,' she whispers into my ear. 'And your mum would be too.'

The biggest smile sweeps across my face as my eyes well up with tears.

'Thank you, Jane. For everything.'

She looks at me and smiles, her eyes glossy. She quickly gathers her things up and leaves the room.

Taking one last look at me before she goes, she blows me a kiss and I smile.

I don't know how to define content or happy. They're both just things we feel. I guess when your time is up, all you can hope for is that you're happy with your life and there are no regrets. Mistakes, yes – we all make them. But as my mum said, we're all human.

Perfectly imperfect ... I'm happy with that.

CHAPTER 37

Saturday 2 March 2019

Jamie

I sat alone in her bedroom for days after she'd gone, not wanting to move anything because she'd touched it last: a glass of water, one of her books, her lip balm. Her bedroom, slowly turning into a museum, gathering dust and memories.

I could still smell her perfume. I just needed to be close to *her* – or the essence of her.

I occasionally brought the girls in and cuddled them, not that they really understood what was going on. I know I haven't been in their lives for very long but they trust me and we get on well. They're both the spitting image of her, the same Cupid's bow mouth and huge green eyes.

For the first two nights after she died, I didn't sleep. Sitting on the blue chair in her room, I stared at the bed in silence, drinking whisky and going through the last twelve years of our lives. I wish I'd been more honest earlier on. I wish I'd told her how crazy mad in love with her I was from the beginning. I wish I'd never held back. I wish I'd been braver. None of that helps me now, though. I just have to live with it.

A huge black hole of death and grief swallows me up. She's been a part of my life for so long, and now she's gone. Just knowing I won't hear her laugh again, see that smile, her beautiful face, breaks my heart. Is it possible to feel physical pain from grief? Because it feels like it.

I'm not the only one struggling. Watching Michael and Ebony go through losing their daughter and sister is utterly heartbreaking. They've been through enough already. Nobody can quite believe it.

'Jamie!' both girls scream, running towards me as I walk through the door. Adelaide jumps right up on me as Evie wraps her arms around my waist.

'Here they are! My little monkeys!' I say, hugging them both as Michael and Ebony appear in the hallway. 'Are you ready for our special trip?'

'Yes! Can we listen to the music in the car and can I bring Moana?' Adelaide begs, shoving a cuddly Moana dolly in my face.

'Definitely yes to both!' I say, enthusiastically.

'Lovely to see you, Jamie.' Ebony smiles, giving me a huge hug as I pop Adelaide down. 'We've just made some coffee.'

'How are you, Ebs?' I ask, as tactfully as I can in front of the girls.

She half smiles, doing the best she can. 'I miss her,' she whispers, the pain she still feels at losing her sister evident in her face. I nod, pulling her closer and kissing her on the side of the head.

Walking into the kitchen, it still feels surreal that she is no longer here in her dad's house where she was both a child and adult. It's also the place she died, very peacefully, one cold night in January as I lay next to her.

'How are you, Jamie?' Michael says, pouring me coffee, Adelaide and Evie nattering in the lounge.

'Just trying to survive each day, you know?' I admit, sitting down at the dining table. 'I feel like I'm constantly switching between crying and being angry at the world. I don't even know what to do with myself half the time.'

It seems a cruel irony that, since I won the art competition, I've been offered so many exhibitions and my work is in much demand. And the one person who encouraged me to follow my dream isn't here to see it.

'You know, Jamie,' Michael says, sitting on the chair next to me. 'Stephanie's mum, Elaine, was the only woman I ever loved.'

'Stephanie told me so much about her – she sounds like an amazing woman.'

'Oh, she was special,' he tells me. 'You just know when you've found a woman like that.'

We share a lovely nod in agreement. Yeah, we both know.

'When I found out that she might be taken away from me, it was like my world was ending. I mean, we'd been through so much I literally couldn't believe it.'

I take a deep breath. It's staggering how much Michael and Elaine's relationship mirrors mine and Stephanie's. It's just not fair.

'We prayed for the worst not to happen,' he says. 'And then it did.' He takes a sip of his coffee, gently placing it back down on to the table. 'And I was so fucking angry, Jamie.'

I do a double take when he says this. Michael does not swear. It sounds unnatural coming out of his mouth.

'Along with grief, in the following years I allowed that anger to consume me for far too long. It affected my relationships with my daughters and those around me.'

'I don't know what to do with it, Michael. I loved her so much and now she's gone. I can't cope with it,' I say, feeling my eyes swell up with sadness once again.

'I feel it too, Jamie. I can't believe she's gone either. But we all have to look out for each other. We can't take care of Evie and Adelaide properly if we are all running around angry. All it does is isolate you from those you love.'

I nod my head and run my hands over my face, hoping I can fend off more tears.

'I see a lot of me and Elaine in you and Steph,' Michael says. 'What you had was the real deal. And I mean no disrespect to your ex-wife and son, but I thank God you were around the last twelve years because you've been the most positive influence on her I've known.'

443

'Thank you, it really means a lot to hear that.'

'I'd never, ever seen her happier than when she was with you. Everyone at the funeral said it too. Your eulogy with the photos and the music, that portrait ...'

I reach for my coffee to stop myself losing it. The funeral was the hardest thing to do. I put together a slideshow of photos of Steph and her family, all set to Michael Buble's 'Close Your Eyes', as the portrait I created of her stood on her coffin.

The final photo in the montage was of a young, fresh-faced, blonde-haired Stephanie, about twelve years old, dressed in a red nightie with daisies on the sleeves. Next to her stood a beautiful, glamorous woman in a red floor-length evening dress. Her long blonde hair was swept to the side, cascading over her right shoulder and a diamond choker around her neck, sparkled in the early evening light, which was pouring into the bedroom they were standing in. They stood next to a dressing table with a three-way mirror, which was full of perfume bottles, make-up, hairbrushes and jewellery. But it was the way they were looking at each other which struck me. Stephanie told me this was the last photo she remembers being taken before her mum took ill, when everything was normal in her world. She was glad she had that memory, though she never remembered what had made her laugh so much, but they're gazing at each other, laughing their heads off, and there is so much love between them.

Mother and daughter.

'Elaine always used to say that the universe knows what it's doing and she was right. But it can also be so cruel, because there is nothing worse than losing the woman you fought so hard for. All we can do is support each other now.'

'Well, you're a very close and tight family. And, in time—' I break off. 'I'll never forget how kind you were to me in difficult circumstances.'

Michael looks at me, frowning, with a confused look on his face.

'Jamie, let me be clear about this,' he says, 'whatever happens, you are part of this family, full stop. You made my daughter happier than she's ever been and Evie and Adelaide could not want for a better step-dad. Whatever happens, you're one of us now.'

The gravel crinkles underneath the wheels as we travel up the familiar driveway and the trees sprout a beautiful selection of fresh green leaves. It's familiar, but different. I've never been here in the spring before.

'Are we there yet?' asks Evie from the back of the car.

I laugh at the sheer cliché of it. She's been asking since we set off. I reply with a big, fat, 'Yep! We're here!'

'Yay! Adelaide, wake up! We're here!' she yells to the little sleeping princess beside her in the car seat, head lolling to the side. Moana has fallen on the floor.

It felt strange, making the phone call.

They all knew Stephanie: Avril, the receptionist, the maître d', the housekeeper – they knew us both. We've been coming here for that long and no questions were ever asked, there was never any judgement. They must have known, but they were always polite and friendly. They became our friends.

It felt right to let them know.

They expressed their condolences with a sadness I hadn't quite expected, calling back a few weeks later, asking if I would like to go today. They wanted to do something nice 'for the girl who loved staying there'.

We park and the kids jump out. Evie bounds up the steps to reception as Adelaide trots up, holding on to my hand. Walking through the door, I'm met by Avril, who comes out from behind the desk and hugs me. She hasn't actually changed that much since the first day I met Stephanie. Her hair is now a grey bob and she still wears the same '50s-style red-rimmed glasses. Turning her attention towards the girls, she comments upon how much they look like their mother as they stand like little soldiers next to the fireplace. Ebony, always organised, dressed them both in dungarees today and they look alarmingly cute. Both have Stephanie's icy blonde hair, but it's got a bit of a curl to it.

We chat to Avril for five minutes or so and she tells us about the thing they've done for Steph, which is so kind of them. She'd love it.

As we make our way outside, the sun breaks through the clouds. It always looks epic when this happens over hills. You feel insignificant and small, which I suppose we are, really. Walking on to the grass, I allow the kids to run free towards the tree. It's looked the same every year since we've been here. I don't know how old it is, but it's one of those really old, thick ones, with sprawling roots and rough bark. It is majestic and imposing, the branches moving freely in the wind.

I see the bench underneath it, facing Heathwood Hall. The same bench Stephanie and I sat on that cold October night and got to know each other.

The night I fell in love with her.

The kids run straight to it, hop on to the seat and start swinging their legs, excitedly. It looks as if it's been cleaned, spruced up, its chunky legs and armrests now a dark, oak colour. But its newest addition takes pride of place in the middle of the backrest.

A small gold plaque, fastened on with tiny gold screws. Engraved, it says:

For Stephanie, who found her fate on the road she took to avoid it

It feels like only a week ago since that night. How can it be that she's gone? I sit on the bench and scoop both girls up, one in each arm, cuddling them both tightly.

'Is this Mummy's bench, Jamie?' Evie asks.

'Yeah,' I reply. 'We used to love sitting here, it was one of her favourite places.'

'I miss her,' she says, burying her head into my torso.

I exhale deeply, trying not to lose it in front of them.

'I know, sweetheart,' I say. 'I miss her too. She loved you very much, you know.'

'Can I have some sweeties now?'

I laugh, reaching in my pocket for the treats I brought her.

'Come on, there's something else I want to show you,' I say, grabbing hold of their hands and walking back towards the Hall.

'I like the lady on the top!' says Adelaide, tucking into her sweets. 'She's pretty, just like Mummy is!'

'Yes, she sure is,' I say, looking at the girl on top of the fountain I've seen so many times over the years. She's still there, blowing her horn or some other weird musical instrument, dancing wildly, having a great time. 'Your mummy loved this fountain. In fact, this is sort of where we met,' I say.

'Did you tell her she was pretty?' she says and giggles.

I laugh. 'Kind of.' Oh, the innocence of being a child. God, I wish I had done.

Then a gurgling sound comes out of nowhere. The cranking and clanking startles Adelaide and she grabs my leg.

'What's that noise, Jamie?' Evie asks.

I look at the fountain, cranking into action as short bursts of water start sporadically pumping out of the top, until, seconds later, it shoots up into the sky and cascades down the three tiers, like a waterfall.

It's beautiful. The girls squeal in excitement as the spray from the water lands on their faces.

Never, in over ten years of coming here, has this fountain ever been switched on. I hear heels clicking behind me and turn around to see Avril walking over, smiling.

'She always used to say, "Why do you never turn that fountain on?" So, we thought we would, for you and the girls.'

I walk towards her, give her a hug.

'Thank you,' I say, welling up. 'She'd bloody love this.'

As Avril releases from the embrace, she smiles, looking a bit teary-eyed.

'Now,' she says. 'I wonder who would like some hot chocolates? Anyone?'

'Me!' both girls shout in unison and Avril takes their hands and leads them into the Hall.

'You take a moment, Jamie,' she says. 'They'll be fine with me for five minutes.'

I nod, thankful for her kindness. I watch them all skip off back into the building and turn back to the terrace.

It's quiet. And beautiful.

The only sound comes from the fountain, a calming, rain-like white noise.

I take a few deep breaths. It's still raw, the grief. It hurts every day. This fountain, that tree, the room upstairs – they're all her. And us.

I take the iPod out of my pocket. Putting the earphones in, I go to the 'songs' menu, close my eyes and scroll through.

'OK, Stephanie,' I say out loud. 'Let's see what you've got for me ...'

Pressing my thumb randomly after a few seconds, I hear a tune I've heard so many times. It's from an iconic film and I recognise it immediately. Such a classic.

The strings slowly build, before that distinctive vocal kicks in.

A smile spreads across my face. I laugh, gently, opening my eyes and looking up to the sky.

'More Than A Woman' by the Bee Gees.

Reading Group Questions

1. *The Day We Met* is an unusual love story in that the romantic leads are both with other people until near the end of the novel. What do you think about this? How does it compare to other love stories you've read?

2. The story is told from the points of view of both Stephanie and Jamie. What did you think to the way the story was told? Was there a protagonist you enjoyed reading about more?

3. Stephanie and Jamie meet by chance. What do you think about the role fate, choice and circumstance play in the novel?

4. Music and art play an important part in Stephanie and Jamie's relationship. What do you think the characters were trying to express with this?

5. Stephanie and Jamie's relationship begins as an emotional affair. Do you think this is worse than a

physical affair? Is it equal in terms of a betrayal or is one more forgivable than the other?

6. Jamie's father leaving when he was young and Stephanie believing her parents had the perfect marriage has a lasting impression on them. To what extent do you think their parents have influenced their approach to relationships?

7. Stephanie changed quite a lot throughout the novel. To what extent did her personal development impact on her relationship Matt? Do you think as people change, they grow apart?

8. Stephanie and Jamie are both reluctant to break up their families. Do you empathise with their situations and did you find them relatable characters?

9. Do you think Stephanie and Jamie should have tried harder to save their marriages? How do you feel about Matt and Helen by the end of the novel?

10. Were you always rooting for Stephanie and Jamie to get together? Did your opinions on Matt and Helen change throughout the novel, and did the characters you wanted to end up together change?

11. Do you believe Steph and Jamie were meant to be? Why? What do you think the novel is saying about the idea of 'The One' and do you agree?

12. How do you feel about the ending of the novel?

Acknowledgements

Sarah Hornsley, you truly are the perfect agent. Thank you for being with me every step of the way. You're my biggest cheerleader and I don't know what I'd do without you.

To my incredible editor, Katie Seaman, who had so much creative vision for this novel from the second I met her. Thank you for your brilliant direction and Beyoncé-inspired editorial comments. Massive thanks to the entire team at Ebury, you've all made this dream come true. Tessa Henderson and Stephenie Naulls – thank you for helping me throw this book into the world.

A million thanks to all of my author friends, far too many to list here. But special mentions go out to Sasha Wagstaff, whose endless support over the past few years has been priceless. Isabelle Broom, thank you for being such a champion and general brilliant person.

This novel wouldn't have been written without the three therapists in my life (they love a triangle, you know). Thank you to psychologist Dr LJ Carter, who met me in a Teesside Park coffee shop back in 2016 and helped me create the complex character which became Stephanie. I'll never forget how you talked about her as if she was real. To clinical psychologist (and very reluctant Dr) Vicky Jervis – I'm not sure how many 'research trips to the pub' we've had, but I'm certain nobody would believe that we actually do just talk about psychology the entire time. Thank you, Amanda Wharton, for making me remember who I am.

I'm sure I have some of the best, most supportive friends anyone could ask for, but it would have been difficult to write this book without Dawn Chaplin, Laura Knights, Andrea Bruce and Caroline Wilkinson.

Enormous thanks to my on-call 'medical team' who allowed me to ask infinite questions about a range of complicated matters. Dr Rebecca Odedun, Dr Tom Poulton and Dr Ross – your compassion, skill and dedication to what you do is beyond admirable. Thank you, Fin O'Leary, for being my source of knowledge on all things completely random.

To my childhood friends, Leanne Weldrake and Melissa Martin – two of the bravest, most inspirational people I know. Thank you for meeting me on that sunny evening in the Black Bull two years ago and sharing your story with me.

To designer/artist extraordinaire, Steve Dobson – I am so very sorry for constantly bombarding you with questions about art for so long. I can't believe I now have informed opinions of my own on such things #ArtChatz. Eternal thanks for all your help on this novel. I'm grateful to the amazing portrait artist Paul Bennett, who also took time to help me with art research. Gisborough Hall in the beautiful North York Moors – thank you for allowing me to nosy around and draw inspiration for the novel. If anyone wants to know what Heathwood Hall looks like in my head – that's it.

Thank you to all the wonderful readers, reviewers, amazing bloggers, people I don't know who message me in the middle of the night saying they can't put my book down. You are the reason we do this.

I'd like to thank 2018 and its trials, tribulations, villains, obstacles and complications for coming at me with great force. You've made me stronger, wiser and a much better writer.

To my kids, my little warriors – you inspire me every single day with your bravery, individuality and resilience. Thank you for allowing me to be part of 'Team Epic' – there's no place I'd rather be. X